NATURAL BORN

A Novel by
John Scofield Prall Jr.

PublishAmerica
Baltimore

ISBN: 978-1-4489-9407-6 (softcover)
ISBN: 978-1-4489-8166-3 (hardcover)
PUBLISHED BY PUBLISHAMERICA, LLLP
www.publishamerica.com
Baltimore

Printed in the United States of America

No person except a natural born citizen, or a citizen of the United States, at the time of the adoption of this Constitution, shall be eligible to the office of President; neither shall any person be eligible to that office who shall not have attained to the age of thirty five years, and been fourteen Years a resident within the United States.

Article 2, Section 1, U.S. Constitution

Whenever the Vice President and a majority of either the principal officers of the executive departments or of such other body as Congress may by law provide, transmit to the President pro tempore of the Senate and the Speaker of the House of Representatives their written declaration that the President is unable to discharge the powers and duties of his office, the Vice President shall immediately assume the powers and duties of the office as Acting President.

Section 4 of the 25th Amendment to the U.S. Constitution

Dedicated to my wife, Sarah, without whose help and encouragement this would not have happened.

PROLOGUE

Philadelphia, Pennsylvania
Thursday, 27 August 2020
9:21 p.m. EDT
"…and God bless the United States of America."

As soon as that clichéd phrase oft spoken by all politicians in America as they ended speeches had escaped his lips, the noise in the hall rose to deafening levels and the crowd surged to its feet. Balloons and confetti began to fall from the rafters of the cavernous building, and flashes from cameras began going off like strobe lights. Navarro stepped around the podium, reached for Kerrigan's hand on the way, took a step forward with her, and raised their arms skyward in victory. The building erupted into even more deafening cheers, the waves of sound washing over the nominees as they smiled and waved.

"Ray, Ray, Ray, Ray," the vast crowd began chanting rhythmically within the cheers.

"And here in Philadelphia the Democrats have now officially nominated Ramon Navarro Jr. to be the first Hispanic candidate for President of the United States," intoned the broadcaster, his voice rising with excitement as he spoke, matching the enthusiasm of the crowd.

The nominees continued to stand center stage, and continued to wave and point at the crowd, as if to say to one individual among the thousands there in the convention center—'I see you and you're important to me.' Ray Navarro, the presidential nominee, was a tall, athletic looking man of forty-five. Standing at 6'3", he towered over his running mate, Congresswoman Fran Kerrigan, standing beside him at 5'4". He had thick black hair, still with no gray, and the olive complexion that betrayed his Mexican heritage, yet the unexpected hazel eyes and the sharp aquiline features and Roman nose showed a longer link back to the conquistadores and the plains of Spain. Weighing in at a trim 218 pounds, he had the build of someone who worked out regularly. Indeed,

Navarro was noted for his almost obsessive attachment to his daily workout; it never boded well for the staffer who tried to interfere with that schedule. The only hint at a chink in his armor was the slight limp as he walked, which became more noticeable as he tired after a long day, the legacy of the war wound he had received nearly twenty years ago in Afghanistan.

Kerrigan, at his side, presented a study in contrast to him. Short and no longer slim, with a resemblance to Judi Dench that was often commented on, she was now in her mid-sixties. Her steel-gray hair was cut at collar length from a center part, and feathered back from her face to reveal wide gray eyes above a small, straight nose and wide mouth. In her youth, Mary Frances Kerrigan had been considered quite attractive, and had matured into a handsome woman, a phrase used regularly by commentators and which she had grown to detest. Nonetheless, she knew that's what she was and that there was nothing she could do to stop the aging process, so she accentuated her good points and worked to minimize her bad. She had been a member of Congress for the past 28 years and the chairman of the House Appropriations Committee for the past six. Born and raised in Philadelphia of Italian and Irish parents, she felt right at home with this city and the raucous crowd that cheered for them, even though she now lived in the suburbs north of it.

"After a long, hard-fought primary contest, these two rivals now stand arm in arm, side by side, ready to do battle in the general election this fall," continued Lou Stevenson, the commentator. "And quite a formidable pair they make. It's hard to foresee that the Republicans will be able to nominate anyone who can match Navarro's charisma and telegenic appeal with the masses, or Kerrigan's experience and connections with the insiders on Capitol Hill. Their best shot will probably be to re-nominate President Thomas, despite the drawbacks associated with that action, given the country's misgivings about the tenor of his administration over these past four years. Certainly no one else has surfaced during their primary season who would seem to be able to give this pair a run for their money."

"I agree with you one hundred percent, Lou," intoned Ken Ingalls, the veteran political analyst who had covered the nominating conventions for CNN for the past three elections, and who would fly out to St. Louis next week to do the same at the Republican Convention when delegates of the Grand Old Party convened there in the heart of the Midwest next Tuesday. "The hold that Navarro has on the psyche of America, and his extraordinary appeal to all types of citizens across the nation, is something I haven't witnessed in my many years in this business. Even compared with Kennedy, or Reagan, or Clinton, or Obama, who all roused fervent enthusiasms from the electorate, Ray Navarro has got them all beat. It's extraordinary."

Navarro and Kerrigan had now moved to opposite ends of the stage at the front of the Convention Center and been joined by their spouses. As with the principals, the two spouses were studies in contrast. Julia Navarro, Navarro's wife of twelve years, was everything one envisioned when the phrase 'Texas woman' came to mind. Tall at 5'9" and well-built, she had cornflower blue eyes and long blonde hair that she wore to her shoulders. Eight years younger than Navarro, they had met in Houston about the time he started his work with local political groups, before he became the Mayor of Houston, and while she was finishing up graduate studies at Rice. As they liked to tell the story, it had been love at first sight, although in reality Julia had had to work to pin Navarro down. It was only through perseverance that she distracted him enough from his civic work to get a firm hold on him and ultimately convince him to get married. To her regret, they had proved to be unable to have children, and so she devoted her energies to her husband's work.

Fred Moscone, at the other side of the stage, was a distinguished senior Senator who had run for President eight years ago, although he had not made it through the primaries of Super Tuesday. He was now sixty-nine and silver-haired, stocky but somewhat overweight due to his love of good food and good wine, although he was still considered to be extraordinarily fit and strong for a man of his age. He had been one of Pennsylvania's Senators for the past 24 years. Having grown up in Little Italy in Philadelphia, he'd gone to Temple, then got involved in the rough and tumble world of local city politics where he stayed for the next fifteen years. It was during this time that he'd met Kerrigan at a fund-raiser. They'd courted for a couple of years, then had finally gotten married in Doylestown, north of the city, when she was still in her freshman term and he was a member of the Governor's staff in Harrisburg. Their only child, a daughter they named Susan, had been born a year later. Susan was now estranged from her parents; they had, in fact, not seen her in over two years, and their last conversation a week ago had quickly degenerated into another shouting contest when she point-blank refused to appear with them at the convention, causing her mother to cry and her father to say things he now regretted, which was the way their arguments now always seemed to end up.

Moscone had been appointed to the Senate by the Governor upon the death of the incumbent shortly after Susan's birth, then had won election in his own right two years later. He had been a Democratic stalwart ever since, and now chaired the powerful Senate Intelligence Committee. Vociferous in his support for his wife's candidacy throughout the primaries, he had left no doubt in anyone's mind that he felt the wrong candidate had won and had now been nominated. That antagonism did not seem to faze Navarro, but it made great fodder for the journalists and columnists who wrote about it, and was a source of great irritation to Navarro's inner circle.

"Why do you think he has such broad appeal, Ken" asked Stevenson. He too was a veteran of several campaigns, although he tended toward investigative reporting of the candidates' foibles rather than the analysis that was the trademark of his partner for the evening. He had looked deeply into Navarro's squeaky clean image throughout the primaries, but had found nothing that would stimulate the prurient interests of his readers.

"The man is a natural born success story. I think it's just a matter of the end result being greater than the sum of the parts," responded Ingalls, who began to tick off those parts on his fingers. "Here you've got a young, good-looking guy who when talking to you is so smooth and so convincing he can make you feel that the sun's shining even when the rain is pouring down. Point for him. He comes from a fairly typical middle-class upbringing, other than that his parents were immigrants from Mexico. Point for him again. He's a bonafide war hero, who served voluntarily in a war of dubious taste after graduating from West Point, and was wounded in action after saving the life of one of his soldiers. Point three. And he's a true Washington outsider, never having been involved in national politics until now. Point four. And after the scandals that ended the promise of the Obama years, and yet another abysmal turn by the Republicans during this last administration, that is a major plus in the eyes of America."

"The way he handled Kerrigan throughout the primaries, despite the heavy hand of Moscone in the background, I'd say he's a natural born politician as well. Nobody really gave him any chance to beat her at this time last year."

"No question about that," replied Ingalls. "The man showed who was the master and who was the amateur. It will be entertaining to watch how the two of them—no, the three of them—get along from here on out."

"What do you make of the notoriety of his birth?" asked Stevenson.

The nominees and the spouses had come together again in the center of the stage. The spectacle was winding down, and they were preparing to exit.

"If anything," responded Ingalls, "the fact that he was conceived in vitro and born to a surrogate mother only adds to his mystery and allure. The man on the street doesn't really understand all that business, of course. He just knows it's not the normal way things are done, so it gives Navarro a sheen of other-worldliness, as if he's somehow different and better than everyone else. The notoriety you allude to only strengthens his candidacy, in my opinion."

The group at the center of the stage were now bidding each other farewell, shaking hands and hugging as if they would really miss each other. Although everyone was all smiles there in front of the cameras, that façade was very shallow. Kerrigan particularly was still smarting from the primary loss to this upstart; she still believed she was the better candidate and would make a better president, and expected she would have to lead him by the hand once they won and got down to the business of governing. She had no doubt they would win, which only smarted more. 'Vice President Kerrigan,' she thought distastefully. 'It almost makes me sorry I accepted.' But she continued smiling, nonetheless, as she chatted now with Julia Navarro.

Navarro, now shaking hands with Moscone, had no reservations about his decision to run. He had been disenchanted with the leftist turn that Democrats had made not so many years ago that had turned out so badly and had alienated so many of their newly won voters. His disenchantment only grew greater as he watched blame being spread indiscriminately by those most guilty for the scandals, with no one being bold enough to accept responsibility for their actions. That wasn't the way he had been raised, and it was not what he believed leaders should do. So he'd decided to move out from the comfortable world he enjoyed in Texas, and try to convince America he had a better way. 'Hopefully I'll be able to continue to convince them,' he thought to himself. 'Although keeping these two from sinking the ship won't be easy.' He looked into the bitter eyes above the smiling mouth of Moscone and knew he'd have his hands full.

"I still find it to be an astounding turn of events that Kerrigan has accepted the Vice Presidential nomination, when only two weeks ago she had said she'd never consider it," said Stevenson.

"Well, Lou, that word actually only came from her staff," Ingalls replied, "so she can say that wasn't what she really meant. I think it's actually a shrewd move on her part. Both she and Moscone have lusted for the presidency for the past decade, but neither of them have been able to grasp that ring. Accepting the Vice Presidency now either puts her in a good position to successfully run in 2028, when she's still not too old, or to run in four years should they lose this time. I actually think that's their real mindset—they've accepted now to show that they're team players, but they're actually hoping for a loss so she can run next time on a more traditionally Democratic platform, since this one will be discredited in the loss."

"Somewhat disingenuous, don't you think?" chuckled Stevenson. "Hard to believe politicians would be that calculating." From his years of investigating, Stevenson knew that, if anything, politicians were capable of doing anything that they felt might advance their chances to get ahead in the cutthroat world of Washington politics.

"Well, I guess we'll find out in a couple years, one way or the other."

Julia Navarro was now saying good-bye to Moscone on the stage. Although she was generally a natural optimist who typically looked for, and usually found, the good in anyone, she had felt an immediate aversion to Moscone when they had first met last week. She couldn't put a finger on exactly where her apprehension lay, but she wouldn't trust him any further than she could throw him. She was glad to end the façade of pleasantries and get back to her husband.

Moscone, for his part, felt an equal amount of distaste, although his was directed at Navarro himself. He had no problem with Julia. Good looking girl, even though so superficial that she'd undoubtedly cause the campaign some embarrassment before the election took place. No, his real dislike was for Navarro. Just another white knight riding in to clean up the town, who would tar everyone who'd labored in Washington for any length of time with the same brush. Just another Boy Scout, and he'd dealt with too many of them throughout his career. 'If only Fran had come out on top,' he thought sourly. But she had come up short, and it was all this guy's fault. 'You won't last,' he thought, staring over at the Navarros. 'What goes around, comes around, my friend.'

"Well, I guess that wraps it up for tonight, folks," began Ingalls. "A historic night to be sure, and a foretaste of historic things to come."

"That's putting it mildly, Ken. I can't wait for the campaign to begin in earnest."

"You've got only about two weeks to wait, Lou. Once the Republicans have chosen their candidates, the fireworks begin. And we'll be right there to cover every detail of it for you, folks, beginning next week in St. Louis. We'll see you then. Good night, America."

The cheers filling the hall continued as the nominees moved off the back of the stage and out of sight.

Philadelphia, Pennsylvania
Friday, 28 August 2020
2:18 a.m. EDT

"You were good, Lou. I mean it. Kept the commentary moving and didn't get bogged down in the minutia. Held your own with Ingalls. It was good." Coryell was doing his best to buck up his notoriously insecure friend, who was once again worried that his performance on screen had been found wanting in the eyes of the nation.

"Thanks. Always good to hear a good review. Too bad we can't get together as often as we used to," answered Stevenson. They had left the Convention Center after things wrapped up about midnight, and headed down to Dave & Buster's on the waterfront below the Ben Franklin Bridge for some burgers and beer. They had finished the burgers, and were now working on their second beer. As they talked, Stevenson kept watching the crowds roaming through the arcade-like restaurant, marveling that they were all out at nearly 2:30 in the morning on a Thursday night—apparently not many people had to work on Fridays in this town. The noise in the place was deafening.

Lou looked over at his long-time friend across the table. Jamie Coryell had been his roommate at Columbia fifteen years ago as they were both beginning their journey in journalism. He still retained his youthful looks even after all that time. They had each set out to change the world, but each had taken a different path. Lou had set his sights on television journalism, while Jamie's true love was the printed word. He had graduated into print journalism, hoping to become a top reporter with some major metropolitan newspaper. Only after he had worked at the *Inquirer* for several years had he realized he would be much happier reporting at a local level, and he had quit and returned to his roots in New Jersey to chase that dream. Both were now thirty-eight, or maybe Jamie had turned thirty-nine by now, Lou could never remember, and both were happy in their jobs. Although Lou admitted to himself that he was always much happier when he was chasing down the nitty-gritty part of some story rather than being front and center on screen to talk about it.

"It would be easier to get together like this if you ever stayed in one place for any length of time," answered Coryell in reply. "Don't you ever feel the urge to settle down and stay put? That's why I couldn't take it on the *Inquirer*—I was always traveling to pin down the details of some story. It got really old after a while." Coryell had been working on his own at the small-town paper he'd bought for nearly fours years now. He rarely missed the stress and high tempo that he'd left behind.

Stevenson took a drink of beer. "You know that's not for me, Jamie. Been there, done that, and it didn't work." Stevenson had gotten married shortly after graduation to a girl both he and Jamie had been friends with at school. The marriage had lasted less than two years and ended acrimoniously, leaving Stevenson with a cynical heart, a huge alimony payment coming out of his paycheck, and a promise to himself never to do that again. "What can I say?" He shrugged his shoulders as if to say it didn't matter to him.

"Yeah, I know," replied Coryell. "Maybe you'll change your mind eventually." He finished off his beer, and signaled to the roving waiter to bring them both another round, then shifted their conversation to a new subject. "Anyway, so what was it like interviewing Navarro?" Stevenson had landed that plum assignment in the days just before the convention began after it was clear that Navarro would win the nomination. "He everything he's cracked up to be?"

"Let me tell you, the man lights up the room when he comes in and really doesn't even know he's doing it. He just has an energy about him and a way of looking at you when he's talking that makes you think he's staring right into your soul. It's no wonder the country's going nuts over him."

"Yeah, but what did you think," persisted Coryell. "Is it all the real deal, or is there some deep, dark secret just waiting to come out?"

"I think he's the real deal. I dug pretty hard into his background during the primaries, just because he seemed too good to be true. And after so much time in this business and doing this sort of thing, I've come to firmly believe that if something looks too good to be true, it most likely is. Particularly when you're looking at politicians who're running for election. But I found nothing on him that people didn't already know about. Former soldiers who served with the guy love him, say he's a natural born leader and a true hero—swear they'd do anything for him. Most of them claim he was short-changed when he was only awarded the Distinguished Service Cross instead of a Medal of Honor for what he did in Afghanistan. People in Houston who've worked with him, and even those who've worked against him, say that they've never met anyone more sincere in his beliefs and more dedicated to doing what he believes is the right thing. The Hispanic community down there—well, throughout the whole southwest, really—they all think he's a saint; fact that he's born on Cinco de Mayo is just icing on the cake. Even growing up in Houston it seemed like he never did anything wrong. Good grades in school, varsity sports where he led the teams, no drugs, no nothing. Just an all-round great guy." Stevenson shook his head as if to say he couldn't believe he couldn't dig up any dirt.

"Sounds like you're falling in love after all, Lou" joked Coryell, smiling. "What do you think of the whole surrogate birth thing?"

"There's nothing there," Stevenson responded, shaking his head. "Parents couldn't have kids after years of trying, so they went to this fertility clinic in San Antonio that had a pretty good rep for success. Went through a few rounds of hormone treatments before finally opting for an in vitro birth with a surrogate the clinic found. Parents never met the birth mother, and Navarro says he's never had any interest to try to find her. I dug around in that a little, but found nothing. Clinic is now closed up—doctor died a few years ago and his wife moved up near Austin. Never seemed to be any problems with it. I think this one's a non-issue."

"That's what it sounded like to me, too. So you gonna vote for the guy?" Coryell knew this was one question that was sure to bring a response.

"You know I never vote for any of these guys, but I'll tell you, if I ever did, he might be the one. Come on, let's go play some games. You're making me uncomfortable with all these intimate questions."

"Wow, that wasn't the answer I expected from you. Guess I'll have to think a little bit about Navarro myself." He got up from the table, grabbed his beer, and started walking to join Stevenson as he headed back toward the video sport games. "Hey, by the way, I've met a girl."

"Now there's an accomplishment," quipped Stevenson. "Honestly Jamie, with the way you keep your head stuck in that paper you've got in Mayberry, I was afraid that you never came up for air, let alone anything else."

"Very funny, very funny. And it's Lambertville, not Mayberry. You should stop by some time and let me give you the grand tour. Then I can introduce you to Sue."

"Sue, huh? Well, maybe after the election I'll get a chance to take a little break. Where's she from, anyway? How'd you meet her?" Stevenson asked as they settled on an electronic batting machine, one of those new types where one of them could swing at the virtual ball that the other threw.

"Well, that's a funny story in itself," began Coryell.

PART 1

CHAPTER 1

Washington, DC
Thursday, 28 April 2022
1:18 p.m. EDT

President Navarro sat at his desk in the Oval Office and pondered his next move. The working luncheon he'd had today with the Vice President and the Congressional leadership, both Democratic and Republican, had not gone as he would have liked. He'd been hoping to gain their support for an announcement he intended to make during the trip to Mexico and Latin America that he was to begin on Sunday. Instead, with the exception of Kerrigan, they'd been appalled by it, and had all advised him to reconsider. 'They're still not on board. Even after all this time, they still don't get it,' he thought.

Navarro had won the election of 2020 by a wide margin, defeating the incumbent Brad Thomas by a tally of 321-217 in the Electoral College, and by 54%-46% in the popular vote. He had won in most of the traditional Democratic strongholds, sweeping New England, except for New Hampshire which acted contrarily after having supported him strongly in the Democratic primary and in pre-vote polling, and winning big in New York and New Jersey. Pennsylvania had proved to be a very close thing, much closer than he had expected, given the presence of Kerrigan on the ticket, and Ohio was a disappointment when he was edged out by a slim margin. He'd won in the Midwest and on the West Coast in what had become recurring Democratic pickups, but failed to post wins in the mountain states, except for Colorado, or in the south, except for Florida. He had been particularly disappointed that he lost to Thomas in Virginia and Michigan, where he had devoted much of his time and energy. His strength, though, proved to be with the Hispanic populations of the Southwest and of Florida, where the states he moved from the red to blue columns sewed up his victory. At the end of the day, it was clear that his mandate to govern rested firmly on the support he enjoyed from that population. Navarro recognized it, as did everyone else who had analyzed the election results, and the policies of his administration for the past fifteen months were always looked at with an eye to ensuring that that support would come again in 2024.

The reason for his support from the Hispanic community came not just because of who he was. Certainly he recognized that because he was Hispanic, spoke the language fluently, and had been born and raised in Texas, he had a natural affiliation with the population. But more than that, it was the way he empathized with them, and with their plight as a caste of unfortunates who were caught between the narco-gangs of Mexico and the unsympathetic Anglos north of the border, that won him their loyalty and devotion. While he had proved to be a good campaigner in other areas of the country as he barnstormed across it during the campaign, the frenzied crowds that he drew everywhere he went throughout the Southwest were what astounded the pundits who analyzed the election, and were what handed him the victory. To a man, the talking heads all foretold that this devotion would not, could not, survive his first months in office, and they all predicted that after that initial grace period he would prove to be not up to the task of governing to the high expectations of those who had voted for him.

But he had proved them all wrong. From his first days in office, Navarro had seemed to be incapable of stepping wrongly as he deftly negotiated his way out of the many sticky problems that his predecessor had left him. He hadn't tried to rush through everything in the first hundred days of his administration, despite the bleatings of the media who clamored that he wasn't taking things seriously enough or moving quickly enough. But Navarro had determined that he would not repeat the mistakes which the Clinton and Obama administrations had made when they came to power, when they had tried to push through an enormously complicated and complex agenda before their honeymoon ended, only to see the train fly off the rails and leave them to slowly pick the pieces up over the next two years. That they had indeed managed to survive the derailment and go on to win second terms in spite of their initial bungling was a credit to the political prowess of those two men more than anything else. But Navarro did not intend to get bogged down picking up the pieces; rather, he planned to gather and maintain momentum and move smoothly to enact his agenda. And that's what he'd been able to do.

It had helped, of course, that he had a Democratic Congress to support his initiatives. His coattails had proved to be long during the election, returning solid Democratic majorities to both the House and Senate after they had been lost in 2016. And even if they didn't necessarily like what he was doing, they were astute enough to recognize that he'd again have long coattails the next time around. He knew that the length of his coattails was in large part due to Kerrigan's effectiveness as the junior member of the ticket. Contrary to what he had expected, both Kerrigan and her husband, Senator Moscone, had proved to be able campaigners and loyal members of the ticket, who had wholeheartedly supported Navarro throughout the election campaign. Indeed, Navarro had come to seek out Kerrigan's advice and to look at her as a confidante off whom he could bounce thoughts and ideas without fear of seeing them being turned against him. He credited her support with the strong showing he had made in the Northeast, and for the win in Pennsylvania particularly, where she had appealed to Democrats who were otherwise ambivalent toward this inexperienced, young guy from Houston. She had helped close the deal, and he was grateful to her for it.

Navarro got up from his desk and began pacing around the office. It was a habit he had developed initially at West Point while he studied, and he still found that he could think more clearly when he was up on his feet and moving. The old wound in his leg ached a little today, a sign he had learned to recognize as precursor to rain. Realizing this, he stopped his pacing and looked out the windows of his office toward the Rose Garden. Although there was no rain yet, the sky had grown overcast—'It's coming,' he thought to himself. For a few moments he thought that it would have been nice if he and Julia could have taken some time to go out and see the cherry blossoms—it was that time of year, and the trees around the Tidal Basin had bloomed right on schedule earlier in the month. 'Too late now, though,' he thought; 'The storm will probably finish them off.' He remembered a visit he and Julia had made to Washington about ten years ago, before he was elected Mayor of Houston. The two of them had spent a wonderful day just strolling along with the crowds as they moved among the trees, enjoying the sun and taking in the scent of the blossoms. They'd then followed it up with ice cream on the Mall, he remembered. It had been only a couple years after they'd been married, and right after Julia's miscarriage, and the trip was a welcome diversion for them at that low point in their lives. 'What a great trip that was,' he thought wistfully. "But you can't go back again," he spoke aloud to the room, and resumed his pacing and focused his mind once more on the problem at hand.

That problem was how to convince Congress and the American people that his vision for the country was worth the pain and effort that would come in the short-term as it was put into place. His slow gathering of momentum had accomplished much during this first fifteen months, much more than his detractors, both inside the party and without, had expected. He had made good on many of the campaign pledges he had made, again despite the naysayers who said it couldn't, wouldn't or shouldn't be done. To the ire of conservatives, he'd normalized relations with Cuba and he'd pushed through legislation that essentially implemented many of the immigration reforms that McCain had proposed fifteen years before. To the ire of liberals, he had refused to repeal the ban on gays in the military and had made tentative overtures to the pro-life side of the relentless abortion debate. And to the ire of all, he had taken action to rectify the problems with Social Security, twisting arms on both sides of the aisle to gain a compromise that was acceptable to all—although barely—yet which was disliked and criticized by all, but which would stabilize that entitlement for the foreseeable future. Yet despite all the ire he had aroused on both sides, he'd enjoyed a consistent and sustained high approval rating across the country; now fifteen months into his administration, his job performance was approved of by 76% of those interviewed, and had never been lower than 66% from the time of his inauguration. He attributed this to the steps he had taken thus far in his term, and because of this high and enduring support, he fully intended to continue to implement the rest of the promises he had made. But now he had come to a point that he had not foreseen, and that would be crucial to his continued progress during the remainder of his term and on into a next, should that come to be. And that was because Navarro had now decided to order extraordinary actions in order to solve a dangerous problem that he had promised to resolve.

The challenge he faced was what to do to eradicate the threat posed to the security of the U.S. by the drug gangs which had destabilized Mexico over the past fifteen years. Although initial, tentative actions had been taken by Bush and Obama, they had largely amounted to throwing money at the problem and had not achieved the grandiose results that their proponents had promised, and which the nation had therefore expected. When the government in Mexico basically disintegrated in 2015 and chaos reigned, essentially leaving the gangs

22

in charge, the Thomas administration sat on their collective hands even as crimes and violence spilled over the border into California, Arizona, New Mexico and Texas, and wished that the problem would just go away. It was largely this inaction to a massive problem that literally threatened the security of the people of the United States, coupled with the forthright manner in which Navarro promised to deal with the issue, that had turned the electorate against Thomas and had so readily ushered Navarro into office. He had spoken forcefully against the inaction during the campaign, promising to act decisively once he was in office, and he had done just that.

On his first day in office in January 2021, he had summoned the leadership from the Pentagon and ordered them to draw up plans to stabilize the border. He gave them broad discretion on how to do this, taking no options off the table. What they had returned with, and what he had approved and ordered implemented, was a modern-day Punitive Expedition that dwarfed the one of a hundred years earlier that had seen Pershing chase Pancho Villa around the deserts of Chihuahua. In April of last year he had ordered III Corps from Fort Hood in Texas, as well as its subordinate units from Colorado and El Paso, and the Marines from Camp Pendelton and Twenty-Nine Palms in California, to move into northern Mexico and secure the border from the southern side. The move ignited a firestorm in Washington and across the world. Congress complained that he had not asked for or received the authority for such an action; the OAS complained that once again the *Norteamericanos* were punishing their southern neighbor for their sins; and the UN complained that the United States was threatening to destabilize the entire Western Hemisphere. But even as these vitriolic debates had gone on, American soldiers, airmen and marines, no longer fettered by operations in Iraq or Afghanistan, had acted to secure the border cities where the narco-gangs held sway, had taken the fight to them directly in their lairs, and had stabilized Mexico to a point where its government could begin to reestablish itself. The initial battles had been won, and won decisively, and Navarro's popularity at home and with the Mexican populace had soared. Although criticism was still heard from abroad, and although the revitalized Mexican government was not yet strong enough to reassert its authority without American support, Navarro's critics within had largely been silenced by success, and his popular support, particularly among Hispanics, had surged even higher. But the job was still not done, and Navarro knew that more drastic measures were needed.

To his chagrin, leading the opposition in Congress was Senator Fred Moscone, who, now that the election was won, seemed to rarely pass up a chance to castigate Navarro for his actions and to predict dire repercussions for the future. Vice President Kerrigan remained aloof, proffering supportive statements for neither her husband nor the President, a situation which increasingly irritated the President when he allowed himself to think about it, while Moscone and the President's staff engaged in running, acerbic verbal battles in the press. The Republicans were merely happy to sit contentedly on the side and egg each one on. It was clear to Navarro that Moscone was intent on embarrassing him so that his re-nomination during the next election would be in jeopardy, no doubt intending that Kerrigan would be the obvious one to pick up the pieces and carry the Democratic banner forward to victory. But he considered himself in the right, and so chose to remain above the fray and not comment on the Senator's strident accusations.

Now, however, had come the time for drastic measures to finish the job. To muddy the waters even more, and to really test the depths of the support he was receiving from the American public, he intended to announce that he planned to keep U.S. forces in Mexico for at least the remainder of his term, and that he intended to expand the operation to ensure that the gangs, as well as their suppliers, wherever they might be in the hemisphere, were targeted and eliminated. During his upcoming trip he intended to convince the leaders throughout Latin America that these extraordinary actions by the U.S. posed no threat to their sovereignty, that the United States had no territorial aspirations in the region, and that only by acting together in concert could they all enjoy a more secure and stable future. Navarro planned to expend much of the political capital that he had accumulated during these first fifteen months on this gambit. He anticipated that the American people, and in particular those from his supporting constituencies, would rally with him in this, but that he would have to work hard to convince the politicians to back him. Hence the luncheon that he'd just endured, in which the leadership had essentially told him—politely, but told him nonetheless—that he was crazy if he thought they'd give him their support. And hence his pacing about the Oval Office.

A knock on the outer door of the office halted his pacing and his thoughts, and he turned to see the rotund form of Josh Caldwell hustle into the office. Joshua D. Caldwell, former Governor of Texas and long-time friend and mentor of Navarro, now served as the White House Chief of Staff. At 62, he was fifteen years older than the President, but had cheerfully set aside his ambitions to help the younger Navarro negotiate the byzantine world of Washington. Although he was a formidable politician in his own right, and a true heavyweight in Texas politics, he looked nothing like the part. Short, round and bald, with his glasses sliding down a crooked nose that hovered above a droopy moustache and a perpetually harried look about him, he could easily have been mistaken for an accountant who rarely came up for a breath of air. In practice, however, he was one of the canniest politicians in the country, who knew how to get things done and was not afraid to push and shove when necessary to make it happen. He'd spent six years in Congress during the Obama years, then had served a term as Texas Governor before becoming Navarro's campaign manager two years before. Following the victory, to no one's surprise, Navarro had named him to be Chief of Staff and chartered him to oversee the transition and develop the master plan to implement his agenda. Navarro relied on him implicitly.

"Afternoon, Mr. President," drawled Caldwell as he entered the room. "I understand your luncheon gave you a bit of indigestion." He grinned at Navarro as he said it, as if to say 'I told you it would.'

"Josh, putting it that way would be an understatement of monumental proportion. They told me in so many words that I'd get their support only over their dead bodies. I thought for a moment that Starkweather was going to go into apoplexy." Dave Starkweather was the Republican Senator from Iowa, and the Minority Leader of the Senate. "He turned red as a beet, and almost forgot to breathe. The others were a little more subdued, but just as opposed to it. The only glimmer of support I got was from Kerrigan, amazingly."

"You knew what was going to happen, but it's better to get it out on the table now than to spring it on them while you're out of the country. At least this way you can counter anything they may leak to the press." The President had asked them all to keep his intentions in close confidence; he did not, however, expect that they would, and in fact was counting on at least one of them to talk to the media 'off the record' about his 'insane' idea. "You know, sir, I wouldn't put too much stock in any support you appear to be getting from the Vice President. I know she hasn't publicly come out against your policies, but her other half certainly has. For my money the two of them are in cahoots, and both bear very close watching. Him particularly, if he's going to be tagging along with you during this trip. I don't trust him for a minute, and you shouldn't either. Can't for the life of me think of a good reason why he asked to be included on the trip other than to make trouble for you. You'll need to be very careful of him while you're gone."

Navarro chose not to rise to this bait. "Heard anything of any leaks yet?" he asked instead, deftly changing the subject.

Caldwell sighed, recognizing that his argument was not going to make any headway with the President today. "Not much, although I did get a call from Lou Stevenson from CNN. He's going to be on the trip with you, remember?" Navarro nodded, conjuring up a mental image of Stevenson as he did so. "He's up in New York rootin' around in something or other, but he's got a whiff of this already somehow. I told him I couldn't give him anything, but that he could try to talk with you about it on Sunday." The President had sat down on the sofa in the center of the office while Caldwell was speaking; Caldwell now sat to face him on the opposite sofa. "Be interesting to hear where his info came from. He usually has closer ties to guys on our side of the aisle." He was referring to the Speaker of the House, Henry Garcia from Florida, the House Majority Leader, Jim Jefferson of Indiana, and the Senate Majority Leader, Tony Igawa of Hawaii. "I don't think Starkweather or Ron McPherson"—the House Minority Leader, from Idaho—"would give him the time of day."

"Maybe I'll invite him up to the front of the plane for a private chat while we're in the air," mused Navarro, staring up at the ceiling. "That ought to drive the rest of the pool nuts. Don't let that out." He snapped his head back down to look at Caldwell. "I'll surprise him with it once we get off the ground. See how good he is on his feet."

Caldwell nodded agreeably. "Sounds good. You know, sir, I wouldn't put it past Franny or the Giant Bug to let this out early, thinking it might throw you off stride."

"Now, Josh," Navarro chided, allowing himself to be drawn in this time. "You shouldn't talk about our Vice President or her influential husband that way." Caldwell knew about two words of Italian—and they were spaghetti and lasagna—but somewhere along the way someone had told him that Moscone could be literally translated in Italian as 'Big Fly.' Caldwell had immediately stored that away, and delighted in frequently bringing it out to needle Senator Moscone, most often in his presence, a fact that served to even further not endear the two to each other. The intense dislike between Moscone and Caldwell was an open secret in Washington, one often commented on with barely suppressed glee in the media.

"Oh, I'm sorry, sir," Caldwell replied guilelessly. "I meant to say the Vice President or Senator Moscone."

"Much better," Navarro chuckled. He leaned back into the sofa, and interlaced his fingers behind his head. "No, I don't think it came from them. The Vice President's been very supportive of most of what we've been trying to accomplish—genuinely so, I think—and I don't think Moscone would set her up to oppose me so blatantly. Like I said, Fran spoke up for me during the meeting in the face of all the criticism I was getting. I'm sure she was sincere about it. And you know she and Fred are practically always in lockstep about what they're doing, even if it may not seem like it on the surface, so I've got to believe he'll ultimately be supportive as well. It would be out of character for them to try to sabotage things now. No, it must be from somewhere else."

"Well, maybe you can get it out of Stevenson in return for some juicy tidbit on the trip." He paused. "You may be right about the Vice President, but I wouldn't trust Fred Moscone an inch. He's still got too much of Philly politics in him. He may be smiling to your face, but he's still trying to slip his dagger between your ribs." As Caldwell began to work himself up about Moscone, the President worked to stifle a smile; he knew that his Chief's main concern was for his welfare, and he knew that he and Moscone got along like oil and water. Caldwell was an inveterate skeptic about anything that had Moscone's name even remotely associated with it. "The man has one loyalty, and that's to his wife, and he'll do anything to move her along. And in his mind, you're in the way. You need to keep a close watch on him every second you're on the trip, because if he can trip you up, he will." Senator Moscone, as the Chairman of the Senate Intell Committee, had asked to travel with the President on the upcoming trip; Navarro had agreed and he was now part of the official party accompanying the President.

"Okay, message received, Josh. I'll be careful. And I'll give it the old college try to get some info out of Stevenson on the plane. So, what else you got before I head out for the photo op with the Villanova crew." Villanova had once again won the NCAA Basketball championship last month, and were coming to the White House today so Navarro could congratulate them. Navarro loved sports, and relished these chances to greet and congratulate champions.

"Just wanted to let you know that a new threat brief has been drawn up by our guys about what you might expect on the trip. Nothing specific, just lots of rumblings down in Mexico from the gangs. Once you're out of there things should calm down. The Service is on top of it, but they want to get in to talk to you about it sometime tomorrow. I think you should take the brief. They're all over it, and there's nothing for you to do, but it would be good for you to hear what they have to say so that we're all on the same page."

"Okay, set it up for wherever it fits best in my schedule, and I'll hear them out." The President got up and headed into the private bathroom just off the Oval Office to straighten his tie and get ready to go. "Listen, Josh, why don't you come upstairs about seven tonight? I'm grilling some burgers"—one of Navarro's favorite ways to unwind was to fire up the grill he'd installed on the Truman Balcony so that he and Julia could relax and pretend they were normal people, at least for a couple hours—"and Julia is fixing her world-famous baked beans. It'll be just like mother used to make." Here he winked at Caldwell. "I know Julia would love to see you, too. And you always cheer her up. What do you think?"

"Well, you know, Mr. President, that I never turn down an invitation to sample Julia's baked beans. Your burgers are questionable, but I can overlook that. You're on. I'll be there at seven. And thanks."

"My pleasure," called Navarro over his shoulder as he headed out of the office. "Wish me luck."

CHAPTER 2

Washington, DC
Thursday, 28 April 2022
7:06 p.m. EDT

"Josh, come on out," called Julia Navarro from the balcony as Caldwell appeared from the Yellow Oval Room. That room, which in the past had been variously used as a presidential study and as a formal reception area, among other things by other presidents, now was used by the Navarros as a family room; it was in this area on the second floor where they typically spent a quiet evening either together or with small groups of invited guests. Caldwell was a frequent visitor, and knew the way well. "You're just in time. Dinner's almost ready—at least my part of it is. You'll have to see if Ray is done burning the burgers yet." The President looked up from a large grill on the far side of the balcony and waved to Caldwell. "I was afraid for a little while that we'd have the fire department show up here because of all the smoke, but I guess he's got it under control now. What would you like to drink?"

"I'll have whatever you two are having," Caldwell responded. He came across the balcony and gave Julia a hug.

"Iced tea it is, then," she said. Caldwell knew that would be the case. Having been friends with the Navarros for most of their marriage, he knew that the President had long ago decided not to drink alcohol, and that his wife supported him by following suit. He himself enjoyed a good Black Russian made with some prime Stoly in the evening after work, and although he knew he'd be welcome to have one if he asked, with no hard feelings or evil looks from his friends, he was more than happy to have an iced tea with them. His main concession was that his would be sweetened, heavily, while they preferred theirs unsweetened.

He collected his tea from Julia and walked to the edge of the balcony to look over the South Lawn and down toward the Washington Monument. It was still light out, although the sun was headed toward the horizon off to his right. The storm that had threatened had briefly come and quickly gone, clearing the sky and leaving the evening delightfully cool and free of the humidity which could plague Washington in the spring and summer. The vista from the balcony was one that he always enjoyed, and he thought that again as he took in the gardens, flowerbeds and blossoming trees that were in view.

He turned to face back to the door from which he'd entered. Julia was now wheeling out a cart loaded with the fixings for the meal. Although the Navarros naturally had an extensive staff that could have done this for them, they generally tried to set aside one night a week when they could do it all themselves. Julia liked to cook—and indeed was a very good one—and she particularly liked to cook for the President. This was their way of allowing that to happen.

Caldwell walked over to where she had stopped the cart and began to help her unload it. A small table had been set out on the balcony for the meal, and he began to set out the dinner plates and silverware while she laid out casserole dishes with the baked beans and potato salad, as well as all the extras—sliced onions, relish, and ketchup. No mustard for the Navarros—they held it as a matter of highest principle that mustard was an inappropriate condiment for a hamburger. Julia set out a refilled pitcher of iced tea, and then turned to face him.

"Come over here and sit down for a bit, Josh, while Ray finishes up," she said, taking his arm and leading him to a set of chairs off to their left that looked out over the lawn. Caldwell couldn't help but admire her gracefulness and unpretentiousness as she folded herself into the farther chair with her legs up under her, and looked off toward the setting sun while sipping her tea. She was now thirty-nine, but still looked as young as when he had first met her years ago. She was wearing jeans tonight and a Rice sweatshirt against the cool air, and had brushed her blonde hair back from her face and swept it into a ponytail. She had on no makeup, and the perfect, unblemished skin of her face that the photographers loved so much still showed no evidence of any damage from growing up in a Texas sun. 'She's got what every other woman works feverishly to get, and she doesn't even try,' he thought to himself, bemused.

Caldwell had first met Julia, and the President for that matter, back in 2011 shortly after he had been first elected to Congress. He had come home to Houston with his wife, Ginny, to engage in some fund-raising after the session had been adjourned in the fall, and had been seated next to the Navarros at the event. He and Ginny had both been immediately enchanted by Julia and intrigued by Navarro. He and Navarro had talked through most of the evening about Navarro's past and about his social work with immigrants in Houston and its surrounding areas, while Ginny and Julia had mingled with the others in the room like long-lost friends. He remembered the pull he felt as Navarro had talked about his life and his work, the feeling of being drawn into the earnest face and the hazel eyes, and remembered thinking that this was a natural born politician he was meeting. He had promised himself then and there to prod Navarro into politics, truly believing he was capable of achieving great things.

And Julia only added to the luster. Here he found a fresh-faced young girl of 27, still practically a newlywed, who clearly adored her husband and who was genuinely interested in the people she was with and the condition of their lives. 'What a perfect complement for Ray,' he had thought at that first meeting. They had talked effortlessly for several hours, actually retiring, once the fundraiser had ended, to the Navarros' home down near the Astrodome and not far from the Rice campus. There he'd had the added pleasure of meeting Ray's mother; his father had passed away some years before. He'd learned about Ray's unique birth, about his time in the service and the wound which ended it, and about Julia's social work with the Houston Department of Education, but mostly he got his first introduction to a special couple that would factor large in his life over the next dozen years. Each time he had returned to Houston from Washington, Caldwell looked forward to seeing Ray and Julia again. He offered Ray encouragement and guidance when he ran for election as Mayor of Houston in 2014, and he was comforted by Ray and Julia when Ginny lay dying of cancer nearly seven years ago. He knew he couldn't have better friends if he'd picked them out himself, and he knew there wasn't anything that he wouldn't do for either of them.

He started as he realized that Navarro was speaking to him. "What are you thinking about, Josh? You've been staring into your glass for about five minutes now." The President was placing a platter with a half dozen huge hamburgers on the table, a concerned look on his face.

"Oh, just thinking about old times. I really appreciate the invite up here," he said, smiling at the two of them.

"Well, old friend, there isn't anyone we'd rather spend a quiet evening with than you, is there Julia?"

"I'll second that," said Julia, squeezing his arm. "You're the best, Josh."

"Well let's eat then," replied Caldwell, and they all reached to begin loading their plates.

After the meal was done and Caldwell had left to go home to the townhouse he rented in Georgetown, Navarro and Julia sat on the balcony looking out into the night. The sky remained clear, and the night sky sparkled with stars. A small sliver of the waning moon hung high in the sky.

"Penny for your thoughts," Navarro said. Julia turned to see him smiling at her, eyes twinkling. She realized she'd been staring off into the distance, mind running in neutral. "You're pretty quiet," he said.

"Oh, you know. Just feeling lazy after a good meal. It sure was good to see Josh feeling so good, wasn't it?"

"Yes, it was. He doesn't really get to unwind very often. Won't do it himself unless I ask him. Too busy trying to keep me out of trouble, I guess."

"Well, you should ask him more often then," she chided good-naturedly. "It really makes me sad thinking about him going home to that empty house so late every night after such a hard day every day." She sighed. "It's a shame Ginny isn't here for him."

"Yup," agreed Navarro. They'd all been devastated when Caldwell's wife had been diagnosed with pancreatic cancer just after he had won election as Governor. She'd died within two months. "It is a shame. Maybe all the work helps him keep his mind off it. I know he did the same as Governor, working unbearable hours just trying to keep sane." He shook his head. "I supposed I'd feel the same way if something ever were to happen to you. I don't know how I could go on. Probably couldn't. Josh is a lot stronger than I am, in that sense. I think I'd just fall to pieces." He looked over at her. "Guess you'd better just stick around." He smiled.

"Well I don't plan on going anywhere," she responded, getting up from her chair and crossing over to settle herself in his lap. "So that's not anything you need to worry about. Besides, you've got more than enough to worry about with this trip coming up. Better keep your mind on that."

"You're right about that. Should be an interesting ten days." He squeezed her. "Though I'm glad we changed the structure of it so that you'd have a role to play. And I'm glad you agreed to come along."

"How can I say no to the President," she giggled, with a mischievous look coming over her face. She got up suddenly and stretched, reaching her long arms up toward the ceiling. She looked sideways at him from the corner of her eyes. "About anything." She brought her arms down, then turned and starting walking into the Mansion. Over her shoulder she said, "You know, I'm feeling pretty tired now. I think I'll go get ready for bed." And she disappeared inside.

Navarro stared after her. "Well, come to think of it, I'm pretty tired myself," he said aloud, then got up quickly and followed her in.

CHAPTER 3

Lambertville, New Jersey
Friday, 29 April 2022
5:25 p.m. EDT

Jamie Coryell shut down his computer and stretched his back. 'Finally done,' he thought. He'd been working for the better part of the day trying to finish up the article on the Shad Fest to run in tomorrow's paper. Between all the phone calls he'd gotten, and all the distractions of people stopping by to talk with him about bits of local gossip—local color, as he liked to term it—the thing had taken forever. At least twice as long as it should have. But he was pleased with the final result. 'Job well done,' he thought, as he wearily got up from his desk in the back office of the building and stared out the window at the remains of the spring day. 'Looks like the weather is going to cooperate for the weekend, too,' he thought, staring up at the sky to the west, which would definitely make everybody in town happy.

Coryell was now almost forty; he was continually amazed at how fast time seemed to go by these days. He remembered back to when he was a kid playing on the streets of this town, how the school year had always seemed to drag by at a glacial pace. How Christmas always seemed to be so far in the future and taking so long to get here that he figured he'd be a decrepit old man before he ever opened another present. But nowadays, it seemed that he'd just taken down the tree when it was time to put it back up again. Maybe he'd run an article about that—might be a good people story to hear other perspectives on how time flies, or crawls, by. He jotted a note to himself on the dry erase board on the office wall, where he always wrote down his random thoughts as they occurred, hoping that he might unconsciously come up with some gold one day.

Most days getting up Jamie now felt the tug of advancing years. His special birthday, as folks cheerfully referred to his 40th, would come next month, although everyone told him that he still looked younger than that and shouldn't worry about being over the hill. He was still pretty fit, played some softball with younger guys in the summer league here and some pickup basketball at the Presbyterian Church gym when it got colder, and tried to work out and run regularly. His early morning jogs through the quiet streets of the town gave him time to think about things to come and what he had to get accomplished each day. He'd actually come to look forward to them. His one main concession to increasing age was the set of glasses that he now had to wear for distance, like when he drove or went to the movies, although he drew the line so far at using them for TV at home, even though he knew that day was coming quickly. He didn't think about the strands of gray that were appearing at the temples of his brown hair, preferring to believe that if he refused to notice them, no one else would either.

Jamie packed up the battered briefcase that he toted into work each day and got ready to head home. He turned off the office lights and locked the door behind him as he left. "You going out for some of the action tomorrow, Alice," he said to the middle-aged woman at the desk outside his door as he walked through the outer office. Alice Metzger was his primary assistant at the paper that he published every Wednesday and Saturday, and had been with him here ever since he'd bought it nearly ten years ago.

"Wouldn't miss it for the world," she replied unenthusiastically without looking up; she was busy on the ads for the morning run. "I'll see you there."

"Okay, don't work too late. See you tomorrow," he answered, and stepped out the door onto Bridge Street. He knew that Alice would stay as long as it took to get the job done perfectly, and then would ensure that the printing crew had everything they'd need to make the run before she ended her day. He knew he couldn't do this without her; he paid her appropriately for her labors, and was glad to do it.

Coryell had been in the newspaper business now for about seventeen years, ever since getting out of college. He'd bounced around a couple places at first, then landed a job with the *Philadelphia Inquirer* where he'd stayed for about five or six years as a city reporter. What he discovered during this time was that he liked being a reporter and was pretty good at it, but he didn't like working in a big city. He found that the items he reported on in Philly were generally pretty depressing, given the soaring crime rate and its nose-diving economy, and even though that meant he was always on to something hot, he'd come to the conclusion that he'd rather be reporting on kinder and gentler things—'Like a Shad Fest," he thought, smiling to himself.

So, after paying his dues in the city, he'd decided to take the plunge and strike out on his own. He'd heard that the local paper here in Lambertville, *The Beacon,* had closed down several months previously when its long-time owner/editor had died suddenly—no doubt due to the stress of the job, the town thought—and that no buyer had surfaced who was willing to take it on. Jamie had had the good fortune to receive a fairly substantial inheritance shortly after graduating from college which he'd saved rather than squandered, unlike what so many of his friends and colleagues did whenever they came into a little cash, and he'd used much of that, plus a substantial mortgage, to purchase the place, lock, stock and barrel. He quit the job in Philly, moved out of his apartment in center city, and moved eventually into a place here in town on, appropriately, Coryell Street. He'd never looked back and couldn't have been happier.

Growing up, he'd always been fascinated by the fact that a street in this town had his name. As a young kid, he thought somehow that made him a little more important than all of his friends, although they naturally didn't see it that way. His pride and boastfulness in that fact had earned him a few fights growing up, most of which he lost, he thought ruefully, but it did have one happy outcome—he credited it with launching him into the world of journalism. After being called a liar one too many times, he'd decided to get to the bottom of the story, and had discovered that in fact his ancestors had actually helped settle the town and had been pretty important people here. In fact, Lambertville had originally been called 'Coryell's Ferry' after the boat service that his great-great-great-great-great-great-grandfather ran here around the time of the Revolution, and it had remained that until some upstart named Lambert showed up and got the town named after him, just because he was a politician. 'Figures,' he'd thought at the time. One of his ancestors, George Coryell, had actually been a pallbearer for George Washington; can't get much more important than that, he liked to say. Many of these ancestors were buried in local cemeteries, and he'd enjoyed hunting through the old headstones to find their final resting spots. He remembered being keenly disappointed and upset when he discovered that many of the early graves he was searching for had been in the Presbyterian Churchyard in the center of town, which regretfully had been concreted over by the church in the fifties to make the gym where he now played basketball! The thought of those graves buried under a basketball court still irked him every time he walked past it as he headed for home up Union Street at the end of the day, as he was doing now. He'd compiled quite a dossier on the subject of the old Coryells from digging around in old records and books in local libraries and historical societies. He still had it in a box somewhere down at the office, along with all his other old files that he stored alongside *The Beacon's* archives. It actually came in handy at one point in high school when he'd had to write a report about something in the community for his social studies class. And best of all, he'd enjoyed doing all the hunting and searching for the details and the facts, and had decided then and there to pursue journalism for his life's work.

Coming back to Lambertville had been an easy decision. Even though he couldn't wait to leave when he graduated from high school in 2000 and left for Columbia, he'd come to realize after four years in New York and six or so in Philadelphia that he wasn't cut out for big city life. Yeah, it had it's moments, like when he wanted to just drop everything and head to the ballpark to watch the Yankees, like he did on so many spring days while at Columbia—never the Mets, though, perish the thought—or to watch the Phillies while he was at the *Inquirer*. Even got the paper to pay for a few of them, or got to use their box and hobnob for free with the big honchos occasionally. But he was much happier here now in a small town, with its slower pace and local color and easy-going friends. And if he wanted to watch some baseball in the spring and summer, there was a great AA team just down the road in Trenton—happily, it was a Yankees affiliate.

Turning east now onto Coryell from Union at the old Ben Franklin store, he mused that Lambertville sat squarely astride the great sport demarcation line that ran through New Jersey. It was a fascinating local phenomena that only natives completely understood: in this central part of the state, there was a constant battle going on for sports loyalties, with one side cheering for New York, which usually meant the Yankees and Giants and Knicks, and the other cheering equally loudly for Philadelphia and its Phillies and Eagles and Sixers. He was of a mixed mind, being a fanatical fan for the Yankees, a loyal fan for the Eagles when they won, and apathetic in general to basketball. He was not a typical case in the town, though, and had been witness to many discussions, sometime quite heated, between representatives of the two blocs. 'I guess the Phillies are okay in a pinch,' he thought, especially since they were in a different league than the Yanks, although he knew they'd never get close to the

Yankees' twenty-nine World Series championships—they were lucky to get that last one way back in 2008, he thought ungraciously.

He was now coming up to his house at the corner of Coryell and George Street. He'd bought this place as a fixer-upper a couple years after moving back to town and buying the paper. He'd lived in a small apartment uptown at first, then had felt able to invest in this once the paper got stable. The house was about 125 years old, and had looked every day of it when he'd first seen it. But it had good bones, as they liked to say, and he'd had enough foresight, plus enough nerve, to be able to see beyond the need for repairs and into what potential it had. His friends had poked fun at him at the time about its 'potential,' but they all agreed now that it was a great place. The house was a single dwelling, unlike many of the row houses that existed in other parts of the town, and Victorian in style. It faced onto Coryell Street, and had a wide covered porch on its front where he liked to sit in the evenings in the spring and summer on the glider he positioned there to relax at the end of the day with either a glass of wine from one of the local wineries or a bottle of River Horse from the town's microbrewery. Inside, the front door opened into a small vestibule that led directly to a narrow hallway heading toward the back of the house, and a stairway heading upstairs. A small living room opened to the left, with another room with a bay window, a dining room he supposed you'd call it, behind it toward the back. The rear of the house had the kitchen and a small mudroom leading out to the backyard, which was just barely large enough to hold the picnic table and barbecue grill that also occupied many of his evenings throughout the year. The yard backed into the service alley, a feature typical of this area of the town, at the rear of the house where he parked his car. The mudroom doubled as a utility room, and held his washer and dryer as well as racks for coats, boots, shovels and brooms. Upstairs the stairway emptied onto a small landing, from which there opened three small bedrooms, one fronting on Coryell, one onto George on the left of the house, and one to the rear. He used the front one as his master bedroom, the center as an office, and the rear as a workout area, where he had a treadmill, a stationary bike, and some weights. He'd furnished the house with a mixed collection of items that he'd either inherited when his parents had died a dozen or so years ago, or that he'd picked up in one of the many flea markets or antique shops that littered the area. It was a fairly eclectic mix with which he'd ended up, but he was very comfortable with it. He liked the house, and looked forward to coming home to it each day.

He'd discovered after he'd purchased the house that it was really in pretty good shape despite its outward appearance, so most of the 'upgrading' that he'd done consisted of improving the electrical system, replacing the roof, and repainting the place inside and out. He also did completely modernize the kitchen and the bathrooms. His one regret at this point was the lack of central air; he had to make do with a window unit in his bedroom to endure the humidity of the summers.

Climbing the front porch to unlock the front door, he paused briefly to admire the quiet street. Each house in this area of town was now nicely maintained, creating a very pleasant neighborhood. Large, mature trees lined the street and surrounded the house, a mix of mostly maples and chestnuts. He chuckled to himself, remembering that as a little boy he and his friends had always taken perverse pleasure in gathering the chestnuts as they fell each fall, hurrying to get them before the thorny pods began to dry out and split open to reveal the hard nut inside, and then throwing them at the neighborhood girls in a bid for attention. Ah, the good old days when the art of attracting female companionship was so simple.

He entered the house, flicked on the hall light, dropped his bag at the foot of the stairs, and headed toward the kitchen. He checked the answering machine on the way, and felt faintly disappointed that there were no messages. He planned to meet Sue for dinner tonight somewhere, but they'd not yet firmed up any plans. He guessed that he'd have to call her.

He was just reaching for the phone when it rang, startling him. He picked it up on the second ring. "Hello," he said.

"Hey, buddy, guess who?" came a familiar voice.

"Lou, how are you?" he replied, immediately recognizing the distinctive gravelly voice of his longtime friend, Lou Stevenson.

"Great. Listen, what are you doing tomorrow?"

"Tomorrow the Shad Fest begins here in town. I'm doing a feature article on it for the paper, so I'll be out and about. It is the social event of the season, you know" he laughed, emphasizing the 'the'. "What's up?"

"Well, I'm up in New York now wrapping up a story, and have to be back in DC on Sunday. Thought I'd swing by Mayberry on the way to say hello. Unless the place will be crawling with too many Shad Festers for me to get into town."

"Hey, that'd be great. I'm sure the Shad Fest will live up to your expectations. How long can you stay? Want to spend the night?" Coryell mentally calculated what gyrations he'd have to go through to produce a second sleeping space in his house, a drill he went through anytime Lou stopped by to visit.

"No, won't be able to do that, I'm afraid. Can only afford a few hours. I'll tell you what's up when I get in. I think I can make it over there early tomorrow afternoon, and then hit the road to get back home after dinner. How's that sound?"

"I think it's a plan. It'll be great to see you. Take your time getting here, and give me a call if you run into any trouble."

"Okay," said Stevenson. "It'll be great to see you, too. Been doing some interesting stuff I'll tell you about. Maybe I'll be able to entice you to come back to the main event instead of keeping yourself hidden out there in the boondocks." Stevenson smiled as he said it, and Coryell could hear the smile in the words.

"Don't hold your breath on that one. You take care. I'll see you tomorrow." He hung up the phone, which immediately rang again. "Hello," he said once more.

"Hey there," came another familiar voice. "I'm finally done and am famished. How about you?" Sue ran a small art gallery across the Delaware River from Lambertville in Pennsylvania.

"I just got in, but I can be ready in about ten minutes. Where do you want to go?"

"Wherever you think. You want me to come there, or meet someplace?"

"How about I meet you in the bar at the Lambertville House, and then we can go down to the Hawke to eat. I'll make us a reservation for 8." The Inn of the Hawke downtown was one of their favorite local places to eat. He looked at his watch, noting that it was now a little after six; still shouldn't be any problem getting a late reservation even though it was a Friday night, he thought. "Sound good to you?"

"Sounds great," Sue replied. "I'll be at the bar by six thirty with drink in hand. Talk to you then."

One of the things Jamie liked about living in Lambertville was that he could easily walk not only to work, but also to a surprising number of pretty good stores, bars and restaurants. He had passed the Lambertville House on his way home from work, so he headed back out the door and down Union Street again. The Lambertville House sat on the corner of Union and Bridge Street, at one of the three stop lights in town. Once he reached Bridge, he walked past the wrought iron railings of the old hotel and up onto its long porch, then pushed through the swinging door into the main foyer and turned right into the bar. Sue, as promised, was already there with, also as promised, drink in hand. And she'd been kind enough to order one for him, too. Glass of pinot grigio for her, and a draft beer in a pilsner glass for him.

"What did you do, fly over here?" he said, climbing up onto the barstool she'd saved for him, leaning over to give her a quick kiss, then grabbing for the beer. 'Very important to do it in that order,' he thought. Her gallery was over the free bridge on Main Street in New Hope, a drive that always took some time no matter what time of day or day of the week.

"Nope, just sailed on through. I think everyone's gone home early to rest up in anticipation of the big event tomorrow." She said that with just the faintest hint of sarcasm in her voice. Sue had grown up in a well-to-do home in wealthy Bucks County outside of New Hope, and frequently showed some good natured condescension toward the more pedestrian sister city in New Jersey. "Cheers," she said, clinked her glass with his, and took a sip of wine.

Jamie had met Sue about three years ago. He'd been writing up a story about local artists, and had made an appointment to interview her late one spring afternoon at her gallery. He was entranced with her when he saw her, but the interview was an abysmal failure. He was tongue-tied, disoriented, and generally incoherent throughout, and he was more than pleased when she took pity on him about halfway through it and suggested that they leave the gallery and go get a drink and only continue talking then. Coryell knew then that this was the girl for him.

Sue was about twelve years younger than he was, but did not seem at all intimidated by that age difference. She was on the short side, about 5'4", and about 110 pounds soaking wet, with an exotic look accentuated by dark hair that she kept cut short. She had the build of a runner, and obviously kept herself in good shape. 'Very good shape,' Coryell had thought to himself as they talked, sneaking an admiring look over the top of his glass as he took a drink. She told him that she'd grown up in Buckingham, about five miles south on Route 202 from New Hope, and had moved into town after dropping out of college four years back to paint. Her parents had been furious about that, she said; felt that she'd embarrassed them. They'd pleaded, cajoled, threatened and even bribed her to go back, but she'd obstinately refused, with the result that they effectively disowned her. They now rarely spoke and even more rarely saw each other. It took several months for Coryell to put two and two together and realize that her parents were Senator Fred Moscone and Congresswoman Fran Kerrigan; he was slow on the uptake since she now went by the last name of Malone. She explained that she'd had it legally changed from Moscone when they'd tossed her out of the house, and that she'd never regretted doing it. Jamie was not so sure that was completely true, but was smart enough not to voice that thought. Once they had grown closer together, he had one time been bold enough to ask her if she was seeing him because she thought or hoped it would irritate her parents. That inopportune question had nearly ended their relationship even before it had hardly begun, and had caused him to go to great lengths to regain her trust and respect. Happily for him, it had worked; he'd been careful ever since to make no further missteps.

"Guess who I got a call from just before you," said Coryell. Sue shrugged and arched her eyebrow as if to say 'I've got no idea.' "Lou Stevenson. Says he's traveling from New York back to DC tomorrow and wants to swing by to visit for a few hours."

"That'll be great," she smiled. Sue and Lou got along well. Jamie had introduced them shortly after the election in 2020, and they immediately hit it off like long-lost buddies. "I'm sure he'll be overjoyed to poke fun at the Shad Fest."

"No doubt." He finished off his beer, and signaled to the bartender to bring them both another round. "He thinks he'll get in about three or so."

The drinks appeared promptly and the empty glasses were whisked away. They enjoyed coming to the bar here rather than to others in town because the service was always great and the bar had a more intimate feel to it. He glanced around now as he took a first sip. Long, polished wooden oval-shaped bar that seated about 15 on tall barstools, backed by a full mirror. About a dozen small tables scattered throughout the room, each of which could seat four. Lights that were always dim, soft smooth music, and no smoke. It was their favorite place to start an evening.

The Lambertville House itself was actually a hotel, with about a dozen fairly high-priced rooms, as well as some party rooms and a small conference center. It had a blue plaque on its outside stone wall identifying it as a National Historic Site. Originally built in 1812 by Captain John Lambert—he of the Coryell family enmity—it had served as the principal way station in the town for many years, and hosted a wide variety of celebrities during the 19th century, including President Andrew Johnson and General Ulysses Grant. At one time, the old hotel ledger bearing those luminaries' signatures had been displayed in the dining area, but it had regretfully been lost when the hotel changed hands in the 1980s. The old hotel had been completely renovated about 25 years ago and transformed into the trendy place it was now.

"What's he doing in New York?" Sue asked about Stevenson.

"Don't know. He said he'd been pretty busy and would tell us about it tomorrow. Sounded pretty excited, actually."

"He needs to slow down," she said. "He's always racing from one place to another, driving like a maniac, trying to run down some new lead on a story he's doing. He's going to keel over from a heart attack if he's not careful. Guys his age have to be careful, you know?" She smirked at him.

"He's younger than me, remember," Jamie replied indignantly.

"Oh, that's right, I forgot," came the innocent response. She batted her eyes at him and squeezed his arm. "But you're in so much better shape."

"That's because I eat right and take my vitamins. Speaking of which, it's about time to head out," he said, looking at his watch. "You want to walk, or take your car?" The Hawke was about two blocks south on Union Street from the Lambertville House.

"Let's walk," Sue said. "It's a great night out. You can tell me about your day as we go."

They finished their drinks, paid the tab, and headed out the door and into the night.

CHAPTER 4

Lambertville, New Jersey
Saturday, 30 April 2022
3:27 p.m. EDT

Stevenson pulled up in front of Coryell's house at about three-thirty on Saturday afternoon. The drive over from New York had taken him just a little under an hour and a half; he hadn't hit any traffic at all to speak of once he'd crossed the Hudson and gotten clear of the Newark area. He was driving his beat-up late model Corvette convertible, built back before GM went bankrupt and shut down, which he parked in front of the house. Jamie and Sue were sitting together on the glider waiting for him.

"You're here," Jamie called out in greeting, getting up from his seat and coming down from the porch to welcome his friend with a hug. "And not a moment too soon. The festivities are just getting underway downtown. If we hurry we won't miss a minute of it." Jamie smiled as he spoke. He knew that Lou put up the false front of a hard exterior—it was like he believed he had to play the role of a big-time reporter, like the ones you saw in old movies, who had to live life hard and fast to be worth their salt. And he knew that he'd act like going to a local festival in a small town, a 'Shad Fest' no less, would somehow demean his exalted status as someone just passing through between big cities. But Coryell also knew it was in fact a façade, and that Lou really would enjoy the time here to unwind a little before sticking his head back in the meat grinder. "I'll bet you've been looking forward to it, haven't you?'

"Oh, it's been at the top of my '25 things to do before I die' list for ages. Hey, Sue, you're looking good, as always." He climbed up the porch steps to give Sue a hug, too. When the hug continued to linger on, Jamie snatched off his baseball cap and hit Stevenson in the back with it. "Hey, break it up there. Find your own girl, buddy. I saw this one first." Stevenson pretended as if he'd heard nothing, finally unclenched from the hug, then nonchalantly reached down into the cooler that sat next to the glider, picked up a beer, popped off the top, and took a long drink. He then pantomimed being surprised to see Jamie standing there and said, "Oh, sorry, were you talking to me? I had my hands full." Then he laughed.

"Yeah, so I noticed," Jamie replied, as he and Sue joined in laughter. They went through this ritual every time they got together. Jamie and Sue both knew that Lou meant nothing by it, and Lou knew that Jamie and Sue knew it. "Let's go."

The crowd began to thicken as they got closer to downtown. The Shad Fest in Lambertville was an annual event that had grown over the years into a two day party which featured local artists and craftsmen, and gave them a venue to sell their wares to the hordes of tourists who now were descending on the town. This year's event was the forty-first, and promised to be a wild one. Already music was blaring from the bands that played in three different locations downtown, and the smell of hamburgers, hot dogs and ribs cooking on the grills, as well as the smell of broiled fish mingling with it, started them salivating before they'd even reached Union Street. As they began to browse through the vendors' stands that had been set up in what seemed to be every available space along the street, and while Sue chatted happily with several local artists that she recognized, Jamie related the origins of the fest to Lou. The festival was so named because of the millions of shad which swarm up the Delaware River each spring to spawn; the shad motif was prominent everywhere, displayed in posters, T-shirts, balloons, and naturally, on the grills. Shad fishing had been a major industry in the area during the 19th century, but pollution in the waters took its toll and all but eliminated it by the 1940's. By the early 80's, though, pollution levels had been pushed low enough that the shad began to return to their ancestral grounds near Lambertville, and the local Chamber of Commerce saw that happy circumstance as an opportunity to promote business. "And that's how a tradition gets started," Jamie said to Stevenson, finishing up, as they walked.

They strolled a little further along the street, then stopped at a grill to buy something to eat. Perversely, both Jamie and Lou detested fish, and the thought of dining on a bony broiled shad was the last thing in their minds. So while many others at the stand happily forked over money for the fish, or even worse, for a scoop of shad roe—sort of a poor-man's caviar that was a local seasonal delicacy and a prominent feature at the fest—they each opted for a plate of ribs and a bottle of beer. They paid for the meal, carried their paper plates a little further down the street, trying not to be jostled in the crowd, and sat down on a picnic bench that was one of several set up in the parking lot across the street from the Lambertville House. While Sue bantered with a vendor across the way, they each began to devour the plate of ribs they'd purchased. It had turned out to be a delightful spring day, exactly what the organizers of the event had hoped for, with a bright sun and light breeze and temperature in the low 80's. Washing the spicy ribs down with the local River Horse beer as they watched Sue admiring some watercolors, they began to catch up on what each other had been doing.

"So why the big rush to get back to DC?" Coryell began. "Must be something pretty hot to keep you from spending the night here."

"Well, my friend," mumbled Stevenson through a mouthful of the fries that had come with their ribs, "you're looking at somebody who's been invited to fly out to California with the President on Air Force One tomorrow. And to be able to conduct running interviews with him throughout the trip to Mexico and Latin America. And to have a spot on the news each night to report on the trip as he makes the swing down there. You may kiss my ring, if you feel the need." He stuffed another forkful of fries in his mouth and studiously acted as if all this was nothing out of the ordinary for Lou Stevenson, star reporter.

"Lou, that's awesome!" Coryell shouted, thumping him on the back. "And definitely well deserved. How did it happen? Did you make a pitch to get the ride, or did the network decide to send you?" Jamie knew that a pool of about a dozen journalists, from both print and radio, as well as a TV camera crew and a few still photographers, normally followed the President during his travels to report on anything newsworthy. For Stevenson to be added to this pool was significant.

"A little of both, I guess," said Stevenson. He was pleased by Jamie's reaction to his news, although he was attempting, vainly, to hide it. Other patrons seated at nearby tables had turned their heads at Jamie's shout, and now were discreetly pointing in Lou's direction and whispering among themselves, clearing recognizing him. Stevenson's growing prominence in the national news scene was more and more frequently resulting in this kind of occurrence, something which he pleased him, although again he vainly tried to hide that feeling; Jamie pretended not to notice so that no more attention would be drawn their way, but inwardly smiled at his friend's good fortune. "I've been pitching the idea for a while," Stevenson continued, "telling them that it would be a great interest story to document what goes on behind the scenes during a major foreign trip like the one coming up. Something where people would be interested not only in the trip itself, and all that was at stake with it, but also in all the activity that goes on behind the scenes to make it happen. And I pushed myself as the one to do it, what with my investigative background and all. Much better than some political analyst"—here he mimed a finger quote to emphasize his disdain for the species—"who can't think below the surface of an issue and basically only reads what's fed to him by his betters. And they bit." He smiled broadly.

"So are you going to be along for the entire trip, or just one leg or so?" Jamie asked. The upcoming trip by the President had been talked about for weeks in the press; it had been sliced and diced and dissected every which way by analysts of every stripe. Jamie knew that the President was taking a large group through Latin America on an extended trip to shore up support for the U.S. in the on-going narco-war. After a quick stop in California to watch the final space shuttle landing, visits were planned in Mexico, El Salvador, Nicaragua, Panama, Colombia and Bolivia during the first week, then would wrap up the second with stops in Argentina and Brazil. Although the public agenda included discussions on the economy of the region as well as several public relations photo ops—the First Lady, who was also going along, would visit several schools and orphanages—and although there would naturally be all the obligatory formal state affairs along the way, the primary reason for the trip was widely known to be to coordinate policy for the eradication of the narco-gangs in Mexico.

"I'll be gone for the whole thing," Stevenson said. "It's my big chance to step up from the limelight and into the spotlight." He paused. "I want you to make a point to watch me every night when I report, then text me about how I did. Be brutal. Tell me like it is, so that by the end of this, I'll be in high demand."

"I wouldn't miss this for the world," Coryell responded. "It'll truly be my pleasure. And you may rest assured that I'll be as brutal as I possibly can." They each took a drink of the beers they'd almost forgotten about during the discussion. "Listen, how would you like to swing by and check out my paper. It's just down the street." He pointed down Bridge Street toward the river. Surprisingly, Lou had never had the opportunity to see it on his previous stopovers in town.

"I'd love it. Been wanting to see what keeps you tied down here anyway. Present company excluded," he added, as Sue came over and sat down with them.

"What are you two grinning about?" she asked. "I've been watching you for the last five minutes, and you look like two little kids who are sneaking cookies. Although two very old little kids."

"Does she always make age jokes?" asked Stevenson, ignoring her. "Just because we're so much more mature, she shouldn't take it personally."

"You just learn to overlook those character flaws," answered Coryell. "I'm confident she'll stop doing it once she grows up." They both swiveled their heads and looked at her expectantly for a rebuttal.

"Just give me a drink of your beer and I'll forgive you for being old," she replied, reaching for Jamie's glass. "So what's going on?"

Stevenson happily related the story once again.

CHAPTER 5

Stevenson nervously paced the tarmac as he and the others waited for the President's arrival. He had been told to be here no later than 3 o'clock; he had made sure he got here well in advance. With something this big, it definitely wouldn't do to get stuck in beltway traffic and miss the take-off. 'That would not go over well at all,' he thought to himself.

He'd left New Jersey late last night. He and Jamie and Sue had enjoyed a great evening after they left the Shad Fest. Jamie had proudly shown him around *The Beacon*, then instead of finding a place to eat in Lambertville, they'd walked across the old free bridge that spanned the Delaware to New Hope on the Pennsylvania side of the river. Once across, they'd turned north on Main Street and headed toward The Landing, one of Sue's favorite restaurants in the town. There, seated outside at a table overlooking the river, they'd enjoyed a great meal. It had been a warm evening with a cool breeze blowing in off the river, and they'd talked easily as they watched speedboats racing up and down the river to their front. They'd all shared a plate of fried calamari as the sun set behind them, then Sue'd ordered pan-seared scallops, which she ate with a local Chablis, while he and Jamie had each had chili with cornbread and beer. They'd stayed there until nearly 10, talking and laughing, then had walked back to Coryell's house where Lou'd fired up the Corvette and headed home. He'd made good time as he raced down I-95, was unlocking the door to his apartment on Quincy Place in DC by shortly after 1, and was crawling into bed by 1:15. He'd slept like a baby and didn't move until almost 10 the next morning.

Once awake and moving, he'd quickly showered and shaved, made himself a cappuccino on his DeLonghi espresso machine—in his opinion, a morning without a cappuccino was like a day without sunshine—then wolfed down a plate of scrambled eggs and bacon while he'd scanned the *Post*. After he'd cleaned up the kitchen, he'd packed the stuff he'd need to be on the road for two weeks, making sure to make it fit into a single suitcase, as he'd been instructed, then had loaded it and his briefcase and laptop into the Vette and headed into town where he'd picked up Pennsylvania Avenue and ridden it east toward Andrews. The day was a little overcast—the paper had forecast rain—but he knew that for the first couple days at least on the west coast the weather was supposed to be great. He'd driven easily through the city, had picked up the Beltway south and then got off at the Andrews exit. He'd had no trouble getting onto the secured base—his name had been provided to the guards at the gate by the White House Press Office so he only had to show his Press ID—and he'd had no problem finding the terminal where he'd been told to park his car and then wait. He'd been waiting now for nearly 45 minutes.

From where he paced he could see Air Force One. The Boeing 787 Dreamliner, emblazoned with the presidential seal on both sides of its fuselage near the nose, a large American flag painted on the tail, and the sides of the aircraft reading 'United States of America' in capital letters, had been brought into service during the previous administration, replacing the aging and costly 747s that had served for the previous 25 years. It technically was not 'Air Force One' until the President clambered aboard, but Stevenson at that moment thought of it as nothing else. When in commercial service, the 787 was a mid-sized, wide-bodied, twin-engined jetliner that would carry between 210 and 330 passengers, depending on variant and seating configuration. This aircraft, however, had been specially built to serve the President, and seated significantly fewer than its commercial counterpart. With more than 4,000 square feet of office space, the aircraft looked inside much more like an executive office suite than an airplane; indeed it was routinely referred to as the flying White House. In it, the President had onboard living quarters, including a private bedroom, bath, workout room and office; his staff had private offices, as well, and a large conference room doubled as a dining area. It could comfortably accommodate 75 passengers and 26 crew.

It had many other 'special' features, too, which differentiated it from a standard 787. It boasted a full-size galley for long trips, a well equipped medical room, an extensive communications suite, and could be refueled while in flight. More significantly, it was hardened to protect it against the electromagnetic pulse generated by a nuclear blast, and had received advanced avionics and defenses to safeguard it against enemy radar and heat-seeking missiles. It was much more of a flying fortress than the old B-17 had ever been.

As Stevenson gazed at the aircraft, he heard the distinctive whop-whop-whop sound that announced the arrival of a large helicopter. Soon Marine One, the military helicopter that shuttled the President around locally, came into view and touched down at the landing pad just outside the terminal. The President and his small party got out of the helicopter and walked directly to the front of the big jet, climbed up the retractable stairway, and disappeared out of sight. Stevenson and the rest of the entourage gaggled out of the terminal and up the rear stairs of the jet. Once on board, they quickly settled into seats, buckled in, and prepared for take-off. In what seemed like only moments, the big aircraft was hurtling down the runway and lifting off into the blue sky. 'No waiting in line on the taxiway when you're flying first class,' he thought to himself, gazing out the window to his right at the suburbs of Maryland which receded into the distance as the plane climbed higher. Within minutes, the plane emerged above the clouds and into the bright sun, then leveled off as they started the cruise to the West Coast.

Stevenson had just dozed off with his laptop opened and still in his lap when he felt a hand gently shaking him by the shoulder.

"Mr. Stevenson?" Stevenson peeled open his eyes to see that a clean-cut young airman was squatting down next to his seat. The crew of Air Force One was composed entirely of Air Force personnel assigned to the Presidential Airlift Group; the pilots and flight officers were typically very senior and very experienced officers, while the stewards and remainder of the flight crew were specially chosen non-commissioned officers. "Sir, the President asks if you've got some time and would like to come forward to see him."

Stevenson sat up straighter in his seat. He stared at the kid for a moment, thinking 'Is he kidding? Do I have time for the President?' He noticed that the other members of the press pool were all watching the exchange carefully. And resentfully, he noted. Many of them had been part of the pool that followed the President around the world to report on his travels for quite some time, yet had never had the chance to do more than say hello to the man. And here was Lou Stevenson, thrown on board out of nowhere and invited not just to talk to Navarro, but to do so in the President's suite in the front of the aircraft!

"Yeah, sure, sergeant. Give me two seconds and I'll be with you." He quickly stowed the computer away, grabbed a notebook and pens and his digital recorder, then unbuckled himself and stood up. "Okay, lead on," he said, and followed as the steward turned and moved quickly up the aisle toward the front of the plane. "Wish me luck, fellows," he called over this shoulder to the rest of the pool. He could almost feel the daggers their eyes shot into his back as he went.

"Lou, come in," the President called out as Stevenson appeared in the doorway. As he had followed the steward through the section reserved for the Secret Service detail and past the office area, he'd thought that he would be meeting the President in the conference room midway down the aircraft. That's where he had been told such meetings usually were conducted. But the steward had continued down the long hallway on the port side of the plane, passing the senior staff work areas and the galley and medical office, until he stood now outside the door to the President's personal office on board. "We'll just be a moment," Navarro continued. "Have a seat right over there and then we'll talk." He gestured to a plush seat against the wall of the compartment opposite his desk.

"Thank you, sir," Stevenson said, then turned to thank the steward for bringing him forward, only to find the young airman had already vanished; the only person in sight was the Secret Service agent standing post outside the office doorway, eyeing him suspiciously. He quickly entered the office and sat down as instructed, and began to look around the compartment.

Navarro sat behind the large executive style desk opposite him, with the requisite telephone and laptop positioned on his left. The compartment had a wainscoting of paneling, with white walls above; several portraits of what appeared to be Texas landscapes hung on the walls. A flat-screen TV, turned on—to Fox News, Stevenson ruefully observed—and muted, was hung on the wall opposite the desk to Stevenson's right. Navarro had taken off the coat and tie he'd worn when he'd boarded the aircraft at Andrews, and was now wearing a light windbreaker with the presidential seal emblazoned on the left chest over an open collared shirt. The President looked well rested, Stevenson thought, which was a good thing given the stress that would undoubtedly come as a result of this trip. Stevenson was always intrigued by the fact that Navarro's hair had yet to show any sign of gray, despite the pressure cooker of a job he was in, and unlike some of his predecessors, notably President Obama, who had seemed to gain a full head of white hair practically from the moment he took the oath of office. He wondered idly if the President dyed it to maintain his appearance of youth, but dismissed the thought as out of character for the man—he didn't think Navarro would care if he had gray hair, he was just lucky to have young genes. Navarro was finishing up a conversation with a man Stevenson immediately recognized as Aaron Post, the Secretary of Defense, who was seated in a chair to the left side of the President's desk. From the look on Post's face he was none too happy about the conversation which had just ended, but the President looked very relaxed, very much in control of the conversation and very sure of his position.

"I understand what you want, Mr. President," Post was saying quietly, glancing over warily at Stevenson. "We'll get to work on it right away."

"Thanks, Aaron. I know I can count on you all. We'll talk more about this later." And with that the Secretary got up and quickly exited the room. The outer door remained open, and the agent remained at his post.

The President leaned back in his high-backed chair, brought his arms up to lace his fingers behind his head, and arched his back with eyes closed, stretching the tension away. He maintained this position for a couple seconds and exhaled deeply, as if offering a silent prayer for strength to see him through trying times with difficult people. Then he opened his eyes, and turned to face Stevenson.

"As you can see, being President is not always fun and games," Navarro said with a smile, jerking his head to the right in the direction Secretary Post had gone. "It's often pretty hard work to convince even your own people to get moving on what you want done, let alone to convince those that don't work for you." He quickly got up out of his chair, came around the desk, and sat down in the chair next to Stevenson. "But that's neither here nor there, Lou. It just is what it is. So, anyway, Lou, it's good to see you again, and thanks for coming up here on such short notice." At this statement the President grinned broadly, focusing the hazel eyes directly on Stevenson's face, clearly enjoying the moment. "I ended up with some free time here on the flight, so I thought maybe we could take a few minutes to talk about the trip. You up for that?"

"Absolutely, Mr. President, absolutely. And thanks for the opportunity to talk." He began to open his notebook to write, and took out the digital recorder. He waggled this at the President as if to ask if it was okay to record the conversation.

Navarro nodded his okay. He watched Stevenson closely as they began speaking. He was impressed to see that the reporter did not appear flustered in the least by the short notice invitation up here, and that he did not appear overly intimidated either by him—Navarro—or his surroundings.

"So, what would you like to talk about?" Navarro famously always began interviews with this question, allowing his inquisitor to start off. He naturally had certain points he'd want to get across during the interview, but he would weave them into the conversation rather than force-feeding them up front. He'd found over the years that this technique for getting his message across worked very well.

"Well, sir, how about if we start with your objectives for the trip?" He'd set the recorder on the edge of his seat nearest the President, so that it would pick up everything clearly, and had pen and paper poised to takes notes during the conversation as well.

"Okay, that's easy. My one and only goal for this trip is to convince our friends and allies in this hemisphere that the gangs of criminals which have gained enough strength and wealth and power to threaten governments must be eliminated, and that only by acting collectively can we ensure that that will be done." Navarro maintained eye contact with Stevenson as he spoke. "It's in all of our best interests to do that; that's what I've got to convince them of. I've got to show them that the United States is acting in all of our best interests and that we'll all be better off in the long run for having acted forcefully now rather than waiting for things to get worse."

"Sir, if I may say so, that sounds like a pretty tall order, especially given the history of U.S. interventions throughout Latin America over the past couple centuries. Do you really think they'll accept it?"

"Well, I know I've got my work cut out for me. But not to try will be far worse in the long run, I'm convinced." As the President spoke, he made short, choppy motions with his hands to emphasize his points, an effect that was not lost on Lou.

"What are your plans if they reject your call for action?"

"I intend to go it alone if we have to. That will naturally make the job more difficult, and will potentially limit the actions that we could otherwise take to neutralize the gangs. Hopefully, it won't come to that."

"Sir, how do you intend to go about this? Are you considering sending forces into other countries, or simply providing support for local forces to take action?" Stevenson took notes as he asked the question, already considering how he would package this for presentation in his evening report.

"I intend to be proactive and strike at the heart of the gangs wherever that may be." Here he put up a hand to forestall Stevenson's inevitable question. "Yes, I know that sounds strikingly close to the Bush doctrine of preemption. But we've come to a point now where the threat has come to us; I consider myself duty-bound to eliminate it. And if that means military interventions, beyond what we've already done, then that's what we'll do." Navarro spoke very deliberately as he said this, clearly aware that Stevenson would report on this conversation later in the day.

"You sound almost like a Republican," Stevenson needled. Navarro smiled at the charge. "How do you think this will go over with your party?"

"Well, honestly, I believe the time has come to not worry about party politics and act in a manner that will best provide security for our nation and its citizens. I'm sure that I'll upset quite a few Democrats by acting this way." 'Fred Moscone chief among them,' he thought silently. "For that matter, I've already upset quite a few with what I've already done by ordering the intervention into Mexico last year. But I believe our success in that action, and the support from across the country that it generated, will buoy us as we take our next step. Which will be potentially a very contentious one." Here he paused. "You see, Lou, I intend to keep our forces in Mexico until at least 2024, and to establish Acting Governors and governments for those Mexican states we've occupied until such time as the Mexican federal government is firmly re-established."

Stevenson stared at him blankly, dumbfounded. Was the President really telling him that he essentially intended to take over the northern states of Mexico? He struggled to regain his wits and his composure. "Mr. President, are you saying that you intend to rule these areas as if they were U.S. territories?" Given the long and oft-times acrimonious state of US-Mexican relations, Stevenson wasn't sure he'd understood correctly.

"No, Lou, I didn't say that at all. What I said was that the U.S. will take the necessary steps to ensure that Mexico gets back on its feet, and that those steps will require us to remain in Mexico for the next couple years. The narco-gangs and drug lords there have caused nothing but death and destruction in those areas for the past twenty years, so much so that there are no local institutions viable enough to do the job. In that void, we will do the job for them until they can do it themselves. I believe that the American people will see the logic of this and will support it, as will the Mexican citizenry which is suffering in those areas. My job now is to convince our allies that this poses no threat to them." He paused to await Stevenson's response.

"Do you think you'll have much success?"

"I do." Again, Stevenson noted, a fervent declaration. The man clearly believes that he knows what must be done and has steeled himself to see it through. "We've already had some back-channel discussions at low levels with most of our allies, and the results of those have been uniformly positive. I anticipate being very successful."

"But what about the reaction in Congress, sir? Do you expect to get their support?" Stevenson clearly was dubious about this prospect, and the President picked up on that sentiment.

"Well, Lou, I know that's going to be a tough sell. I was just having that conversation with Secretary Post when you came in. I have held preliminary discussions of this with the Cabinet, and I plan to continue those discussions again tomorrow by video-teleconference in California. Secretary Post is not yet fully behind the endeavor, to say the least. As you arrived, I was instructing him to have the planners in the Pentagon begin working on the specs for the operation. You probably noticed he was none too pleased."

Stevenson nodded, still writing. "Yes, sir. I could tell he wasn't happy about something." He finished scribbling and looked up at the President. "I think you're going to get similar reactions from several other members of the Cabinet, as well as the Vice President."

"You know, it's interesting you mention her. I held a working lunch with her and the Congressional Leadership the other day—you can imagine their initial reactions," here he smiled, "and she spoke up fairly forcefully in support of this policy. I can honestly say I believe she'll publicly proffer that same support once I announce this during the trip."

"Sir,"—here Stevenson chose his words carefully—"I have to say that all this is an extremely optimistic prognosis. At the least, your announcement will create some degree of ill-will within certain sectors, both at home and abroad; at the worst, those opinions will dominate the debate regardless of the logic and promised benefits of your actions. I don't think you can underestimate the amount of distrust that exists toward the United States throughout Latin America."

"You're right, of course, Lou. And I recognize that fact. I'm not naïve about the difficulties that we'll face. But I have to believe—optimistically, as you say—that our arguments will prevail." Stevenson again noted the almost serene state the President was in, clearly comfortable with the decision he'd made. 'I hope you can keep that up,' he thought.

"Sir, shifting gears a little, do you worry at all about the threats that these actions may generate? I don't mean only to the U.S. itself, but more personally, to you." Navarro shifted in his seat, and stretched out his leg. Stevenson wondered if the talk about a threat caused the old wound to act up, or was it just sitting still for so long that did it. "There have already been several instances of the gangs publicly posting a bounty on you, and lately we've received a number of reports indicating that the drug gangs don't intend to go quietly into the night. Don't you think that these actions will only stir them up more?" Stevenson looked up to see what reaction the President would exhibit to that statement.

"Again, Lou, of course, you're right. There is always the possibility that some group may do something bad just because they oppose the policies we have. I can't be driven by that. I've got to put that in its corner and move forward." He again emphasized his point with his hands; interesting how he does that, Stevenson thought. "In that light, I'll tell you that we've received no hard intelligence indicating that any specific threat exists in any portion of the trip. That's to me personally, to the official party, or to any targets in the U.S. or along the way. Our guys have been focused on that for weeks now, and there is nothing credible that's turned up. I expect the trip to go off without a hitch." He paused, and smiled. "Perhaps we should compare notes about the threat. Maybe you're getting some intell that we're missing."

"Well, sir, I'm sure there's nothing we've got that you haven't heard about already. I just hope you're right." At this moment, the door to the right of the President's desk, which opened into the private presidential suite in the nose of the aircraft, opened and Julia came into the room. Stevenson struggled to get out of the chair and onto his feet as she entered, juggling his notepads as he did so, but she waved him back into the chair and dropped down next to the President.

"Lou, I asked the First Lady to stop in while we talked to see if you had any questions for her. Hope you don't mind." Stevenson noted that Navarro had immediately reached out to hold Julia's hand as she sat down.

"Not at all, sir. It's very much appreciated. Mrs. Navarro, thank you for taking the time to talk with me." Lou smiled as he spoke. This was the first time he'd met Julia Navarro, and as with everyone who met her for the first time, he was entranced.

"Please, call me Julia. May I call you Lou?" she asked, smiling back.

"Of course, absolutely," he gushed. He felt like a little schoolboy and had to forcibly act to regain his composure. The President was watching him with a bemused look on his face. Stevenson had no doubt that he'd seen this kind of reaction before.

"Wonderful, Lou, wonderful," she said. "First tell us a little about yourself. You're from Long Island, right?"

"Yes, ma'am. Julia. Yes. Born and raised there, then went to school at Columbia, then on to CNN, where I've toiled ever since."

"But you've built a pretty impressive reputation there," she continued. "That's why Ray requested that you come along. He was impressed with you when you interviewed him during the campaign a couple years ago, and has been impressed by your work since then." She looked at her husband.

"Now, Julia, you're not supposed to tell him that. Lou, ignore her; I never really like anybody's work." The President effected to put a stern look on his face.

"Yes, sir, that's what I thought she meant." Inwardly Stevenson glowed with pride at the unexpected compliment. "What about you, Julia," he asked, turning back to face her. "How did you and the President meet?"

"Oh, I saw him at a Board of Education meeting down in Houston one night. He was passionately advocating a policy change to the school board that would help the children of immigrant families do better in schools. I knew then that he was the guy for me. Of course, it took me a little longer to convince him of the same thing, but perseverance does pay off, I guess. Anyway, I introduced myself to him and basically invited him out on a date, and things took off from there."

"Sir, is that the way you remember it, too?"

"Oh, absolutely," said the President with feigned sincerity. "Seriously, do you think I'd contradict whatever answer she gave you?"

"No, sir, I suppose not," chuckled Stevenson, jotting a note. "And then you were married after a fairly whirlwind courtship." Reams of paper had been written about the life history of the first couple. "Do you ever regret getting involved in politics and being caught in the public eye?" Here again Stevenson looked up to gage their reactions.

The President and Julia looked at each other momentarily, as if they were unconsciously trying to decide who would field the question. Finally, Julia responded.

"No, Lou, I don't think either of us has any regrets about politics or being in the limelight. Sure it can get tedious once in a while being chased around by nosy reporters,"—here she reached out and poked Stevenson in the arm— "but all in all politics has helped each of us to accomplish the things that are important to us. Ray has been able to develop programs that have provided help for people who have nowhere else to turn, people who are really just like his parents were seventy years ago, and I've been able to work on programs to improve our schools and education. That success is a fair trade for the flashbulbs that occasionally go off in your face. Wouldn't you say so, Ray?" She looked over at Navarro.

"Julia's right, Lou. Politics has enabled us to do wonderful things, and has positioned us now to do even more. There are no regrets."

"No regrets at all?" Stevenson persisted, looking at Julia.

"Well, I'm sure you know the one disappointment we've had in our marriage," she responded. She'd often encountered questions of this sort before, and had become adept at answering them. "Every marriage wants children, and we haven't been able to have any. That's a tough thing even in a normal situation, let alone when it's in the public eye. Is that a disappointment for us? Sure. Is it a blessing, as well? Well, maybe. I'll tell you that when I had the miscarriage way back when that ended any chance I could get pregnant again, we were both devastated for a time. But then we both realized that this was nearly the same situation that Ray's parents had found themselves in shortly after they were married. It drew us closer to Ray's mother, and to his father in spirit since he was already gone, and it held out hope that other avenues for children still remained open to us." She looked over at Navarro. "You know that Ray is a 'test-tube baby.'" She smiled and Stevenson nodded. "It doesn't seem to have hurt him any. So we've been discussing the idea of an in vitro baby for ourselves, before we get too much older." She paused to let this sink in. Stevenson had stopped writing, having not been prepared for this intimacy and not knowing how he should handle it.

"Lou," began the President, "we'd appreciate it if you'd keep that to yourself for the moment. If you were to report that, it would create a great deal of chatter that will distract from the importance of this trip. When we're ready to make an announcement, if we're ever ready, I promise you that you'll be the first to know." Again, he turned the hazel eyes full on Stevenson. "Can I count on your confidence?"

"Yes, Mr. President. Julia. You can. I promise you that not a word will come from me. Thank you for your trust."

"You're very welcome, Lou," Julia said. "I knew I could trust you the moment I met you here. And I'm a very good judge of character, aren't I, Ray?"

A short knock on the door interrupted them before the President responded. The same young steward was standing in the open doorway.

"Mr. President. Mrs. Navarro. We've got about an hour until landing in California."

"Thanks, Jim. We'll be done in a moment." The steward vanished again, leaving only the agent in sight. Stevenson noted that he continued to watch as if he expected him to attack the President with the digital recorder or the pen he held in his hand.

"Well," said Julia, getting up. "I'll be going. Takes me longer to get ready than him, you know. It's been a pleasure talking with you, Lou. I hope we have a chance to talk some more while we're on the trip." She smiled at him.

Stevenson stood. "I'd like that very much, Julia. Thank you. It's been a pleasure meeting you."

Julia crossed over to Navarro, leaned over and gave him a quick kiss on the top of his head. "Mr. President, may I be excused?" She smiled down at him.

"You are excused, Mrs. Navarro," he responded. "I'll be in in a moment."

"Good-bye, Lou." And she was quickly out of the room, closing the door behind her. They both stared after her for a few moments.

"Mr. President, if I may be so bold, you are one lucky man. I can see why everyone loves her."

"I am indeed, Lou. I don't know what I'd do without her. I can tell you that I certainly wouldn't be here today if we hadn't met, and I don't know how I'd do this job now if I didn't have her to talk to at the end of the day." He got to his feet, signaling that the interview was concluded. "Well, I guess that's all we've time for now. I, too, will look forward to talking with you some more while we're on the trip. I'll be interested to hear your reaction to some of the goings-on, and I'll be interested to get your read on our audience. If you can help me with that, I'd appreciate it."

"Certainly, sir, I'd be glad to give you my impressions." He began to pack up his things and prepared to leave.

"Oh, by the way, Lou. Josh Caldwell asked me to say hello to you. Says he admires your work, and would like to talk with you about it sometime. Says you shouldn't get all of your info from the opposition"—meaning the Republicans—"like you did in New York."

"New York?" Stevenson drew a blank. "No, sir, I was up there following a lead I'd gotten after talking with Senator Moscone about homeland security issues. We had talked about the growing number of private companies doing classified work for the government, and it had piqued my interest. Nothing newsworthy, yet, unfortunately. But if Mr. Caldwell would like to talk with me, I'll be more than happy to talk with him."

'Very interesting,' thought Navarro to himself. 'I wonder what Fred is up to.' He reached out to shake Stevenson's hand. "Okay, I'll let him know. He'll be pleased to hear it. Good-bye, Lou. Happy landings."

"Thanks, sir. And thanks for the talk." The President stood by the outer door and ushered Stevenson back into the custody of the steward, who escorted him back to his seat with the rest of the press pool. This time the daggers from their eyes all went into his chest as he came down the hallway and buckled himself back into his seat.

CHAPTER 6

Edwards Air Force Base, California
Monday, 2 May 2022
10:08 a.m. PDT

The double clap of thunder from the sonic boom of the orbiter startled the onlookers and rattled the windows of nearby buildings. Those who were new to the experience looked at each other nervously, while the many veterans of these landings smiled knowingly. Many times residents of southern California had believed they were experiencing an earthquake, as they heard this noise and felt these rumblings. Local police and emergency services had come to anticipate a rash of 911 calls whenever a shuttle landing occurred on Edwards' runways.

About 500 official spectators had gathered this morning in the grandstands set up along Edwards' main runway to watch this final descent of a space shuttle. An additional several hundred were gathered just east of the sprawling air force base to watch in an unofficial status, jostling for prime locations at which to use their long-lens cameras and high-power binoculars. Many of these had been here many times before to watch a landing. They dispensed advice to the newbies about what was happening and what to expect next. Several of the more enterprising were hawking T-shirts bearing shuttle logos and slogans such as 'I witnessed the end of the Age of Discovery,' a nod to the name of this last orbiter in the U.S. space shuttle fleet.

The day was perfect for the event. Clear skies, no humidity, temperature in the low nineties—but it was a dry heat, as the locals liked to say—with visibility that seemed to go on forever. A dry, flat lakebed in front of mountains rising in the distance, this area of the high desert of southern California seemed tailor-made for aircraft and spacecraft landings. And indeed it had been used for just that purpose by the United States for the past 90 years.

Edwards Air Force Base, officially designated as the Air Force Flight Test Center, was established here in the Mojave in 1933. It was named after U.S. Air Force test pilot Glen Edwards, who died while testing the Northrop Flying Wing in 1948, one of many dozens of test pilots who had met similar fates while pushing their aircraft to the limits of their design. Located in the Antelope Valley, it covers nearly eighteen square miles of essentially uninhabited land far from distractions and far from prying eyes. Strategically located next to Rogers Dry Lake, a desert salt pan whose hard surface provides a natural extension for the base's runways, the location and the excellent year-round weather made it a perfect site for the testing of experimental aircraft. It was here that Chuck Yeager piloted the Bell X-1 that first broke the sound barrier in 1948, causing the characteristic sonic booms to be heard for the first time, just as they were heard again today. And it was here that many other less well-known, yet more potent, aircraft in the U.S. inventory had had their flight characteristics tested and perfected.

NASA began to use Edwards for the Space Shuttle program following the start of the program in 1972. 13 test flights of the Space Shuttle Enterprise, whimsically named after the stalwart starship in Star Trek, were conducted here, and Shuttle Columbia made the first landing here in 1981. Edwards continued to serve as NASA's primary shuttle landing site until 1991, when the construction of runways and service facilities at the Kennedy Space Center at Cape Canaveral made that a more favorable, and more favored for cost effectiveness, landing location. Nonetheless, Edwards remained as the primary backup, and many shuttle missions ended here in the high desert when the weather in Florida was uncooperative.

The spectators now craned their heads and necks as the orbiter became visible in this final portion of its descent. The 100-ton spacecraft was now moving more like an airplane than a spaceship, as its rudder and wings gradually became more active and responsive as air pressure built up. At this point in the flight path, the shuttle was actually an enormous glider flying in unpowered flight, since its engines contributed nothing to the landing sequence. During this final approach, the shuttle dropped to the runway about twenty times faster and seven times steeper than a commercial airliner does when it lands, and was still traveling at more than 200 miles per hour when the main landing gear touched the runway.

A collective 'Ooh and aah' had left the lips of the crowd as the landing gear was deployed by the crew and locked into place about fifteen seconds prior to touchdown, and loud cheers and applause broke out when the orbiter lightly kissed the desert surface with a puff of smoke from its wheels as the rubber burned and as the drogue parachute burst from its tail and slowed it to a stop. The crowd continued to cheer for many minutes, watching the large view screens that were set up around the grandstands on which the descent had been visible to NASA's long-range observation cameras well before it became visible to the naked eye. For several minutes, while service vehicles raced to meet the shuttle in the desert, and while its fuselage cooled from the inferno of the re-entry and the poisonous fumes of its attitude control jets dissipated, the shuttle remained silent. Then a moveable set of stairs was rolled against its side, the door was opened, and the crew of Discovery emerged into the California sun. The Air Force Band, which had been waiting for the moment, burst into life and the crowd cheered again.

President Navarro led the cheering in the official party, which included not only the President and First Lady, but also the Secretaries of Defense and Interior, the NASA Administrator, the Governor of California, California's two Senators and several other members of Congress, to include Senator Fred Moscone of Pennsylvania. An entourage of this size was not usually on site to witness a shuttle landing, whether it was here in the middle of nowhere in the Mojave or in the more hospitable climes of central Florida. This flight, however, marked the end of the line for the venerable spacecraft, as the Shuttle Program now officially ended to be superseded by the Constellation Program, representing the United States' first steps back to the moon and on toward Mars. The shuttle had been originally programmed to end service about ten years earlier, but developmental problems with the Orion spacecraft, the manned capsule within Constellation, had caused its demise to be extended so that transportation to and from the International Space Station could still occur without total dependency on Russian spacecraft. But now the day had finally come, and the shuttle would now be viewed only in the Smithsonian.

This day was also special for Navarro because one of his former roommates at West Point, Colonel Dick Jenkins, was the Command Pilot for this final flight. Navarro had been sorely tempted to intervene with Dave Forrest, the NASA Administrator, to get Jenkins assigned as the Commander when crew assignments were set up for this mission about two years ago right after he came into office, but he had restrained that urge. He was subsequently pleased to find out that it had worked out as he had hoped anyway; he never made even the smallest inquiry to see if Forrest was trying to butter him up or not. He averred that he was pleasantly surprised by the whole outcome, and that he knew that Jenkins was the right man for the job.

"Welcome home, Dick," said Navarro, extending his hand toward Jenkins as the crew emerged from the van that had brought them from the spacecraft back to the reviewing stands. They were all wearing their flight suits, which smelled faintly metallic to those who got close. They all walked somewhat unsteadily, and all appeared tired. 'Fifteen days in space will do that to you, I guess,' Navarro thought. "Welcome home to all of you, and job well done."

"Thank you, Mr. President," replied Jenkins, saluting and smiling. "It was our pleasure to be of service. I just wish it didn't have to end." The rest of the crew, composed of both military officers from all services as well as civilians, men and women, all nodded in agreement. It was clear to Navarro that the crew had been selected not only for their technical expertise, but for their demographics as well. Forrest clearly understood the significance of the moment, and NASA's place in it. The President, glancing over at him, thought to himself, 'I may have to keep a closer eye on Dave; he's a very smooth operator.'

The crew happily shook hands with the President, First Lady, and the rest of the VIPs, then patiently posed for pictures and spoke with the many reporters who were also present for the landing. The Secret Service kept a tight rein on things, ensuring that no one idly approached the President or his party, and that the media crowd was kept at a safe distance. Even though many of them had travelled with the President out here, in the minds of the agents each one was a potential threat and was treated as such. Stevenson was able to work his way toward Jenkins and speak with him after he finished with a reporter from Los Angeles. He then started moving to the van that would take the official party to the helicopters for their next leg of the journey. Most of the assembled group moved to either head home or to go ahead to Los Angeles to prepare for the President's speech tonight. Stevenson, though, was travelling with the smaller group that was going with the President and First Lady by helicopter to help open a new library in Victorville, about twenty-five miles southeast of Edwards on I-15. They would be there for about an hour, the President would give a short speech, basically a teaser for the major address he would make later in the evening in Los Angeles, the First Lady would help cut the ceremonial ribbon, and then they would all get back on their helicopters and fly to rejoin the rest of their party in L.A. The trip to Victorville was a nod to the First Lady's emphasis on primary education and child development, as well as a good public relations visit to maintain goodwill for Navarro in a state critical to his reelection hopes. It was a small detour that no one felt would have an impact on the more important trip to Mexico and beyond.

Reaching the helipad, the group boarded the waiting helicopters—the President and VIPs in Marine One, and the reporters in two other aircraft—and buckled in as the crews starting their rotors turning. When they had reached their operating rpm's, the aircraft lifted off into the clear blue sky and headed southeast toward Victorville.

CHAPTER 7

Victorville, California
Monday, 2 May 2022
2:27 p.m. PDT

Victorville, California is a city of about 100,000 people situated in the high desert astride I-15 between Los Angeles and Las Vegas. It was founded in the late 1800s near the narrows of the Mojave River soon after a railroad station was built there. The abundance of good water and the availability of rich bottom lands led to agricultural development shortly after the establishment of the railroad depot. Near the turn of the century, large deposits of limestone and granite were discovered, and since then the cement manufacturing industry had emerged as the single most important industry of the Victor Valley. The city was noted for having the largest enclosed regional shopping center between San Bernardino and Las Vegas, the Mall of Victor Valley. It was adjacent to this mall that the new Library of Victorville had been constructed on Petaluma Road.

Julia Navarro had long been a proponent of harnessing the power of the internet to bring higher education and learning within reach of more of America's citizens. Beginning with her graduate work at Rice, and continuing on through Navarro's tenure as Houston's Mayor, she had championed the development of high-tech institutions for research and learning. Throughout Texas, she had worked at the grass-roots level to goad local school boards and municipalities to bring their institutions into the 21st century. Now as First Lady, she had intimately involved herself with the workings of the Department of Education to foster nationwide development. Nowhere was this having a greater effect than in the Hispanic communities of the American Southwest, and this new library was one of the cornerstones for that development to be put in place in southern California.

A large crowd had gathered to witness the opening. Many had come because of their interest in the library itself. Many more had come to get a closer look at Julia Navarro, whose face continually graced the covers of magazines across the country and whose musings filled their pages. And many more had come to applaud Ray Navarro for his successes. It was a phenomenon that had become typical of his presidential appearances.

The library itself was a sleek, modern looking building. Two storied, with floor to ceiling glass windows on its front side, it had been designed to look like a place in which knowledge would collect and from which it could be easily accessed. A small seating area had been established to the left of the main entrance behind a small platform on which a podium with the presidential seal rested. It was here that the President and First Lady and other speakers would make their remarks. The platform itself was bedecked in the requisite red-white-blue bunting, and balloons and streamers adorned the front of the building. A large banner that read 'Welcome President & Mrs. Navarro' was strung over the front doors.

The crowd had begun assembling early in the morning, and by noon was estimated at 2,000 or more. Once again, the Secret Service, along with the California Highway Patrol, was aggressively keeping the crowd in line, establishing areas for the general public, for the media, and for the invited guests and VIPs. Those entering these areas were required to pass through metal detectors and to have all bags searched; the services were taking no chances with the security of their principals. In general, those enduring these measures were complacent about it, having long ago become accustomed to similar procedures when boarding planes and trains at stations and terminals across the country. A cordon of police from the Highway Patrol was posted in front of the library, between the speaker's platform and the public seating area; the officers were positioned about six feet apart along the front of the building, and were alertly watching the crowd while they waited for the arrival of the President's helicopter. A group of CHP officers on motorcycles were idling softly to the right of the building, prepared to escort the Governor of California from the site in his limousine once the ceremony was concluded; he was heading to an engagement in San Bernardino and had opted to travel by road for the short trip there rather than fly and be accused of wasting his taxpayers' money.

In the media area, local news stations, as well as the major networks, had set up control vans to orchestrate their broadcasts. They all wanted to be able to report on the President's remarks, as it had been made known that they would establish context for the evening's address. Missing out on these would put the stations behind the curve for later reports, and none wanted to place themselves in that position. A crew from the CNN office in Hollywood had been one of the first to arrive and set up their control van, and it was to this location that Lou Stevenson would head as soon as the helicopter in which he was flying landed on the temporary helipad that had been established in the new library's parking lot.

The arrival of the helicopters was staggered to allow the media and minor guests to arrive and get situated before the President and the official party touched down. This phasing was done primarily by the airspeed of the aircraft themselves; Marine One, which was capable of flying much faster than the other two helicopters, deliberately lagged so that a ten minute interval was created during the flight from Edwards. The phasing also allowed the first two aircraft to touch down and discharge their passengers, and then to lift off and relocate to the Southern California Logistics Airport, the former George Air Force Base on the northwest of the city near Adelanto, where they would refuel and wait until the ceremony was completed; they would then return to the helipad once the President had departed, reclaim their passengers, and make the final leg into Los Angeles. The ten minute headstart before the landing of Marine One would give the guests time to find their seats, under the watchful eye of the security services, and allow the members of the media pool to check in with their controls and get set up for the broadcast.

Stevenson hustled off the helicopter as soon as the doors opened, walked straight out from the doors to get out of the arc of the rotors, then veered to his left to where he knew the CNN van was located. The blades of the helicopters never stopped turning as the passengers disembarked, and the wind created by their rotation blew up a large cloud of Mojave sand that dusted the areas next to the helipad, causing people to shield their eyes and hang on to their hats. As soon as the last passenger had cleared the landing area, the two aircraft lifted off again, the whine of their turbines gradually fading away as they disappeared to the northwest.

As Stevenson climbed the three steps into the control van and opened its door, he was greeted with the familiar controlled chaos of live broadcasting. A control station in the center of the van faced multiple flatscreen panels showing the feeds from the camera crews that had been set up outside;

different shots showed the speaker's platform, the helipad, and the general crowd itself. Sitting in the center seat of the control station was Lynn Moggio, today's broadcast producer, flanked by two assistants who would help give direction to the camera crews and broadcasters, one of which would be Stevenson, and to talk back with the studio in Hollywood. Moggio was an old acquaintance of Stevenson's. They had worked together on numerous occasions before, so Lou did not expect to need much in the way of instruction prior to the beginning of the broadcast. He was not to be disappointed.

"Hey, Lynn," began Stevenson as he entered the van. He nearly had to shout to make himself heard over the din inside. Moggio was talking with the guy in the seat to her right as he came in, and glanced up at him and waved as she continued to issue instructions. "Got anything for me?"

"Hey yourself," she responded. "Nothing different than any other time. Just be yourself. Listen to what the man says, and tell us what he meant to say. Where should he set up, Joey?" she queried to the assistant on her left.

"Just to the left side of the platform should give us a good shot of the podium and the building. Camera 2 is already positioned there," the aide responded.

"Got that, Lou?" Moggio asked, even as she spoke into her microphone directing a camera to reposition. "Go get ready. Give us a sound check once you're there." She waved him away and resumed talking into her headset.

"Okay, got it. Be back with you in a couple minutes." He departed the way he came in, marveling at the silence outside as he shut the door. 'I am really glad I don't work that end of things,' he thought to himself as he moved quickly toward the left of the building in search of Camera 2.

He found his spot, about seventy-five feet to the left front of the podium, did a light test with the on-site director and a sound test with the control van just as Marine One appeared and landed on the helipad in a swirl of desert sand. The Silverado High School Band, invited to provide music for the ceremony and positioned to the right of the main entrance, struck up an amazingly good version of 'Hail to the Chief' as the President appeared in the doorway of the aircraft, eliciting a roar from the enthusiastic crowd which had been waiting for his arrival. He waved to them to acknowledge the applause and saluted the Marine sergeant who had jumped out of the rear of the helicopter and positioned a set of steps at the foot of the doorway so the President could exit. As the President waved, the First Lady appeared at his side, drawing an even larger ovation from the crowd. The couple then descended the steps and walked quickly across the tarmac of the parking lot to the speaker's platform in front of the library, followed by the other VIPs who had travelled on the aircraft with the President: the Secretary of Defense, Aaron Post; the Governor of California, Jim Marshall; and California's two Senators, Stephen Hartwig and Garrett Sutphin. They were met on the platform by the Secretary of Education, Walter Hodges, who had arrived in Victorville earlier in the day. The crowd continued to cheer, and the high schoolers continued to play, as the President alternately shook hands with the people on the platform and waved to the crowd. As he did so, the pilots of the helicopter that brought him powered their engines down, so that by the time the entire official party had made it onto the platform and was settled in their seats, the aircraft was quiet and its blades were still.

At various points throughout the crowd, newscasters could be seen facing their cameras and speaking earnestly into their handheld microphones. All were saying basically the same thing in preparation for the speeches—they described the helicopter's landing, they described the President's arrival and the reception he received, and they described the First Lady's wardrobe. Everyone recognized that it was just filler, taking up time until the speakers began, but each journalist did it nonetheless. Stevenson was no different, speaking in hushed, urgent tones to his viewing audience.

"The President and Mrs. Navarro have now climbed onto the speaker's platform and are greeting those already assembled there. In attendance are the Governor of California, James W. Marshall, California Senators Hartwig and Sutphin, as well as members of the President's Cabinet. The President and First Lady have arrived here after viewing the final landing of a space shuttle earlier today at Edwards Air Force Base, about forty miles from here. They've arrived here under warm, sunny skies, and have brought this crowd to a frenzy. You might think they were movie stars, given the reaction they're receiving. The President and Mrs. Navarro are now approaching the podium, where Governor Marshall will introduce them as the ceremony begins." Camera 2 framed Stevenson just to the left of the podium, so that his head and shoulders appeared in the foreground, with the VIP seats appearing behind his left shoulder and the podium, where the President and First Lady now stood, to the right side of the screen.

As Stevenson finished this sentence, the loud roar of a motorcycle sounded from the right of the crowd. Stevenson had just a moment to glance to his left over his shoulder, where he caught the image of a racing CHP motorcycle, and to register what seemed to be the sounds of gunfire, before the world lit up and he was knocked off his feet. Immediately, he felt a roar of superheated air blast over him, and a deafening noise thundered, drowning out every other sound. As soon as the heat passed by, black clouds of smoke began expanding throughout the area. The smell of cordite filled his nostrils, and the taste of it coated his mouth. He pulled himself to his knees, coughing as he did so because of the smoke. He shook his head slowly, trying to clear it. His ears were ringing. When he lifted his head to look around, the scene he saw was one of carnage.

The main entrance to the new library was devastated. Every window in the glass front of the building had been shattered; it was obvious that the falling shards had inflicted injuries on many of those below, in addition to the havoc that had been caused by the blast. People in the public area were beginning to get to their feet—although many forms lay still throughout the area—but the VIP area was obliterated. Surprisingly, Stevenson thought, he did not see much fire. Some small flames were evident here and there, but there was no large conflagration. But as he peered through the smoke toward the spot where the President had been standing, he could make out no one.

As he looked around, he slowly became aware of the noise. Not only were there moans and screams from those injured by the blast, but the earpiece that still was lodged in his right ear was screaming at him. He heard Moggio's voice yelling.

"Lou. Lou. Lou. Answer me. Tell me what's going on. Tell me what you see."

He was surprised to see that his cameraman and director also appeared to be uninjured—shaken, without a doubt, but uninjured—and he motioned to them to get ready to broadcast.

"Lynn, I'm here, I'm here" he yelled into the mike. "Give me a second to get it together."

"Hurry up, Lou," she yelled back unsympathetically. "If you're not hurt, you should be talking to me. What happened?" Stevenson heard the whine of sirens now adding to the din around him. Ambulances that had been positioned across the street from the library in the mall parking areas were now screaming into the blast area, accompanied by what seemed to be every police car and fire engine in all of southern California.

Stevenson gathered his wits about him and began to speak to the camera. "Lynn, a devastating blast has just occurred at the site of the new library being dedicated by the President and First Lady here in Victorville. I don't know yet what happened, but it appears that the entire VIP section has been destroyed. I can't tell you the fate of the President—I don't see him anywhere—but I'll see if I can work my way a little closer. Stand by." He began making his way forward toward the site where the podium had been. He could see that the podium had been blown about fifteen feet to its right by the blast, and that a deep crater, black and smoking, now existed just to the left of the speaker's platform in the area where the band had been playing. As he got closer, he could see ambulance crews now aiding the wounded who were scattered throughout the area. Police and secret service agents were working hurriedly to establish a cordon around the blast site; he knew that this was not only to protect those that were still living, but also to preserve what was now a crime scene.

"Lynn, the scene here is unbelievable. It appears that a bomb was detonated just to the right of the main entrance as you face the building. Are you getting this shot?" he asked to the cameraman, motioning with his hand in the direction of the devastated library. "Okay, okay. The kids from Silverado were in that area—I can't see anyone moving there. To the left of the entrance, where the speaker's platform was, there is not as much destruction—but the podium is gone, and the blast has carried all the seats that had been positioned there away. I can see some movement in the area, as well as numerous bodies on the ground. Medics and police are now swarming the area." He coughed from the smoke.

"Lou," she intoned in his ear, "what can you tell us about the President?"

"Lynn, I can't see him anywhere. The area where he and Mrs. Navarro were standing while the Governor spoke is gone. It's just gone. Wait—there's a big commotion happening. Secret service guys are going nuts. Now the medics are running over to where the agents are standing. Can't see what they've got, but from the way they're placing themselves around the area, I'd say they've found the President and that he's still alive. I can't see any movement, so I'd have to guess he's injured. Now they've got an ambulance backing in there. Wait, wait—another cluster. More guys racing around. Stand by, let me see what I can find out." He turned to the cameraman. "You stay here and keep filming—don't move, just stay put. I'll see what I can find out, then come back." And he headed off toward the ambulances.

He had to fight his way forward. Smoke continued to foul the air, making both breathing difficult and visibility murky. The fire crews were swiftly putting out what few fires existed, but the smoke was still terrible. The cries of those wounded in the blast were increasing, adding to the calls of those now rushing to provide aid. He worked his way up to the front edge of what had been the general seating area; the remains of the speaker's platform were about twenty feet to his front. He could see that rescuers were performing a triage of sorts, by-passing some bodies that lay still while hurrying to aid those that were moving. More ambulances had been brought forward, and medics were beginning to load victims into them.

There was a sudden high-pitched whine off to his left, and he turned in that direction just in time to see the President's helicopter lift away from the helipad and fly away. 'Why would they leave now?' he thought, then had the answer provided as two smaller helicopters with large red crosses painted on them swooped in to land in its place.

He turned his focus back to the blast area and tried to move forward again, only to be stopped this time by a disheveled Secret Service agent. "No further, pal," the agent yelled to him, placing a hand in his chest to stop him from moving further forward. The agent was covered in soot, and his once neat suit had tears in the arm of the jacket and in both knees; an ugly looking sub-machine gun was in his hand, and he clearly was not inclined to get into any discussion about his order.

"What about the President?" Stevenson shouted back to him. The agent shrugged his shoulders and waved off in the direction of the first ambulance that had arrived. As Stevenson looked in that direction he saw a stretcher with a bloody body on it being lifted into the rear, then saw the doors slammed shut as the ambulance raced away, siren screaming. "Is that him? Where are they taking him? Is he dead?"

"Not dead. Not dead. But hurt bad. Don't know where they're going."

"Who else is hurt?" Stevenson watched as more bodies, some moving in pain and some still, were lifted onto stretchers and either loaded into additional ambulances or set aside to wait their turn. "What about the Governor or the First Lady?"

"Don't know," the agent said distractedly, his head continuing to swivel back and forth as he watched the area. "Not sure. The Governor's dead, I think, but I haven't seen anyone else. You need to get out of the way now while we deal with this. If you're not hurt, go back where you were and stay put." The agent moved away abruptly to intercept others who were coming forward to gawk at the spectacle.

Stevenson turned around and began to run back to his camera, but immediately tripped over something and fell on his knees, tearing open his left pant leg and scraping his shin. Looking behind him he saw that the obstacle was the decapitated body of a man; Stevenson noted perversely that the corpse still had a tie neatly knotted around the remains of the neck. He clambered shakily to his feet, only to find that he had fallen in the pool of blood that had come from the body. His hands were now sticky with it, and the front of his shirt was covered. He began running again, frantically wiping his hands on his shirt as he ran.

"Lou, what happened to you?" asked the cameraman, staring at his ashen face and the blood that covered his shirt. He and the director were still in the same spot; they had been continuously filming since Stevenson had left. The director moved forward to see if Stevenson needed any help.

He waved her away. "Nothing. I'm fine. I fell. Lynn, can you hear me?" he shouted into the mike he had retrieved, stuffing the earpiece back into his ear. "The President has been severely injured and has been taken away by ambulance. I don't know where, but probably to wherever the nearest hospital is. Initial report says the Governor has been killed. Got that from a Secret Service agent. Nobody knows anything else at the moment, or at least they're not saying. The scene is absolute chaos. I couldn't identify any other bodies, but there're dozens all over here. Ambulances are hauling some away, some are being flown out on medevacs, but I'd estimate I've seen at least twenty-five dead on the ground. What do you want me to do now?" He turned around as he spoke to stare back at the scene.

"Lou, pack up your guys there and head off to the hospital. See who's being brought there and what's going on. Nearest one is only a couple of blocks from you, Desert Valley Hospital, east on Bear Valley Road. Go there, then call back in."

"Okay, got it." He tossed the mike to the director. "Let's go. We're going to head to the hospital to see what's there. Which way to your car?" She pointed off in the direction opposite the destroyed building. "Good," he said, "let's go."

The sirens and cries of the injured continued as they ran to the other side of the parking lot, piled into the car and headed off.

CHAPTER 8

Washington, DC
Monday, 2 May 2022
6:35 p.m. EDT

"Madame Vice President, Josh Caldwell here. We have a situation. I need you to come over to the Situation Room immediately." Caldwell was speaking in quick, urgent tones on the phone. Vice President Kerrigan had taken the call in her ceremonial office in the Eisenhower Executive Office Building across the street from the White House where she had just concluded a reception with the new Swedish Ambassador. She had been preparing to head back home to the Vice Presidential mansion on the grounds of the U.S. Naval Observatory off of Massachusetts Avenue in northwest Washington where she was to host a dinner in the Ambassador's honor later in the evening.

"Josh, what's going on? Jess said he didn't know what you wanted." Jess Dougherty was the Vice President's Chief of Staff. He had been her long-time legislative assistant while she served in the House, and had loyally moved with her when she won the Vice Presidency two years ago.

"A bomb went off where the President was speaking in California about a half hour ago. He's been injured, but we don't know how bad. Things are pretty sketchy right now. Robby's going to give us the latest as soon as you get over here." Dan Robinson—'Robby'—was the Director of the Secret Service.

"A bomb?" Kerrigan sounded dumb-founded. "Where, at Edwards or L.A.? How bad is the President?"

"We don't know how bad he is. Robby should be able to tell us some more. The bomb went off at the ceremony in Victorville. No other details. Listen, I gotta run. Keep this close hold until we know more. Get here as fast as you can."

"Josh, wait. What about Fred? Was he there, too?" Kerrigan knew that her husband was part of the President's party for the foreign travel, but she didn't know if he had intended to accompany Navarro on his itinerary before Mexico.

"No. He was at Edwards, but he had headed down to L.A. to get ready for the dinner tonight instead of going to Victorville. He should be okay. Gotta go. Get over here quick." The phone clicked dead in her ear.

Kerrigan reset the phone in its cradle and sat down in her chair, trying to clear her mind. She reached out and hit the intercom button on her phone, and dialed in Dougherty's extension. "Jess," she began. "Get the car ready to take me across the street right away. Then come in here." She powered down the laptop she'd been working on, then waited. Fifteen seconds later a knock sounded on her outer door and Dougherty entered.

Kerrigan began speaking before he could utter a word. "Listen. There's been an assassination attempt on the President in California," she began, not even thinking about Caldwell's request to keep the news quiet for the moment. "The Service is going to give us a brief across the street in a little bit. I need you to cancel my things for tonight—offer my apologies, offer to reschedule, whatever you think is right—and clear my schedule for tomorrow. Things are iffy right now." She started gathering up her things and headed for the door. "And get Senator Moscone on the phone and ask him to call me as soon as he can; he should be in L.A. now." She halted and turned to face him. "Got all that? Any questions?"

"How bad is the President," Dougherty asked.

"They don't know yet. We should know more after the brief. I'll let you know when it's over."

"Okay, got it. The car's waiting for you downstairs. I'll track down the Senator and ask him to call"

"Thanks, Jess," Kerrigan said as she swept from the room. "Talk to you later."

Lambertville, NJ
Monday, 2 May 2022
7:12 p.m. EDT

"Jamie, Jamie," cried Alice Metzger from the front office of *The Beacon*. "Are you watching this on the news?"

"I've got it," Coryell called back, standing up at his desk and staring slack-jawed at the screen of the TV. The TV on the table in the corner of his office ran continuously on mute throughout the day while Coryell worked. He normally flicked it back and forth between CNN and Fox, depending on the mood he was in, so he could keep up with what was happening in the outside world. It was on CNN now, and he had turned the sound on to listen to the 'Breaking News' that was blasting from it.

"I can't believe it," said Metzger, coming into his office and standing next to him to stare at the screen. They had just been getting ready to close up shop for the night when the report came on.

"…and there are unconfirmed reports of dozens dead among the audience who had gathered to watch the President and First Lady dedicate the new library," intoned the commentator from the set. "As yet, there is no report on the condition of the President. Neither the White House nor government officials on the scene are offering any comment. To repeat, a bomb exploded just over an hour in Victorville, California where President Navarro was participating in a ceremony opening a new library. There are reports of significant numbers of casualties, but no word yet on the condition of the President, and no report of how the explosion occurred or who is responsible for it. We take you now to our local affiliate in California." The scene switched from the talking head to one of the devastated area in Victorville.

"I can't believe it either," agreed Coryell. "I wonder if Lou was there," he said suddenly. He began fumbling with his cell phone, scrolling through to find Stevenson's number. It was an emergency number the Stevenson had told him could reach him at any time, day or night. Coryell had never used it before, but now felt compelled to do so. He pushed connect and held the phone to his ear, listening as it searched for the signal, then began to ring.

"Oh, Jamie, I hope he wasn't there," Metzger said, reaching out to touch his arm. She knew how close the two were. "I'm sure he's okay."

Suddenly the phone connected and Coryell began shouting into it. "Lou, Lou, hello, it's Jamie. Are you alright? I just saw the news. Were you there?" The connection sizzled with static.

"Jamie, yeah, I'm okay," Stevenson yelled back. "Sorry I can't hear too good right now. Was about fifty yards from the blast when it went off, and it really rang my gong. Unbelievable. I'm okay, though. Trying to see who's being checked in at the hospital now. Gotta go. I'll talk to you later." The connection went dead.

Coryell snapped the phone shut. "He's okay, he says." He sagged down into his chair, still watching the screen which now shifted from a scene of the destroyed face of the new library to one of medevac helicopters lifting off from the area next to it and flying away. "He's okay. Says he'll call me later." He looked over at Metzger. "Said he was right there when it went off. He's checking the hospitals now to get some updates."

"What did he say about the President?" Metzger asked.

"He didn't say anything," replied Coryell. "And I forgot to ask. Hopefully he's okay, too."

"You're right about that," Alice shot back brusquely. "I hate to think about things if Kerrigan is in charge." Metzger had never minced any words about her dislike of the Vice President or her husband. She knew them both from living and working in the area all her life, and had actually met the two during election campaigns at various times in the past. She had not been impressed by the meetings.

Coryell did not reply as he continued to watch the story unfold. But he thought to himself: 'I wonder what Sue will think of all this.'

Washington, DC
Monday, 2 May 2022
7:18 p.m. EDT

Within five minutes of leaving her ceremonial office, Vice President Kerrigan walked into the Situation Room in the basement of the West Wing of the White House. Everyone stood as she entered, and she quickly motioned them back to their seats as she looked around the room. She saw that Caldwell had assembled the principals of the Crisis Action Team in record time. She noted that the seat at the head of the long conference table was vacant—waiting for her, she presumed correctly—and that Josh Caldwell was occupying the chair to its right. On the left was the National Security Advisor, Oliver Holcombe. Occupying other chairs in the room were the Deputy Secretary of Defense, Jared Radcliffe; the Secretary of State, Michael DiMarco; and the Chairman of the Joint Chiefs, General Sam Fuller; as well as the heads of the CIA and FBI and another half dozen Cabinet officers and staffers. 'Interesting,' she thought, as she noted with distaste the presence of the White House General Counsel, Rich Pregent, among those assembled farther down the table; Pregent rarely was invited to participate in meetings of this type. At the foot of the table, standing next to a briefer's lectern, stood the Secret Service Director, Dan Robinson.

Kerrigan swiftly took her seat as the doors closed behind her. "Okay, Josh," she said, addressing Caldwell. "Are we ready to go?"

"Yes, ma'am, all set. Robby, go ahead."

"Thank you, sir." Robinson was an athletic looking man of fifty-six, of medium height, with a haircut that would have made any Marine proud. He always dressed impeccably, and even in this pressure situation looked like he was ready to pose for the cover of GQ if someone asked. He had been in the Secret Service for twenty-six years, the last three as Director, having been appointed by President Thomas and kept on by Navarro when he assumed office. He had a well-deserved reputation as an effective, no-nonsense administrator, and had worked hard to modernize the Service and keep it the best in the world. He got right to the point of the briefing.

"Madame Vice President, ladies and gentlemen. At 3:06 Pacific time, approximately one hour ago, a bomb was detonated outside the new library in Victorville, California where the President and First Lady were presiding over the ribbon-cutting ceremony. The President was severely injured in the blast. He was transported to Desert Valley Hospital in Victorville where he is currently undergoing emergency surgery. Initial reports indicate that he sustained injuries to his head, chest and left leg. He is currently listed in critical condition, pending the conclusion of the surgery which is expected to take at least another hour.

"The bomb appears to have been delivered by a suicide bomber dressed as a California Highway Patrol officer and riding a CHP motorcycle. Various reports indicate that just prior to the blast a motorcycle which had been idling with other CHP vehicles to the side of the library suddenly raced in toward the speaker's platform and then exploded. We are reviewing video from the networks now to verify if this is correct. We're also in communication with CHP to ascertain if one of their officers is missing. We should know both answers within the next half hour."

"Robby," the Vice President interrupted. "What is the extent of other casualties?"

"Ma'am, preliminary reports list twenty-four dead and another forty-seven injured, some of them critically. Killed in the blast were Governor Jim Marshall of California, as well as Senator Gary Sutphin and Secretary of Education Hodges. Secretary Post was injured, although apparently not severely."

"And how many of your agents?"

"Ma'am, four were killed outright by the explosion, including Marv Whitaker, the President's head of detail. Six others were injured, although two later died at the hospital." Here he paused. "All of them had young families. We've already initiated steps to support them through this ordeal."

"Robby, what a tragedy." Kerrigan shook her head. "Please let the families know that if there is anything they need, all they need do is ask. Relay our condolences to them and thank them for their sacrifice."

Robinson stared stiffly at the Vice President, thinking her response a little too canned, a little too trite, working to hold his emotions in check. "Thank you, Madame Vice President. I'll be sure to do that." He paused again. "Regretfully, I must also tell you that Mrs. Navarro was apparently severely injured in the explosion; we have not yet ascertained her status."

"No," gasped Caldwell. "Not Julia, too. Robby, please ask your senior agent on site to determine her status as quickly as possible." He turned to face Kerrigan. "If she has been truly injured in the attack, you can bet that there will be calls for action to avenge her from one side of the country to the other. There'll be anger enough about the President being attacked, but it won't compare with what follows when word gets out that Mrs. Navarro has been injured, too. We've got to get on top of that immediately."

"Agreed," responded Kerrigan. "Robby, please make that a priority."

"We will," he replied.

"Do we know yet what type of bomb it was?" asked General Fuller.

"No, sir, not precisely. Not yet. But it does appear to have been contained within the motorcycle that I mentioned earlier. I would not want to jump to conclusions, but that type of delivery device is typical of the drug cartels that have operated in Mexico. I have a forensics team moving to Victorville now from L.A.; they will arrive within an hour and should be able to verify the accuracy of my statement shortly after that."

"Ollie," Kerrigan said, speaking to the National Security Advisor to her left. "What's your thought on this? Is this an isolated incident or something bigger?"

"Ma'am, I'd have to say that it's an isolated incident. We've seen nothing to indicate that any widespread threat exists. There have only been general upticks in the noise level over the past couple weeks as the President's trip was announced, and those correlated most closely with threats outside the country. I'd be surprised if there was anything more to it. "

"Ma'am," interjected Loren Fitch, the Director of the FBI. "I'd concur with Dr. Holcombe's assessment. We have not been picking up anything that would indicate a widespread threat aimed across the government."

"Okay," responded Kerrigan. "So, we have to wait for Robby's next update until we know the President's condition. What else do we need to do, Josh?" She turned to her right to face Caldwell.

"I'd recommend we direct an increase in the security level at all government facilities until we get a little more clarity here." Kerrigan nodded her approval. "Naturally, we also need to prepare a statement for the media; I've already got Barb"—Barb Singletary, the White House Press Secretary—"working something up that we can release when we're ready."

"Okay, good. I'd like to review that once she's got it ready. Anything else?" asked Kerrigan.

"Yes, ma'am," answered Caldwell, pausing deliberately. "We need to consider transferring the President's power to you as prescribed in the 25th amendment. I've tentatively called a Cabinet meeting for tomorrow morning to discuss that." Around the room, heads turned to look quizzically at each other.

"Josh, do you think that's really necessary? I mean, we don't even know the President's full condition yet. Moving too quickly like this might be taken the wrong way around the country and across the world."

"Ma'am, with all due respect, it's something that has to be considered." Rich Pregent was now speaking from the end of the table. "The amendment makes it very clear that in the event of a President's disability, his powers and authority must be transferred to the Vice President, or whoever is next in the prescribed line of succession, as quickly as possible so that no void in leadership exists in the government. I don't believe you have a choice in the matter."

Kerrigan bridled at this comment from the lawyer, but held her tongue. Ignoring Pregent, she continued speaking to Caldwell. "Alright, Josh, convene the Cabinet for tomorrow morning. The sooner the better, I guess, if we're to believe Rich." She glared down the table. "What time have you set?"

"We're currently scheduled for 8 o'clock," replied Caldwell.

"Okay, 8 it is. Robby, anything else?"

"Nothing yet, ma'am."

"Good," said the Vice President, rising from the table. Everyone stood as she did so. "We'll reconvene, along with the rest of the Cabinet, upstairs at eight tomorrow morning to discuss the 25th. I'm not particularly happy about this, I want you to know. I think it's premature. But we'll talk it through and see where it goes. Good night, everyone."

She left the room to silence.

CHAPTER 9

Victorville, California
Monday, 2 May 2022
4:42 p.m. PDT

Stevenson had made his way into the Emergency Room of Desert Valley Hospital, and was trying to make sense of the scene before him. It had taken him quite some time to get this far; the police had the entrance to the emergency room drive-up blocked off when he and the crew had pulled up, and they hadn't been able to talk their way through. They had then pulled around to the main entrance of the hospital, and happily found that it had not been restricted yet. Stevenson sent the camera off to film arriving ambulances, with instructions to get as close as possible, while he entered the hospital with the intention of getting into the emergency room through the 'back door.' After a few wrong turns in the building, he'd been successful, since the security guys were only focused on the outer doors at the moment.

He knew he'd have to work as fast as he could while he had the chance. He expected to be accosted by someone in authority at any moment, then hustled from the room by hospital security, or police, or secret service and either removed from the building or placed into temporary custody. He'd been in similar situations before during his investigative career, so he knew he had to move quickly.

The scene in the room was nearly as chaotic as it had been at the library. A steady stream of stretchers bearing bloody bodies was flowing into the room, where a team of doctors and nurses were frantically working to sort through them. He could see that they were triaging the arrivals as they were brought in. Doctors and nurses were shouting back and forth to one another, issuing instructions and requesting assistance. Those arrivals with apparently life-threatening injuries were hustled deeper into the hospital, presumably for emergency surgery or other measures, while those who were less serious were being staged along the walls of the room and the adjacent corridors to wait. As Stevenson passed among them, he could see that most appeared to have cuts and bruises, maybe some broken bones, but no trauma from the explosion or its aftermath. He assumed that those injuries were the ones being wheeled further in. He looked at the faces as he went by, trying to recognize some. Most were strangers, but he could identify a man he knew was a Secret Service agent, another who was California's senior Senator—'Here's one situation where you won't get any preferential treatment, buddy,' he thought as his gaze slid past the senator with the blood-stained shirt—and yet another who had been on the helicopter with him when he arrived at the library from Edwards. He saw no sign of the President, or any others in the official party. Glancing around the room, he noticed another set of stretchers that were being placed in an adjacent room and left unattended. As he made his way there, he saw that they were being sent there by one of the triage doctors, who would examine the body on arrival, shake his head with shoulders slumped down, then wave the bearers toward the room. Stevenson realized that these were the dead being set out of the way of those who still had hope. He made his way to them to see if he could recognize anyone.

Most of the bodies were not covered; there had not been time for body bags or anything else, so Stevenson could see them all clearly. Several of them had traumatic injuries, clearly resulting from proximity to the blast and from flying debris. Several of the dead were members of the high school band, still in their uniforms. He recognized the Secretary of Education, and remembered he had been standing to Navarro's left when the explosion went off. His gaze slid to the next stretcher, and he sagged against the wall as he recognized the mutilated body of Julia Navarro.

Stevenson could see that the First Lady had apparently been struck by flying glass, as well as bearing much of the brunt of the blast wave. The left side of her body was literally in shreds, with jagged gashes on her neck and left shoulder. Her blonde hair was matted to her skull with blood, and the light yellow blouse she'd been wearing was black and sticky. Stevenson felt himself gasping to breathe, leaning with both hands against the wall to steady himself. He realized that he'd been talking with her only a few hours ago, when she'd been so full of life and vitality. And now that was all reduced to a bloodied mess. Stevenson, no stranger to the sight of terrible and horrific things during his career, felt as if he was going to be sick.

"Are you injured?" a voice asked him. "What are you doing here? You alright?" Stevenson turned to see a security guard facing him, looking warily at the blood on his shirt. "You need to be out of here. Come on with me, and we'll get a doctor to look at you."

"No, I'm all right, just a little disoriented," Stevenson said. He let the guard lead him away from the dead room and back into the main area.

"You wait right there and somebody will see to you as soon as possible."

"Okay, thanks." Stevenson waited until the guard was out of sight, then got up and left the room, and went to rejoin his crew.

CHAPTER 10

Washington, DC
Monday, 2 May 2022
11:21 p.m. EDT

Caldwell sat slumped at his desk in his West Wing office, staring at, but not seeing, the images on the TV screen flickering in front of him. He held a tumbler of scotch against his temple, as if that would help him concentrate; it was his third of the night, and the night wasn't over.

He had decided not to go home to Georgetown after the press conference. He'd had things to arrange before the Cabinet session in the morning, things to see to, and—the bottom line—he just didn't want to be alone in the big house on this night. At least here he had other people around, even if they were all busily working in other offices. He could sense their presence, and their presence let him know he wasn't alone.

Singletary had handled the press conference well, he reflected, delivering the terrible news without emotion, and fielding their probing questions as if she were discussing something of no consequence, rather than something that struck at the core of the national psyche. The press corps had actually been relatively respectful, not clamoring for attention, not trying to outshout one another, but patiently receiving the news and waiting their turn to query the Press Secretary.

The President's condition was now more fully known. He had suffered serious injuries to the left side of his body, the side that had been presented to the blast when the explosion occurred. The wounds to his chest and left shoulder were relatively superficial; sutures had been required to close the cuts that had come from the flying glass, but no vital organs had been injured and there was no doubt among his attending surgeons that he would regain full use of his left arm in time and with therapy. The wounds to his head and left leg, however, were much more catastrophic. When he had arrived at the hospital, his lower leg and knee had been mangled by the blast and were hanging by shreds to his body; the doctor's had immediately determined the leg could not be saved and had amputated it just above the knee. He had also sustained a broken pelvis, which would require him to be in traction for an extended period. The physicians were of mixed mind as to whether he would recover enough to walk again, even with a prosthesis. The head injury was the most traumatic. Again, flying glass had marred his face, requiring 155 stitches to sew up the gashes that had been opened from temple to chin down his left cheek, and to reattach his dangling left ear. But the blast wave had knocked the President unconscious, the concussion causing the brain to swell, which in turn had required that he be placed into an induced coma while the skull was opened to relieve the pressure caused by the swelling. He still remained in the coma, with no clear prognosis about when he would awaken. Caldwell had been told that injuries of this sort could sometimes heal without aftereffect, while at other times patients would linger in the coma until they just slipped away. Caldwell groaned as he thought about his vibrant friend lying in that condition.

The press had received that news stoically, with clinical questions regarding future treatment and prognosis. Likewise they had received the news of the other deaths—Jim Marshal, Walt Hodges, Gary Sutphin, and the others—in a sanguine manner, as if the cruelties imposed on these public servants were just part of the job. But when it was announced that Julia Navarro had also been killed, they broke down. Beloved as she was, they could not accept her passing so easily; clearly, it was not part of her 'job' to be placed in harm's way. The reports following the conclusion of the press conference had all been of a similar vein, with somber announcements of the President's condition, followed by emotional reports of the First Lady's death.

Caldwell could almost not shake the feeling that he was in a waking dream. He could not believe that these two friends, ones he had so recently shared a pleasant meal with, ones who had been so much a part of his life for the past dozen years, were gone. Gone in an instant. True, Navarro was not gone yet, but it felt like he was. His prognosis was certainly not encouraging, and Caldwell had a foreboding he couldn't get rid of that Ray wasn't coming back. He had said he'd do anything for them, and now he found he could do nothing. He couldn't get a grip on it. The scotch was the only comfort he had.

Calls had begun to come into the White House from around the world from other leaders offering condolences and asking if they could help in some way.

Caldwell knew that some were sincere, but that most were not, and after the first few he decided to refer them all to the State Department to answer.

He had called Kerrigan with the updates on the President's condition as they came in. She had returned home to the Naval Observatory after the Sit Room meeting, and seemed to be receiving all the bad news in what Caldwell felt was a callous manner, remaining very unemotional and showing no signs of grief or remorse. He thought again of how much he disliked her, and her detestable husband, and resolved to remain true to Navarro's agenda until the time he woke again. He didn't know how Kerrigan would act once she assumed power—and it was now a fairly foregone conclusion that she would receive that authority when the Cabinet convened in the morning—but he felt sure it would not be in the way Navarro would want her to act.

Taking another long pull of the scotch, Caldwell got up and walked out of his office, going to find the Press Secretary to see if there were any further updates at the end of this bleak day.

CHAPTER 11

Washington, DC
Tuesday, 3 May 2022
08:00 a.m. EDT

Vice President Kerrigan walked into the Cabinet Room at 8 sharp. All stood as she entered, and all sat when she sat. She didn't offer any greetings on the way in. She had sought her husband's advice on the phone last night, and they had concurred that it would be best to conduct this meeting formally and in a purely business manner, without any of the usual preliminary pleasantries.

She pointedly did not sit in the President's chair; she and Fred had agreed that she should not seem presumptuous, and she did not want to cause any distraction to the purpose of the meeting. Glancing around the long table, she noted that all seats were filled by the principal Cabinet officer, with the exception of Defense, Interior and Education, which had the Deputies representing their absent superiors. Every seat along the exterior walls of the room was also filled with a staffer of some sort. Clearly word of the purpose of the meeting had spread and generated keen interest. Kerrigan was willing to bet that the struggle to gain entrance to the meeting and occupy those seats had been intense, cutthroat even—no one wanted to miss this moment in history. She intended to remedy that situation. Looking to her right rear, she found Josh Caldwell sitting in his usual position in the corner of the room, with General Counsel Rich Pregent to his side.

"Josh, I want everyone who is not a cabinet officer, with the exception of you and Rich, to clear the room."

Heads along the table all swiveled toward Caldwell to await his response, while most of those along the walls began squirming in their seats.

"Madame Vice President, I don't think that's a wise idea," Caldwell began. "Each secretary here may require the advice of the aides they've brought. Our discussion promises to be unprecedented. I'd recommend…"

"Josh," she said, cutting him off abruptly in mid-sentence. "Just do as I asked please. The cabinet secretaries will have to think for themselves." Turning back to face the table, she continued, "Everyone who is not a cabinet officer or representing one will leave now." She glared around the room at all those who had no need to be there.

Slowly, grudgingly, the staffers packed up their bags, got to their feet, and began to exit the room. Some stopped momentarily to hand their principal a file folder or sheaf of papers, or to offer some parting words of advice, but the room cleared quickly. Kerrigan sat with her hands folded, glancing around the room as it cleared, silent. The door finally closed behind the last to depart, and the 15 cabinet officers, along with Caldwell and Pregent, were left alone with the Vice President.

"Madame Vice President," Caldwell began, clearly irritated at being cut off before, but was immediately silenced as Kerrigan held up her hand.

"Josh, drop it. Let's move on with what we've got to do." She paused to gather her thoughts, cleared her throat, then began to speak, slowly and without emotion. "Ladies and gentlemen, our purpose here today is to consider invoking the 25th Amendment to declare the President incapable of performing his office because of disability. I would like to do this in a straight-forward manner, without any pontificating or histrionics. I will ask Mr. Pregent, the White House General Counsel, to explain the particulars of the amendment and what it requires of us, then will ask Governor Caldwell to update us on the President's status. After that we'll discuss the issue as necessary, then vote on its implementation. Are there any questions or comments?" It was clear from her tone that she neither wanted nor expected any response, and she was not disappointed. "Very well, seeing that there are none, we'll begin. Mr. Pregent, if you please."

Pregent stood and began to speak from his position at the wall of the room. "Thank you, Madame Vice President. Ladies and Gentlemen, good morning." Pregent was a thin man of moderate height, bespectacled, of French Canadian heritage; now sixty-two, he had been appointed as General Counsel by President Navarro one year ago. "The 25th Amendment to the Constitution, which clarifies presidential succession, was passed by Congress in 1965 and ratified by the States in 1967. It was initiated largely as a result of the assassination of President Kennedy in 1963, which resulted in Vice President Johnson, who had a history of heart problems, assuming the Presidency. It also acknowledged advances in medical technology and technique, with the resulting capability to maintain an injured person's life for extended periods of time, even though the patient was completely incapacitated.

"The amendment is structured to address three contingencies. First, what happens when a president dies while in office or is removed from office by impeachment or resignation. Precedent had been long established, beginning in 1841 when Vice President John Tyler became president following Harrison's death in office, that the Vice President becomes the President when this occurs. The 25th states this outright, without ambiguity. He does not merely 'discharge' the duties of the president; he is the new president. This situation has occurred eight times in the nation's history, most recently in 1974 when Nixon resigned and Ford became President.

"Second, it allows for the case when a sitting President determines that he is unable to discharge his duties effectively. This is a case where a president may be temporarily incapacitated, typically due to a medical procedure. When the President informs the President Pro Tem of the Senate, and the Speaker of the House, in writing, of his incapacity, the Vice President is designated as the Acting President and authorized to discharge the duties of the office. The President remains the president, but is unable to act; the Vice President is not the president, but is authorized to act as one. When the President determines his incapacity has been overcome, and he again informs the Congressional leadership of that in writing, he is once again authorized to act as president. This clause of the amendment has been invoked a handful of times in recent years by Presidents Reagan, both Bushes, and Thomas, at times when they were sedated for medical procedures." Pregent paused and looked up from his notes as some muted laughter was heard.

"Must be a Republican thing," quipped Bob Powell, the Attorney General, irreverently. Others chuckled around the table.

The laughter stopped abruptly as Kerrigan rapped her knuckles on the table. "Gentlemen, please. We've got a serious issue to deal with here, and I'd appreciate your full attention, not sophomoric humor." She glared at Powell. "Mr. Pregent, continue."

"Thank you, ma'am. The third contingency is what we are meeting to consider today. It is the case where a president has been disabled, by whatever instance, and is unable to declare himself incompetent and transfer his powers. The amendment then allows the Vice President and a majority of the Cabinet to declare, in writing, to the same Congressional leadership, that the President is unable to execute his office. In this situation the Vice President is declared the Acting President with authority to discharge the duties of the president. This situation remains until the President recovers sufficiently and can declare to Congress in writing that he is again capable. This last declaration can be challenged by the Vice President and Cabinet if they feel it's improper or premature, in which case it is adjudicated by Congress. This clause of the amendment has never been invoked before."

He paused and looked around the room. "Are there any question thus far?" Seeing none, he continued. "Very well. On a side note, the amendment also prescribed how to fill a vacancy in the Vice Presidency, although this is not of interest to us today. It has been utilized twice since ratification: first, when Gerald Ford was selected to replace Agnew after he resigned the office; and second, when Nelson Rockefeller was selected to replace Ford after he became President following Nixon's resignation.

"So, the situation is this. If you, the Cabinet, determine that President Navarro has been disabled to the extent that he is unable to perform his duties as president, you may, by majority vote, so notify Congress, in which case Vice President Kerrigan will be declared Acting President. There are no specifications about what characterizes a disability, nor of what discussion must be entertained, nor of how a vote should be conducted. You are literally establishing precedent here today.

"Madame Vice President, unless there are any questions, that concludes my synopsis of the 25th."

"Thank you, Mr. Pregent. Please be seated." Looking around the table, she asked, "Are there any questions?" Seeing there were no indications of any, she turned to Caldwell and said, "Governor Caldwell, please provide us with a current update on President Navarro's condition."

Caldwell stood wearily, and also began speaking from his position along the wall of the room. He spoke in a monotone, clearly upset by what he had to report. "Madame Vice President, members of the Cabinet. The President's condition is largely unchanged since the last reports we received last night. He remains in critical condition. He spent six hours in surgery yesterday at Desert Valley Hospital in Victorville following the assassination attempt. He has been stabilized, and plans are being made to fly him to Walter Reed here in Washington as quickly as possible; it's anticipated that this will be possible within a week's time. The injuries he sustained to his chest and left arm are largely superficial and not a long-term threat to his health. He has had his left leg amputated at mid-thigh—a traumatic injury, to be sure, but not life-threatening. The right leg, which had sustained the wound in Afghanistan years ago, is considered viable, but he has suffered a fractured pelvis, which may ultimately leave him unable to walk again even with a prosthesis. Again, traumatic, but not life-threatening. Most seriously, however, are the blast injuries he sustained to the head. Although there was no penetration by flying shrapnel, the blast wave caused a severe concussion which necessitated cranial surgery and required that the President be placed into an induced coma. He remains in that state. It's also now been determined that he suffered a fractured skull, most likely due to being knocked down by the blast. The surgery is believed to have been successful, and the prognosis for his full mental recovery is considered good at this point, but the doctors intend to keep him in this induced coma for an extended period until the swelling of the brain diminishes. Even after it has gone down, they are unable to predict precisely when the President will regain consciousness." Caldwell stopped speaking, and pulled a handkerchief from his pocket to wipe his face, which had turned ashen as he spoke. It appeared as if he was going to continue, but then abruptly sat down.

"Josh, are you alright?" Kerrigan asked, looking at him closely. He nodded that he was okay. "Do you have anything else for us," she persisted.

"No, Madame Vice President, I've nothing to add."

Kerrigan stared at him dispassionately, but inwardly thought to herself, 'Caldwell, it looks to me like you've been in the booze again. You're about at the end of your usefulness here. Something may have to be done with you, old friend.' And then aloud, "Very well, Josh, thank you." She turned back to the table.

"Ladies and gentlemen, I propose we act in this manner. We must determine if President Navarro is unable to act as president. We will do that by taking a public vote, not a secret ballot. I don't believe there should be any secrets to this decision. If we make that determination, that an incapacitation does exist, I will ask Mr. Pregent to draft a letter to Congress informing them of our decision, signed by all of us, which I will then deliver personally to the President Pro Tem and the Speaker. Does anyone have any issue with that process?"

It was clear from the body language of some around the table that there was a fair amount of uneasiness. Kerrigan presumed it had to do with the lack of a secret ballot. 'Too bad,' she thought. 'None of you will be able to hide this time.' She shared the general view that most people were often very bold and forthright when things could be done without anyone else knowing about them; politicians were the worst of the bunch in this regard. She had no intention of letting any of them get away with that.

Kerrigan waited a few seconds longer; still no one voiced an objection. "Very well," she said. "Since there are apparently no objections, we will proceed. The subject is open for discussion. Does President Navarro's current condition, as delineated for us by Governor Caldwell, make him unable to execute the duties of the office of president?"

For the first several moments, the heads of the government's executive departments looked around the table at each other as if they were school children who had been called on to recite. Finally, the silence was broken by Mike DiMarco, the Secretary of State.

"Madame Vice President, I believe there is nothing to debate here. President Navarro, regretfully, is clearly unable to act as president. The man is unconscious, with no prognosis that he will awaken any time soon. And even if he awakes, there is no guarantee that he will not be mentally impaired as a result of his injuries. We simply cannot adopt a wait and see attitude, hoping that his impairment will be very brief, and hoping that no crisis occurs in the interim. I'm ready to vote now to declare a disability."

"Thank you, Mike. Are there any other comments?" She swiveled her head to look around the table.

There were none. Although several others around the table felt compelled to speak—they were, after all, politicians who could sense the historic import of this moment, and hence the need for them to be remembered by history as actively contributing to the decision—no one else voiced anything different than had the Secretary of State. All concluded that President Navarro was incapacitated as a result of the injuries sustained in the assassination attempt, and was therefore unable to function as president.

When Vice President Kerrigan called for a vote by polling each member around the table, all fifteen Cabinet officers voted affirmatively. Kerrigan made it unanimous.

"Very well," she said. "We are of one mind. Mr. Pregent, please prepare the letter we discussed earlier to inform the Congressional leadership of our decision. Indicate in there the reasoning behind it, and state that the vote was unanimous. Everyone here will sign it"—here she stared pointedly at the people seated around the table—"and then I will deliver it."

"Yes, Madame President," Pregent began. "I'll…"

"No." Kerrigan immediately cut him off. "Let me make this completely clear to everyone. Ray Navarro is the President of the United States. He is temporarily incapacitated, and I will act in his stead. But I am not the President. I will have no one address me as such, and I will not pretend to be such. I will discharge the duties of the office, but that is all. Is that perfectly clear to everyone?" Heads nodded all around the table. "Good. Please ensure that your departments are clear on that as well." She turned toward Caldwell. "Governor Caldwell, please schedule a meeting for me with the President Pro Tem and the Speaker in the Speaker's ceremonial office in the Capitol today at the earliest opportunity. And for all, I expect no word of this meeting to be made public until I have delivered that letter."

"I will do my best," Caldwell spoke sullenly. He clearly was unhappy with the results of the day.

"Ensure it happens, and the sooner the better. Rich, I want that letter back in this room within thirty minutes; Governor, I want it signed by all within the hour." She stood up, catching most off guard, causing them to climb hastily to their feet. "I'll be in my West Wing Office." The Vice President had both a working office in the West Wing—one which Kerrigan rarely used—as well as the ceremonial office across the street in the Eisenhower Building. "Bring it to me there when it's completed." And she swept out of the room before anyone could offer any comment.

As soon as she had left and the door closed behind her, the room exploded into conversations. Pregent quickly left for his office upstairs to draft the letter. Caldwell alone remained seated and silent. 'One way or another,' he thought to himself, 'I will ensure that Ray Navarro resumes his office. That woman is not going to hijack his presidency while I have any say in the matter.' He got up without speaking and went to his office to arrange the meeting.

CHAPTER 12

New Hope, Pennsylvania
Tuesday, 3 May 2022
1:14 p.m. EDT

"…in an historic turn of events, Fran Kerrigan now occupies the Oval Office as President of the United States," intoned CNN's commentator Ken Ingalls on the television across the room. It was a very pleasant spring day, and Jamie Coryell had walked across the bridge to New Hope just before noon to join Sue for lunch at Fran's Pub, a little place on Main Street that was not overly frequented by tourists. They had found they could get a good sub there, eat it at the counter, and talk quietly with each other throughout their meal. Today, though, midway through their meal, this story had broken into the regular program, and thoroughly disrupted their peace of mind. They were each stunned by the news.

"Well, to be precise, Ken," interjected Mitzi Fletcher, another of CNN's stable of political analysts, sitting at the news desk with Ingalls, "Ms. Kerrigan remains officially the Vice President, but is authorized to discharge presidential responsibilities as Acting President. She made that point several times during the brief press conference she held in the Capitol following her meeting with Senator Cherry, the President Pro Tem of the Senate, and Congressman Garcia, the Speaker of the House, at which she presented them with a letter signed by her and the entire Cabinet indicating their determination that President Navarro is no longer capable of acting as president."

"You're right, of course, Mitzi. For those just joining us, the 25th Amendment was invoked today to…"

Jamie turned to Sue as the news continued and said "Well, I guess that means you'll get a Secret Service detail to protect you now." He smirked at her. "Could cramp my style, you know."

"Don't even say something like that," she responded dryly, a deadpan expression on her face. "I'd refuse it if it were offered. Again. I had to do that two years ago when she got elected Vice President. The last thing I want is to be known only as her daughter, and not my own person. I hope no one makes the connection." She stared at him. "It certainly better not make its way into print."

"Won't be because of me, if it does," Jamie replied, eating the last of his sandwich, "but don't bet that word won't get out. Somebody on some tabloid will become interested in you, just because your family situation is newsworthy, and they'll try to track you down; wouldn't be very hard, truthfully, despite the name change. And if your mother is now president—or at least acting as the president—you've just become even bigger news. Prepare yourself, 'cause it's coming."

"Man, I really hope you're wrong," Sue moaned. "That is the absolute last thing I need." She looked at him quizzically. "You don't think that Lou has figured it out, do you?" They had never told Lou who Sue's parents were.

"I wouldn't doubt it. Lou's a pretty sharp cookie, you know. But even if he has, he wouldn't use you like that. Don't worry about him."

The commentary on the TV continued, with Ingalls and Fletcher now recounting the list of injuries to Navarro, and running through the preliminary details that had been put together for Julia Navarro's funeral.

"I really hate news people," said Sue, a look of distaste on her face. "Present company excluded, of course," she quickly corrected herself, smiling at Jamie. "But they're all ghouls. You can practically see them drooling over the spectacle of that funeral while the President fights for his life, unconscious, not even aware that his wife is dead. They really need to get a life. Maybe contribute something positive for once, instead of just gloating over the bad stuff." She huffed disgustedly and stuffed a piece of apple pie in her mouth.

"That might be a little harsh," responded Jamie. "Somebody's got to tell about the bad stuff, too."

"Yeah, but they don't have to act like they're enjoying it."

"I suppose," Jamie said. He took a sip from his mug of coffee. No pie for him today. It'd been a long winter, and he'd decided to lose a bit of the extra that had somehow grown around his waist. He daily cursed his slowing-down metabolism. "How do you think your mother will do in the job?"

"She'll be great," responded Sue immediately. Even if they didn't see eye to eye about many things, Sue respected her mother completely. "She's wanted to be President practically her whole life. It's what she's worked to achieve for the last thirty years. Everything she's ever done politically has been viewed with an eye on that prize. I think she wanted it even more than my father did when he ran for the nomination back in 2012." She chuckled. "The hard part now will be getting her out of the office if Navarro ever wakes up."

"Seriously?" Jamie asked, suddenly interested. "Now that would be a story to tell."

"Well, you better not be the one to tell it. Both of my parents are not people you want to mess with. And they'd definitely consider a story like that messing with them."

"Oh, just kidding," Jamie said, although in his mind he'd already begun to turn over the possibilities. He looked at his watch, then signaled to the waitress for the bill. "Man, time flies when you're having fun. Gotta run," he said, standing up and digging for some cash. "I do have a paper to publish, you know. I'll see you later." A quick peck on the cheek and he was out the door.

Sue turned back to the TV and resumed eating the remains of her pie, a pensive look now on her face as she listened while the commentators droned on. "Good luck, Mom," she said quietly to herself.

CHAPTER 13

Washington, DC
Tuesday, 3 May 2022
3:22 p.m. EDT

Fran Kerrigan walked into the Oval Office upon her return to the White House from the Capitol and stood staring at the President's desk. Known as the Resolute Desk, it had been a gift from Queen Victoria to President Rutherford Hayes in 1880, and had been used off and on by presidents ever since. Ray Navarro had chosen to keep it in the office when he moved in, just as Brad Thomas had done before him. Famously, it was the desk in the 1962 photo taken of young John Kennedy Jr. playing underneath, peeking out of the kneehole panel, while his father, the President, worked above. The desk had been constructed from the timbers of *HMS Resolute*, an abandoned British ship discovered by an American vessel and returned to the Queen of England as a token of friendship and goodwill by the United States. When the ship was retired from service by Great Britain, Victoria'd had the desk constructed at the Royal Naval Shipyards, and then presented to the President. Hence, it's name.

Kerrigan had no intentions of using the desk. No intention of using the Oval Office, for that matter. She intended to make good on her word that she would be only the Acting President, functioning as a caretaker for President Navarro until he resumed his office. Instead, she intended to work out of the Vice President's Ceremonial Office across the street from the White House. She knew it had been done before—Nixon had maintained a working office in that building—and she knew the efficiency of the White House would not be hampered in the least by her working from there. 'And it won't be so bad for my image either,' she thought. 'Will strike the right note with people if I'm not seen as a usurper. And the election is only two years away.' She smiled to herself.

She'd told Caldwell of her intention earlier in the day. He'd not been one bit happy, and had told her so. She'd abruptly dismissed his objections and told him to get on with it. She smiled again to herself. She knew a confrontation would come, that one had in fact been brewing for some time now between herself and Caldwell, but now she had the upper hand. 'Come into my parlor, said the spider to the fly,' she thought.

She was walking slowly about the office as she thought these things to herself. 'No, no need to change anything of Navarro's. The office, the Residence'—the living quarters of the President and his family within the White House—'all of it can remain untouched. Until I can have it for myself.' She turned and was about to leave the office to head across the street, when she suddenly felt compelled to give herself one small indulgence. And as she moved behind the big desk, and sat down in the President's big upholstered leather chair, she sighed contentedly. 'Yes, I'll be here in my own right before long,' she thought. And smiled again.

Then abruptly she got up from the chair and left the office. It was time to go to work.

PART 2

CHAPTER 14

Washington, DC
Tuesday, 20 September 2022
10:23 a.m. EDT

Acting President Fran Kerrigan was at her desk in the Eisenhower Executive Office Building reading an analysis of the upcoming mid-term elections that had been prepared by the Democratic National Committee. She'd found that she enjoyed working in the office, away from the hubbub of the West Wing. It had required some adjustments on the part of her staff, and the President's staff, but she felt it was worth it. She often thought that if she ever became President in her own right, she would maintain a working office over here and use the Oval Office for ceremonial functions. Nixon had done something like that, 'So why not?' she thought. The analysis she was reading offered a prognosis that was good for the party, and it appeared very likely that they would avoid the typical loss of seats in Congress that the party of an incumbent President experienced during the mid-terms. 'All in all,' she mused, 'the attack on Navarro has turned out to be a good thing for us.' The country was still sympathetic to his plight, a situation that Kerrigan stoked every chance she got. She knew that if that sympathy could be maintained, her chances for election to the presidency in 2024 would get even better, particularly if Navarro's condition didn't.

It had now been nearly five months since the attack on the President. In that time, his situation had stabilized, but the doctors still were unable, or unwilling, to predict when he might awaken. Or even if. Numerous experts had been consulted about his state, but no consensus had developed. They just didn't know. In general, his wounds had healed well, which was a tribute to his strength and stamina. He was expected to regain full use of his left arm, and to experience no lasting effects from the largely superficial wounds to his chest. His fractured pelvis was healing as expected, but the team of doctors at Walter Reed that was overseeing his care, and carefully monitoring his progress, was of mixed mind with regard to whether he would regain his ability to walk. They were also of mixed mind with regard to the depth of the injury to his brain. He was no longer in an induced coma; indeed, the medicines that had placed him in that state had been discontinued shortly after his transfer from California to Walter Reed last May, but he had not awakened since that time and still remained unconscious and unresponsive. The doctors put him through an intense regimen of physical therapy to keep his body from atrophying while his mind healed, and all of his vital signs were satisfactory. But when he would come out of it remained a mystery.

In the aftermath of the assassination attempt, following the designation of Kerrigan as Acting President, there had been a great deal of recrimination and finger-pointing at all levels of government as folks tried to figure out exactly what had happened and why. The FBI was quickly able to determine that the suicide bomber, one Miguel Ascencio, had been a legitimate member of the California Highway Patrol; indeed, he was a 14-year veteran of CHP and had received several commendations throughout his career. Some deeper digging by the FBI into his background, however, had turned up some relatives in Mexico who were involved with the drug gangs—some of them had been killed during the intervention that Navarro had initiated, others captured by the U.S. Army and were now incarcerated in the Super-Max in Colorado—as well as a bank account that contained significantly more money than a CHP sergeant would be expected to possess. When FBI interrogators questioned those relatives, and interviewed several of Ascencio's colleagues in CHP, it became clear that the man had been intensely angry at the President for the attacks in Mexico, that this anger had been flamed even hotter when his relatives were killed or thrown into prison, and that this had in turn converted him to a willing recruit for the gangs that were searching for a way to strike back. When word of all this leaked out—the fact that a known malcontent was placed in a position to provide protection for the President—as it inevitably did, even though a public release of the FBI's report was not intended, heads rolled in California as a incredulous populace demanded that somebody be held accountable for allowing a person like this to go unnoticed.

Kerrigan saw in this an opportunity to demonstrate that she was now firmly in charge, and to set a precedent defining the scope of an Acting President's authority. The Secretary of Homeland Security, Frank Fitzrandolph, had long been a critic of Kerrigan and her husband; he was also an ally of long-standing of Josh Caldwell. Fitzrandolph was also from Pennsylvania, although from the Pittsburgh area, and had served in Congress until he was nominated by Navarro for the Homeland Security position in 2020. While in Congress, he had locked horns with Senator Moscone on several occasions, criticizing him for his perceived, but not proven, links to the unsavory elements of Philadelphia politics, and for Moscone's efforts to influence the disbursement of funds from the state government to the eastern half of the state at the expense of the west. They had also battled more recently over Moscone's criticism of the President's actions in Mexico. Kerrigan had come in for her share of this criticism from Fitzrandolph largely from a 'guilt by association' rationale; consequently, there was absolutely zero love lost between them, and Kerrigan now saw an opportunity to pay the bill in full. One of her first public actions was to flog the Department of Homeland Security during a news conference for their inability to predict and prevent the attack, and to call for Fitzrandolph's dismissal. He had protested that DHS could not have known about Ascencio, that no intelligence by any agency at any level predicted any attack within the U.S., and that he and his department were being made scapegoats for the debacle. Kerrigan's demand for his resignation caused heated debates within Congress about whether her authority included appointing and dismissing officials within the executive branch, as well as heated debates about where fault for the security lapses should be placed. Behind the scenes there were angry discussions in the Cabinet and with Josh Caldwell about the merit of the action to dismiss Fitzrandolph. In the end, though, Senator Moscone had shut down the congressional rhetoric, and Caldwell found himself outvoted by the other cabinet members. Fitzrandolph was dismissed, and Kerrigan emerged with a precedent that said an Acting President was every bit as powerful as a real President, which had been her goal all along. Getting rid of Fitzrandolph, and sticking Caldwell in the eye in the process, was just an added bonus.

She had moved quickly to press her advantage, nominating men who had supported her failed presidential bid to fill the Cabinet vacancies in the Department of Education, in place of Walt Hodges, who had been killed in the Navarro attack, and in Homeland Security, replacing the now departed but unlamented Frank Fitzrandolph. There was some sniping in the press about 'stacking the deck', but there emerged no challenge to her authority to make the nominations. Continuing to press, she intended shortly to begin making judicial nominations to see if any opposition appeared to that.

Kerrigan finished reading the DNC report and set it aside, looking out the window toward the White House. It was a lovely day out, not too hot and with no humidity—perfect baseball weather, she thought. She and Senator Moscone were going to attend a ballgame tonight out at Nationals Stadium. For once, Washington's baseball team appeared to be heading for the playoffs, and she'd thought it would look good for her to attend. Moscone hated baseball— he was a football and hockey nut—but he had agreed to go along, and would no doubt portray the most avid Nationals fan you could imagine, at least when the cameras were pointed at him. She intended to use the time to relax a little.

She glanced over to her scheduler. Next on her plate was receiving an update on the medical status of Navarro, something she had been getting weekly ever since the attack. There had been little change in these updates for the past several weeks, and Kerrigan realized they were becoming almost a distraction in their commonality. She found that she had to force herself to focus on what they contained.

A knock on her outer door informed her that the briefers were ready; the door opened as she rose from her desk and Jess Dougherty entered. He continued to function as her Chief of Staff here in the Executive Office Building, while Caldwell ran the staff in the West Wing, although she had begun to shift more responsibilities toward Dougherty, fully intending to marginalize Caldwell's influence as much as she possibly could. It sometimes amused her that Dougherty and Caldwell resembled each other somewhat; both were of mid-height, and both were overweight. As she thought this, it occurred to her that they both bore a passing resemblance to her husband as well. 'Funny how similar packages can hold such very different contents,' she thought to herself. Dougherty was followed through the door by the President's physician, Major General Glenn Webster. Navarro had maintained the tradition of having a military doctor as his primary physician when he came into office. Webster had been one of the team of doctors who had overseen then-Captain Navarro's rehabilitation following his wounding in Afghanistan in 2003, and Navarro remembered him well. He had sought him out and asked him to be the 'Physician to the President' following his election, and Webster had readily accepted. Now, once more, nearly twenty years later, Navarro was again in his care for rehabilitation, only this time the stakes were much higher. Webster understood this well, and had forcefully taken charge of his patient's care, demanding much from the staff of Walter Reed, and fiercely defending his treatment plan in the face of an onslaught of unsolicited advice from both within the medical community and without. His success thus far in stabilizing Navarro and beginning his rehab even while he remained comatose was one of the few areas on which both Kerrigan and Caldwell were in agreement.

"Good morning, Madame Vice President," Webster greeted her as she came around the desk to meet him. Gray-haired, but with piercing black eyes, Webster was a Cajun from rural Louisiana who'd gone to medical school on the Army's dime thirty-five years before, and then stayed in the service even after he had paid his dues because he found that he liked the challenges. He was known for his straight-forward, no-nonsense, all-business manner, and did not suffer fools well. He had not yet formed an opinion as to whether Kerrigan fell into this category. "It's a pleasure to see you again." He firmly shook the outstretched hand she offered him.

"Thank you, Doctor. It's good to see you again as well." She motioned for him and Dougherty to take seats at the long conference table in the center of the room, and took one opposite them as Webster opened his materials to begin the briefing, handing each of them a short two-page summary of the President's status this week. "And how is our patient this week?" she asked.

'A little bit flippant today, aren't we?' Webster thought to himself. He looked up from his papers and proceeded to speak to her without referring to his notes, watching her expression carefully as he did. "Well, ma'am, I'm pleased to report that although he is much the same as previously, there has been no regression. His vital signs all remain good. His wounds and broken bones are all healing nicely, as we would expect, and the low-grade infection we had noticed last week has been successfully treated with the regimen of antibiotics we introduced. His physical therapy is maintaining his body tone so that there is no significant degree of muscle loss or rigor. I believe I can confidently say that if he were to awaken today, he would be moving around without much assistance within days." Kerrigan nodded as he spoke, reading the paper that he had given her as she did so.

"What about his head injuries?" Kerrigan asked, flipping to the second page of the summary. "Is there any sign of improvement there?"

"No, ma'am, unfortunately there has been no change. His brain activity remains normal, and there is no sign of any bleeding or scarring within the cranium. All of the wounds due to the surgeries have healed normally. He's just not awake. His body is still resting itself. When he wakes is something, unfortunately, that I still can't predict for you."

"Is he still being sedated, Doctor," asked Dougherty while examining the summary, "or is he just in the coma on his own?"

"He's essentially now on his own," replied Webster, shifting slightly in his chair to speak with Dougherty, who sat to his left. "As I said, we have been giving him antibiotics to ward off the infections, but he has been weaned from the other drugs we'd been giving him before. In my opinion, he is in no pain, and his body will heal itself more quickly if we don't numb it unnecessarily."

"Very well," said Kerrigan, somewhat annoyed that Dougherty had entered the conversation. "I'm glad to hear he has not regressed. Hopefully, he will begin to move forward shortly. Is there any change in his treatment that you envision for the near future?" It was a query she always made, mainly because it was a question that she was always asked when discussing Navarro's progress.

"None, Madame Vice President." He had shifted in his seat again to face Kerrigan directly.

"Okay, then I guess that's it. Thank you for coming to talk with me again, Doctor. We'll meet again next week." She looked at Dougherty to confirm that a spot on her agenda would be reserved for General Webster's report, although in her mind she was already thinking ahead to the next item on her schedule for the day. "Is there anything else?"

"Well, ma'am," began Webster. "There is one thing of interest." Both Kerrigan and Dougherty looked at each other in surprise at this statement. Usually Webster had nothing to add to his report and departed the office quickly to return up 16th Street to his office at Walter Reed.

"And that is?" asked Kerrigan.

"Well, as you know from what I briefed you on a couple weeks ago, I was concerned that we ascertain whether there was any history in the President's family of illnesses or genetic disorders that might impinge on his recovery. To determine this, I requested that the medical files of the President's parents, Ramon Sr. and Theresa, be pulled from the HHS databank so that I could review them." As part of the reform of health care in America initiated at great expense during the Obama Administration, a massive databank had been established of medical records for all Americans. Overseen by the Department of Health & Human Services, this database linked records entered at treatment facilities across the country so that data on a patient entered at one location could be readily and easily accessed at any other by an authorized user. While this program had without doubt increased the efficiency of healthcare, allowing test results, lab information, doctor case notes, and prescriptions to be reviewed by many physicians without a need for repeated, duplicative tests, and had thereby reduced costs, it did spark a storm of protest about the privacy of an individual's medical history that was still being debated. One significant piece of the information stored in the database was a DNA sample in all personal medical files. "My starting point in this analysis was to look at the DNA prints of the Navarros to see what genetic problems we might need to consider. Now, Mrs. Navarro had submitted a DNA sample when the program began in 2014, a couple of years before she died in Houston. The President's father, as you probably know, had died in 2000, well before this program was initiated, so there is no sample available in the database for him. There are only digital records of his health history." Another portion of the program had been to digitally transfer all HHS files, to include those from Medicare and Medicaid, to the database. "Surprisingly, what I found when comparing the DNA of the President's mother to his DNA is that there is no correlation between the two." He stopped talking to look at them, pivoting his head from one to the other.

"What does that mean?" asked Kerrigan, clearly perplexed. She often felt that Webster purposely did not state clearly what he meant merely to see if she could be caught short, a tendency that annoyed her to no end. "That there are no genetic problems that link the President and his mother?"

"No, ma'am. What it means is that there is zero chance that Theresa Navarro was the President's biological mother." And again he paused to let this sink in.

Both Kerrigan and Dougherty stared back at him blankly. Webster's eyes stared passively at the Acting President, waiting for her to make the connection on her own, and he could almost watch the wheels turning in her head as she worked it out. Finally, Kerrigan understood what he was saying.

"Not his mother? But how can that be?" she asked, almost talking to herself out loud. "It's well known that the President was born in vitro via a surrogate. Everybody knows that. So how can she not be his mother?" Webster's information just didn't make any sense.

Webster waited another moment, then stated it plainly for her. "It can only be if the egg taken for the in vitro fertilization was not Theresa's, but someone else's. Whose, I have no idea; it doesn't matter. But I can assure you that he is not her real child."

"How can you be sure?" asked Dougherty. Kerrigan's eyes snapped over to him, but he had turned to face Webster and didn't see her reaction, although Webster did. "Have you conferred on this with anyone else?" Already in his mind he was leaping several steps ahead in seeing the significance of this disclosure.

"Mr. Dougherty, I have shared the data with four other doctors, all of them specialists in DNA analysis. It was done anonymously, of course, meaning they weren't told anything about the patients in the case. I provided them with the two DNA samples, the President's and his mother's—I mean, Theresa's—I guess I'll still call her his mother—and asked for their analysis. All of them confirmed my conclusion that the two individuals are not biologically related."

"Well, so what?" replied Kerrigan, taking back the initiative in the conversation. "So what if she's not his mother? What if another egg was used for the process? Nothing's changed. We just won't know about the President's predisposition for genetic disorders."

"Ma'am," began Dougherty, "I believe what the good doctor is alluding to is not the medical aspect of this set of circumstances, but its political overtones. If Theresa was not party to the in vitro, perhaps Ramon Sr. was not as well." Webster nodded as he said it. "And that would place us in a situation where an 'unknown,' in terms of citizenship, was now the president." Kerrigan huffed impatiently. She was growing more annoyed that Dougherty was now lecturing her, and doing it in front of Webster. "Ma'am, please, hear me out. If the President is not the biological child of either Ramon Sr. or Theresa, there is the chance that he is not legitimately a U.S. citizen."

"Stop," interrupted Kerrigan. "Stop right there. Jess, are you seriously saying that Ray Navarro may not be a U.S. citizen?" She laughed as Dougherty appeared as if he was about to speak once more. "No, there's no way that can be. The man's a natural born American, a born and raised Texan. He's a bonafide war hero. He's been in politics and the public eye for at least a dozen years, so he's had his life publicly dissected by the press. It's inconceivable."

"But just consider," persisted Dougherty. He could now read the annoyance on his boss' face, and wanted to make this point before she cut him off completely. "Yes, even if he's not the child of Theresa—let's presume that Doctor Webster's correct about that, as no doubt he is—he's still a citizen if he's the son of Ramon Sr. But what if that's not the case either? What if he's the biological child of neither one?"

"So what," responded Kerrigan irritably. "If he's not their biological son, he's essentially an adoptee. And adopted children have been Presidents before; President Ford was adopted. If he was born here and adopted by the Navarros, he's a citizen and eligible to be president."

"Precisely," said Dougherty. She had made his point for him. "IF he was born here. But what if that part of his life story as we know it is not true either? What then?"

Kerrigan opened her mouth to respond, then promptly closed it and sat back in her chair. She sat staring at Dougherty across the table, her mind racing. Could it be even remotely possible that Ray Navarro could not legitimately be the President, because he was not legitimately a U.S. citizen? 'Where would that leave us?' she wondered to herself. She needed to talk to Fred about this so they could figure out what to do, how to approach it.

"Okay, gentlemen." She spoke very slowly and deliberately, looking them each directly in the eye in turn. "No word of this is to leave this room. Is that clear?" Both heads nodded to her. "Doctor, is anyone else aware of what you've determined?"

"Only Governor Caldwell, ma'am. I needed some help in getting the records from HHS, and he had told me to come to him if I ever needed anything for the President's treatment. When I asked for the files, I explained what I was doing. I must say he wasn't very happy with my plan, but he cooperated. I have not told him of my conclusions, however. Beyond that, as I said, my request for corroboration to my colleagues was done anonymously, and I've talked with no one else about it. The records, of course, of the President and his mother exist in the HHS files, and people there are aware that I requested to see them. But I've told no one else of my conclusions."

It took all of Kerrigan's self-control to keep herself from exploding when Caldwell's name was mentioned; she could feel the blood rising to her head. Instead, she merely said, "Good. You are to keep this all to yourself for the time being. And I want you to gather up any notes or other documentation you put together regarding this and provide it to Mr. Dougherty by tomorrow. No copies are to be made. If you have need to review it again, you may do it here.

Is that understood?"

"But, ma'am, I need to have a copy of my notes readily available so that I can refer to them as we continue to adjust the President's treatment as we move forward." He had noticed her reaction to Caldwell's name, and wondered why that would be. 'Perhaps they don't get along; I'll have to remember that,' he thought.

"Doctor, I don't believe I was unclear. There will be no copies. Everything will be sent here. Is that clear?"

"Yes, Madame Vice President. Perfectly clear."

"Jess, clear?"

"Yes, ma'am. Completely. I'll secure the file in my safe when the doctor gives it to me tomorrow." He motioned to the outer office as he spoke.

"No, please give it to me. I'll maintain it personally. And I'm not kidding about keeping a lid on this. Any idle speculation in the press about Ray Navarro would do no one, and certainly not the country, one bit of good." She looked from one to the other. "Very well, gentlemen, that will be all for today." She stood, and they got to their feet as she did.

"Good morning, ma'am," said Webster. "Thank you for your time." And he exited the office, thinking that he now knew exactly in which category Kerrigan fit.

"Jess," she said once the doctor had gone and the door had closed. "Get Senator Moscone on the phone and tell him I need to speak with him here as soon as possible. But it must be this afternoon, and it must be here. Whenever he's available, clear two hours on my calendar so he and I can talk without interruption."

"Yes, ma'am. No problem."

"And tell Governor Caldwell that I'll need to cancel my meeting with him today." She and Caldwell routinely met briefly at the end of each day in her office to go over the doings in the West Wing. "Tell him it's because I'm going to the game tonight and I've decided to get there earlier than we'd planned. Then you give him the rundown on the President's status. Only don't mention a word about what Webster told us." She smiled to herself as she said this, imagining Caldwell's reaction to the snub she was handing him. "Then get Liz Barton"—the Secretary of Health & Human Services—"on the phone and instruct her that no requests that come to HHS, from anyone, and I mean anyone, regarding the President's health status, or that of anyone in his family—including Julia's—are to be answered without my personal approval. Okay?"

"Yes, ma'am. Got it."

"Thank you, Jess." She turned abruptly to head back to her desk, signalling that the discussion was ended and he was expected to leave. He did so immediately, silently closing the door behind him.

Kerrigan sat back down in the big chair behind the desk, but did not take up any of the work that was waiting for her attention. Instead, she stared out the windows to her right and began turning things over in her head, thinking what a lovely day this final day of summer was turning out to be.

CHAPTER 15

Washington, DC
Tuesday, 20 September 2022
3:42 p.m. EDT

The knock on the door caused her to look up sharply from the file she'd been reading, and she unconsciously reached up to remove the reading glasses that she wore. Although she did not hide the fact that she had to use them, Kerrigan's vanity still compelled her not to be seen wearing them if she could help it. Her staff had strict instructions not to allow any photographs to be taken of her with them on, and she had been successful thus far at excluding them from her historical legacy.

The door cracked open and Dougherty stuck his head in.

"Pardon the interruption, ma'am, but Senator Moscone just called to say he'd be here in five minutes."

"Thank you, Jess. Show him in as soon as he arrives, then ensure we're not disturbed while we talk." They had been over this already, so he knew what was expected, but she saw no harm in re-emphasizing the point one more time.

"Yes, ma'am. And the car will be ready to take the two of you to the ballpark from here once you're through." Both she and Moscone would change clothes here prior to leaving. They'd put on something more comfortable and more appropriate for attending a baseball game than their business suits.

The door closed and she went back to reading the file while she waited for her husband's arrival. She was reviewing a handful of dossiers that the staff had put together on potential judicial appointments. There were vacancies that needed to be filled in four district courts—in New Jersey, Iowa, Utah and Oregon—and more significantly in the 5th U.S. Circuit Court, which had responsibility for Texas, Louisiana and Mississippi, something near and dear to the heart of Josh Caldwell. She intended to send her nominations to the

Senate first thing next week. Her nominations would be of persons who had supported her candidacy two years ago, and who would undoubtedly support her again two years from now. Most likely Navarro, and by extension Caldwell, would not have even considered them, but as before, she intended to make a statement with these nominations that in every way but name she was the President and would act accordingly.

The door opened again abruptly and Moscone burst into the office. His entries into a room were always like the arrival of a force of nature, and Kerrigan smiled at the sight of her husband.

"Franny," he practically shouted, in his loud Philadelphia accent. "How's my favorite president doing, *cara mia*?"

Moscone was now seventy-one years old, but showed no signs of slowing down. Still possessed of a full head of white hair, still overweight, and with a booming voice that was often mimicked by late night comedians as a much louder version of Sylvester Stallone's, he relished the rough world of Washington politics and had proved himself a master at that strange and unforgiving art. He was one who believed implicitly in the adage that a successful man is one who keeps his friends close and his enemies closer, and Fred Moscone had a well-earned reputation for being as good and steadfast a friend as you could ever hope for, and for being the most ruthless and vindictive enemy that you'd ever fear to get. He was a man who had openly lusted for the presidency for his entire life in politics, only to see it slip from his grasp ten years ago. He was now vicariously pouring all those energies and aspirations into the presidency of his wife. Which is exactly how he thought of it—her Presidency. It didn't matter a whit that the upstart who'd kept her from it still breathed. Franny was the President and he intended to do all he could to keep her in that seat.

"Fred," she said, coming around the desk and grabbing his arm to lead him to the upholstered chairs at the far end of the room. "Thanks for making time to come over. You will not believe what I've got to tell you."

"Did he die?" he asked hopefully.

"No, something that might be better." She teased him with that thought, letting him wonder what it could be, drawing out the suspense. She could see his mind turning over the possibilities, but not coming up with a good conclusion.

"What could possibly be better than that?" he responded finally.

"It does us no good if he dies," she said dispassionately. "He'll then be revered. A martyr, the boy wonder who could do no wrong and who was going to clean up the world, if only he hadn't been so tragically cut down in his prime." She shook her head. "No, you know that's no good to us. What is good is if his reputation is taken away, he's discredited, he's the butt of everyone's joke instead of their hero."

"Alright, Fran," Moscone interrupted, growing impatient. He understood her point; they'd discussed this subject off and on several times, never coming to any resolution because there was nothing to hold on to. "What have you got that's made you so excited?"

So she told him the tale that Webster had related to her earlier. He immediately grasped the significance of it, putting the pieces together and connecting the dots even more quickly than Dougherty had. She knew this by the way his dark eyes lit up and became very still while he concentrated, while his breathing became quicker. She was glad he was there for her; he'd know exactly how to put this information to best use, for both of them, and in such a way that no one would see their hands on it.

Finally he spoke. "You did right, Fran, to tell them to keep a lid on this. Having this come out and finding out it's not true, that there's nothing to it— that would just make everybody look silly. No, this will have to be handled very carefully." He paused, thinking. "You know, I know some guys who may be able to look into this. I'll get hold of a couple and ask them to do some digging around." Kerrigan smiled as he said this because Moscone always seemed to know somebody. 'That's what comes from the bare-knuckle backrooms of Philadelphia politics,' she thought. This background, coupled with nearly thirty years in DC, much of that dabbling in the dark world of the intelligence community, made Moscone a very formidable man who most people went out of their way to remain on the good side of.

"You'll have to be very discreet," Kerrigan cautioned, even though she knew as she said it that it was unnecessary; Fred would ensure that no word of this got out if he didn't want it to.

"*Cara mia*, please." A pained expression danced across the round, Italian face. "You know I'll take care of everything. You don't worry about a thing. I'll handle it for you. Don't I always?"

"Yes, Fred, you do. Thanks. I couldn't do this without you," she responded, meaning every word of it sincerely.

"You betcha, *carissima*" he said. "Now here's how I think we should deal with this."

118

CHAPTER 16

Washington, DC
Tuesday, 20 September 2022
5:18 p.m. EDT

"Whaddya mean, she doesn't want to meet tonight?" Caldwell shouted into the phone at Dougherty.

"Josh, I'm just the messenger. She told me to tell you that she was going to head to the stadium earlier than she had planned, and asked me to update you on the President's status this week."

"I already know his status," Caldwell snapped back. "I check on it with the hospital every day, not just infrequently so that I don't get some bad press." Caldwell was fuming about this. He knew his blood pressure was soaring upward; 'Doc won't be happy about that,' he thought idly. He knew full well that Kerrigan was trying to maneuver him out of a job by whittling away at his responsibilities, his authority, his access to the levers of power. And he knew in his heart that the puppetmaster pulling her strings from behind the scenes was Moscone. But Caldwell didn't intend to go quietly into the night. No, he intended to stay right here and keep the ship afloat until Ray was back in the seat. 'Then we'll see who gets out-maneuvered.'

"You listen to me, Jess," he said slowly in what Dougherty thought was a menacing voice. "You listen to me. Ray Navarro is still the President of these United States. Don't let anybody fool you about that. And nothing is going to change that unless he has the misfortune to die, and I've already asked the Service to be doubly alert so that some mishap doesn't regretfully happen while he can't protect himself." He paused momentarily to let the import of those words sink in. "And I'm fully confident—based on the DAILY reports I'm getting about his progress—that he'll be up and around here before you know it. So you better tell your boss, the Acting President,"—he said the words facetiously—"that I'm not going anywhere anytime soon. You got that?"

"I got it, Josh. I got it. Believe me. I'm just the messenger here." His anger was rising also, and he worked to keep it from showing. He supported Kerrigan completely, as he had done for years, and rarely sat idly by while she was attacked by a political opponent. He waited a moment, then continued more quietly. "Listen, Josh. You better tread carefully. There's stuff going on that you don't know about. Explosive stuff." He stopped, knowing he'd already said too much. "That's it. You've got the Acting President's message. If you don't need an update on the President, I won't give you one. Good night, Josh." He hung up, pondering whether he'd gone too far.

Caldwell replaced the phone in its cradle, sat back in his chair, and tilted his head back to stare up at the ceiling. 'I wonder what that was all about,' he thought. 'What has she heard that's got Dougherty so cocky?' Caldwell actually liked Dougherty. He enjoyed working with him as they coordinated the activities of their two offices, appreciated the way he always tried to accommodate Caldwell's requests, could always be counted on when he'd committed to something. He could even appreciate his loyalty to his boss, so extreme that the press sometimes castigated Dougherty about it, labeling him Kerrigan's 'lap-dog' or 'poodle.' Caldwell felt almost sorry for him at times, thinking about what it must be like to work for Kerrigan; then he'd remember that Jess had been doing that for long before the election, and his pity would vanish. 'He chose the bed, now he's got to sleep in it,' he thought. He also knew that Dougherty would do almost anything to protect Kerrigan's reputation and to promote her ambitions. So what happened today that would fire him up? 'Must be the meeting with Webster,' he concluded. He knew Kerrigan's schedule; it was made available to the offices in the West Wing as a matter of course. 'Everything else on the schedule today was routine. Yet after she talks to Webster, she clears her afternoon, summons the Giant Bug, and then starts poking at me. I guess we'll just have to find out what went on.'

He picked the phone back up and dialed the number to Walter Reed from memory.

"This is Governor Caldwell, the President's Chief of Staff," he began to the secretary in Webster's outer office who answered the phone. "I'd like to speak with General Webster, if he's available. Yes, I'll wait. Thank you." The line went to hold, playing canned military march music.

'Okay, Franny, what are you and the Giant Bug trying to pull?' he wondered while he waited.

CHAPTER 17

Washington, DC
Tuesday, 20 September 2022
7:38 p.m. EDT

The climb back to consciousness felt like he was swimming through syrup. He could barely move his limbs, and he could feel the pain where the bullet had hit his leg. He could still hear the noise of the gunshots, could still smell the acrid bite of the cordite, could still hear the shouts around him, could still feel the cold of the early Afghan spring air. He remembered seeing Sergeant Zimmerman get hit by the sniper's bullet, and remembered the light and heat of the explosion that followed. He'd crawled out of the vehicle, which had been flipped over by the blast but miraculously remained in one piece and not on fire, although it now lay tipped on its side. He remembered dragging his driver from it and hauling him off to a covered position. 'Medic, I need a medic,' he'd heard himself shouting, doing what he could for the soldier with the broken leg until the medic dashed in to help him. He remembered running as fast as he could and diving into the dip in the ground next to Zimmerman, hearing the zip and whine as the bullets passed by him. He'd reached out and dragged Zimmerman down into the hole with him, and had begun to work to stop the bleeding from the wound in the chest where the sniper's bullet had, unluckily for Zimmerman, found a crease in the vest that he wore to prevent such mishaps. He'd begun calling to his lieutenant to move the men forward out of the kill zone, when the whoosh from the RPG passed over him to explode in the face of the building to his rear. Again, he felt the blast and the heat; again, he felt the pain as he was thrown forward on his face into the front of the hole; again, the smell of the cordite and sulphur. Then the pistol was in his hand and he was firing it into the face of the bearded madman who had come screaming up toward him, then watched as the body thumped heavily into the hole with him and lay still, then firing again as a second raced up. Next, running again, now with Zimmerman over his shoulder, legs pumping like he used to do in football games when he pounded toward the goal line. He headed back to the shelter where he'd left the driver, bullets whining past him and kicking up dirt around him as he raced for safety. Almost there, only to be knocked to the ground like he'd been hit with a club, and the fire began to surge from his thigh and spread to his whole body, so bad he could taste the color of the pain. Then he saw nothing but black.

But now he was trying to emerge from the black, dragging himself up to the light just as he had dragged and carried the others. Swimming harder, the light getting closer and brighter. Finally, forcing his eyes to open—only to realize he was in the wrong place, and that things were not right. He still felt the pain, but now it was in the wrong leg and in his head. It was no longer cold, and there was no bright sun in the clear mountain sky; now he stared up at bright fluorescent lights in a quiet room with ceramic walls. The noise had gone away, and he heard only soft chirping sounds like so many distant insects. He struggled to sit up, wanting to check on Zimmerman and the others, but found he could not move.

"He's awake," shouted the nurse excitedly. "Quick, get the doctor." The other one picked up the phone to summon Webster to the room. "Rest easy, Mr. President, don't try to move. Just lie easy."

Navarro heard the nurse's command and decided to obey. He was exhausted from the effort to get to the light, and now gratefully slid back under. At least he knew that Zimmerman was okay. 'I'll just sleep a little longer,' he thought.

"When," Kerrigan shouted into the phone. "Robby, when did this happen?"

"Just about fifteen minutes ago, Madame Vice President," responded the Secret Service Chief. He'd been called by the agent in charge of the President's security at the hospital, as he'd instructed, once Navarro regained consciousness. Naturally, the man knew no details; that would have to come from Webster and the other doctors. But he'd relayed the information to Kerrigan immediately anyway, because that's what she'd told him to do. "I've got no other details, other than he awoke briefly and is now sleeping again, although my agent reports that the doctors believe it's normal sleep and not the coma that it was."

"Thanks, Robby, very good work." She clicked off the line and punched the speed dial button on her secure cell phone for Dougherty.

"Jess, call out to Walter Reed and get me Webster on the phone. I'm told the President's awake, and I want confirmation of that. Yes, that's right, he woke up. Just a little while ago. No, nothing else. Just get him on the phone. Thanks." Again she clicked off the line.

The agent had come to her with the news in the middle of the third inning, with the Washington nine trailing 4-0 already. Now she had to decide how to handle it. Should she leave immediately? That might set tongues wagging with speculation if she abruptly left in the middle of the game. Should she sit here through the entire game? If Navarro was indeed awake, she'd be criticized for enjoying herself at his expense while he fought to regain consciousness. What to do? She went back to her seat and whispered the news to Moscone, who visibly reacted to the words. After a few moments, Moscone had suggested that he leave now to go to the hospital, where he'd get the full report on Navarro's status, then call her with it. That way she wouldn't get folks all excited by rushing out prematurely, but would get credit for sending a responsible representative to ensure the President's well-being. And it let Moscone mercifully leave this miserable game early. She agreed, and he quickly left.

Webster rushed down the hall from his office to the isolated room in the ICU that had been set aside for Navarro. The room had been equipped with more equipment than a typical ICU room had, in an attempt to plan for any possible contingency that might occur as the President recovered. It was also manned full-time by a team of two nurses, and had a doctor specifically designated to cover that room as a priority. Outside its door, two Secret Service agents kept round the clock vigil, ensuring that no one other than those cleared by Webster entered the room.

Webster had been preparing to head home to his house in Laurel when the call came. "There's nothing to do," he'd calmed the excited nurse, "just ensure that he's comfortable and that his vitals are all stable. I'll be down right away." Then he found himself racing down the hall as his adrenaline kicked in, too.

The agent in charge came up to him as he approached the door. "Sir," he began matter-of-factly, "I've got to phone this in. Wanted you to know." Webster understood that the man wasn't asking permission, just telling him what had to be done. He nodded.

"Okay, thanks," he replied, and brushed past him and into the room. He knew that the call would inevitably cause more calls to come his way, but he'd just have to handle that when it happened.

He was pleased to see that the room was not in an uproar, rather that the two nurses—one male, one female—had things under complete control and were managing everything perfectly. No fuss, no hysteria, just professionals doing what they did best. He reflected that Army Nurses were some of the best people he'd ever met, and knew he was lucky to have them working with him here.

"Okay, tell me what you've got," he said coming into the room, addressing the female major who was the senior nurse there. His black eyes flicked over the readouts coming from the sensors attached to Navarro's body, even as he looked over the still body of the recumbent president. He liked what he saw.

"Doctor," she began, "the President opened his eyes at 7:38 and looked around the room. It was clear to me that he was aware of his surroundings and responding to them, although he appeared somewhat disoriented by them. He appeared to attempt to sit up, but could not, then immediately fell asleep again. His breathing and pulse increased rapidly as he did this, but his other vitals have remained stable throughout the period. Pulse and respiration are now normal again."

As she finished this statement, they saw the President's eyes flicker open again. This time he did not struggle, but remained still, looking around the room and moving his head slightly. His eyes locked onto Webster's when he found them.

"Mr. President," Webster began. "Please take it easy and don't try to sit up or move."

"How long?" Navarro's voice croaked out weakly from dry lips. He swallowed, then said, more strongly, "How long have I been here?"

"It's been about five months, sir. You were injured in an assassination attempt in California. A bomb exploded, and you were injured. You're in Walter Reed. You were moved here right after the attack, and I've been with you ever since." Webster smiled down at the President's pale face.

"Thanks, Glenn," Navarro said. "I wouldn't want to be with anyone else." He glanced around the room, taking in the two nurses working quietly, checking all of his vitals. He saw all the equipment set against the walls, and noted the tubes and wires dangling from various points of his body. "How am I?" he asked.

"You're doing very well," said Webster, "especially now that you're awake. What can you remember?"

"I don't know," replied Navarro. "I think I'm confused, mixed up. I was dreaming about the explosion, but then I was back in Afghanistan. I remember the leg. But that was before." He paused, trying to concentrate. Trying to summon up the memories of this incident. And could not. "I don't remember this. Last thing I've got is the shuttle coming down." He swallowed again. "Tell me," he commanded.

Webster hesitated momentarily, then decided to forge ahead. "You received injuries to the left side of your body from the blast. Some wounds from flying glass, but mostly from the blast. Most serious was the TBI"—traumatic brain injury—"that's had you in the coma all this time. That was what I worried about most. You had some deep cuts on your face, shoulder, and chest—they're all basically healed, and I expect any scarring to fade with time. And you had a fractured pelvis and serious leg injuries. The right is okay, but, I'm sorry to tell you, the left has been amputated." Navarro blanched as he said this, and Webster quickly looked over to the nurses and glanced at the readouts on the monitors; he was gratified to see that all remained well. "There was no choice, it was too damaged. The leg has healed fine, but we don't know if you can walk." Navarro closed his eyes at this, and Webster thought he had lost consciousness again. But then the lids raised, and the hazel eyes cleared, and a look of determination fixed itself on his face.

"Alright, Doctor. So this is a little worse than last time." He spoke firmly, albeit grimly; Webster again was pleased with the strength in his voice. "I'm ready to do what you want me to do to get back." The voice appeared to fade as the President tired with the effort. With an effort, he rallied himself and said "What's first?"

"First, Mr. President, is that you continue to build up your strength. I want you to sleep. We'll give you a little something to help you with that. Then when you awaken next—and you'll feel much stronger then, I promise you—we'll be ready to work." Webster smiled down at him, even as he signaled the nurses to administer the sedative.

"Fine, fine," said Navarro as he began to fade. Suddenly his eyes briefly cleared. "Where's Julia?" he asked urgently, causing the nurse to gasp.

"Later," said Webster. "We'll talk later. Go to sleep now."

The hazel eyes closed and Navarro slept.

CHAPTER 18

Washington, DC
Tuesday, 20 September 2022
9:03 p.m. EDT

'I'm a popular guy today,' thought Webster to himself ruefully. 'First the call from Caldwell, then Dougherty, then Kerrigan, and now I've got Moscone coming in personally. It just keeps getting better.' Webster had thought he'd finished dealing with all these people after he'd left Kerrigan at her office shortly before lunch, but just around dinner time the calls started coming.

He'd been surprised by Caldwell's call. It had been fairly clear to him after talking with Kerrigan that she and Caldwell did not get along; this call had confirmed it to him. Caldwell asked probing questions about the meeting with Kerrigan, trying to find out what had been discussed without actually asking that question. Webster had pled an inability to provide a response due to the directive given to him by Kerrigan—something that very obviously did not sit well with Caldwell—but, since he felt he owed Caldwell something for helping him obtain the records in the first place, he mentioned in passing that the files he'd obtained had been very illuminating. He didn't say they'd been discussed with the Vice President, and he didn't say precisely why they were illuminating, but he figured Caldwell was probably sharp enough to pick up on the cookie crumb he had dropped there. That seemed to be the case, because Caldwell was quickly mollified and told Webster that if he needed any additional help in the future, to not hesitate to ask.

Dougherty had caught him just after he'd finished seeing the President. That conversation was over very quickly, as Dougherty was only relaying the message to call Kerrigan. Although Webster felt that Dougherty wanted very badly to ask about Navarro's situation, he did not do so and Webster did not offer anything.

Kerrigan's call was also brief. She asked him for a confirmation of what the Secret Service had told her, which he provided, and for a prognosis, which he did not. He explained that he would have to monitor the President's condition during the night, and that he could update her with a better status in the morning, but that he couldn't do that now. She seemed very agitated through the entire conversation, something that Webster found very intriguing. As the conversation was ending, the Vice President informed him that she was sending Senator Moscone to the hospital to get a first-hand report on Navarro's status, and that he was to be given every cooperation. Webster stoically received that news, but outwardly groaned as he replaced the handset.

And now Webster was waiting for the Senator's arrival, reviewing Navarro's data as he did so. He had many things he wanted to get done, and dealing with a senator who happened to be the Acting President's husband was not one of them. So he set up a consultative meeting for first thing in the morning with the team that was overseeing Navarro's care; he ordered blood tests and another EEG; and he reviewed the reams of telemetry that were streaming in from the President's sensors. Just as he finished with that review, without preamble Moscone burst into his office.

"Good evening, Senator," Webster began, extending a hand as he moved toward the big man standing in his doorway.

"Evening, Doctor," Moscone replied, not moving forward to reach the extended hand, but waiting for Webster to come to him. "The President asked me to get an update on your patient's status for her." He eyed Webster carefully, interested to see the reaction that came from his demand.

Webster stopped in mid-stride and withdrew his hand, stared back at Moscone and replied in an even tone. "If, Senator, you're referring to a request made by the *Vice* President, and if she's interested in the current medical status of *President* Navarro, I will be happy to provide you with that as she's asked me to. However, if you've been sent here by someone masquerading as the president, then you're out of luck." It was clear from his tone and manner that he was not intimidated by the big man in the least.

"Well, of course, that's who I meant, doctor," Moscone replied, smiling easily and returning the volley. "The Acting President has sent me to get an update. May I have that please?" And without being invited, he moved into the office and sat in the chair facing Webster's desk.

'So this is how you want to play it,' Webster thought, returning to his seat. 'Well, let's play.' And he proceeded to provide Moscone with a bare bones summary of the President's rise to consciousness. He described what was currently being done, and outlined what he intended to do next, but would not provide a guess as to his prognosis for full recovery until they could evaluate him further in the morning.

Throughout the interview, Moscone blustered and bullied in an attempt to get more information; he demanded to be allowed to see Navarro, something that Webster refused outright; and he threatened to have Webster removed from his position if he didn't become more cooperative, at which Webster inwardly chuckled to himself. Throughout, Webster remained impassive and provided only the minimal amount of information necessary. At one point during the meeting, he actually wondered to himself why he was doing that, why wasn't he being more forthcoming, more accommodating. And as he thought about it, he decided it was because he basically did not like the man now pacing his office and berating him, nor did he like his wife, who he again concluded fit into the category of persons that he did not suffer well. In the end, Moscone realized he was going to get nothing more and departed in a huff with the instruction for Webster to call Kerrigan with an updated status first thing in the morning. Webster could not recall the last time he had been so glad to see someone go away.

He thought about that for a few moments, continuing to stare blankly at the doorway through which Moscone had exited, then suddenly decided that since everyone else was calling him, he might as well be making a call, too.

He'd called the number a handful of times over the past several months, but even so had to look it up in his Outlook contact listing. Once he found it, he dialed and when a weary voice answered—"Hello?"—he related one more update on the President's recovery.

CHAPTER 19

Lambertville, NJ
Wednesday, 21 September 2022
11:33 a.m. EDT

"What a scoop, Lou," Jamie Coryell said into the phone. He'd just finished reading the story that Stevenson had filed early that morning that told the world the news of the President's miraculous recovery. Every other reporter, and every other news agency, was now playing catch-up. Stevenson had refused to divulge the source of his information, saying only that he had received the news during the night, and CNN was again on top of the news world because of him. "Was it hard to corroborate the facts before you sent it out?"

"Not really, although I didn't have any independent verification beforehand. This source is someone I've talked with plenty of times over the past several months, and he is most definitely in the loop on these kind of things. I had no doubt that the information was true. I just had to write it up to leave myself a little wiggle room and to ensure that the source remains unknown—at least to everyone but me." Coryell could hear the smile in his friend's gravelly voice over the phone. 'You sound tired, my friend,' he thought, but didn't say that to Stevenson. He let Stevenson continue to ramble on, glorying in the telling of the tale, knowing that such words of concern would only be brushed aside anyway.

"So what happens next?" Jamie asked.

"Well"—again Coryell could hear the big smile over the line—"because I was the first on the scene, so to speak, Josh Caldwell called me up and invited me to go with him to Walter Reed to talk with the doctors directly and to see Navarro, if he's up to it. Probably happen sometime next week." Stevenson laughed. "Not five minutes after I hang up on him, Kerrigan's office calls and says she wants to talk to me, too, but only after I've finished with Caldwell. Sounds like a juicy power struggle brewing to me, and little ol' me playing both sides off each other." Again, the laugh. "I love it."

Coryell thought that Stevenson sounded like a little kid who'd just found the key to the candy store. It reminded Jamie of the time, while they were at Columbia, when they had picked up a couple of Pace University nurses in a pub in Greenwich, told them they were airline pilots just in town for a couple of days on a layover, then proceeded to spin a convoluted tale of where they'd been and what they'd done and how great flying around the world was. Those nurses had lapped up every word, and Stevenson had had the time of his life inventing the most outrageous lies to tell them. 'They were really mad when we finally told them,' Jamie chuckled to himself, remembering. Ah, the good old days. Anyway, it was good to hear Lou in such high spirits.

They chatted for a few more minutes, then each claimed that they had to go. "Don't work too hard up there on the *Mayberry Tattler* now," Lou said, getting in one final dig before hanging up.

"Don't worry about me," Jamie laughed in reply. "You just keep doing what you're doing. And if you need any help, let me know." The phone clicked dead, and Jamie found himself staring at it momentarily, surprised with the sure feeling that Lou was actually going to need his help shortly.

CHAPTER 20

Washington, DC
Wednesday, 21 September 2022
2:47 p.m. EDT

"Yes, I'm sure," said Glenn Webster in response to Caldwell's question. They were speaking in his office at Walter Reed, to which Caldwell had come to see how the President was doing. In a misfortune of poor timing, Navarro was still sleeping, so his Chief of Staff had not been able to see him yet. In the meantime, while waiting, he was explaining to the doctor what he intended to do, and seeking his advice on whether it would be okay. "He was stronger this morning than he was when he woke up yesterday, and all his vitals remain good. I think you'll have to go slowly, but he should handle it well." Webster was actually more concerned with Caldwell, who clearly had not slept well, if at all, the night before, and who looked much the worse for wear.

"Well, I sure hope you're right," Caldwell responded. He could see the concern in Webster's eyes, but mistook its object, thinking he was really worried about the President's weakened condition. "I just think it's the right thing to do. And the sooner the better. And I think it should come from me, and not somebody else." Webster clearly understood who that 'somebody else' was, while Caldwell silently completed the thought to himself—'someone who only wants to tell the press how wonderful they are, and how concerned they are about Ray Navarro, when they're not concerned about him in the least.' He could feel the anger welling up inside, and he forced himself to take some deep, slow breaths to calm down again. "You're sure he'll be able to handle it?" he asked the doctor once more, a worried look again on his round face.

"Yes, I believe so, Governor. This kind of news is always hard for anyone to take, particularly someone in a weakened physical and emotional condition. But I've known him a long time, and I know he'll undoubtedly begin asking for her soon, so he'll have to be told. It will do no good to delay the inevitable. And

I agree that you, being his closest friend here in the city, should be the one to tell him. I'm sorry, but I think that's the best way." As he spoke, his door opened and his receptionist told him that the nurse attending the President this shift had just called to say that he'd awakened again. "Thanks, Nancy," he said, "tell them I'll be right down." She nodded and left to make the call.

"Well, Governor, look's like he's ready for you." He smiled sadly at Caldwell, who was sitting in his chair like a man with the weight of the world on his shoulders. "Don't worry, he'll be glad to see you, and a visit from a friend is probably the best medicine he could get right now." He stood up as he spoke. "Come on, let's go."

They left Webster's office and headed down the long hallway to the left. They were in the administrative section of the building, Caldwell knew, and were heading through the labyrinth of hallways toward the patient wings. Walter Reed was an enormous place, with more than 5,500 rooms and over twenty-eight acres of floor space. Named after famed Army Doctor Major Walter Reed, who led the team that confirmed in 1900 that yellow fever is transmitted by mosquitoes rather than direct human contact, the hospital that became the Army's flagship medical center on the east coast opened its doors at this location in northwest Washington in 1909. Now in 2022 it was still going strong, Caldwell noted, as he and Webster swept past full rooms. Even though Congress had decreed that the hospital be closed by 2011 and combined with nearby Bethesda Naval Hospital in the hopes of producing efficiencies, as well as saving some money, for one reason or another that event had yet to transpire, and Walter Reed continued to provide the same premier service for the Army that it had for the previous century.

Descending three floors and exiting an elevator, the two entered the critical care ward of the hospital. Caldwell had been here at times in the past with Navarro as they visited wounded servicemen and women from the Mexican incursion, as well as the many other hot spots around the globe in which the military had placed people in harm's way at the country's behest. This visit, though, had a heightened urgency about it, and Caldwell could feel himself growing more anxious as they approached the isolated suite of rooms that had a very large man, unmistakably a Secret Service agent, standing outside. The agent nodded in recognition to Webster and Caldwell as they approached, and held open the door for them to enter the suite.

Inside, Caldwell saw that it was basically no different than any other hospital area—maybe a little bit larger—but was just a suite of three rooms segregated by itself which uniquely housed only a single patient. It looked the same, felt the same, smelled the same, had the same kind of stuff buzzing and chirping and beeping. As he and Webster approached the bed, Caldwell could see that Navarro was awake and alert, although thin and drawn and looking pretty weary. But the hazel eyes were clear, and they glittered with pleasure at seeing Caldwell come through the door.

"Josh, you are a sight for sore eyes," exclaimed the President.

"Mr. President," Caldwell began, then had to pause to gather himself as his throat choked up while he took in the livid scars on the left side of Navarro's face, the swath of bandages on his head, and the empty space at the lower portion of the bed where the left leg should be. He recovered momentarily, and no one else in the room commented on the emotion. "Mr. President," he continued, "you're the one who's a sight. I can't tell you how good it is to see you again."

"Thanks, Josh. I gotta tell you, I'm glad to be back." He looked over toward Webster. "All thanks to you, Doc." He smiled appreciably.

"You're welcome, sir," Webster replied. "But you're not out of the woods yet. Tomorrow we'll start you on some testing and some therapy to see how extensive the damage is to your pelvis and your remaining leg; try to figure out how that will affect your ability to walk. And we'll continue to check out your brain function, although I'm reasonably confident at this juncture to say that you're okay in that department." He paused. "The therapy and tests will be pretty stressful initially. Pretty painful. Do you think you're up for it?"

"You can start poking and prodding right now as far as I'm concerned," rejoined the President. "I'm ready to go. All I need is some real food and I'll be right as rain."

"Well, that may have to wait a little while, too, until your body gets strong enough for something more substantial than the liquids you've been fed all these months." He looked over to Caldwell, who nodded. "Well, Mr. President, I'm going to go review some of your current data, then I'll be back to check up on you later. While I'm gone, Governor Caldwell has some things to talk about with you."

"Thanks, Doc. See you later." He watched as Webster left the room, and noted with interest that he asked the nurse on duty in the room to leave with him. 'Josh must have something sensitive to tell me,' he thought. Then 'I hope

Fran hasn't done anything dumb' passed through his mind, and he hoped that wasn't the case. He watched Caldwell pull a chair up to the bedside and sit down.

Caldwell settled himself into the hard, straight-backed chair and steeled himself for what he had to say. 'If only there was an easier way,' he thought; but he knew there was not. He stared at his knees, trying to put together the right words. He almost laughed at himself, because if there was one thing he'd never been accused of in his past, it was a lack of words. But they'd all but deserted him now. Gathering his resolve, he took a deep breath, then looked up at Navarro. The President was looking back at him with a bemused expression on his face.

"Whatever she's done, it can't be that bad, Josh," he said. He was feeling a little light-headed from the pain medication, which was doing its job of keeping his pain at bay. 'Working almost too well,' he thought. 'Maybe I'll need to ask Glenn to ease up on me a little.'

Caldwell, still alone with his own thoughts, didn't understand the President's comment at first. "Whatever who's done?" he asked. "Who are you talking about, sir?"

"Fran, of course. Aren't you here to tell me about some problem that she and Fred have caused?"

Caldwell took a deep breath again, then plunged ahead. "No, sir, I'm not. I wish that's what I had to tell you." He leaned in closer to the bed, thinking what a terrible blow this will be, and how unfair it was to have to deliver it to a crippled man still in his hospital bed. He looked at Navarro's face, and saw that lines of concern had formed amidst the scars now that he'd been told it didn't have to do with Kerrigan. 'Just get it over with,' he told himself.

"Mr. President—Ray—it's about Julia." He watched Navarro pale when he used his first name, something he hadn't allowed himself to do since the younger man had been elected to the highest office in the land, and then blanch even further at the mention of Julia's name. He felt his eyes watering up and his throat choking as he continued. "I'm sorry. In the attack when you were injured, in California, she was killed. I'm sorry. This is the last thing I want to tell you. But she's gone." The last words croaked out as a tear washed down his left cheek.

Navarro said nothing, but laid his head back on his pillow and stared at the ceiling. He remained silent in that position for what to Caldwell seemed an eternity. Suddenly his eyes closed and his face crumpled and the tears flowed freely. He turned his face away from Caldwell, not to hide the emotion but to save his friend from being uncomfortable at this display of his grief. Caldwell sat silently at his side throughout, slumped forward in his seat, futilely trying to think of something of comfort to say, and staring forlornly at his friend. Finally, Navarro composed himself and turned to face Caldwell.

"Josh, thanks for being the one to tell me. I've been in and out of it so much since last night that I haven't had a real coherent conversation with anyone yet. I was dreaming about her actually. I was wondering where she was and when she'd come to see me. I had hoped this wasn't the reason she hadn't been by, but I think that I knew in my heart that it was." He sank back into the pillow again. In a quiet voice he asked, "Did she suffer, Josh?"

"No, she was killed outright in the explosion. She felt no pain. She didn't suffer."

The eyes closed, and he held them that way as he spoke. "Well, if there's anything good in all this, that's one thing to be thankful for." He paused. He wanted to change the subject; he couldn't take it all in right now. He wondered if he was still dreaming, but realized all too well that this was all too real. So instead, he opened his eyes as he refocused himself, turned his head to look at Caldwell and said "Josh, tell me about the rest of it. Who was behind the attack? Who else was hurt? What are we doing about it now?"

"Sir, do you think this is the right time for this. Let's wait until you've gained a little more strength." He noted wryly that he'd slipped back into speaking formally to Navarro without even being conscious about it.

"No, I'm okay. And it will help take my mind off the… the other thing." He couldn't bring himself to form the words 'Julia's death.' "Tell me now."

So Caldwell quickly ran him through the entire tragic story. He described the aftermath of the explosion, named those dead and injured in the attack that the President knew, told him of the initial surgeries he'd received in Victorville and the subsequent ones he endured after his return here to Washington. He explained the outpouring of grief that had washed in from around the world— condolences and offers to help, from common people as well as the high and mighty—told him of the identification of his attacker and his apparent motives. Finally, he described Julia's funeral.

Caldwell had taken personal responsibility for the funeral of the First Lady. Like Ray, Julia had also been an only child whose parents were also already deceased, so there was no other family to take charge. With the President still fighting for his life, Caldwell felt compelled to act in his stead, rather than allowing the service to be monopolized by Vice President Kerrigan. A public memorial was held, with mourners in their thousands passing by Julia's closed coffin in the East Room of the White House. A state funeral service was conducted in the National Cathedral. And a private interment was conducted in Arlington Cemetery, with Julia's burial in Section 60 of the cemetery so that when Ray was ultimately buried there next to her, he would be surrounded by other soldiers he had served with in Afghanistan. The entire series of events was a cathartic experience for the nation which was watched by a mesmerized world.

Caldwell paused in his narrative to see how the President was bearing up. Once again Navarro's eyes were closed, although Caldwell could tell by the tight expression on his face that he was not asleep. As if he could feel Josh's eyes on him, Navarro opened his and said, "Thanks for all that, Josh. She would have appreciated that you were the one to do it. Now tell me what Fran's been up to."

Once again, Caldwell led the President through the events that had transpired over the past five months while he slept. He told of the departure of Fitzrandolph, of the new appointments made to the Cabinet and the nominations posted for the judiciary. He told Navarro of some of the policy changes being discussed within the Cabinet, and of the tension that was ramping up between him—Caldwell—and Kerrigan. Finally, he told the President of the discussion he'd had with General Webster regarding the HHS files and Kerrigan's reaction to it.

"I don't yet know what that means. I haven't had a chance to check up on it, and I can't make the pieces of the puzzle fit together. I didn't press Webster, because he clearly feels constrained by Kerrigan's directive to him; but if you ask him about it, I don't believe there would be any such reservation." He looked at Navarro pensively. "I think you should. I can't figure it out. Why would she react so strongly to something that seems so innocuous? We need to know what it is about those files that set her off."

"You're right, of course, Josh," responded Navarro. He was clearly losing steam, the immensity of the discussion taking its toll. He could feel the overpowering urge to close his eyes and sleep some more, and only by force of will was he able to continue to focus on Caldwell's words. But he was losing, and Caldwell could see it now.

"Sir, I think that'll be enough for now. You rest some more, and I'll come again later tonight or tomorrow, whenever the docs think it'll be okay." He stood up and pushed his chair back against the wall, then returned to the bed and laid his hand on Navarro's shoulder. The President appeared to be sleeping again already. "Good," he said. "Rest up. Then we'll begin to get you back into the driver's seat." He turned and left the room.

Navarro opened his eyes to watch the retreating back. 'Thanks, Josh,' he thought, 'for everything.' And then, more bleakly, 'What am I going to do without her?'

CHAPTER 21

Washington, DC
Wednesday, 21 September 2022
9:12 p.m. EDT

Acting President Kerrigan was brooding in the living room of the Vice Presidential mansion on the grounds of the U.S. Naval Observatory in northwest Washington, pacing back and forth and thinking about all that had recently transpired, a glass of *recioto* in her hand. This strong, sweet, red wine came from the Valpolicella region of northern Italy west of Verona from which the Moscone family originated—indeed, a Villa Moscone still stood, surrounded by vineyards, near the small town of Negrar—and she and Fred had grown to enjoy it considerably. She and her husband had finished a quiet dinner earlier and were now discussing options for how to best handle the implications of the events of the last two days. He sat on the settee that faced out toward the broad porch that wrapped around the front of the mansion, watching his wife pace and occasionally offering one-word comments as she talked aloud. They had been sitting out there on the porch earlier in the evening, but now in late September the sun was already setting earlier and earlier, so they'd been driven inside by the cool air. He also was sipping a glass of *recioto*.

As his wife continued to pace, Moscone thought to himself that he liked living here much better than when they were in their townhouse in Georgetown. He liked the size of the three-story, 33 room, 9,000-plus square foot Queen Anne style Victorian mansion which had been the official residence of U.S. Vice Presidents since 1975; it went well with his oversized persona, he acknowledged, immodestly. The senator recognized that he was an egotistical man who enjoyed being the center of attention, but he viewed this as an asset rather than as a character flaw. He tended to lean toward being bombastic instead of reticent as a matter of course. And this big house suited him.

He sipped his wine and refocused his attention on Kerrigan. "Franny, stop pacing. You're getting yourself all worked up over nothing." He waved a big hand at her. "Come over here and sit down so we can talk." He scooted his large bulk over to the right side of the settee so that his wife would have room to sit beside him.

She did as he asked, still talking aloud as she sat. "Fred, I just can't tell you how mad I am about Caldwell. Twice today—not once—but twice, he gets in to see Navarro over at Walter Reed, but each time I have Dougherty call over there Webster tells him that Navarro is sleeping and shouldn't be disturbed." She took another sip of the strong wine and started to stand again to resume pacing.

Moscone reached out and pulled her back down before she could get started. "Here, *cara mia*, just sit and relax," he said, draping a big arm across her shoulders and pulling her in close. "All that pacing isn't going to do you any good. It'll just rile you up some more. Listen, I've been thinking it through, and here's how I think we should play things." As he spoke, Kerrigan stopped fidgeting and turned on the settee to face him.

"Tell me," she said. "Tell me what you've come up with."

"Okay," he began. "First, nothing really has changed yet." Her eyes flew open wide at this, and her mouth opened to protest, but he forged ahead. "No, wait. Listen. It doesn't matter if Navarro is awake, he's still not able to do anything until the Cabinet says he's capable again. What we've got here is a man who's just come out of a long-term coma, with traumatic physical injuries, the full extent of which nobody's even sure about yet. There's no way the Cabinet's just going to hand power back to him until he's gone through a substantial rehabilitation period. So, in the meantime, you're still effectively the President, just as before."

"Fred, I understand all that. But I accept that it's going to end. I'm only the Vice President"—here her face unconsciously scowled—"and Ray Navarro is going to be back in the White House as soon as he's able. I know that. I can deal with that. No, I'm upset with Caldwell, and the way he's acting. What are we going to do about him?"

Moscone was silent a moment, realizing he had misjudged his wife's emotions. He then realized that if he handled things right, maybe he could kill two birds with one stone.

"Franny, you still need to push ahead. For all intents and purposes, you're still the President, and every day you're setting precedence and creating a legacy. You can't act as if Navarro is going to come back, because maybe he won't. If the Cabinet thinks he's too weak to resume—and they're the only ones that matter, really—or if, perchance, some questionable information regarding his birth and pedigree somehow became common knowledge, then maybe he won't be back at all. You're all that matters right now."

She was nodding as he spoke, silently acknowledging his logic.

"So what should we do about Caldwell?" she asked.

He began to tell her what he was thinking. Although he didn't tell her everything that was rolling around in his mind.

CHAPTER 22

Washington, DC
Thursday, 22 September 2022
7:47 a.m. EDT

Navarro had awakened in the darkened room early, shaken by the dreams. He was back in the Army again, but now earlier, shortly after his graduation from West Point. He'd been walking a long time, he realized, and he was tired. It was dark, or just getting close to dawn, that time when forms begin to be visible but still seem like shadows. He was in a long file of other soldiers trudging across an area of scrubby pines and other sparse trees, a place where small farms and houses used to be but were no more; he knew suddenly that he was once again in his training as a Ranger, and marching on a patrol through the north Georgia mountains. As the dawn got brighter, he noticed the soldier in front of him wore no helmet like every other soldier in the patrol, but instead had long, golden hair. Abruptly, the soldier turned her head to glance at him over the shoulder and he recognized Julia. He wanted to ask what she was doing there, but couldn't speak. As he reached out to grab her shoulder, she suddenly vanished from his sight into the earth with a loud, long scream that pierced his soul. Looking at the place where she'd been, he saw a hole in the ground, an old abandoned well from one of those long-vanished farms. He'd shone his flashlight into the well, and could see Julia's face looking up to him from the waters at the well bottom, pleading with him for help. He'd called out to his comrades for help, but they could not hear him and kept marching past, oblivious to his cries. He'd struggled to reach down into the well, only to find he couldn't touch Julia's outstretched fingers that strained for him, and which then sunk under the dark waters into the silence. 'No, Julia, come back,' he cried, and awakened himself with her name on his lips, opening his eyes to find the duty nurse rushing to the bedside to settle him.

From there the day had gone downhill. Webster had appeared with a neurological specialist in tow, and they had wheeled him into a 'torture chamber' where they poked and prodded to determine the extent of the damage caused by the crushed pelvis. Electrodes where attached to him, dye was injected, pictures taken, his one leg and one stump moved and lifted and twisted, all the while the pain swirled around him—only to conclude that he would not walk again. Ever. 'Simply put,' they told him, 'there are no signals from your brain reaching below your lower back. Although your legs, even the amputated left one, are functionally intact and your wounds have healed, they are unable to work.' They had told him they were sorry, and he wanted only to scream at them 'What do I do now?' Instead he thanked them for trying, told them to begin teaching him to use a wheelchair or walker or whatever as quickly as possible, and asked them for some pain medicine.

He was sweating and exhausted by the time they wheeled him back into the room six hours later, and he was grateful as the pain began to blur into a mist and he could close his eyes and talk to Julia again.

CHAPTER 23

Washington, DC
Thursday, 22 September 2022
7:11 p.m. EDT

Stevenson was working at his desk in the small room he used as a home office, preparing himself and organizing his thoughts for the interview he'd have with the President next week when he accompanied Caldwell to Walter Reed. He was playing catch-up, downloading files of work that he'd begun or completed at the office downtown, or digital voice files from interviews he'd conducted. He'd long ago got in the habit of putting copies of everything he did onto a flash drive, then bringing it home to download onto a portable hard drive that he used as a personal archive. That way he figured if anything ever happened at the office and his stuff got corrupted, he'd have a clean copy of everything so he could restart. It was a system that had worked well in the past, particularly on one notable occasion where a virus had gotten through the office server's firewall and he'd found his desktop's hard drive erased when he booted it up one morning. From that point on he ritually performed this exercise every week.

He glanced up from his laptop to look out the window. He loved working in this room. The house on Quincy, one of a series of old row houses that was in a formerly run-down area of the city that had been rehabilitated before the housing bubble burst a dozen years ago, was situated on an east-west axis, so that from this window he could look out to see the Capitol dome glowing in the distance. It was a sight of which he never grew tired, whether the gleam was from sunlight during the day or from the myriad floodlights during the night. He stretched his back and reached to his right for the deep red glass of Argentinian *Malbec* he was drinking. This was his deep, dark secret, the fact that he was a closet wine snob; most people assumed that only beer ever passed his lips. But over the years he'd come to relish a glass of good wine with a meal at the end of a day, and he always stocked a substantial and varied collection of wines. He sipped the wine now, savoring it, as the voice files being downloaded were automatically processed by the sophisticated voice recognition software he used which translated the voices into a word file that could be read and printed out. 'Much easier than hiring a transcription service,' he thought to himself, as he remembered the way things used to work when he was getting started in the business, now so long ago. Seemed like the advances in computer technology just kept coming. Sometimes it was hard to keep up.

Stevenson had bought this place about eleven years before, shortly after his divorce and the sale of their suburban monstrosity down in Woodbridge. His ex had moved back to New England—from which he hoped she'd never leave so he wouldn't have to see her again—and he had hunted around for a much smaller bachelor pad he could use as he started out on his own, newly alone. He was fortunate to have wealthy parents up in New York who were willing to front the money to purchase the place for their only child and to renovate it for him as a tax shelter, and he dutifully mailed them a check each month as repayment; happily, housing prices were again climbing after having reached their nadir in the Obama years, and now his equity in the place was fairly substantial. When he'd got it, it had still been a rundown shell, but it was in a neighborhood that was being revitalized by up and coming young people just like him, and he could sense the potential it had. Since then, he had basically gutted the place and had it rebuilt to create bigger, brighter rooms with an open feel. It had two working fireplaces, one in the living room that fronted onto Quincy and one in the master bedroom above it. He'd had a fully modernized hi-tech kitchen installed in the back—he enjoyed cooking for himself—which had a small eat-in area and which opened out onto a back patio and garden, where he often puttered around. There were three bedrooms, including the master and the one he used as his office, and a functional wine cellar—a necessity—down a steep set of stairs to the basement. On weekends he frequently enjoyed prowling antique and bric-a-brac shops in off-the-beaten-track places in DC, as well as going to flea markets throughout the Maryland and Northern Virginia suburbs, looking for unique items to install in the home. As a result, guests were typically surprised when they entered from a non-descript Washington street to find themselves confronted by a handful of antiques, fine paintings, chandeliers, crown molding and such. Not many, given the state of his finances, and certainly not as much as he coveted, but enough to make the place stand out. Stevenson felt a great deal of justified pride in his home.

He drew his attention away from the evening sky and back toward his work, now intending to plough through the mail that had been accumulating. He worked through several pieces of junk mail, tossing them unopened into the trash, and several bills, which he set to the side to pay later, before coming to a package that had been delivered to the house that day via Fedex. He ripped open the top and pulled out a sheaf of papers from inside, as well as a cheap flash drive that had come from Staples.

'What's this all about' he thought, looking at the envelope for a return address and finding none. He began to flip through the pages, quickly stopping as he realized what he had, then starting again to read them more closely. "You've got to be kidding me," he said aloud to the room, then set them down on the desk and reached again for his wine so that he could think.

Stevenson had been burned by anonymous stuff once before, and he'd learned from that regrettable experience to tread warily whenever something came to him without invitation and without confirmation. So he knew the first thing he'd have to do is try to confirm the validity of these documents. Fortunately, that should not be that hard given the wide net of contacts he'd developed over the years investigating stories related to the government. He could probably get hold of his friend in that agency tomorrow, show her the documents, and merely ask her to confirm that they were legit. Wouldn't put his friend in a compromising position since she wouldn't be providing the files, she'd only be saying they were real. And he could ask the science guys at his office to put him in touch with someone who could verify these test results; again, that could all be done anonymously, so they'd be no more the wiser for their efforts. And if both proved correct, he'd have a story to write, and he realized it would be a good one.

He pondered if the source of the package was important to him. Naturally, he wondered about the motives of the sender, and knew he'd have to take that into consideration if this developed any further. It would be interesting to know who'd sent them, but in the end it really wasn't important. He supposed that the guy would eventually be getting around to money—everybody who sent stuff in like this was ultimately looking to be paid for their trouble—but he knew the bureau would handle that if the story was good enough. No, that didn't matter; not yet, anyway. The bottom line was: if the documents were valid, where they came from didn't matter—they were news despite the motive of whoever sent them. If they weren't valid, there would be no story, and so where they came from still didn't matter. He was already visualizing himself laying out the story on televisions across the nation, knowing it would be good. 'But do I really want to do this?' he thought. 'Maybe I should give Navarro a chance to comment on it first. I could broach it with him when I see him next week.' He stood up and started pacing around the small room. 'But if I wait 'til then, somebody else might break it first. I think I gotta go with it now.' No, it'd have to be now. And with that decision made, he began to sketch out what he would write if the legitimacy of the documents was confirmed, unconsciously humming to himself and sipping his wine, because he could feel that this was one story that wasn't going to go away.

CHAPTER 24

Lambertville, NJ
Tuesday, 27 September 2022
6:34 p.m. EDT

"And he wants us to come down to visit this weekend so we can talk," Coryell said to Susan, as he grilled a couple steaks on the small patio behind his house. "Says you wouldn't believe the mail he's been getting—both pro and con—since he reported the story last night on the news. He sounds a little overwhelmed by it all, truthfully." He expertly flipped the two ribeyes over and slathered on another dose of his home-made marinade, then closed the grill to wait another nine minutes, his prescribed grilling time from which he never varied. Jamie claimed he grilled the best steaks in the world because of his precise timing, although others—many others, in fact—disputed this.

"Why's he want me to come along?" Sue asked. She was dressed in jeans and an old Columbia sweatshirt of Jamie's. The day had been a bright, sunny one, but the air had now cooled, portending that true fall days and evenings were not far away. She had walked over from New Hope a couple hours earlier and met Jamie at his office in *The Beacon*, then had strolled with him uptown, talking about Stevenson's exposé which she had seen on the news last night. "I hate Washington. Plus you guys will sequester yourselves out on his back porch and talk shop, and expect me to keep you refilled with nachos. Plus I hate Washington, did I say that?"

"I know, but Lou sounded almost beat. Not like him at all, particularly after a big win like this one. I think this mail he was talking about is getting to him." Jamie plopped down next to her at the battered picnic table which sat by the grill and stretched out his legs while he waited for the steaks to be ready. He looked over at her. "Plus it'll be fun to get away. The weather's supposed to be great, we can hang out, do nothing, go do the tourist thing, whatever." He smiled plaintively. "Please come with me."

"Oh, alright," she said, feigning exasperation, "I'll go. But you better pay attention to me, or else." She held up a small fist and waved it in his face, glaring at him. Then she laughed and took a drink of her beer. "Maybe we can swing by and see Mommy and Daddy while we're down there. Wouldn't they be surprised?" She laughed again, although this time somewhat more tentatively.

Jamie wondered if she was asking him if he wanted to meet her parents. Generally, they were off limits; Sue didn't like discussing them, and rarely did. He'd never before heard her say she was thinking about visiting them. Jamie could tell at times that she missed seeing her mother. But her father was a more complicated story, one that Jamie had not deciphered. Sue was always much more wary and more careful when talking about Moscone.

He looked at her and said carefully, "Do you want to visit your folks while we're there?"

She said nothing, merely stared at her mug of beer, swirling it idly as she did. Finally she responded "You know, Jamie, I think I do. I haven't seen them in over two years now. I think I'd like to do that." She looked up at him, as if asking for his approval.

He nodded to her. "Then we'll do it," he answered emphatically. He'd long believed it would be good for her to reconnect with her parents; plus he was curious about them. "So how do you do that? Do you call to make an appointment, or do you just drop in?"

"First of all, it's WE, not just ME. You're coming along too, buster." She was waving the fist around again. "I may need a driver for my getaway, and you're it. And I think it would be best to just call once we're down there so they don't get too much advance notice. Less pressure that way." She waggled her head up and down once forcefully, as if to cap that statement with an exclamation point.

Jamie glanced at his watch and then jumped up. He'd waited ten minutes, and now fretted that the steaks would be ruined. But he was mollified to find they could be salvaged, and he removed them from the grill and plopped them onto plates, then ran quickly through the back door into the house to load some cole slaw and scalloped potatoes on them, and returned to the picnic table so they could eat.

Sue confirmed that the steak was okay while still chewing her first bite. "Jamie, this is great. I think ten minutes is definitely the way to go. You better switch up from here on out."

He agreed that the meat was okay, but still would not budge on the orthodoxy of nine minutes. Soon they both lapsed into silence as they ate.

Eventually, as her plate grew empty, Sue asked, "So what do you think will be the fallout from Lou's report?" On the news last night, Stevenson had very carefully laid out all the details that he'd confirmed from the medical reports, and then skillfully led his audience to possible conclusions of their import. He'd told about the DNA comparisons of the President's file and his mother's, and how they showed they could not be related, and explained how although a DNA sample from the President's father did not exist, details from his father's other records seemed to corroborate the case that the President was not the natural born child of Ramon and Theresa Navarro as the country had long thought. He'd then reviewed the qualifications for a President—that he be at least thirty-five years old and a resident of the U.S. for at least fourteen, and that he be a 'natural born' citizen—and then discussed the implications that a birth of questionable pedigree might have. Newspapers and news outlets across the country had been filled with articles based on Lou's story, and the editorial pages were already shouting for the issue to be looked into. To this point, members of Congress and other politicians had yet to raise their voices— undoubtedly waiting to see which way the wind began to blow, Jamie thought ungenerously—although that was sure to come quickly enough.

"What do I think?" Jamie echoed. He took a drink from his mug to buy himself a moment to gather his thoughts, then said "Well, I think I would have waited a little longer to check things out. Lou told me he received the information anonymously. I'm always leery of something like that. I'd want to know a lot more about who sent it to me—and why—before I went public with it." He stood up and began clearing the table, talking as he did.

"Jamie, stop. Sit down," Sue said. "I'm not done yet."

"Oh, sorry. Nervous habit. I always find myself making busy work when I'm talking aloud." He sat again. "Anyway, presuming it's all true, and disregarding the source for the moment, it leaves us with Navarro as effectively an adopted child. Nothing wrong with that. But it then begs the question of where this child was born, and although his birth certificate does say El Paso"—Stevenson had researched this and included that fact as part of his report last night—"people will say that if one fact about him is false, then what else is too? I think there'll be a lot of energy expended over the next several days and weeks in examining the other details of the President's life, as well as that of his parents."

"So the fact that he's not really Ramon and Theresa's natural born son doesn't matter?"

"Nope. It will only matter if he was not born in El Paso like his birth certificate says."

"But Texas has verified that the certificate is true, didn't it? They had to do that before the election. I'm sure I read that."

Jamie nodded patiently. "True, but like I say, if one piece of Navarro's life is not accurate, people will be looking for other pieces to be wrong too. It's just the nature of the beast, unfortunately."

"Well I hope nothing comes of it. I think President Navarro's a great man who's been doing great things. He needs to get back in office and keep working, not be looking over his shoulder trying to defend himself from someone taking cheap shots at him."

"I hope so, too," Jamie answered. "I guess when we get to talk with Lou we may get some more details." He started clearing again, now that Sue had finished her steak and relinquished her plate. "How about some dessert to wash that all down?"

"No, thanks," she responded. "I'm stuffed. Let's go sit on the front porch and finish our beers and you can tell me what you're printing in the paper this weekend."

"Sounds good to me." He held open the back door so they could head through the house and out to the front porch. He continued talking as they went. "I'm actually thinking of including an article about this struggling artist I've discovered over in New Hope. Young thing, little wet behind the ears, needs all the help and encouragement she can get. I'd be doing her a big favor."

"Oh, yeah?" Sue said, as they settled onto the glider on the porch. "Tell me about her."

CHAPTER 25

Washington, DC
Wednesday, 28 September 2022
9:13 a.m. EDT

"I want to know how those files got released," said Kerrigan. She was standing behind her desk, facing Josh Caldwell, the President's Chief of Staff, Jess Dougherty, her Chief of Staff, and Liz Barton, the Secretary of Health & Human Services, dressing them down as if they were recalcitrant high school students who'd been caught cheating on a test. "It's inconceivable to me that any medical records, let alone the President's and his parents', could be made public, but to have it done in such a way that it casts his Presidency in doubt is beyond the pale." She was clearly livid at the breach, her face flushed and voice pitched high, and the recipients of her tirade offered no vocal rebuttals, although at least some of them did so in their minds. "Liz," Kerrigan continued, "I want a full-fledged investigation into this. I want to know how it happened and who's at fault. Who had access. Who stands to gain. And I want a preliminary report by the end of the week."

"But Madame Vice President," Barton began.

"No buts, Liz. I want it done quickly and I want it done right. Understood?" She clearly was going to broach no argument.

"Understood, ma'am. I'll have my people get right on it. I'll have the report on your desk by Friday night."

"Very good. Thank you, Liz." She was bringing herself back under control and talking more slowly. "We'll talk then." Barton turned to head for the door and exit the room.

She turned to face Caldwell and Dougherty. "Josh, Jess, I want you to do the same with the staff. Examine who had access and who might gain from such a release. I'd like your initial impressions by Friday also." She paused. "Questions?"

Caldwell was about to speak, but decided not to. 'There's only one person in this room who might benefit from this,' he thought to himself, 'so I'll definitely look into it.'

Instead he said "I'll inform the President when I visit him later today. He should be told of this immediately."

"I agree," said Kerrigan. "And I want to be there with you when he's told. He needs to know that he has my full support in this." She smiled tightly at Caldwell, knowing she'd trapped him. "When are you leaving to head out there?"

Caldwell knew he was caught. He couldn't refuse to allow Kerrigan to join him, and he couldn't now say the President was too tired or otherwise unavailable. He'd have to take her along. 'Shoulda just kept your mouth shut, Josh,' he admonished himself. To Kerrigan he said, "I'm leaving the West Wing at 3:30 to head out to the hospital."

"Good," she said, "I'll pick you up there then. Jess, please arrange the car to take me to the White House to pick up Governor Caldwell at 3:30 and then take us out to Walter Reed. We'll be out there for what, Josh, about an hour?" Caldwell nodded. "Good, afterwards the car can take me home then return the Governor to his office." She sat back down at the desk. "Thank you, gentlemen, that will be all."

She stared at their backs as they departed the room. 'Did you really do it?' she thought. 'And what do you hope to gain?'

CHAPTER 26

Washington, DC
Wednesday, 28 September 2022
4:07 p.m. EDT

"Fran, how good to see you," said Navarro as the Acting President came into his room with the Chief of Staff and General Webster. "It's been a long time." He flashed his smile at her as he sat in the wheelchair; he'd been practicing maneuvering around on the thing, and was starting to feel fairly comfortable with it.

"Mister President, it's good to see you, too, finally. I was out here last week a couple times to visit, but you were never awake." In truth, Kerrigan had come out to the hospital once, and then finding Navarro asleep, spent the time interrogating Webster about his prognosis; all other times she'd had Dougherty call, only to be told, in essence, 'Don't come.' "Governor Caldwell was gracious enough to agree to come with me today." She glanced over at Caldwell, who had continued to the President's wheelchair and laid a hand on his shoulder. "Please allow me to extend my most sincere condolences over Julia's loss."

Navarro lowered his head suddenly as she said this, and seemed to deflate momentarily into his chair. But, reviving quickly, he answered, "Thank you, Fran, thank you very much. It's a very great loss. I'm still trying to get used to it." He looked up at her, wondering how sincere she truly was, and decided that she did indeed mean the words, that it was not an act.

"Sir, if there's anything Fred or I can do, please ask. If it's in my power, I'll do it."

Caldwell stifled a grunt at this, not believing a word she said. 'I'm watching you like a hawk, lady,' he thought to himself. 'You and the Giant Bug. And I'll get to the bottom of it, you can count on that.'

"Thanks, Fran," Navarro answered. He proceeded to demonstrate his increasing prowess with the wheelchair. He was gaining in strength every day, and now spent upwards of three hours each day rolling along the halls and corridors of the hospital, a Secret Service agent trailing not far behind, getting the feel for his 'wheels', as he called them, and gradually increasing his upper body strength. He would also have use of a self-propelled wheelchair, and would begin practicing with that soon to get the feel of it, but he'd said he wanted to begin with the basics. So he propelled himself along by hand, greeting surprised staff and patients as he rolled along.

"Looks like you're becoming a pro at that," Caldwell said. "You're not pushing yourself too hard, are you, sir?"

"Not at all, Josh. Webster here keeps me on a short leash. Only lets me work out on it for a few hours a day, although I'm sneaking in a little bit more than he thinks." He winked at the doctor good-naturedly. "But when I get tired, I rest. Don't worry about me, I intend to get back to work as soon as I can."

"That's very good news, Mister President," said Kerrigan dubiously. She thought that Navarro looked pale and drawn, clearly not the robust man he'd been. 'That's to be expected, naturally,' she thought. Then to him, "I'm keeping the seat warm for you, sir. Just let me know when you're ready to come back, and you can move into it with my blessing." Caldwell stared at her thinking 'You don't fool me for a second.' She pretended not to notice his look, and continued "When do you think you'll be ready to return?"

Webster interjected. "Not for at least another week, I would estimate. The President's recovery has been remarkably fast, and he is steadily getting stronger. But all too often there is a little relapse as the body adjusts itself which might hinder his return. We will all"—here he looked and spoke directly to the President—"have to be patient and not rush things."

"Of course, doctor, of course," said Kerrigan. She paused. "Doctor, would you excuse us for a few minutes? Governor Caldwell and I need to speak with the President about a few items." She looked at him expectantly.

"Yes, ma'am. Of course. I'll be in my office should you need me. Just ask the nurse to call me."

"Thank you, doctor. And I would like to speak with you and Governor Caldwell together once we've finished here, so please keep yourself available." She smiled at him, although her eyes remained dark.

Webster nodded affirmatively, and quickly left the three alone.

Kerrigan looked toward the President, while Caldwell pulled over two chairs in which they could sit. Navarro was clearly getting better. The scars were fading, he was without question getting stronger, the wide swath of bandages on his head had been removed and replaced with a smaller one covering the entry point of his inter-cranial surgery. The paralysis did not seem to be affecting his spirits. All in all, he looked like a man on the road to recovery. She wondered how he would take this latest bit of news.

"Mister President," she began, once she and Caldwell were seated. "We need to make you aware of a disturbing development which was made public on the news two nights ago." And she proceeded to describe Stevenson's exposé and its inferences, and to tell him of what actions she was taking to get to the bottom of it. "I promise you, sir, we'll discover how those records were released, and the perpetrators will be punished."

Navarro was silent throughout her narration, only occasionally glancing over to Caldwell to gage his reaction. Once she'd finished, he said "Fran, thank you for the update. Makes me wish the good doctor would let me have a television in here so I could keep current on things myself, but he says at this point it will only tire me out. Soon though, I think. Anyway, I don't think this report's something to worry about. Sure, we should find out how the files were leaked to prevent that from happening to someone else in the future, but I don't know that we—I—need to respond to this. The media is trying to get us to swing at an outside curveball. Just let it go."

"Sir," Caldwell began, "don't you feel the need to address the accusations that Stevenson's made, that you're not the natural born child of your parents?"

"Josh, I can't see that it would do any good. I'm astounded by the news—truly. I find it hard to believe that it's true, and I certainly don't believe my parents deceived me about my birth. If what Stevenson said is a fact—and it should be pretty easy to evaluate whether it is or not—then they never knew it either, just as I did not." He looked from one to the other. "But what does it matter, really? It's just another twist thrown on top of my already unusual birth."

"So you don't want us to respond to this?" asked Kerrigan incredulously. She had expected Navarro to explode with anger, as she would have done had her private life been publicly ripped open.

"No, Fran, it's not worth it. I'll just focus on getting better, and you and Josh just focus on keeping things running smoothly." He smiled again, hazel eyes twinkling. "Wait 'til I tell Julia about it, though. She'll be mad, too, like you are."

"What?" Kerrigan asked, staring at him blankly. She looked over to Caldwell, noting the concern on his face. "You're going to talk with Julia?"

"Oh, I mean in my dreams," Navarro responded hastily, waving his hand at her. "Don't worry, I'm not losing it. It just helps me settle down and sleep. It's not like she answers back or anything." He yawned. "It does feel like it is getting to be that time. Another round of pain medication, and another nap. The high points of my day."

"Well, then, Mister President," Kerrigan said, standing up, "we'll leave you alone to rest. Thank you for talking with us, sir. Get well quickly."

Caldwell was also on his feet. "I'll see you tomorrow, sir."

"Thanks, Josh. Bye, Fran. Thanks for stopping by." As they exited the room, two large orderlies entered and lifted Navarro from the wheelchair and gently laid him into the bed.

"Josh, what was that all about?" she asked Caldwell once they'd entered Webster's office. They'd been silent in the hallways, not wanting anyone to overhear parts of their conversation. "Does he think he's talking with Julia? Doctor?"

"No, ma'am, he does not," replied Webster. They were all sitting in the overstuffed chairs positioned around a small coffee table in the forward area of Webster's large office. "He's merely going through the normal stages of the grieving process for his wife. In these initial stages, the surviving spouse often 'talks' with their departed loved one, telling them about their day and what's going on in their life. It's the brain's way of filling the void until the rest of the psyche catches up. If the President says he's talking to Julia now, you can rest assured it won't last for long."

"Well, that's good to hear, at least. How much pain medication is he on?"

"He had been on morphine for several weeks while he was initially injured, but now is getting only Vicodin. He's getting less than the maximum dose, and I expect that to be decreased even further in the next several weeks as he gains in strength."

"Is there any chance of him becoming addicted to it?"

"What kind of question is that?" Caldwell asked angrily.

"It's a legitimate one, and you know it, Josh," Kerrigan shot back. "As you know full well, whenever there's a traumatic injury like this for which pain medication is employed over an extended period, a risk of addiction exists. I want to know how General Webster is handling that." She swiveled her head back to Webster.

"It is a legitimate question, one we take very seriously. And Vicodin can be addictive, but I see no indication at this point that the President is receiving more than is warranted. As I said, we will begin to wean him from it soon, once his strength has returned. I don't anticipate he'll have a problem." He paused, and looked significantly at both of them. "Remember this man endured traumatic injuries once before, at which time he also was prescribed pain medication, and he came through that with no hint of any addiction. I'm confident he'll do it again this time."

"Well, that also is good to hear, isn't it, Governor?"

"Yes, ma'am, it is. Although I expected to hear nothing less."

"Nor did I, believe me." She looked to Webster again. "And any signs of depression, doctor?" She could feel Caldwell bristle again at the question, but she held a hand up to forestall the explosion. "Josh, I just want to know if he's dealing with his grief appropriately, or if it's going to affect his complete recovery. Doctor?"

"Again, ma'am, I see nothing that would lead me to think he's not proceeding through his grief normally. It will take some time for it to run its course, but he will come through it. Again, I am fully confident in saying that."

"And when will that be?" she asked. This was the real question she'd wanted to ask all along.

"Unfortunately, ma'am, I am unable to hazard a guess about that. Everyone is different. He could be fully recovered mentally and far enough along physically for him to return to the White House next week. On the other hand it could take months. We will just have to take it one day at a time."

"Very well, doctor, I think that's all of my questions, for the moment at least. Josh, do you have any?" Caldwell shook his head silently. "None. Okay, well then I guess we're through. Thank you, doctor, for your attentiveness to your patient." She rose from her chair to leave, Caldwell rising as well, then turned back to address Webster once more.

"Oh, doctor, by the way, did you ever mention the discussion we had in my office last week to anyone else?" She eyed him carefully as she spoke.

"No, ma'am, certainly not," Webster replied hotly. "You instructed me to keep what we discussed in confidence, and I have spoken to no one about it."

"Good. Be sure you keep it that way." She glanced over to Caldwell. "The Governor and I are trying to plug a leak. I'm glad to hear it's not you."

Webster black eyes didn't move from her. "I've not spoken about the contents of our meeting, and I won't. Perhaps you should inspect your own house, ma'am," inferring that Dougherty might be the cause of the problem.

"Careful, doctor. I'll take care of my business, don't you worry. You just make sure yours remains in order." She spun on her heel and swept out of the room, heading to the elevator to descend to the waiting limousine.

Caldwell began to move to keep up, but not before he also cautioned Webster to be careful.

Webster watched them go, glad to be rid of them both. Then he turned to head back downstairs to check on Navarro.

CHAPTER 27

Washington, DC
Wednesday, 28 September 2022
10:17 p.m. EDT

Stevenson was working at the desk in the home office again, when his cell phone rang. He set what he'd been working on aside—it was a follow-up to his original story with more pieces filled in from inquiries he'd been making in Texas—and answered it without thinking since he only gave this number out to a few people, and had diligently made sure that other unwanted nuisance calls never rang on it.

"Stevenson," he said into the phone.

"Good evening, Mister Stevenson," a voice said into his ear. The voice had a metallic sound to it, as if it was being masked somehow; sounds of traffic and crowds were audible in the background.

"Good evening, yourself. Who is this?"

"This is your pen-pal, Lou. I'm the one who sent you the Fedex package. I'm glad you put it to good use. You don't mind if I call you Lou, do you?"

Stevenson sat up straight in his chair and focused his attention on the caller. "Who are you? How did you get this number?"

"Not important," said the voice. "I'm sending you another package. Look for it in a few days. More exciting stuff." The connection ended.

"Wait, wait," he shouted into the dead phone. He realized it was futile. He looked at the phone now to see the number from which the call had been made, but it was masked as unknown. He set the phone back down on the desk, and tried to think through the implications of the call, when suddenly the phone came to life again.

He tentatively picked it up and flipped it open, saying "Stevenson."

"Stevenson, Josh Caldwell here." The words sounded somewhat slurred, as if the man'd been drinking, Stevenson thought. "I just wanted to commend you on the hatchet job you did on the President after he'd been so gracious to you in the past. Really considerate of you, especially when he's crippled and in the hospital and can't defend himself."

"Governor Caldwell…" he began, only to be cut off by Caldwell's flood of words.

"Just wanted you to know how much I appreciate it, and tell you that if anything like it happens again, I'm going to crush you." The venom in Caldwell's voice rang through the phone. "And don't think I won't."

"Governor, if you think you can threaten me and…"

"Can it," Caldwell shouted. "Just remember what I said. Oh, and by the way, you can forget about that interview at Walter Reed we'd talked about. You're not getting near the place." And once again the connection abruptly ended.

Stevenson stared at the phone in disbelief. And almost jumped out of his skin when it rang a third time.

"Stevenson," he said questioningly.

"Mister Stevenson," came a loud voice, "Senator Fred Moscone here. Hope I'm not calling you too late."

"No, Senator. Not too late. I'm wide awake, believe me. What may I do for you, sir?"

"Well, Stevenson, I naturally saw your report on the news the other night. Amazing stuff, with some considerable implications. You did a great job with it, by the way. I'd like to talk with you about it, and wondered if you would be good enough to come by my office tomorrow about ten o'clock. Would that work for you? Do you know where my office is?"

"Yes, sir, that would be fine. And I'll be able to find your office. Can you tell me what your interest in the story is, sir?"

"Now, Lou," Moscone laughed, "you wouldn't want to spoil all my fun by letting the cat out of the bag early, would you? No, you just come by tomorrow and we'll talk. Don't be late now."

"No, sir, I'll be there. Thanks for the invitation."

"My pleasure, Lou. My pleasure. See you tomorrow." He laughed again, and once more the connection was broken.

Stevenson stared at the silent phone for a long time, almost anticipating that it would ring once more with another disturbing call. 'Maybe I should have thought about this story a little more before going ahead with it,' he thought as the silence continued. 'Maybe it wasn't such a good idea, after all.'

He decided to forego any more work for the night.

CHAPTER 28

Washington, DC
Thursday, 29 September 2022
9:53 a.m. EDT

The following morning had turned out to be warm and clear, so Stevenson had decided to catch the Red Line at the New York—Florida Avenue station, a couple blocks from his house on Quincy, and ride it downtown to Union Station. He frequently did this when the weather forecast looked good so that he wouldn't have to fight the traffic. Even though he didn't have the added hassle of finding a parking place if he did drive—he could park in the employee's lot at the CNN Bureau office—he just liked to walk to and from the stations, and to ride the train. Most people thought he was crazy, but he found it put him in a better mood.

He had decided today not to go to the bureau office first; that would have involved some backtracking, and he'd have been forced to ride the train when the crowds were heavier. So instead, he had left his house shortly after nine, exited Union Station at about nine thirty, and was now walking down 1st Street and approaching the Hart Senate Office Building where Senator Moscone had his office.

Stevenson admired the vista of the office building as he approached it from the north. The third of the Senate's three buildings that housed the working offices of the nation's senators, as well as numerous committee and sub-committee meeting rooms, the Hart Building had been in use only since the mid-80's. Unlike the other two Senate buildings, the Dirksen and the Russell, the Hart Building has a distinctly more contemporary look than the neo-classical style of the others. A nine-story structure with over a million square feet of office area, it provides its Senators with two-story duplex office suites that allow an entire staff to work with its principal in connecting rooms which feature movable partitions, allowing them to reconfigure the offices to fit each

Senator's needs and style. Situated farthest from the Capitol, the building has an underground connection linking it to the Capitol Subway under the Dirksen Building, by which Senators can be whisked easily to and from the Senate's chambers for official business.

Stevenson entered the building through its east doors and crossed the high, central atrium of the building, headed for the skylit semicircular staircases at the far side. As his destination was only on the third floor, he had decided to climb the stairs rather than ride up in the elevators. He admired the centerpiece of the atrium, Alexander Calder's mobile-stabile, *Mountains and Clouds*, as he did so. This monumental piece of sculpture combines black aluminum clouds suspended above black steel mountains and rises 51 feet high within the center of the building; Stevenson was always struck by the simplicity of the sculpture's design when he saw it, yet could appreciate Calder's genius as he climbed the stairs and perceived he was climbing the mountains of the sculpture and moving up into its clouds as he did. He paused momentarily to take in the view of the atrium once he reached the third floor landing, then turned and headed along the balcony to the entrance of Moscone's office suite.

Upon entering the suite, Stevenson was greeted by the receptionist, a pretty dark-haired twenty-something, and was immediately ushered into Moscone's office. "He's just next door talking with Senator Igawa"—Tony Igawa of Hawaii was the Senate Majority Leader—"and will be back here in a moment. Please make yourself comfortable." She smiled at him, indicating a comfortable chair facing the Senator's large desk, then left him alone in the room.

Stevenson glanced around the big office somewhat self-consciously and apprehensively while he waited. 'Wonder if these places have surveillance on them,' he thought nervously, surprised that he'd been left alone in the powerful man's private sanctum. He knew full well that Moscone chaired the Senate Intelligence Committee. Would that cause some extra security to be installed in his office? He dismissed the thought quickly—no Senator would have a system installed that could watch him while he worked—and then realized as well that this more 'public' office area was not the sanctum anyway; that would be wherever the Senator's private office in the Capitol Building itself was. Somewhat reassured, he began to look around the room and noted that the walls of the paneled office were covered with photographs of Moscone with the rich and famous—millionaires, politicians, movie celebrities, sports stars—although Stevenson found it telling that no photo of President Navarro was featured on the wall. In every photo, the Senator's broad face smiled back as he shook his acquaintance's hand. He noted with interest how the Senator aged over the timeframe of the photos, some showing him with a full head of dark, wavy hair, and some showing him with the silver coiffure that he now sported. Only the big man's weight showed no sign of change; in each, he dominated the picture, his oversized persona showing right through the photograph.

As he was looking at the photos, the door to the office suddenly flew open and Senator Moscone strode into the room, hand extended and a big smile on his face. "Lou, thanks for dropping by. It's good to see you again." Then, noticing Stevenson's attention on the photographs, "Hey, those are some great shots, aren't they? It sometimes amazes me, when I take a moment, to see how many people I've met over the years I've been here in office. Amazes me, it really does."

"It is quite an assembly," Stevenson offered cautiously. "Tell me, sir, who would you say was the most memorable person you've met?"

"Well, Lou, I guess it would be too easy to say that that person is my wife," he waved a big hand toward his desk where a portrait of the Acting President sat. "Even though it is. But if I exclude her from consideration, I guess I'd have to say that meeting the Pope a few years back was my most memorable. This picture here." He pointed at a photograph hung prominently at eye level. "We got to travel over to Rome for it, had a private audience in the Vatican, Swiss Guards and all that. Very impressive affair. You know, my parents emigrated here from Italy after the war, so getting to go back to the 'old country' for such a meeting meant a little something extra for me. It was a very special day."

"Yes, sir, I can see where that would be quite a thrill."

"It was indeed, Lou, it was indeed." Moscone continued, draping an arm across Stevenson's shoulders and guiding back toward his chair. "But of course that's not why I asked you to stop by today."

"No, sir, I realize that," Stevenson said, sitting down expectantly and watching as the Senator moved around the big desk to sit in his own chair.

"No, I want to talk with you about that exposé you broadcast the other night. Riveting stuff, I thought." He smiled at Stevenson, although the smile did not extend to his dark eyes. "I'd like to know where you got your information," he said bluntly.

"Sir, you know I can't reveal my sources." He sat up straighter in the chair. This was what he had expected to talk about, and what he'd prepared to answer. "As you well know, if I did that, I'd never get another lead on anything."

Moscone's face darkened slightly, and his voice lowered. "Yeah, I know all that." He paused, still staring into Stevenson's eyes, and leaned back slowly in his chair. "You see, Lou, my concern is the motive of whoever sent you this stuff. Don't get me wrong, I don't doubt for a second that it's accurate. But if I ask myself who's going to be seen as benefiting from this manna from heaven that you've received?" He leaned forward suddenly, still holding Stevenson's eyes. "You know, I think you don't know where it came from. In fact, I have no doubt that you got it anonymously—I can read it in your face. So what's everyone going to think about that? Everyone will conclude that the most logical answer for its source that is that Fran Kerrigan, my wife, the nation's Acting President for the moment, is that person. So I've got grave concerns about motive. You following me?"

"Absolutely, sir, although I won't confirm that I got this anonymously." Moscone grunted dismissively as he said this. "But I did go to some length to verify the accuracy of the information provided, and it's indisputably accurate." He hesitated. "I believe the motive of my source is irrelevant."

"Well, let me tell you that you're mistaken," Moscone roared back at him, standing up from his chair and looming over the desk, face reddening, big voice filling the room. "It is completely relevant! It is the only thing that's relevant in the entire tale you've spun." He visibly calmed himself with some effort, and sat back down in his chair again, leaning his arms on the desk and intertwining his fingers. "Listen, carefully to me, Lou. I think your so-called source is none other than our illustrious presidential Chief of Staff, Josh Caldwell. It only makes sense that he's the one. He has access to all that information you released, he knows none of it really affects Navarro's status"—Lou noted that the Senator neglected to refer to Navarro by his title, 'President'—"so it won't hurt him in the long run. A little short-term embarrassment maybe, but the country's sympathy for the man will overcome that quickly. No, the rationale for him feeding you this story is solely to embarrass and discredit my wife." Here his voice lowered ominously. "And I don't take kindly to anyone doing that."

Stevenson sat stunned by the outburst, trying to connect the dots and see if they made sense. Sure, Caldwell could be the source, but a great deal of supposition on Moscone's part went into that conclusion. Any number of other people could equally be the source, some with ulterior motives and some just eager to publicize a discovery they came across. He considered whether a motive to discredit Kerrigan held water. 'A long shot,' he thought silently. Aloud, he replied "Senator, I don't know what you expect me to say. My information is accurate and I…"

"Here's what I expect," Moscone cut him off, reddening again. "I expect not one word to come from you that infers that the Acting President is in any way the source of this information. I expect not one word that the Acting President can expect to benefit from this situation. And I expect you to be very circumspect with regard to what you report on in the future when you receive information from unreliable sources." Again, he calmed himself, and again his voice lowered. "And if my expectations are not met, as I said before, I won't take it kindly. Are we clear on that, Lou?"

Once more, Stevenson sat stunned. 'Is he threatening me?' he thought to himself. He knew very well the stories of Moscone's past, when he was a hard-nosed ward boss in Philadelphia who brooked no challenges and tolerated no opposition; he knew also the stories of Moscone's reach within the intelligence community. But, a threat? 'Couldn't be,' he thought. So aloud he replied, "Senator, I will report on whatever I find to be true and accurate, regardless of where it leads. I…"

Abruptly, Moscone was on his feet and coming around the desk, interrupting once more. "Lou, we're done here. Don't tell me anything else. Not another word. Just remember what I said and don't make a foolish mistake, because I don't tolerate fools, or mistakes." He stood over Lou with his hands clenched at his side. "You can find your way out, I'm sure."

Silently, Stevenson got up and headed for the door. As he opened the door to the outer portion of the suite, he hesitated, half turned and began "Senator, I…"

"Thanks for coming by, Lou," Moscone cut him off a third time. "I'll look forward to your next report. You have a good day now. And remember what I said." And with that, he turned his back and headed back toward his desk.

Stevenson silently exited the office, closed the door behind him, and started walking slowly toward the stairs to depart the building and head back up to his bureau office, all the while thinking to himself, 'What was that all about?'

CHAPTER 29

Washington, DC
Friday, 30 September 2022
4:03 p.m. EDT

Jamie and Sue pulled up in front of Stevenson's house in Washington shortly after four o'clock. They had left Lambertville right after lunch, wanting to get past Baltimore and into the DC area before the notorious capital Friday afternoon rush hour started. The day was a little overcast—there was a forecast for rain over the weekend—and temperatures were turning cooler, particularly in the evenings. 'Won't be long before the leaves start turning,' Jamie thought as they'd headed south out of Lambertville on Route 29—'River Road' to the locals—along the east bank of the Delaware. They were riding in Jamie's new Ford hybrid, taking it out on its maiden long-distance voyage. Coryell had purchased it about a month before, after his late-model VW Jetta finally gave up the ghost, and was very pleased with it so far. After passing through Washington's Crossing, they'd picked up I-95 and had followed it through Philadelphia and Baltimore all the way to DC without any problem to speak of. Other than a little backup of traffic at the tolls just south of Wilmington, something that Jamie could not ever remember not happening, they'd encountered no delays and made great time, reaching Washington in just a little over two and a half hours. Now on Quincy, Jamie found an open parking spot on the street just a couple houses down from Stevenson's, expertly wheeled the Ford into it, and shut off the vehicle.

"We're here," he said, looking over to Sue in the passenger seat, raising his voice slightly to wake her up. She had fiddled with the radio for the first thirty minutes of the trip, flipping around trying to find a soft rock station to listen to, and had eventually passed out and stayed that way for the rest of the trip. "Time to wake up," he continued, nudging her shoulder.

Sue started slightly at his touch and then went through an extended stretching routine to rouse herself. "What time is it?" she asked, squinting at him. "Wow," she said, when told, "you made great time. Musta been flying, huh?" She unlatched her seatbelt and arched her back.

"Just moving along with the rest of the traffic," Jamie replied. "You ready?"

"Ready," she answered, opening the door. "Do you think he's here this early?"

"He said he'd be here about three, so I guess so. We'll soon find out." He popped the trunk to pull out their overnight bags as he got out of the car.

The street they were on did not appear to be in the best of neighborhoods—Jamie had noted a few bars and several vacant buildings not far away as they drove in—but most of the houses here on Quincy appeared to have been recently renovated. Indeed, a couple looked like they were still having work done, as evidenced by the scaffolding erected across their fronts. There were a few trees on the street, although not to the extent of the streets in Lambertville, and parking spaces clearly came at a premium—it looked like Jamie had lucked into the last spot available. He wondered idly where Lou parked. The only people Jamie saw was a group of men talking in front of a house about halfway down the street.

Lou's house somewhat resembled a New York brownstone, they observed as they approached. A half flight of stone steps led up to the front door, while another few led down to what Jamie presumed was a basement entrance. The door was on the left side of the house, flanked to its right by two sets of windows, with matching sets on the second story above them; a gabled roof capped the building. He and Sue climbed the steps toward the massive wooden front door with the wrought iron knocker on it, and were about to reach out to ring the bell when the door opened and Stevenson greeted them.

"Hey, guys. I saw you pull up from the window. Come on in."

Both Jamie and Sue reached out to give Lou a hug as they entered, and Jamie noted that Lou eyes flicked up and down the street apprehensively as they did. He also noted that Lou quickly bolted the door and set the security alarm as soon as they were inside.

"What a great house," Sue said, looking around the entryway foyer and peeking into the living room to her right. She had never been here before, and had only heard a description of the house from Jamie. As an artist, she could appreciate the architecture of the building, as well as the ways in which Lou had fixed it up. "Where did you get all this great stuff?"

"Oh, here and there," responded Lou, clearly pleased with Sue's reaction. "I always keep an eye out for interesting things that might look good here whenever I'm out and about. Here, let me give you the nickel tour."

He proceeded to lead them through the house, describing to Sue what the room had looked like when he'd moved in and what lengths he'd gone to to fix it up. She admired the details of each, particularly noting the art work that he had on the walls. None of it was anything particularly valuable, but all of it was unique—and she enjoyed looking at each item. They moved through the living room, dining room and kitchen on the first floor, then climbed the stairs from the foyer up to the second and took in the three bedrooms. Then they backtracked and headed to the lower level via a stairway from the kitchen. This was a steep set of stairs that led to two small rooms. "Watch your step coming down," Lou called out. "These can be pretty treacherous if you're not careful." One room housed Stevenson's improvised wine cellar—an impressive array of bottles lying in racks—and the other a TV room, equipped with a 60" plasma flatscreen on one wall and a rack of DVDs along another, and a surround sound system that Jamie imagined could blow out your eardrums if you weren't careful. A door from the TV room led outside toward the front; this was the door Jamie had noted earlier.

Jamie had seen all this before, but he dutifully tagged along and agreed with every squeal of delight that Sue sounded when she spied something else that intrigued her. Ultimately, she pronounced the house a marvel and told Lou how wonderful he was to have fixed it up so beautifully.

"Well, thanks," Stevenson said. "I do like the place. It's a great place to come home to after a long day or a long trip. And it's convenient to most everything I need when I'm working here."

"How about the neighborhood," Jamie asked. "You got any problems with crime or anything else?"

"Not really," Lou replied, shrugging his shoulders as he spoke. "Washington can be a rough town, so you just have to be careful. I've never had any problems, though."

"Good," said Sue.

"I noticed some guys hanging around out on the street when we pulled in," Jamie persisted. "Is that kind of thing typical?"

"Not really," said Lou carefully. "That's just started recently. I kind of want to talk to you about it actually, but later. After we eat. I've got all kinds of culinary delights planned for you."

He was true to his word.

CHAPTER 30

Washington, DC
Friday, 30 September 2022
5:49 p.m. EDT

"Thank you, Liz," Acting President Kerrigan said to the Secretary of Health & Human Services, Liz Barton, as the report was handed to her. They were sitting at the big conference table in her office. "Tell me what it says."

Secretary Barton had arrived about five minutes earlier, and had been escorted into Kerrigan's office almost immediately by Jess Dougherty. He remained in the office with her, seated on her left, his large frame a noticeable counterpoint to her petite size; Kerrigan smiled inwardly at the disparity between the two.

Barton had pushed her people hard to complete the investigation into the release of the President's medical records. She thought they had done a great job, given the limited amount of time with which they'd had to work, but she didn't delude herself that the report was comprehensive. It covered the bases with regard to what had happened, but barely scratched the surface regarding how to preclude a repeat. She intended to make that point clear when she presented her department's finding to the Acting President.

"Madame Vice President," she began, "let me start by saying that what I'm presenting to you today is essentially an executive summary. A comprehensive report, detailing findings of what occurred and how it occurred, and with recommendations as to how to prevent a recurrence in the future, will not be available for at least two more weeks." She watched Kerrigan closely to assess whether this statement would earn her a tongue-lashing. Concluding from Kerrigan's lack of reaction that she was safe for the moment, she continued. "At that time I'll be able to present you with a complete report of the investigation."

"Fine, Liz, fine," Kerrigan replied, blithely. "Just give me your preliminary findings."

"Thank you, ma'am. My investigators determined that the records were accessed by only one party, General Webster from Walter Reed. Since the request was outside the normal means for requesting a record—which is granted only to medical personnel directly involved in the case of the person in the file, or upon the request of family members when legally empowered— my records managers were reluctant to release either the President's mother's datafile, or the digital copies of his father's records, but acquiesced to the request once Governor Caldwell directed them to do so. They should not have. The records were provided directly to Doctor Webster, not to anyone else. I have issued instructions that no files related to the President or his family are to be released to anyone without your explicit approval, and have directed that a refresher training program be conducted for all records managers throughout the department to ensure that everyone knows the rules, and that a repeat doesn't occur again." She stopped to await Kerrigan's comments.

Kerrigan received the information passively, pondering the implications of it as Barton spoke. She had felt sure that the investigation would show that only Webster had received the files—just as he'd said—and that Barton would not be able to show who had released them to Stevenson. It was clear to Kerrigan that tracking down this leak would be nearly impossible unless Stevenson actually divulged his source—which she did not believe he would do—so whoever she chose to punish as the leak would probably be the wrong one. But she knew equally well that she needed to publicly demonstrate that she was moving decisively to stop the intrusion into the President's privacy, so she would just have to select a scapegoat. And she decided to make that Webster.

"Okay, Liz, thank you for this. And thank your people for producing it so quickly. I'm sure they had to put in some long hours to comply with my request." She nodded her head and stuck out her hand. "Good job. Have a good weekend. If I need anything else, Jess will let you know."

Barton quickly got up and departed the office.

Once the office door had closed, Kerrigan turned to Dougherty and said, "Jess, find out for me if Governor Caldwell is still across the street. I need to speak with him."

"Josh, Fran Kerrigan here," she said into the phone once she'd been patched through to Caldwell. Dougherty had found him at work in his West Wing office and had informed Kerrigan. He had raised an eyebrow when

Kerrigan told him she'd call Caldwell herself—it was not typically her style to dial a phone and wait to be connected—and he'd left her alone to make the call, thinking 'This should be good.'

"Madame Vice President, good evening," Caldwell responded. "To what do I owe this honor?" he questioned suspiciously.

"Josh, I'll get right to the point. Liz Barton just gave me her look into the release by HHS of the President's parents' medical files. Her conclusion is that only General Webster received the files, and that therefore the leak originated there."

"Ma'am, I don't believe for a moment that Webster would have given Stevenson that information."

"Nor do I," responded Kerrigan, testily, "but be that as it may, his flouting of the rules to request and receive the files"—she hesitated momentarily to infer to Caldwell that she was aware of his role in the request—"is the root cause of the problem, and its something that has to be dealt with. Publicly. I've decided to remove him as White House Physician, suggest that he retire quietly to forego any further action, and assign his deputy to the President's care."

"You cannot do that," Caldwell exploded, standing up at his desk as he shouted into the phone. "Webster is President Navarro's personal physician and only he can remove him. You're overstepping your bounds here, and you know it."

"Josh, you're wrong, and you know it. It is perfectly within my authority as Acting President to appoint, or remove, the White House Physician, to move military officers onto the retired list, and to ensure that the medical care of an incapacitated president is handled appropriately." She smiled to herself as she said all this, knowing that Caldwell was once again trapped. If he opposed her on this, it was perfectly within her authority to remove him as well. "You are to inform General Webster that he is relieved of his duties effective immediately, and you are to schedule a press conference for Monday morning to announce his resignation and retirement. Get Barb"—Barb Singletary, the White House Press Secretary—"working on that at once." She paused. "And if you ever speak to me in that tone again, I'll have your resignation on my desk so fast your head will swim. Understood?"

Caldwell seethed at his desk. He knew there was nothing he could do as long as she was in power. 'But that won't be long now, will it?' he thought. 'I've just got to keep things steady until Ray is back.' He could see she was pushing him to snap back at her and give her the ammunition she needed to remove him also. 'Fat chance of that, lady.' So instead he said simply, "Understood," and silently fumed as she hung up without another word.

He leaned back in his chair and stared at the ceiling for several moments, not moving. Then he reached for the phone once more and placed the call to Webster. "General, I will be out to Walter Reed at 7 o'clock. I need to speak with you privately, and I need to speak with the President. Will that be possible? Good. Yes, please let him know I'm coming. I'll need his full attention, and don't want to surprise him."

CHAPTER 31

Washington, DC
Friday, 30 September 2022
9:33 p.m. EDT

Later that evening, after they had gorged themselves on the huge meal that Stevenson had prepared, they moved out back onto Lou's patio to savor the evening. Lou had brought out oversized plates of gnocchi with walnuts in a gorgonzola sauce and buttered polenta with mushrooms, accompanied by soft Italian bread, and all washed down with two bottles of his favorite *Amarone*, a strong red wine from northern Italy that he enjoyed; Jamie and Sue had to force themselves to stop eating, they'd enjoyed it so much. The rain still had not come, but they could tell the sky was overcast even in the dark, and they could feel the breeze beginning to pick up, portending the arrival of the storm. They were seated in chairs placed around the fire pit that Lou had in the center of his small yard; the embers there were now glowing red and producing enough heat to ward off the night chill. All three of them had small glasses in their hands from which they were sipping *grappa*, the clear, bitter Italian brandy that traditionally serves as an after-dinner drink following a heavy meal.

Lou and Sue each sipped at the *grappa* appreciably, while Jamie's face immediately screwed itself into a knot as the fiery spirit crossed his lips. "Oh, Lou, this stuff is awful," he choked out. "It tastes like that white paste that everybody used to eat when you were a kid in grade school." He looked over at Sue, who was swirling her glass slowly, clearly savoring the taste. "Don't tell me that you like this stuff?" he said to her.

"It's an acquired taste," she purred, taking another sip and reaching out to take one of the cherries that Lou had marinated in the stuff, which she promptly popped into her mouth. "Try one of these. They're even better."

He looked at Lou, who was staring quietly at the coals. "I think you two are in cahoots, that's what I think." He downed the rest of his glass, squeezing his eyes together in the vain hope that it would dampen the taste, and quickly turned his glass upside down on the table to show that he was through. He looked back at Sue again. "I can't believe you're enjoying that."

"Oh, I practically grew up on this stuff. When I was a kid, almost every meal finished with either this or a glass of *limoncello*"—the sweet lemon liqueur produced in the Sorrento region of southern Italy near Naples and the Amalfi Coast—"and I was allowed to start tasting it when I was about ten. Like I said, it's an acquired taste."

"Well, no more for me, thanks." He reached out to poke at the coals in the fire, sending up a small shower of sparks into the night sky. He leaned back in his chair and turned toward Stevenson. "Okay, Lou, something is clearly bothering you. You've been distracted all evening. What's going on?"

"Whadya mean?" he asked tentatively.

"Come on, it's me," Jamie said. "I know you. You're barely talking, staring into the fire like some mystic. You're poking at your food when you usually wolf this stuff down. You're as jumpy as a cat. Something's got you worked up. What is it?"

"He's right, Lou," Sue chimed in from the other side of the fire. "Even I can tell something's bothering you."

Stevenson sat quietly for a moment, staring into the coals.

"Come on," persisted Jamie. "You can trust us."

Lou leaned back in his chair and gave out a long sigh. "I know I can, guys. You're practically the only two I think I can trust, particularly in this town right now." He paused, then looked up at them grimly. "I think I've stumbled into some trouble, and I don't know what I should do."

"What?" asked Jamie, suddenly concerned. He had thought that Lou might not have been feeling well, or was stressing over a deadline at the job, or something like that. "What do you think's wrong?"

"It's this story," Lou said. "You were probably right, by the way. I probably should have been more careful with an anonymous source. But I checked into it, and everything checked out. I'm sure the information is true, so I didn't think the source's motive was important." He looked at them again. "Well, now he says he's sending more stuff—better stuff, he says—plus I've been basically threatened by both the White House Chief of Staff and by your father, Sue, to make sure not to write anything damaging to Navarro or your mother, respectively."

"Wait, what?" Sue shot forward in her seat. "What do you mean, my father and my mother?"

"Oh, give me a little credit, will you?" Lou responded. "Don't you think I figured out long ago who you were." He smiled at her. "Wasn't really that hard, you know. There're lots of photos around of you as a kid, and some of the MySpace junk you posted when you were a teenager is still out there." Now he grinned at her. "Nice beach photo, by the way."

"Stop, stop," she shouted. "I'm not responsible for that picture. It was a dare." She buried her face in her hands. "So, how long have you known this?"

"A few months after I first met you. I was doing some research on our new Vice President, and there you were. I thought about telling you that I knew, but figured if you wanted it to be a secret, it was okay with me."

Jamie had been listening silently to all this with a bemused expression on his face. Now he reached out to massage the back of Sue's neck. "I told you he was sharp. But I bet he hasn't told anyone else, have you, Lou?"

Stevenson shrugged his shoulders. "No. Like I said, if you want it kept quiet, it's okay by me." Now he leaned forward to speak to Sue. "But don't kid yourself. This isn't something you can hide. Your childhood and your family were too public. It's just waiting for somebody to connect the dots like I did."

Sue dropped her hands and shook her head. "Well, I supposed I always really knew that, but was just hoping it wouldn't happen. Okay, so what did Mommy and Daddy say to you?"

"Wait, first, what did this guy say to you?" interrupted Coryell, again poking the fire.

"Well, first I got a phone call from Caldwell. On Wednesday night. No, wait, actually first came the call from the source." He stopped abruptly, then said. "I gotta get a name for this guy. You know, something catchy like *Deep Throat* was for Woodward and Bernstein." *Deep Throat* had been the pseudonym given to the inside source who provided information to the two Washington Post reporters as they exposed the coverup of the Watergate scandal by the Nixon White House. In 2005, *Deep Throat* was revealed to have been Mark Felt, the Associate Director of the FBI during the Watergate era. "I think I'll go with *The Shadow*—you know, Lamont Cranston, 'Who knows what evil lurks in the hearts of men? The Shadow knows.'" He looked up at them expectantly, then continued when they offered no reaction. "Anyway, *The Shadow* calls up first on Wednesday night while I'm working late, on my unlisted cell phone number, and tells me he's glad I put his package to good use and he's sending me more in a few days. Then hangs up. No discussion, nothing else."

"It was a man, though?" Sue asked.

"Definitely sounded like a man, although he was disguising his voice somehow. Sort of muffled. And it sounded like the call came from a public phone. Lots of noise in the background."

"Did the package come yet?" asked Jamie.

"No, nothing yet," Lou said, shaking his head. "So then, a few moments later, Caldwell calls. Again on the same cell phone. He basically tells me he thinks I stabbed President Navarro in the back and that if anything like it happens again, he's going to crush me."

"Crush you?" Jamie asked incredulously. As a newspaperman, he was well aware of the love-hate relationship that politicians had with the press, but instances of blatant threats were very rare. "His exact words?"

"Exact words," said Stevenson. "He sounded a little drunk, actually." He smiled ruefully. "Needless to say, his invitation to go with him to visit Navarro no longer holds. Anyway, he says his piece—no discussion—then hangs up on me, too, and almost immediately the same unlisted cell rings again. This time it's Sue's father and he's inviting me for an office call, which I naturally gleefully accept."

"The fly coming to the spider," Sue said in her best, spooky voice.

"Exactly," continued Lou. "So I go down to his office the next morning—yesterday morning—and after first chatting me up a little, he then asks where my info came from—which I say I can't tell him. Then says he thinks Caldwell is behind the whole thing to embarrass Kerrigan—he thinks Caldwell is *The Shadow*, by the way—and then basically says that if I do anything to embarrass her with this, he'll ensure that I sleep with the fishes. Not his exact words, but that was the inference."

"He can be pretty intimidating, can't he?" said Sue, without a smile.

"Definitely can," agreed Lou. "So after the Senator tells me that we're done, I start heading back to my office. And as I'm walking, I get the feeling I'm being watched. And ever since, every time I turn around it looks like there's some guys watching me or following me or just hanging around, like you saw out on the street." He looked from one to the other, face now pale in the weak moonlight that filtered through the clouds, a worried look on his face. "I think they're Secret Service. I think Caldwell's got them watching me."

"Lou, how can you think that?" Jamie asked. "Even Caldwell can't just turn the Secret Service loose on you for writing something embarrassing about the President. If you haven't threatened him, they're not interested." He looked closely at him. "You didn't make some off-hand remark that could be construed as a threat, did you?"

"No, nothing. I mean, I like Navarro. And I really liked his wife. Threatening him is the last thing I'd do." Coryell could see Stevenson's trembling as he talked. His friend was clearly overwrought by the stress.

"Tell you what, Lou," he said, concern in his voice. "Why don't we call it a night? Sue and I will clean up, you get a good night's sleep—'cause I bet you haven't had one lately—don't answer any phone calls, and tomorrow will be a better day. You'll see. Once you're rested, you won't feel like someone's after you. Don't you think so, Sue?"

"Absolutely," she said, getting up out of the chair and going over to Stevenson. "Come on, Lou. Jamie's right. Some rest is what you need when you've been working so hard and having to deal with disagreeable people." She helped him to get up out of his chair, and pointed him toward the house's rear door. "Let us take care of all this, and you go to bed."

"Okay, guys. Thanks. I think I will." He started plodding despondently up the back steps. At the door, he turned and said, "I'll see you tomorrow," then disappeared into the house.

Jamie and Sue watched him go. Both sank back down into their chairs when the back door had closed.

"What do you make of all that?" Jamie asked.

"Well, I think he's just spooked by everything that's going on. Like you said, the Secret Service wouldn't be interested in him if he's made no threat, and although my father can be pretty ruthless when he wants something, even he wouldn't have guys following Lou around. That's not his style. He'd be—I don't know—more direct somehow. So I think Lou's just stressed out like you said. Some rest is what he needs."

"I sure hope you're right," Jamie replied. "I hate seeing him like this." He leaned over and squeezed her hand. "Thanks again for coming down here with me. If it was just me with him, I'd probably start getting spooked, too."

"Yeah, yeah," she said. "My pleasure. Come on, let's get this stuff cleaned up and put away. I've got to gather my strength to call the folks tomorrow and tell them I'm in town. After that, I may be spooked along with the rest of you."

They got everything cleaned up and put away in fifteen minutes. Jamie made sure the fire was damped down, and that all the doors of the house were locked. After which, they spent a quiet night.

CHAPTER 32

Washington, DC
Sunday, 2 October 2022
11:33 a.m. EDT

Sue and Jamie pulled up in the Ford to the guard post where guests were stopped prior to admittance to the Vice President's mansion at the Naval Observatory. The agent on duty there quickly verified their identities and checked their names against the admittance list, then passed them through without a second look. Jamie had expected it would be a little more difficult somehow.

As he headed toward the parking area to which the agent had directed them, he glanced over at Sue in the passenger seat. She was staring straight ahead, hands folded in her lap where she clasped and unclasped them repetitively; she was white as a ghost. He reached across and put his hand on top of hers, saying "Don't worry. Everything'll be fine." She smiled wanly back at him, as if to say, 'Don't count on it, buddy.'

Yesterday they had spent a quiet morning at Lou's house, getting up late and enjoying a lazy morning of reading the paper and eating breakfast. Stevenson had seemed in much better spirits after a night of good sleep and no phone calls, for which Jamie was grateful. They had ridden the Metro into town, where they'd strolled around the Mall for most of what was a lovely afternoon. Lou had spent much of it surreptitiously looking around to see if they were being followed—they weren't, Jamie'd decided—while Sue had gamely tried to gather up enough courage to call her parents to arrange a visit.

She'd finally decided to call her mother's office and basically make an appointment. That way she'd avoid a potentially bad phone call which might result if she called direct, and it would give her parents an easy out if they didn't want to see her—they could just claim their calendars were booked, which probably wouldn't be too much of a stretch. Sue'd been sure that her mother's office would be open even on a Saturday afternoon—it was—and that she'd be able to set up the visit. Her call had initially gone to a switchboard operator, who had relayed it to Jess Dougherty once she understood it was not a joke.

"Miss Malone," Dougherty'd said after coming on the line. "What a pleasant surprise. Your mother will be thrilled to know you're in town."

"I'm not so sure of that," she'd replied, and laughed self-consciously. "Do you think she'd have some time tomorrow when I could drop by?"

"She's got most of the day open, actually," he'd responded. "Nothing until a dinner party at the mansion at six." He'd hesitated. "May I ask if there's any particular purpose for the visit, or are you truly just dropping in? She'll want to know."

Sue had considered momentarily how to respond to this, then had decided Dougherty was just doing his job. "No, no hidden agenda," she'd responded. "I'd just like to say hello, and introduce them to a friend of mine. It's been a while, you know?"

"Yes, I know. Occasionally she'll mention that she'd like to see you. Hold a moment and I'll ask her when a good time would be." The phone had shifted into music before she'd had a chance to object.

A few moments later, her mother's excited voice had sounded on the line. "Susan, of course you can come over tomorrow. We would love to see you. And a friend, huh? How wonderful! Of course he's more than welcome, too. What are you doing in Washington? You should have called earlier so that we could arrange something special." Sue had involuntarily bristled at the implied criticism, but decided to let it pass. "I know your father will be overjoyed to see you, too. It's been much too long. Why don't you plan to come at noon, and we'll all have lunch and catch up." Kerrigan's voice had raced faster as she'd talked longer, excited with the conversation. A few more brisk comments and the Acting President had been off, leaving her only daughter gasping for breath in the rush.

Staring up now at the mansion, Sue took a deep breath and said, "We're on," then opened the car door and stepped out into the rain. The weather had shifted dramatically overnight, and a cold, fall rain was steadily coming down; the forecast predicted much the same for the next couple of days. She and Jamie ran quickly toward the front door, which opened before they could ring the bell to reveal Acting President Kerrigan and Senator Moscone—Kerrigan with a big smile on her face and staring at her daughter, and Moscone grimly staring at Jamie. A third person was standing behind them, not recognizable at this point. 'I can see how this will go,' he thought, entering the foyer of the residence.

"You're here," Kerrigan gushed, wrapping her arms around Sue in a big hug; she was clearly delighted to see her daughter, and Sue was clearly relieved at the reception. "Susan, let me look at you. Oh, this is wonderful, isn't it, Fred?"

Moscone was also smiling, although not as broadly as his wife. He was also more focused on Jamie's presence than on Sue's arrival. "Yes, it is wonderful to see you, Susan," he answered. "Finally." Sue pretended not to hear the remark. "And who is your friend here?"

"Jamie Coryell, Senator," Jamie interjected, holding out his hand toward Moscone. The big man extended his carefully and shook Jamie's briskly in a firm grip. "It's an honor to meet you, sir," Jamie continued.

Moscone looked him over cautiously. "It's a pleasure to meet you, too, young man. Allow me to introduce Susan's mother." He guided Jamie toward Kerrigan as he spoke. "And this is the Acting President's Chief of Staff, Jess Dougherty," he continued, indicating the third person Jamie had noticed before, who stepped forward to shake Jamie's hand, shifting a pile of folders into his left hand as he did.

"Madame Vice President, I'm very pleased to meet you," Jamie said, now extending his hand to her.

"A pleasure, Mr. Coryell. Any friend of Susan's is most welcome here." She gave him a taut smile, perfunctorily shook his hand, then turned her attention back to Sue. "Susan, I'm sure that you two must be hungry. Why don't we move into the dining room and enjoy our lunch? We can talk while we eat," she continued, guiding her daughter from the foyer, with her arm around her waist, and into the dining room to the right.

"Jess, I believe we are through for today," Senator Moscone said to the big man on his left. Although both men were about the same height as Jamie, they both clearly out-weighed him significantly.

"Mr. Dougherty, nice to meet you," Jamie said as Dougherty headed for the door.

"Yes, the same," Dougherty replied, giving Jamie an odd, intense look as he did, before exiting into the rain. 'You're a strange one,' Jamie thought, then refocused as Moscone asked him a question.

"And what is it you do, Mr. Coryell?" Senator Moscone asked as they followed Kerrigan and Sue into the dining room and moved toward the table.

The table was the antique wood convertible type with a central pedestal that could seat six in its smallest configuration, or be expanded to comfortably seat twenty when fully expanded. There were place settings laid out on four sides of the oblong table at the moment, with a vase of wildflowers in the center.

"I'm the publisher of a small newspaper where I live in New Jersey," Jamie responded, looking around the room as he did. They were in one of the so-called turret rooms of the mansion, a round room with windows on three sides that opened out onto the broad veranda. The table sat in the center of the room, with additional chairs and a buffet along the wall from which they entered.

"A journalist," Moscone exclaimed, then burst out laughing. "Franny, did you hear that? We've let the wolf in amongst us lambs. Susan's friend runs a newspaper." He threw a big arm across Jamie's shoulders. "Mr. Coryell, you've brightened my day. I can now face this evening's monotony. A journalist," he said again, shaking his head and laughing once more.

Kerrigan looked at Jamie warily, murmuring "How interesting."

Sue glared at her father. "Daddy, Jamie runs a very fine newspaper. He does a very good business up there. Don't you pick a fight with him."

"Oh, I don't mean anything by it, Susan, you know that," Moscone responded. "It's just that, at times, we have a somewhat adversarial relationship with members of the fourth estate. I'm sure you understand." He turned to face Jamie, his dark eyes gleaming. "No offense meant."

"And none taken, sir," Jamie said. "I don't cover national politics in my paper anyway," he continued, smiling.

"Well that's even better, then. Let's eat. I don't know about you two, but I'm starving."

"We're eating light today," Kerrigan said, waving her hand toward the buffet where a light lunch of sandwiches, potato salad and iced tea was already set out, "because of the dinner we've got scheduled for some members of Congress here this evening. That won't be as enjoyable as this meal will be," she said, chuckling as she squeezed Sue's hand. "I hope you don't mind."

Moscone and Jamie brought the sandwich tray and the potato salad to the table, while Kerrigan and Sue filled glasses with the iced tea. Then they sat down, the men on the long edges of the table and the women on the smaller, and proceeded to chat throughout the meal. Sue surprised herself by having a very enjoyable time, while Jamie was made to feel comfortable by these two important people. They talked about Sue's gallery, its successes and its disappointments; of Jamie's life history in Lambertville; and they tip-toed carefully around Jamie and Sue's relationship. They finished the main meal in what seemed like the blink of an eye, then moved out onto the veranda for a light dessert of strawberries with cream and steaming mugs of coffee.

They settled into cushioned chairs around a small coffee table, and continued to talk.

"And what brings you down to Washington now, Jamie?" Kerrigan asked. At some point during the lunch, Moscone and Kerrigan had transitioned to a more informal address mode for Coryell. Thinking back, Jamie couldn't identify exactly when it had begun, the transition was so seamless and easy.

"Well, ma'am"—the informality did not go both ways—"my old college roommate lives and works down here, and he invited us down for a quick getaway. He's got a place he's fixed up over on Quincy. We're really just here to relax a little." He popped another strawberry in his mouth.

"What's your friend do down here?" Moscone asked.

Jamie hesitated, knowing he'd stepped into a bad area, but could not think of any way out. "He's also a journalist, actually," he replied carefully.

"Really," said Kerrigan. "How interesting. What's his name? Perhaps we know him."

"Lou Stevenson," Jamie said, quickly following with gulp of coffee. Out of the corner of his eye he could see Sue watching the exchange incredulously.

"Lou Stevenson," Moscone said, suddenly interested. "He works for CNN, right? Yeah, I know him. He does good work. You know who he means, don't you Franny?"

"I do," Kerrigan answered. She was looking at Jamie with more intensity now. "He's the one who first reported that the President had come out of his coma, and who recently presented the exposé on his medical records. Am I right?"

"Yes, Mother, that's him," Sue said. She was watching her father closely. "He said he came to see you the other day, Daddy, and that you threatened him." Jamie shot her a look that said 'Don't start trouble,' but to no avail.

Moscone laughed. "Threatened? No, not me. I don't threaten people, I just talk to them. Sometimes they might misconstrue what I say, but I never threaten." He glanced over at Kerrigan, who remained silent. "We had a nice chat about the report he made on the news the other night, and I asked him to be careful of his sources. Whenever you get some anonymous tip in the mail that looks like it'll stir up trouble, I think you've got to be very cautious of it. That's only being a responsible journalist, don't you think, Jamie?"

Jamie laid down his mug and spoke quietly. "Senator, I occasionally rely on anonymous information in articles I write. But I'm always careful to corroborate what I've been given as best I can, and only use the material if I believe it is true. I know for a fact that Lou does the same. If he reported on a story, you can take it to the bank that he checked out his information and believes it is true."

"Well, that's very good to hear," Moscone responded evenly. "I could tell that Stevenson could be counted on the moment I first laid eyes on him. I'm sorry he took our conversation the wrong way," he continued, looking at Sue. "Perhaps I should call him up to make sure everything's okay."

"No, Daddy, I don't think that's necessary. Lou is fine. And you can be sure that he'll do the right thing with whatever news story he gets his hands on." She stared at her father defiantly as she spoke.

"Okay, enough talk about the news," Kerrigan interjected. "That's too much like work, and I was enjoying our afternoon too much to be drawn back into that too soon." She spoke to Jamie. "Please let Mr. Stevenson know that I—we—think very highly of his work, and always look forward to seeing it."

"Thank you, ma'am, I will. I know he'll appreciate that."

At about three o'clock, Kerrigan said that, regretfully, she and Moscone had to get ready for the dinner that evening. Jamie and Sue quickly packed themselves up, said their good-byes, and departed, both reflecting that, all in all, it had been a surprisingly pleasant afternoon. As they left the mansion, they noted happily that the rain had stopped and the sun was feebly attempting to break through the clouds. They climbed into the Ford and drove off, waving farewell to Sue's parents, who dutifully stood in the doorway and waved back.

Once the car was out of sight, Kerrigan and Moscone stepped back into the mansion and closed the door. "Very interesting afternoon, don't you think, Franny? What do you make of Coryell?"

"He seems very nice," she said distractedly, clearly thinking of something else. "Susan seems quite taken with him. It's quite a coincidence about his relationship with Stevenson, don't you think?"

"It does seem to be a small world," Moscone replied. He was already considering the possibilities that relationship held for him.

CHAPTER 33

Washington, DC
Monday, 3 October 2022
11:41 a.m. EDT

"Fran, thanks for coming over," President Navarro said as his Vice President walked into the room at Walter Reed, Admiral Callahan at her side. Don Callahan had been Webster's deputy, and was still in shock to find that he'd been elevated in position; he had first talked with Navarro in this role yesterday, a discussion that did not go well. He remained near the doorway as Kerrigan proceeded into the room.

Navarro had asked Caldwell to tell the Acting President that he wanted to speak with her as early on Monday as possible; he was somewhat put out that her earliest convenience was close to noon. "I want to speak with you about Webster. Donnie, you can wait outside, please." Callahan left quickly and shut the door behind him.

Kerrigan had expected this confrontation, knowing it would come as soon as she had told Caldwell to discharge the doctor. She had announced her action to the Congressional leadership over dinner the evening prior, and had informed the Cabinet at the meeting held earlier this morning. Although there had been some concern expressed about the wisdom of her action, there was none with regard to her authority to act.

She was somewhat surprised by Navarro's appearance as she entered the room. Where before he had appeared tired and thin, he now looked better rested and was clearly putting on weight. His scars continued to fade, although that would naturally require months until they became truly unremarkable, and his agility with his wheelchair had moved forward by leaps and bounds. Only some heaviness around the eyes betrayed the fact that he was still recuperating and still receiving medication.

She sat down in a chair next to a small end table in the room—something there for use by a visitor as they waited, or read, or napped—and waited for

Navarro to maneuver the wheelchair next to her.

"Mr. President," she began, "General Webster was removed from duty because he was the root cause of the unauthorized release of the medical records of you and your parents. He willfully disregarded procedures to obtain the records, and as a result caused both your privacy to be violated and considerable embarrassment to this administration. It was an act I did not feel could be left unaddressed."

"But he is my doctor, Fran. Mine. You have overstepped your authority to direct a change to my medical care without my consent. I expect him to be reinstated immediately." Navarro spoke softly, but was clearly upset.

"I'm sorry, sir, but I will not do that." She looked at him evenly as she spoke. "I believe it to be in your best interest, as well as the administration's, to have another physician appointed. Doctor Webster was too close to you to provide objective care, in my opinion, which led to his breach of procedures."

Navarro stared at her, thinking that the moment of conflict that he'd expected for so long had finally come. He saw that Kerrigan believed she was in the driver's seat, and that he could have nothing to say in the matter. 'Well, you're wrong about that, Fran,' he thought to himself.

"So you won't agree to allow me to have the doctor of my choice, is that what you're saying?"

"I'm sorry, Mr. President, but I can't."

"Or won't?" Navarro asked softly, then continued in a stronger voice. "Very well, Fran, I can see that your mind is made up. I had hoped that once I expressed my wishes, that you would change your instructions. Apparently, that's not to be." He looked at her steadily, holding her eyes as he spoke. "I guess that will be it, then. Thank you for coming by."

"Certainly, Mr. President," she said. She paused momentarily, waiting to see if Navarro would speak again. When nothing came, she continued. "I think this is all for the best, and that once you've recovered fully, you'll see that this has been the right course of action. Rest assured that your welfare is foremost in my mind." She stood and moved toward the door. "I'll try to get over to visit with you again tomorrow evening, sir."

"No, Fran. That won't be necessary. You've got a great burden on your shoulders, and you should focus on that. The weight of office, as they say. There will be no need for you to come here again." Navarro spoke very slowly and deliberately as he said these words, and could feel the pain suddenly flaring behind his eyes as his anger rose. His face, however, remained a mask.

"As you wish, Mr. President," Kerrigan responded. "Good day, sir." And she swiftly left the room.

As soon as she had gone, Navarro sagged into his chair. The effort to maintain his composure had sapped his strength and allowed the pain to surge through. The pain was still with him every day, but the medication that Webster had provided for him kept it in check. He motored his chair over to the nightstand next to the bed, and reached for another dose of the pills, even though it was an hour or so before he was due. 'What's one hour,' he thought sourly, swallowing the pills with a drink of water. 'I'll sleep better, and get to talk to Julia about how to handle this. She'll know what's best.'

He rang the buzzer next to his bed to summon the nurses, who would help lever him into the bed so he could sleep. Then he'd summon Caldwell.

CHAPTER 34

Washington, DC
Tuesday, 4 October 2022
7:12 p.m. EDT

Stevenson walked toward his house along Quincy, daydreaming about the next renovation he intended to pursue in the townhouse. He was coming from the Metro station after work, and was somewhat disheartened to realize that the days were growing shorter very quickly. It seemed to him that summer had just been here, and now leaves were turning and it was already dark at seven o'clock. 'Might have to stop walking pretty soon,' he thought; he was reluctant to walk the dark streets during the winter, not only because of the inclement weather, but also because it posed too great a risk. Muggings and robberies were unfortunately still relatively commonplace in most sections of the nation's capital.

When he reached his home, he quickly bounded up the front stoop and inserted the key to open the door. As he did, his eyes fell on a Fedex package leaning against the railing on his right. He started momentarily as he registered its presence, then reached down for it, involuntarily looking around the vacant street as he did so. He quickly stepped into the house, deactivated the security alarm, and shut, locked and bolted the door. Once inside, he reactivated the alarm once more.

This was a much thicker package than last time. He was confident this was the promised package of new information. Whereas his previous correspondence from *The Shadow* consisted only of the medical files and the flash drive, this was an 8 x 11 inch box, 2 inches deep that had a heft to it that made Stevenson feel assured it was stuffed with documents. As before, there was no return address, and as before, his address was printed on a stick-on label, not handwritten. There was no way to tell who had sent the package.

Stevenson walked back through the house, turning on lights as he did. It was not something he typically did, normally being frugal and conscious of his electrical usage, but now he wanted as much visibility as possible. The old anxieties came back, and he found himself thinking back through the day to remember if he'd noticed anyone watching him. Nothing came to mind. In the kitchen, he popped open a Sam Adams—this situation called for a beer, he decided—and proceeded upstairs to his office to examine the package.

Once upstairs, be began to boot up his laptop when his cell phone rang. He checked the caller ID, but got no listing. Warily, he answered it. "Hello? Stevenson here."

"Did you get the package?" came the voice. Same metallic sound, same background noise.

"I just found it. How did you know I was home?'

"I just know," *The Shadow* answered. "You'll find this package much more interesting than the last. Put it to good use. I'll be watching you." The line clicked dead.

Stevenson set down the phone and found his hands shaking. He was sure no one was following him, yet the guy knew as soon as he got into his house. Needing to do something, he quickly walked through the house again, checking the doors and windows, making sure nothing was out of place. He found that nothing had been touched. All was as he had left it, and all doors and windows were secure. He was alone.

Returning to the office, he ripped open the package. As he'd suspected, it was full of documents, some of them copies of what appeared to be medical reports once more, some of them other official looking documents, and a sheaf of papers that appeared to be a report of an investigation of some sort. Another flash drive also fell out of the box.

Flipping through the papers, he decided to begin by reading the investigative report. He took a long pull from his beer, and began scanning the document to get a feel for its contents. Almost immediately, he sat up straight in his chair and began to read it word for word. "Unbelievable," he said aloud. "This can't be true." He knew if it was, *The Shadow* was right—this was much more interesting than last time. And potentially much more dangerous.

'What am I going to do now?' he thought.

CHAPTER 35

Washington, DC
Wednesday, 5 October 2022
9:12 a.m. EDT

The weekly Wednesday morning Cabinet meeting had only just begun when the room was thrown into turmoil, and the agenda thrown out the window, as President Navarro briskly wheeled himself into the room.

"Good morning, everyone," Navarro sang out as he rounded the end of the long conference table and headed down toward his normal seat, adroitly maneuvering his wheelchair around obstacles without any apparent difficulty. Recovering slowly from the shock of his unannounced entry, the Cabinet chiefs hastily began to clamber to their feet. "Please, everyone, stay seated," the President said. "I just felt so good this morning when I woke up that I wanted to come down to see you all. I was hoping that the Cabinet still met on Wednesdays, and I can see that things are still as they were." He arrived at his place and waited while the aide who had been following him removed the chair so that he could wheel himself into position at the center of the table. He looked evenly at Acting President Kerrigan as he waited.

"Mister President." The words were seemingly on everyone's lips at the same moment. "So good to see you."

"You look wonderful."

"How do you feel?" A round of soft applause began spontaneously. And finally from Kerrigan, "Sir, you should have let us know you'd be coming. We would have waited until you arrived." She glanced over at Caldwell, who had followed the President into the room and had now assumed his position against the wall, as if to say, 'This is your doing, I know it.'

"Now, Madame Vice President," Navarro began, "that would have spoiled the surprise. And I do so like surprises," he continued, a hint of a smile on his lips. The hazel eyes remained fixed on her, but did not join in with the smile.

Kerrigan, along with the rest of the Cabinet, stared openly at the President, trying to gage his condition. Some faces showed pleasure, some relief, and some displayed hints of frustration as a result of his unexpected appearance. They all noted a much reduced version of the vital man who had once before occupied that place at the table. They noted the scars on the face, the damaged left ear, the slight palsy of the left arm. They could not avoid seeing and considering the implications of the wheelchair. And none of them missed the occasional fleeting winces of pain that crossed the President's face.

Kerrigan began to speak, saying "Sir, allow me, on behalf of the entire Cabinet, to welcome you back to the White House. I know I speak for all of us in saying that it does each of our hearts good to see you up and around. You have been sincerely missed at this table."

"Thank you, Fran, for those kind words. And thank you all. It is good to be out of that hospital." He looked around the table, catching the eye of several members of his Cabinet and giving them a quick smile as he did. He noted the absence of Walt Hodges and Frank Fitzrandolph with feelings of loss and bitterness, respectively.

"Sir," Kerrigan said, "we had just begun the meeting shortly before you entered. Secretary DiMarco"—the Secretary of State, Mike DiMarco— "was about to update us on the upcoming NATO summit in Paris next month." This meeting of the Heads of State and Foreign Ministers of the 31 member nations of the Alliance would be the first to include Georgia and Ukraine as full members. It also would be the first to convene in Paris since the Headquarters was moved back there following the dissolution of Belgium into two separate nations, Flanders and Wallonia, three years earlier. "You are more than welcome, of course, to attend the meeting," she continued, then hesitated. "Naturally, we would not want you to jeopardize your recovery by over-exerting yourself too soon." At those words a hush fell over the room.

"Thank you for your concern, Fran. But, with apologies to Mike, I propose a change to today's agenda." As he said this Josh Caldwell appeared behind him and handed him a manila folder. Navarro opened it and removed a single sheet of paper, which he handed to Kerrigan. "Madame Vice President, Ladies and Gentlemen," he said, addressing the entire assemblage, and looking from face to face as he did, "this is a copy of a letter I will deliver to the President Pro Tem of the Senate and the Speaker of the House this afternoon. In it, as required by Section 4 of the 25th Amendment to the Constitution, I affirm that I no longer have a disability that precludes me from executing the office of President, and that I am ready to resume the duties and powers of that office immediately. Although it is not required, I naturally wanted to make all of you aware of that first, so that I could assure you of my competency." He paused and let the silence build. "Does anyone have any questions for me?"

There was silence in the room. Finally, Secretary of State DiMarco broke the ice. "Mister President, I can think of nothing more wonderful than you being well enough to resume your office. Although we all have done our best in your absence, the nation—and the world, I might add—has hoped and prayed for your recovery. I don't say that to disparage our worthy Vice President, who has done admirably in your absence." He glanced at Kerrigan, who nodded her head modestly at his comment. "But it is you that everyone has waited for." He looked around the room, seeing the heads of most nodding as he spoke, realizing that he was speaking for most of them. "But, sir, despite that desire for your return, we certainly don't want you to act prematurely or hastily. We don't want you to put yourself at risk if you are still recuperating from your horrendous injuries. We can all see the physical impact on you of the explosion, and we can only surmise that the extent of the emotional impact is just as traumatic." He pivoted in his chair now to look Navarro directly in the eyes. "So if I may be so bold, why do you believe you are ready to resume now?"

Navarro smiled at him. "Mike, everyone, rest assured that I am fit for office. You can see my scars, yes. But they are only superficial evidence of injuries that have healed. I still have to undergo therapy to strengthen my left arm and chest, yes. But that does not preclude me from office. I cannot walk, yes. And never will." Here he paused momentarily, closed his eyes and took a deep breath. "I'll tell you that that is the most difficult thing for me to accept. That I'll never again walk, run, stand on my own, stride into a crowd to greet people and shake hands. That's the most difficult. But we've had a President before who also could do none of those things, and he's reckoned as one of our greatest. So I tell you I am ready, and willing, to resume."

"Sir, may I ask about your head injury?" The question came from The Attorney General, Bob Powell. "You were in a coma for months, and awakened only a couple of weeks ago. Has that had any lasting effect on you?"

"No, Bob, there is none. I've undergone extensive tests, and all have shown that there is no evidence of any permanent brain damage. I'll admit I was tired at first after waking, and tended to drift back into sleep frequently, but that was just my body recuperating. Once my strength returned, I have noticed no ill effects. I'm ready to go."

"Mister President." This time it was Kerrigan who spoke. "May I ask, sir, how dependent on narcotics you are at this point in your recovery?"

"That is uncalled for." Caldwell had shot to his feet from his seat against the wall. "The President's use of medication prescribed for him by his physician is irrelevant."

"It is completely relevant, Governor," Kerrigan shot back. "If the President is regularly under the influence of narcotic drugs, whether at the direction of his physician or not, is of the utmost concern to us. Requiring extensive pain medication to deal with his injuries, even if they are healing properly and his recuperation is proceeding normally, may cloud his mind and his judgment. That is critical to us and can't just be ignored!" She slapped her hand down on the table in front of her to punctuate this last statement.

"Josh, it's alright, I've got it," Navarro said, waving Caldwell back into his seat but still staring at Kerrigan. And then directly to Kerrigan, "Fran, I am taking only the pain medication prescribed for me at the rate prescribed, and am in no way impaired because of it. I've felt no more lingering results from it than I have in the past when I've taken Sudafed. There is no dependency."

She smiled stiffly at him and responded "Thank you, sir, for clearing that up;" paused briefly, then spoke dramatically "May I ask, sir, if you still speak with Julia?"

Caldwell again shot to his feet. "You are completely out of line…" he began, only to be forestalled by Navarro's upraised hand. The other voices around the table that had erupted in dismay were also quieted by the gesture.

Navarro looked at Kerrigan coldly. "Fran, in this instance, Governor Caldwell is right. You are out of line. To attack me by using my late wife to impugn my competency is loathsome. Don't ever say that to me, or anyone, again." The words fairly dripped with venom as Navarro spoke, shocking many at the table because of their directness but also because they were out of character for the man.

Kerrigan was also shocked, and had paled noticeably at his vehemence. "Mister President, I did not mean to say anything negatively about Julia. I…"

Navarro cut her off. "Thank you, Madame Vice President. Apology accepted." He wheeled himself back from the table, pivoted, and headed for the door, Caldwell in his wake. "Please excuse me now, ladies and gentlemen, but I have an appointment on Capitol Hill. Continue with the meeting. I will be back in my office, at work, this afternoon, and business, as they say, will return to normal. Good day." Again, those around the table hastily climbed to their feet as the President left, only this time he did not tell them to keep their seats.

As soon as he had left, the room exploded into pandemonium, with each Secretary talking excitedly to his or her neighbor about what had just transpired.

"All right, all right," Kerrigan said, raising her voice to be heard over the din, and banging her hand on the table. "We have a meeting to conduct, so let's settle down. Secretary DiMarco, you were about to talk with us about NATO. Please continue."

As the Secretary of State began his briefing, Kerrigan thought to herself, 'Wait 'til Fred hears about this.'

CHAPTER 36

Washington, DC
Wednesday, 5 October 2022
7:02 p.m. EDT

"What an amazing turn of events, Lou," CNN analyst Ken Ingalls said to his guest, Lou Stevenson. "I can't think of anything that is comparable to it either for political drama or just plain American history. President Navarro has literally returned from the grave and reclaimed his office."

"It truly is amazing," agreed Stevenson. "For those of you just tuning in, in a stunning turn of events today President Navarro met with the President Pro Tem of the Senate, G.W. Cherry of Colorado, and the Speaker of the House, Henry Garcia of Florida, and announced to them that he is ready and able to resume his office, and provided them with a letter to that effect as required by the 25th Amendment. The President met with them just before noon today, and was reportedly back at his desk in the Oval Office at work this afternoon."

"But that's not the end of the story, is it, Lou?"

"Well, Ken, it could be the end unless the Cabinet wants to dispute the President's fitness to resume his office. If they do, they must state in writing to the Congressional leadership that they believe he is unfit, in which case Congress will decide. And that will take a two-thirds vote of both houses, so it would clearly have to be evident that President Navarro is not fit for Congress to take such an action."

"Why so difficult, Lou? If the members of the Cabinet—those he works with most closely and who are charged with executing his policies and programs—believe he is incapable, then why should it be so difficult for Congress to concur with that? Why the two-thirds vote?"

"Well, Ken, the presumption is always that the people's choice, the elected President, is the individual who should be in office. We don't want to permit a system where a cabal of disgruntled department heads, coupled with a hostile

Congress, can remove the President at will simply on the pretext of disability. If the President says he is fit, then it's presumed he is."

"Doesn't he have to be given a clean bill of health from somebody?" queried Ingalls. "I mean, surely he can't just check himself out of the hospital, announce to the world that he's as good as new, and immediately take up the reins again as the most powerful man on earth." The commentator put a perplexed expression on his face for the camera. "If I'm injured, I can't just leave the hospital and go back to work, so why should he?"

Stevenson chuckled, playing along with Ingalls' argument. "You're right, of course, Ken. The President can't just check himself out, and he didn't. His departure from Walter Reed was okayed by the Acting White House Physician, Admiral Don Callahan, who said he no longer needed to remain there and that he was strong enough to resume work."

"Well, that makes me feel better, then," said Ingalls, sarcastically. "Wouldn't want him to have a setback from overwork, would we?" He paused momentarily before launching into his next question. "Now, on a related note, Lou, what effect do you think your recent exposé on the President's unusual birth circumstances will have on this?" Ingalls was referring to the revelation that President Navarro was not the natural born child of Ramon and Theresa Navarro, as he had been supposed to be for his entire life.

Stevenson hesitated only briefly before answering; the knowledge of what was in his second package still left him thunderstruck, but he was not yet prepared to make that information public. Because of its nature—and because of the unnerving phone calls he had received when he released the original package—he wanted to be as sure as possible of its veracity. He had already initiated some queries, using an investigative agency he'd relied on before to discreetly look into the facts he'd been given. They were now down in Texas working to corroborate that information for him; he expected to receive their initial report within days.

"Truthfully, Ken, I don't believe it will have an impact. If anything, it's just another interesting facet of the Navarro mystique, but it has no relevancy to this discussion of his competence for office."

"Well, Lou, it will be interesting to see how this unfolds. Again, ladies and gentlemen, President Navarro today resumed his office as President of the United States when he…"

"Oh, shut it off, will you, Fran," Moscone said. They were both watching the news report on the television in the living room of the Vice Presidential mansion. Kerrigan had hastily closed out a number of actions awaiting her signature as Acting President, to include the nomination of several federal judgeships, before Navarro's meeting at the Capitol. She knew that even if the Cabinet ultimately disputed his fitness, any act she took after that meeting would be invalidated. So she had closed out all those things that she deemed important, and had Dougherty pack up the rest and ship them back across the street to Caldwell to sort through. She expressly did not ask him to let Caldwell know what they were. 'He can figure that out for himself as he tries to pick up the pieces,' she thought. 'If they want to get back in the game this abruptly, they're going to have to start at full speed.' She was still bitter about the President's comments during the Cabinet session in the morning and the manner in which he'd delivered them. So having cleared her desk, so to speak, she then instructed Dougherty to cancel all her appointments, and left the office early and headed home. Moscone joined her at home shortly before six, and they ate their dinner largely in silence as they watched the news. "They're not saying anything new, they're just filling airtime."

Kerrigan continued to stare at the screen while she poked at her food. "I'm just concerned that this is all too soon. If the timing felt better, I wouldn't be bothered by any of this. But I don't. It feels wrong. So I feel obligated to challenge him to prove his fitness, but I don't know how to fight this, Fred. Or even if we should. I don't even believe the Cabinet would support me if I tried to convince them that he's not fit, and even if I did, it would look to the world like I'm trying to steal the job. I don't want it to appear that way. Public opinion's in his corner right now, and would turn on me in a heartbeat if I make a move, and then there'll be no chance of an election in two years. Plus there's no telling what a vote in Congress would do." She looked over to him. "Maybe it would just be best to step aside as required, put on my supportive face, and let the chips fall where they may. What do you think?"

"You're probably right, Fran, it's a no-win situation. But I think we can probe a little bit to gage what kind of support we'd have. You check through the Cabinet, and I'll ask around through Congress. If things seem favorable, then perhaps we can reconsider. But I think that unless Navarro collapses, we're just going have to sit tight for now."

"Okay, Fred. I agree. I'll discreetly canvas the Cabinet and we can compare notes tomorrow. In the meantime, I'll just put on my happy face for the world and act as supportive as I can stomach." She looked at the TV again, where Stevenson continued to talk. "I guess it's good that the thing with the medical records didn't get any traction," she said, and snorted disgustedly to herself.

"Yeah, too bad about that," Moscone answered, glaring at Stevenson's image on the screen. "But you never know what else might happen. These things have a way of growing bigger than people initially expect if you just give them enough time." 'And particularly if you just give them a little shove,' he thought silently to himself, a grim smile on his face.

In the White House, at the same time, Josh Caldwell was also urging that the television be shut off. "Sir, you've got to rest. If you push yourself too hard, too fast, you'll have a relapse and will provide the ammunition people need to attack you." He stood up from the chair where he had been seated watching the screen, and moved behind the President's wheelchair to assist him. He glanced at Stevenson's image on the screen, and said with distaste, jerking his head toward it, "Besides, those guys will twist the truth into knots just to make themselves sound good. And that guy Stevenson is among the worst."

"Oh, I don't know, Josh. I thought he was a pretty likeable fellow. And Julia liked him, too. So he can't be all that bad." He smiled wearily at he said it.

"Don't bet any money on it, Mr. President. You'd lose, I'm telling you." He grabbed the handles behind the chair. "Shall we go?"

"I suppose so," said Navarro. "I do feel like I'm running out of steam. And I can tell it's time for another pain pill." Caldwell began pushing him out of the Yellow Room, turning left down the long second floor hallway toward the President's suite.

"It's about an hour early, actually," said Caldwell, "but if you're going to bed now I suppose it's time to take it so you can sleep well."

From the time Navarro had awakened from his coma at Walter Reed until now, much work had been done to make the White House ready for his return. His bedroom had been transformed, with all the furniture removed—although he had demanded that some reminders of Julia be retained—and replaced with items specially designed for the handicapped. Similarly, the bathroom had been reconfigured to accommodate the wheelchair, and railings had been installed to enable Navarro to lift himself between the chair and other areas, even though he was not yet strong enough to do it. Nonetheless, he insisted on trying and insisted that he would master it in relatively short order. The room next to his bedroom, formerly a private sitting room for the first family, was now set up as accommodations for the pair of military nurses that lived in the residence around the clock. It held a bed in which one of the two could sleep if necessary, as well as storage cabinets and emergency kits stocked full of supplies and medications that the President might require. Much of the design employed was modeled after that which FDR used while he lived in the White House in a similar capacity nearly a hundred years earlier; the particulars had been updated, of course, but the principles remained the same.

All of this implementation had been orchestrated by General Webster. Navarro's first act of this day as he'd resumed his office had been to reinstate Webster to his former position; the doctor met the President and Caldwell in the bedroom now as they wheeled in.

"Good evening, Mr. President. Good evening, Governor. Just wanted to be sure everything was in place before I called it a day." He looked closely at Navarro. "May I ask how you're feeling, sir?"

"I'm feeling like I'm ready to go another fifteen rounds," quipped the President, smiling in an attempt to mask his fatigue. A wince of pain flashed across his face. "Actually, I feel like I've just run a marathon. I'm whipped." Navarro actually knew from which he spoke. While Mayor of Houston he had run in the Houston Marathon about five years earlier; he didn't do well, finishing near the bottom of the pack, as he could not run with much speed due to the war wound to his right leg, but he did complete it. It was one of his proudest accomplishments, although he swore privately to Julia that he'd never make that mistake again.

"As I'd expect you to be after such a day," Webster answered sternly. "You're going to have to be careful to pace yourself or you run the risk of seeing yourself back in the hospital." Without waiting for an answer, he looked up at Caldwell. "That's going to have to be your job, Governor, because he won't do it on his own. I used to be able to get him to take care of himself, in spite of himself, because I'd get Julia to make suggestions. You'll have to do that now."

"Doc, if you're suggesting that Josh is going to be a stand-in for Julia for me, I can assure you that you're wildly wrong." The President looked up and down Caldwell's massive bulk as he said it, shaking his head.

Webster ignored him. "You're going to need to be sure to get at least eight hours of sleep each night, and more if you become fatigued. Might not be a bad idea to build some rest time into your schedule each day. You're going to have to cooperate with the nurses, too"—he waved his hand toward the two nurses, both male, who were preparing the bed for the night—"when they want to check on your vital signs." He pointed an accusing finger at the President, and put on a stern face. "I vividly remember what kind of patient you can be, and if I hear of any shenanigans from them about you, you'll have to answer to me." Navarro had been noted for the fits he'd given his medical handlers at Walter Reed when he had recuperated there under Webster's care from his wound in 2003 and 2004.

"Yes, mom," Navarro responded in a sing-song voice, "I'll behave and play nice." He gave Webster a weary look, but with a gleam in his eye. "Truly, Glenn, I'll be good. I'm too tired to be otherwise. Yet."

"Good," said Webster. Then, looking at him more closely, asked "Have you got any pain right now, or are you just tired out?"

"My arm and chest are fine," Navarro said, pumping his left arm up and down. "I do have a little headache"—he pointed at the left side of his forehead—"but not too bad. Just a dull ache behind my eyes. The legs are the worst. The right one aches like always, but the left one is killing me. Isn't that weird?" Although he rarely acknowledged it, and even more rarely allowed anyone else to notice it, the old wound in his right leg pained him continually throughout the years; he had learned to mask it from himself so that it became essentially background noise and nothing more.

"The left?" Caldwell asked perplexed, looking down at the void below Navarro's left thigh. "How can that be?" He looked over to Webster.

"It's actually not at all unusual, and truthfully I'd be surprised if it didn't. It suffered the most trauma, and the nerves still don't know what happened. Your brain thinks the leg is still there because the nerves are telling it that it is, but they're also saying it's in trouble, which the brain interprets as pain." He gave Navarro a compassionate look. "You may always feel phantom pain like that, although it should lessen with time."

"Just my luck," said Navarro, grunting as the nurses helped muscle him into the bed. "Two bad legs, one missing and one not working, and both of them hurt."

"We'll give you something for it, Mr. President," said the senior nurse, a Navy lieutenant.

"Ah, I thought you'd never ask." Then, turning to Caldwell, he said, "Josh,

I'd like to start meeting with each Cabinet officer individually tomorrow. I want to talk with them one on one so they can see me for themselves without any peer pressure. We'll need to get them all in before Friday, so nobody can try an end-around on us and say I'm not capable yet." He accepted his medicine and a glass of water from the nurse, then lay his head back on the pillow and closed his eyes. "I think I'll sleep now. Good night, guys. Thanks for everything. I'll see you in the morning."

"Good night, Mr. President," both Webster and Caldwell said simultaneously, then turned and exited the room, extinguishing the light as they went.

"And Julia, I'll see you in just a bit," Navarro whispered into the empty room, still with his eyes closed.

In Lambertville, at the same time, Jamie Coryell clicked off his television and headed upstairs. He'd been watching the Yankees earlier as they were heading toward a victory over Seattle in the American League Divisional Series, but had flicked over to CNN as the news broke in about the President's resumption of power. He watched Stevenson with a critical eye, and again thought his old friend did well in his growing role as one of the network's rising stars. He and Ingalls clearly worked well together, anticipating what each other was going to say, and supporting each other in their responses.

Coryell did think Stevenson looked somewhat tired; the eyes looked a little strained. 'Must not be getting enough rest,' he thought, as he began climbing the stairs toward his room. 'Maybe I'll give him a call this weekend to suggest he come visit and unwind a bit.' He figured that since the hoopla surrounding Stevenson's exposé with the medical files was now overshadowed by the President's surprise return, the pressure would be off and he could relax.

He couldn't have known how wrong he was.

CHAPTER 37

Washington, DC
Friday, 7 October 2022
11:56 p.m. EDT

The ringing of the phone startled Stevenson awake. He fumbled for the light and looked at the clock. "Midnight," he said aloud. "Who's calling me at midnight?" Even as he said it, he knew who it was.

He'd gotten home late from the office tonight. He was worn out from the week, and felt like he was coming down with a cold. 'Too early for flu season,' he thought; but it felt like the flu. He'd heated up a couple of slices of old pizza and tried to watch a little TV, but found his attention continually wandering, so he'd headed up to bed around nine.

Despite the news events of the week, he didn't think the pace of the news cycle was affecting him. He'd been in the business now for nearly twenty years, and up near the top now for the past couple, so he was used to the pressure to get a story and run with it. No, that wasn't wearing on him. But he did have the feeling again that he was being watched, and he did think occasionally that he noticed someone following him, that the same handful of people always seemed to be nearby. That was what was weighing on him. And he knew it was all related to the package.

"Stevenson," he mumbled into the phone, having snatched it from its cradle.

"Good evening, Lou," came *The Shadow's* metallic voice. "We haven't spoken in a while, so I thought I'd give you a ring. Not too late for you, is it? I didn't think you looked like you were feeling well today." A faint chuckle sounded in Stevenson's ear.

"What do you want?" Stevenson responded sourly, swinging his legs to the side and sitting up on the edge of the bed. Although his heart leapt into his throat at *The Shadow's* comment about watching him, he chose to ignore it even though his pulse was now racing.

"I want to know what you're doing with my story, Lou, because I haven't seen or heard anything about it. And it's very big news." The voice lowered menacingly. "I expected you to have reported it by now. If I can't rely on you, I'll have to find somebody else to grace with my largesse. And I want you to know that I really, really hate it when I can't rely on someone."

"I'm still checking it out," Stevenson countered. "I don't even know who you are, let alone whether I can trust you. I'll report on it when I'm good and ready." He could feel his temper rising as he talked, taking affront at the presumption of the voice on the phone.

"You're not trying to find out who I am, are you, Lou? Because I'd take that as a very unkindly gesture. If I felt you were trying to do that, I'd be very angry with you, and people don't last very long when I'm angry with them."

Stevenson's mouth dried up at the implied threat. "Listen," he choked out. "I'm just checking out your facts. It'd be better to be able to say where they came from, but I'm only checking the facts."

"Good, Lou, good. I like that much better." *The Shadow* paused. "I know what you've got those guys down in Texas doing, and I know they owe you something soon. Maybe you should hustle them up, because I expect you to report on this first thing next week. As you know, the pace of things has picked up, and we don't want to wait too long, do we?" Another pause. "And make sure you keep all of this, my files and your investigation, to yourself until that report is made. If I feel you're spreading word of our conversations around, or that you're sharing these files with anybody, or that you're trying to tip somebody off about it, I'll be very angry again. Are we clear?"

"Clear," said Stevenson quietly.

"Fine. Good night then, Lou. Sleep well. And make sure this hits the news next week." The call disconnected.

Stevenson replaced the phone in its cradle and stared at it, trying to think about what he should do. As he made up his mind, he reached for the phone again, but withdrew his hand before picking it up. 'Could they possibly be tapping my phone?' he thought suddenly. He looked around the room. 'Could they have the place bugged, or have stuck in cameras?' He shook his head, deciding he was being overly melodramatic, but decided to use his cell phone instead, figuring they'd have to be really sophisticated to be capturing his cell signature, whereas tapping a hard line can be done by almost any run-of-the-mill amateur. He pushed the number 6 key on the phone to speed dial the number he wanted, and waited for it to connect, pacing nervously around his bedroom. After four rings the connection was made.

"Hi, Lou," Jamie Coryell answered. "What's got you calling so late? You never used to be a night owl. You know, it's actually kind of funny that you are calling, because I was going to give you a ring in the morning. What's up?"

"Jamie, can you talk?" Stevenson asked anxiously.

"What do you mean, can I talk?"

"I mean, are you alone where nobody will overhear us?"

"Sue and I just got home from a movie, and now we're sitting in her apartment having a drink."

"Hi, Lou," Sue shouted in the background.

"Lou, what's wrong?" Jamie asked, sitting up straighter in the chair on Sue's balcony and focusing his attention. He could hear the anxiety in Stevenson's voice, which he knew was not the sign of anything good. "Tell me."

"Jamie, listen, I need to ask you a favor."

"Sure, Lou, anything. You know that. What do you need?"

"I just had another phone call from *The Shadow*. Very bizarre, very scary. I got that second package I'd told you about in the mail last week, and it is some explosive stuff. He's pushing me to report on it right away, but I told him I needed to check out the facts first. I'd actually connected with some guys down in Texas to do that for me, who should have some answers for me in a couple of days. But somehow, *The Shadow* already knew that. I can't figure out how he knows so much about what I'm doing. Anyway, he's very threatening, telling me to not share the information or leak it to the wrong people or whatever." He paused for breath, realizing he was talking in rapid-fire fashion. "And I think I'm being followed around again."

"What? Lou, are you sure?" Jamie exclaimed, his voice clearly saying that he didn't believe him. "Why do you think that?" He paused, then getting no response, continued. "If you really do, maybe it's time to go to the police. I don't know—don't you think you're just a little overwrought by all this stress. I mean, the reason I was going to call you was to invite you up here to unwind a little. Thought you were looking a little too tightly wrapped on the TV." As he spoke, Sue reached over to lay a reassuring hand on his shoulder. "Anyway, so what do you want to ask me?"

"I want to send you a copy of all my files on this, plus the investigative report when I receive it. I don't feel safe having it only here. I'll send it to you, and if something happens, you'll still be able to report the story."

"Lou," Jamie said very carefully, not liking the tone of his friend's voice. He began an attempt to calm Stevenson's obviously frayed nerves. "What do you think's going to happen? You must be getting yourself all worked up over nothing, buddy. You're watching too many movies, or something. Nothing you've got can be that important, can it? Why would anyone want to do something to you, anyway? What motive have they got?"

"I don't know," Stevenson mumbled into the phone. "It's this package I got; this guy keeps pushing me to make it public. For a while I thought it was Caldwell doing it. Thought he was feeding me fake stuff to somehow have it backfire on Kerrigan and Moscone. Then I thought maybe it was them, trying to discredit Navarro. Now I don't know. I can't figure any of it out. Maybe it's somebody else. I just think I need to stash another copy of all this, and you're the safest one I could think of. Sorry for asking you this."

"No problem, Lou, just send it to me whenever and I'll keep it in the safe at my paper. In the meantime, you definitely need to get some rest before you have a nervous breakdown. Okay, buddy?"

"Okay," Stevenson answered. "Thanks, Jamie. Really, I mean it. You can't imagine how much better that makes me feel."

"Good. So what do you think about coming up here?"

"No, this weekend won't work. I've got a couple other things to check out—not related to this mess—then have to get ready for the debates next week." Stevenson had been tapped to moderate a debate organized by the League of Women Voters that showcased a panel of Republican Senate hopefuls against a panel of Democratic Senate hopefuls. It was a new twist to try to generate some voter enthusiasm for the off-year elections coming in November. "But I'll take a rain-check and plan to come up next weekend. How about that?"

"It's a date," Coryell said. "Good night, Lou. Rest up." And the call ended.

Stevenson snapped the cell phone shut, turned out the lights, and lay back down in bed. But sleep eluded him for much of the night.

Coryell also closed his cell thoughtfully, turned to Sue and said, "I think Lou's in trouble. Listen to this." And repeated the story to her growing disbelief.

And on Quincy Place, not far from Stevenson's door, a non-descript van drove slowly down the street.

CHAPTER 38

Washington, DC
Saturday, 8 October 2022
10:33 a.m. EDT

The eleven men and four women who comprised the Cabinet all arrived at the Vice President's residence at the Naval Observatory within twenty minutes of each other. Chauffeured cars pulled up to the front door, discharged their passengers, and quickly drove away to parking areas at the rear of the mansion to wait. The day had dawned clear and cool, but a fall wind now had picked up, pushing scudding clouds across the sky, a foretaste of things to come. The extended forecast predicted rain and daytime temperatures in the fifties for the next three days.

As they arrived, the Cabinet chiefs were greeted by the Vice President and ushered into the dining room, where they found the table fully expanded with seats for them all, as well as coffee and pastries laid out on a buffet against the wall. With the arrival of Secretary of Veterans Affairs Gabe Carkhuff, Kerrigan called on everyone to find a seat at the table so they could begin. Surprisingly, all complied in a relatively swift manner.

"Thank you all for coming today on such short notice," Kerrigan began once they were seated. As she spoke, she remained standing at her place in the center of the table. "First, please allow me to apologize to you all for the irregularity of this, but I felt it was our constitutional responsibility to address the President's fitness, and I felt it would be better done here than in the Cabinet Room in the West Wing." As she spoke, her eyes roamed the table, taking in the faces and body language of those assembled. Most appeared non-committal, as if this was just another meeting, although some sat facing her with dour expressions and folded arms. "So, to address the business at hand then, our purpose is to decide if we collectively believe that President Navarro is capable, or not, of resuming his office as President and taking up those duties and responsibilities again. As we did when we invoked the 25th several months ago, we'll discuss the matter until everyone is satisfied, then take a vote. If the majority votes to declare him competent, that will be the end of it; there will be no record of the vote, so that there will be no stigma if someone votes against the matter. If a majority believes he is not yet fit, we will again draft and sign a letter to send to Congress stating such." She sat down, saying "The floor is now open."

As before, there was silence initially as the Cabinet chiefs looked around the room at each other to see who would go first. Finally, Secretary of Agriculture Rob Fulper broke the silence.

"Madame Vice President," he began, "I believe there is nothing to discuss. The President has stated he is fit, and his doctor has confirmed he is fit on the basis of examination and tests. As you are well aware, we have each had an opportunity in the last couple of days to speak with him at length on an individual basis,"—Caldwell had moved mountains to get every Cabinet officer into the Oval Office with Navarro, where they each spent about an hour alone with him—"and I for one am fully convinced that there is no reason he should not resume his office. With the exception of a need for additional physical therapy, some medication, and obviously an inability to walk, he is just as capable as he ever was."

"Madame Vice President," interjected Secretary of Defense Aaron Post, "I disagree." Post was now recovered from the relatively minor injuries he had suffered in the California attack, and had been back in the Pentagon for the past two months. "While I agree with Rob's assessment of the President's physical state—that he requires therapy and medication but is otherwise in good health—I found his mental state somewhat disturbing during my meeting with him. More than once during that session his attention wandered and I had to repeat what I had just said to him. Very uncharacteristically for him, he was very brusque with me during our discussion, cutting me off several times and showing irritation with what I was telling him."

"Aaron, what time of the day did you see him?" asked Secretary of Transportation Jonas Pittenger from across the table.

"Late on Thursday, about four thirty," replied Secretary Post.

"I had the same experience, Madame Vice President," said Pittenger. "My meeting with the President was yesterday at three o'clock, and he was decidedly out of character compared to the man he was. I had the distinct impression that he was in serious pain the entire time we talked."

"I saw nothing like that," said Secretary of State DiMarco, now joining the fray, "and my interview was after Aaron's on Thursday. I found the President to be very congenial and fully in command. I cannot think of one reason why we should not accept him at his word."

The discussion continued around the table for the next hour. Some at the table expressed an interest in reviewing the President's medical records to help them assess his capabilities, while others argued that was a gross infringement of his privacy. Some believed there should be some sort of probation period established, during which the President would essentially have to be on his best behavior, so to speak; that concept was discarded quickly as both unworkable and unconstitutional. Most in the room indicated that they saw no difference in the man now from the man he was six months ago, with the exception of his physical injuries, while others had noted instances of behavior that were not at all in keeping with his character as they knew it before the attack.

Finally, Vice President Kerrigan rapped on the table to signal she believed the time for discussion had culminated. "We've heard many arguments, and I believe everyone has had a chance to speak their peace. Does anyone have anything further to add before we vote on the matter?" Again, heads pivoted around the table, but there was no indication that anyone wanted to talk further. "Very well," said Kerrigan, "in that case we will put the matter to a vote. We are voting to determine if we, as the Cabinet, in accordance with Section 4 of the 25th Amendment, concur that President Navarro is fit to resume the powers, duties and responsibilities of his office as President, as he has stated he is. A 'yes' vote will agree with that, meaning that he is fit, while a 'no' vote will disagree, indicating a belief that his disability still exists and that we should report that to Congress." She looked around the table as she spoke. "All those in favor, please raise your right hand." She, and everyone else, looked around the table, counting hands. "Thank you. All those opposed, please raise your right hands." Again, all counted, after which Kerrigan formally announced the result. "Thank you, ladies and gentlemen. The measure has passed, twelve to three. We therefore will not challenge the President's ability, and our work here is concluded. I thank you all for coming, for your forthrightness during these discussions, and for your vote. I'll see you all again next Wednesday during the regular weekly meeting with the President. Our meeting today is adjourned."

Swiftly, the cars cycled from the parking lot to the front door, picked up their distinguished passengers, and headed out into the rain that was now falling.

Kerrigan saw them each to the door and watched them go. Then, when the last had departed, she turned and walked through the living room and out onto the veranda, where she sat, lost in thought, watching the rain as it fell on the gardens.

CHAPTER 39

Lambertville, NJ
Wednesday, 12 October 2022
5:21 p.m. EDT

Jamie Coryell had been struggling in his office at *The Beacon* all afternoon trying to finish his preparation for the series of articles he intended to write on the demise of the family farm in Hunterdon County, the county in which Lambertville was located. For weeks he had been interviewing old farmers and visiting the sites of the old farms in the southern part of the county, all of them now long gone. At one time, and not too long ago, practically the entire county had been farmland. But as commuting to and from the New York and Philadelphia metro areas had become easier, causing newcomers to move into the county to escape the urban areas, most of that farmland had been turned over to developers and built up into houses. Those few farmers that had hung on eventually found themselves feeling like pariahs on their ancestral homesteads, branded as roadblocks to progress for holding down the tax base and for threatening the health of their neighbors because of the fertilizers and pesticides they used to up their yields. As the newcomers took over local governments, what the farmers could do and how they could do it on their own land became more and more restricted. This phenomenon, coupled with falling crop and dairy prices and the skyrocketing cost of operations once federal farm subsidies were phased out in the Obama years, drove those last farmers out of business. True, there were still 'farms' in the county, but they were generally owned by the wealthy who farmed as a hobby more than anything else.

Coryell knew that this series of articles would probably not sit well with the people of the area. He intended to be very frank about the fact that the absence of farms had stolen the soul from the county, and to be very frank about where, in his opinion, the blame for the situation lay. Nobody liked to have an accusing finger pointed at them, he knew. 'Too bad,' he thought. 'They should have thought about that twenty-five years ago.' He intended to publish the first of the series in next week's Wednesday paper.

But he was struggling because it was so nice outside and his mind kept wandering. Lambertville was in the midst of an Indian summer right now, with temperatures in the mid-seventies, a gentle breeze blowing to cool things down a little, and a bright, blue sky with big, fluffy cumulus clouds. He and Sue planned to go see a performance of *Cats* this evening at the Bucks County Playhouse in New Hope; he'd been looking forward to it all day, knowing it was one of Sue's favorite shows. Even though he found it to be bizarre, he knew he'd enjoy it because she enjoyed it. He'd found himself all afternoon staring out the window of his office when he should have been focused on his story. "Just focus," he said out loud, chiding himself. "Focus and you'll be done." He tore his eyes from the window and back to the computer screen.

A soft knock on his door startled him. "Come in," he shouted, and the door cracked open to reveal Sue's red-eyed face peering in at him. "Sue, what's wrong?" he said, jumping up from his chair and coming around the desk to meet her. Jamie knew that she rarely, if ever, got so emotional that she went to tears, so he couldn't imagine what could be so bad to bring this on.

"I came over as soon as I heard," she mumbled, sniffing into a tissue and dabbing at her eyes. "Jamie, I'm so sorry."

"Heard what?" he asked, perplexed. "Tell me what's wrong."

"I saw it on TV, on the news. Haven't you seen it?" she asked.

"No, I've been shut in here all afternoon trying to write, and not doing very well at it. What is it?"

"It's Lou," she sniffed, the tears flowing again. "They say he was killed in an accident in his home." She leaned into him and buried her face in his chest.

Jamie felt stunned, like he'd just been punched in the stomach and had all the wind knocked out of him. He stared out into the outer office, seeing Alice standing behind her desk watching him; she was also crying. "Killed how?" he asked finally. "What kind of accident?" Alice was now moving to switch on the TV to CNN to see what was being reported.

"I'm not sure," Sue answered. "The report said he'd been missing from work, and was found at home when the police went to check on him. Jamie, it's terrible. I'm so sorry for you."

Alice had the television on now, and Jamie moved forward to be able to watch the report. Details were still coming in, the newsman said, but

Stevenson's body had been found early this morning after being missing from work yesterday. He lay at the bottom of the stairs leading down to his basement; the initial report indicated that he appeared to have accidentally fallen down the steep stairs and broken his neck. More information would follow, but that was all they knew at the moment.

Jamie sagged down into a chair and continued to stare at the TV, trying to come to grips with this revelation. 'Lou's gone,' he thought dismally. He thought of how much he was looking forward to his friend's upcoming visit this Saturday. His mind began to unconsciously scroll through a series of memories: Lou in college, always chasing girls, but rarely catching one; Lou down in the dumps after graduation when he couldn't find a job right away; the high point of Lou's wedding, and the low point of his divorce. He saw Lou's work through the eyes of a reader at first, as he read the investigative reports Lou filed early in his career, and later through the eyes of a television audience, as his friend became an established presence at the bureau and on the national news scene. He pictured Lou when they'd seen him last during their visit to Washington not so long ago, remembering the anxiety and concern, and later the increasing nervousness—a fear, almost a paranoia, Jamie thought—that came through on the telephone just the other night. He pictured in his mind the steep stairs from that visit to the house, remembered thinking that a person'd have to be careful on them. But he remembered the handrail also, and the non-skid treads that Lou had placed on the steps. He remembered how cautiously Lou had moved up and down them each time as he'd get another bottle of wine or they'd head down to watch a Blu-Ray. And suddenly, he wondered if this was really what it seemed.

CHAPTER 40

Lambertville, NJ
Monday, 17 October 2022
5:13 p.m. EDT

Sue and Jamie arrived back in Lambertville around five, having made good time returning from Long Island. They'd left Bayville shortly before three, and had not hit any traffic or construction—a minor miracle, Jamie thought—as they headed west on I-495, cut across Manhattan, and took the Lincoln Tunnel into New Jersey. Sue had been silent for the entire ride back, staring out the passenger window of Jamie's Ford, occasionally dabbing at her eyes with a tissue.

They had driven over to Long Island yesterday for Lou's viewing, which had depressed them so much that they'd decided to forego the bayside dinner they had planned, and instead grabbed a quick bite at Taco Bell to stave off their hunger and then headed straight to their hotel. The funeral service this morning had been somewhat better, although the sight of Lou's bereaved parents had almost done them in. 'How do you cope with the loss of your only son,' Jamie had wondered silently to himself, and hoped he'd never have to find out. The graveside ceremony had been held in the Locust Valley Cemetery, a century-old, non-denominational memorial just outside Bayville which is notable for its landscaping; it looks and feels much more like a woodland garden than a traditional cemetery with rows of granite and marble; Jamie thought that Lou would have been very pleased with it. A fairly good-sized group had attended both the funeral and the graveside service afterwards; Jamie'd noted several senior people from CNN in attendance, as well as Ken Ingalls, who had become a *de facto* on-air partner of Lou's over the past couple of years.

The weather, unfortunately, had turned nasty, with a cold mist blowing in off Long Island Sound. Jamie and Sue had departed quickly once the service was concluded, not wanting to fall into the melancholy that often follows a funeral of someone too young to die, nor wanting to stand out in the coming rain. They'd offered their condolences to Lou's parents, commiserated with them briefly, then headed home.

"Here we are," Jamie said, pulling into his reserved spot in the small parking lot behind *The Beacon*. He maneuvered the car into his space, shut off the ignition, and looked over to Sue. "How are you doing?"

"Fine," she said, "I'll be fine. I just can't believe it's happened. Makes you think about things, you know?"

"I know exactly what you mean," Jamie replied. "I've been thinking the same." They headed into the back door of the building, Jamie using his key to unlock it, then holding open the door for Sue to enter.

"Hey, Alice, we're back," Jamie called out as they entered.

"Welcome home, you two," she responded. "How was it?"

"Very nice, I guess," Jamie said. "It was a funeral, what can you say?" He walked over to his message box to see what was new. "Anything happening here?"

"Nothing," she said. "Big pile of mail for you to go through, but that's about it."

"Okay, then," Jamie responded, picking up the wire basket into which all the incoming mail for *The Beacon* was deposited when it arrived. It did appear to be an unusually large amount for a Monday. "This all came today?"

"All today," she answered. "Lucky you." She grinned at him.

"Thanks a lot. I'll take it with me and go through it at home tonight. Sue and I are heading out to reflect a little bit"—he glanced over at Sue as he said it— "but I'll be in bright and early tomorrow to get things finished up for the farm series."

"No problem," Alice responded. "Take your time, come in late. Take as much time as you need. I know it's been a rough couple of days for you, so you deserve it. I'll handle things here until you get in."

"Thanks, Alice. I couldn't do it without you."

"I know," she said, smiling. "Have a good night."

Jamie finally got home shortly after nine o'clock. He and Sue had gone to eat dinner at the Hawke once again, and had enjoyed a fine meal. They'd spent much of the time reminiscing about Lou, remembering his quirks and the funny things he'd done. It was all part of the grieving process, Jamie knew, so he'd enjoyed talking about his old friend, and was happy that Sue was feeling better. After they'd finished, he'd driven her across the bridge to her apartment on Main Street in New Hope, both of them amazed at how early it was now getting dark. Then he had returned to his house on Coryell Street.

Jamie parked the car on George Street to the left of his house, then entered through the back door, carrying the basket of mail from the office with him into the kitchen. He flicked on the lights as he entered, then removed and hung his jacket on the hook by the back door. He suddenly noticed that he was very tired; obviously the events of the weekend, coupled with the long drive, were now taking their toll. 'Getting to bed early probably isn't such a bad idea, anyway,' he thought, as he fixed the coffee pot so that it would be ready to perc when he got up in the morning.

The loud ring of the phone startled him. He glanced over at it on the wall—it was a Yankees sport memorabilia phone, dark blue with the New York logo on the receiver—and wondered who would be calling him now. He walked over to it, skirting the island in the center of the kitchen, and snatched it from its cradle before the third ring.

"Hello," he answered tentatively.

"Good evening, Mr. Coryell," came a metallic voice from the phone. "I hope you had a nice trip to Long Island."

Jamie's mouth dried up at the call. He could feel the blood draining from his face, sure that if he looked in a mirror he'd be white as a ghost. He had no doubt about who the caller was. 'Is this what Lou felt like when he got this call?' he wondered.

"Who is this? What do you want?" he asked.

"I'm an acquaintance of your lately departed friend Mr. Stevenson," the voice replied. "Very unfortunate accident, that. Very unfortunate. Stairways can be such dangerous places if you're not careful."

"What do you want?" Coryell asked again slowly, heart pounding in his chest.

"I want you to be more enthused about my material than Mr. Stevenson was," came the response. "You've received a package in your mail today. It contains the material I provided to him to examine, as well as the report from the investigators he hired to verify what I'd sent. They did a very good job, by the way. Very thorough. I'm sure you'll find it to be very enlightening."

"I haven't seen any package," Jamie said, moving over to the basket he'd set on the island when he entered, and began flicking quickly through its contents. "I just got home." Even as he said it, he came to a box, letter-sized and about four inches deep; he could tell from its heft that it was full of papers.

"You'll find the box. I want you to read it, and then report on it. Soon. If you wish, take a little time to verify its contents, just as Mr. Stevenson did. But don't make the mistake he made of deciding it was best not to go forward with it. That made me very angry with him. I wouldn't want to get that way with you."

The implied threat chilled Jamie. 'Is this guy saying he caused Lou's death?' he wondered. "Don't threaten me," Jamie responded, although his voice quavered as he spoke. "What if I just decide to go to the police with this instead?"

"That, my naïve friend, would be most unfortunate. Not only for you, but for your little girlfriend, too. Most unfortunate. I'd advise strongly against doing anything so rash." A chuckle rang through the line. "Just read the file. We'll talk again later."

The phone clicked in Jamie's ear, and he stared at it for a moment, almost unwilling to believe the conversation had happened, then replaced it in its cradle when it started to chirp angrily at him for not hanging up. He sank down onto one of the high barstools set next to the island, trying to think about what he should do. If it was just him, he'd just go discreetly to the police—maybe not the local ones, but he knew some State Police officers who lived in town—and they'd figure it out. But he couldn't jeopardize Sue. He knew he couldn't even tell her about the threat; she'd demand that he go to the police, no matter the consequences for her. He thought momentarily about trying to convince her to accept Secret Service protection, but realized that discussion would go nowhere with her. No, he'd talk with her about the call and the package, but not about what the voice had said about her.

He reached out for the package and removed it from the basket. It was a standard post office shipping box, addressed to him care of *The Beacon* in Lou's handwriting. The postmark showed it was mailed last Tuesday, the day of Lou's death in the fall. Jamie tried to work out the timeline in his mind. 'He must have mailed it, then been attacked,' unconsciously not even considering that Lou's death was an accident. 'Where's it been since then?' he wondered to himself as he ripped open the box to review its contents. As he'd suspected, it was full of papers, separated into three manila folders. A computer flash drive also fell from the box as he pulled out the folders.

He began to gingerly go through the files. The first folder he saw contained some of Lou's notes, sheets of paper which were drafts for an article he had considered writing. They were incomplete, with annotations here and there indicating that certain facts needed to be verified. The second folder contained a dossier that was obviously that provided by *The Shadow*—Jamie noted ruefully that he'd adopted Lou's dark moniker for the voice; it was appropriate, he thought. The dossier laid out an astounding series of accusations about President Navarro and the circumstances surrounding his birth. Throughout the document, Lou had jotted down notes; his thoughts, his questions, his need for more information. Jamie could feel Lou's concern with the document, his fear that it was fraudulent. 'For good reason,' he thought, reading the file in disbelief; 'I can't believe it either. If this stuff is true it will cause all kinds of trouble, for all kinds of people.' He set the folder aside and reached for the third.

As he opened it, he saw that it contained a thick, in-depth investigative report prepared by a group called the Trova Agency based out of San Antonio. Jamie was familiar with the firm; Lou had spoken of them many times in the past, and had told Jamie that if he ever needed something looked into with complete discretion yet complete thoroughness, these were the guys to do it. He began to read the report.

And became more and more agitated the more he read. 'These guys are saying this is all true,' he thought in astonishment. 'How can that possibly be?' He remained seated at the island well into the night, reading of an amazing train of events that had transpired nearly fifty years earlier, but which would reverberate across the country today. 'If it gets reported,' he thought, then remembered *The Shadow's* menace. 'What am I going to do?' he thought. And then to a point out in the distance, 'Lou, what have you got me into?' He finally closed the files, shut off the lights, and headed upstairs shortly after two in the morning to go to bed.

But as he lay in the dark, sleep would not come.

PART 3

CHAPTER 41

Near El Paso, Texas
Tuesday, 6 May 1975
6:34 a.m. MDT

"The stupid girl. If she isn't hurt too bad, I may kill her myself" muttered Acevedo to himself as he raced through the West Texas morning. The sun had crept over the horizon in his rear view mirror about an hour before, and he could already feel the heat beginning to rise after the cool of the night. The promise of a hot day did nothing to improve his mood as he approached the outskirts of El Paso on I-10. He'd been driving now for seven hours since leaving San Antonio after he'd received the frantic phone call, and he still had at least an hour to go until he was able to cross into Juarez. And that was if he had no problems getting through the city and across the river, which was not likely if his luck held true to form. "Stupid girl" he cursed again.

The front seat of his beat-up '69 Impala was littered with coffee cups and candy wrappers, and the ashtray overflowed with spent Marlboro butts. The back seat held his overnight bag containing the change of clothes and toilet kit that he had grabbed before rushing to get on the road last night. He'd have much preferred to be driving his Lincoln, but he wouldn't dare take that into Juarez if he wanted it to retain its value. Plus the Impala was much less memorable, and he wanted to be as unmemorable as possible right now.

He glanced at himself in the rear view mirror and thought that he was starting to get too old for this kind of nonsense. Even though he was only forty-seven, trips like this, plus dealing with all the other problems that arose with his special business, made him look and feel older. Staring at his face, he noted the clipped moustache needed a trim. Patting down what remained of the hair covering his bald head, he chuckled to himself and thought that rarely was he taken to be a doctor when people first met him. "I suppose that chain-smoking all those cigarettes doesn't help," he said out loud, as he lit another one and stubbed out its predecessor in the overflowing ashtray. It did keep his weight down. Only a little over 5 feet 7 inches to begin with, he carried only 153 pounds on his gaunt frame. Anyway, maybe only a couple more years of this business and he'd have enough to get rid of the clinic and settle in up toward Austin where his wife was from. For the moment, though, each of these girls was worth big money to him, and he was not ready to give it up yet.

He had received the call just after he had finished a quiet dinner at home last night from the girl's idiot boyfriend and her frantic grandmother, both jabbering so fast in Spanish that he could barely make out what they were saying, even though he was fairly fluent in the language. Had to be, to be successful at the kind of work he did. Finally getting them to slow down, he was able to piece together that the girl had been in an accident of some kind and was in the hospital. Only when they told him the hospital was in Juarez did he almost jump through the phone. The one thing he had told the girl was that she had to stay in El Paso if she wanted to get paid, and now she was lying in some Mexican hospital. If she hadn't been the key to making the whole thing work at the moment, he would have hung up on them. Instead, he had told them he'd be there in the morning to sort things out.

He'd left his house at midnight and had driven straight through with only quick stops in Van Horn and Fort Stockton to get fresh coffee and more cigarettes, as well as fill up on gas. It irritated him even more when he thought that he'd just been out here last week when the other girl delivered, and that he'd have to be back here again in another month or so for the third one. He hated the drive. He'd told his wife only that he had to go check on an emergency at the clinic out west. When she'd wanted to know where he was going and why he was in such a rush, he said that he'd be gone only a couple of days at most, and not to worry about it. At least she was good enough and smart enough to accept that at face value. He'd have to make it up to her when he got back home.

There wasn't too much traffic on the road as he rolled into town, admiring again the sight of the Franklin Mountains rising west of the city, practically the only thing he enjoyed whenever he was forced to come out here. He knew that much of the business of El Paso was on the west side past the mountains, and on the north near Fort Bliss and up toward White Sands. Not too many commuters coming from this direction except tumbleweeds, he thought, as he watched one the size of a Volkswagen roll along next to the interstate, driven by the never-ending wind.

As he neared the exit for I-110 and the border crossing, he thought about what he needed to get done. He'd have to find the hovel that the girl's grandmother lived in and figure out which hospital they'd taken her to. If she wasn't too banged up and the baby was in no danger, he could probably afford to let her stay there to mend for a day or two before getting her back across the border again. If she was in serious shape, he'd need to move her quickly so she could get better treatment in the city, although that would mean paying out a bunch of bribes, which would mean his profit margin for the deal, perish the thought, would go right into the toilet. Hopefully, it wouldn't come to that. He then needed to stop by the house on Raindance where he kept the girls, to make sure the last one understood not to sneak back south across the river like this one had.

Finally turning off I-10 and heading for the crossing, he was relieved to see that there was no backup of cars waiting to cross. There'd been days when he'd waited in line in the sweltering sun for what seemed like hours to get through the crossing and across the river. Maybe today would turn out okay after all, he thought, as he approached the booth and pulled out his passport to wave at the customs officers. Maybe everything would work out.

Neither he, nor his car, nor his passport was even looked at as he was waved across the border into Mexico.

CHAPTER 42

Ciudad de Juarez, Mexico
Tuesday, 6 May 1975
8:06 a.m. MDT

The old woman blamed herself. If only she'd paid more attention to Elena, and to the friends she hung out with, maybe none of this would have happened. She blew her nose and dried her eyes again. It seemed like she hadn't been able to stop crying ever since the news came. She was sitting in the shade outside her home, fanning herself, swatting at the flies that swarmed around her and trying to ignore the heat. The swamp cooler on the roof of her home had given up the ghost last week, and she had no money with which to get it fixed, so she was forced into the shade, and forced to move with it as the sun arched across the sky throughout the day.

She involuntarily glanced at her house as the beat-up Chevy pulled up and the little man got out. She liked this little place on Lago de Patzcuaro where she'd lived for so long. Although not glamorous, its stucco walls and red tiled roof had been more than enough for her and the girl and the girl's mother—her daughter—before she had run off and disappeared. 'I failed with that one, too,' she thought.

Elena's boyfriend, Manuel, was swaying in the hammock in the back. A good-for-nothing lout, was her opinion. Now eighteen, the boy had not finished school and was content to run around the edges of the gangs that infested the city and brought so much grief to so many families. He had treated her granddaughter badly even before she got pregnant, and then could think only of getting her an abortion so that he could get out of the mess. Probably would have happened, too, if she hadn't put her foot down and her granddaughter hadn't met the little man who was now coming to talk to her.

She had been distraught when Elena told her she was pregnant. She was only fifteen. She had had such high hopes for the girl, and now they would go nowhere. Only when she had heard of Dr. Acevedo and his work had she seen a glimmer of hope. All the girl had to do was go with Acevedo to El Paso on a work visa for his clinic there, and he would take care of all her medical bills during the pregnancy, then take the baby for adoption once it was born. And for their time and trouble, as if they had another legitimate option open to them, he would give Elena five thousand U.S. dollars as she returned back home. It had all seemed to be an answered prayer.

And then yesterday Manuel had shown up on her doorstep and shattered that illusion. "There's been an accident," he'd said. "Elena got hurt and is in the hospital. And my car has been totaled," he'd moaned piteously. It was clear which was the more devastating thing to him. "I'm lucky that I wasn't hurt too badly, too." She'd wanted to race right to the hospital, but the boy said they should call Dr. Acevedo first to let him know so that their money wouldn't be jeopardized. So she'd made the call, trying vainly to control her emotions, then told the boy to go away and got her neighbor, Señor Alvarez, to drive her to the hospital. And then her world had collapsed.

Acevedo dreaded the conversation he was about to have, because he knew it would take forever with this woman and he didn't have the time to spare. He glanced at the house and wondered how anyone could live there. So tiny, so run down. Yet the yard where the woman sat was kept as well as could be, so that at least was something. Still, he wanted to get this over with and get on to the girl at the hospital. He flicked his cigarette into the street and walked up to the house.

As he approached, he looked at the woman more closely and realized she'd probably been awake and crying ever since she'd called him on the phone last night. The eyes were puffy, the nose red, the gray hair pulled loose from the tight bun it was habitually kept in. Off to the right he saw the boyfriend getting out of the hammock, as if he'd just awakened from a nap. He noted the stringy, black hair and scraggly beard, as well as the deep-set black eyes and the perpetual smirk. 'Trouble's going to find that one sooner rather than later,' he thought to himself. 'He's not going to be around for very long.'

That in itself was somewhat of a comfort, because if this boy and Elena had not been nearly identical younger versions of the couple who had paid for this baby, he would not have wasted his time and effort on them. As it was, this baby would fit the bill very nicely. Whether a boy or girl, and the parents-to-be knew he couldn't guarantee a specific gender for them, the baby would resemble them so closely that they would have no doubt it was their child. As it should be when you've been told that your own in vitro baby is coming from a surrogate.

The woman was getting up to talk to him, but before she could speak the boyfriend jumped in. Speaking in Spanish, the boy said, "This isn't going to affect our arrangement, is it, Doc?" Responding in kind, Acevedo replied, "That depends on the situation, now doesn't it?" Although he was clearly of Hispanic heritage, Acevedo's Mexican ancestors had arrived in Texas well before it became part of the U.S. He felt no more Mexican than any other Anglo in Texas. But his appearance did help out business, and it certainly helped out when he had to come out here, so he made an effort to get better at speaking Spanish to foster the image. The woman pushed the boy out of the way and began to speak.

"It's terrible, Doctor" she said, starting to cry again. "She has always been such a good girl, truly." She dried her eyes on her apron and looked at him as if to say, 'I dare you to challenge that.'

"Yeah, yeah, a good girl, but I told her to stay in El Paso. What's the story with that? What was she doing here? What kind of accident was she in?"

"That accident wasn't my fault," chimed in the boyfriend. He was almost shouting to talk over the old woman. "That truck came out of nowhere, man, and rammed into her side of the car. I didn't even see anything, then the next thing I know there's nothing but flashing lights and sirens around. My head got banged pretty good. I had to get a couple of stitches and the thing is still killing me." He made a face as if to show how much agony he was in.

"Why was Elena over here?" Acevedo persisted.

"She wanted to come over for Cinco de Mayo. You know it's a better deal over here than in El Paso—more parties, more fun—and she'd been cooped up in your place forever. She wanted a little action. So she called me and I picked her up." The boy spoke defiantly.

"Then I guess the deal's off," replied Acevedo brusquely. Both the woman and boy began to protest. "Listen, I told all of you that she had to stay at my place over there until the baby was born. I was doing you a favor here. All you had to do was wait the six months from the time you came to me with this trouble and the time I took the baby off your hands. But since you don't listen, since you had to bring her over here for a party even when she's eight months pregnant, I guess I'll go home. The party's over. None of you are any use to me now." He started to make as if to return to the car.

"Wait, wait, Doctor, please," the woman said, clutching at his sleeve and pulling him back. "What am I to do now? It's all so terrible. Now I'm all alone." Both she and Acevedo ignored the boy who stood by sullenly.

"I don't know what I can do, or why I should do anything," said Acevedo. He could feel victory coming, knowing that the bluff of departure would start them pleading. He could cut their price in half and they'd be grateful to have it. "What hospital is Elena in? If she's stable enough by now, maybe I can get her transferred back across the river and we can work from there. Where is she?"

The woman started crying again. The boy looked dumbfounded. "But, Doctor," she moaned pitifully, "Elena is dead. She was dead by the time she got to the hospital."

Hospital-General de Ciudad Juarez, three kilometers from the center of the city on the Avenida Paseo Triunfo de la Republica, is a state-run facility that caters to the poor and indigent of the city, unlike its newer and fancier relatives nearby that are state-of-the-art and cater to the wealthy and to Americans who come south for 'medical tourism.' That phenomena of middle-class Americans coming to Mexico for cheap drugs and exotic treatments that are not available or approved in the U.S. was nothing new, but it was becoming a booming business. Acevedo made a mental note to see how he might get involved in those lucrative referrals once he returned home.

He and the woman had raced there right after she dropped the bombshell on him. "What do you mean, dead?" he'd shouted. "Why didn't you tell me this last night?"

"We didn't know, then. I couldn't get to the hospital until later."

"What about you?" he'd said, rounding on the boy. "Why didn't you tell me?"

"I didn't know anything, man" he'd replied. "I got hurt, too, you know. I can't help it that she got it worse. But you can still help us out, right?"

Acevedo had ignored the question and turned back to the woman. "Are you sure she's dead? Did you see the body?"

"No, doctor. But that's what they told me. Then they told me to go away." She'd continued to cry as they spoke.

"Well, maybe you heard wrong. If there's a body, I want to see it."

He'd shoved the woman into the car and left the boy standing in the street and raced away into the morning.

The hospital was a large brick building, probably built right after the war, but which did not look like it had been upgraded since. He was lucky to find a place to park the Impala in the crowded parking lot across the street, although he wasn't optimistic about what shape the car would be in once he got back to it. He congratulated himself again for being smart enough not to bring the Lincoln. He got out of the car with the old woman in tow and entered the building.

The place was a madhouse. Even now, at 10 o'clock in the morning, sick and injured people jammed the waiting room while harried nurses and orderlies raced back and forth. The room itself was dirty and had that hospital smell that he hated. 'Remind me never to get sick in Mexico,' he thought. He and the woman elbowed their way up to the counter, drawing curses and angry comments from those they passed.

"I'm Doctor Acevedo," he began, speaking to the tired looking receptionist at the counter. He thought to himself that if the woman looks this bad only three hours into her shift, she's in for a very long, hard day. "This woman's granddaughter is my patient. She was brought here after being in a car accident yesterday, and then died here. I want to see the body and talk to the doctor that treated her."

The receptionist looked him over, decided he wasn't worth arguing with when she had a whole roomful of people waiting to argue with her, so she told him to go down the hall to his left to see the hospital administrator. "He'll be glad to help you," she smirked.

They marched down the hall, banged on the door indicated, and went in. Acevedo knew immediately that he could do business with this man.

The administrator, Señor Ramirez, indeed turned out to be a true businessman. In his early sixties, tall but overweight, he had the look of a tired bureaucrat who had retired on the job and was always looking for something to make his life easier. When Acevedo had introduced himself and the woman, and had asked to be taken to the body, Ramirez had bluntly asked what was in it for him. And so began the time-honored dance with which Acevedo was so familiar. After a brief negotiation, Ramirez was a hundred dollars richer and

Acevedo was in the morgue, where he received the second great shock of his morning. Elena was indeed dead from massive head trauma, but the baby she carried had been delivered alive and was doing well in the nursery upstairs. And Acevedo saw his opportunity to turn this lemon of a situation he'd been handed into lemonade.

First, though, he had to deal with the woman and make sure she and the idiot boy believed the matter to be closed. "I've verified it," he said to her sympathetically back in the waiting area as she cried. "She died instantly," he exaggerated, "there was nothing that could have been done to save her. If she'd only stayed in El Paso as I asked we would have none of this trouble now." He had to keep himself from gloating. "But to do what little I can to make it easy for you, I've arranged for her burial. And I'll give you five hundred dollars from life insurance I bought on her." He thought that was a nice touch, even as he made it up. Paying her only five hundred bucks would both make him look good in her eyes and would keep her from causing any trouble. And he could well afford it since he had planned to pay ten times that for the baby which he'd now get for about half that if things went right. She accepted the money on the spot, resigned to her situation and happy to get anything out of it, and he packed her off in a taxi to go home, saying he would finalize the remaining details here so she wouldn't have to be troubled by them.

Ramirez had readily understood what Acevedo wanted, even if he didn't understand all the details of it. And he had readily agreed to take care of things for the nominal price of fifteen hundred dollars. This price bought Acevedo disposal of the body—Ramirez would pack it off to the pauper's cemetery immediately. It bought him the baby—one less patient for the hospital to deal with. And, most importantly, it bought him the elimination of all records of the baby's birth—they hadn't been completed yet anyway, and Ramirez said he'd remove all trace of it from the accident report. All the world would know would be that Elena had been mortally injured in a tragic accident, largely caused by the negligent driving of her worthless boyfriend, and that she and the baby had died as a result of her injuries prior to arriving at the hospital.

"My friend," said Acevedo, shaking Ramirez's hand, "it has truly been a pleasure to do business with you."

"The pleasure has been mine," answered Ramirez, smiling broadly. The cares of the morning that had been evident on his face when Acevedo banged on his door had now vanished.

"Perhaps we can help each other out again sometime in the future," Acevedo said coyly. He looked straight into Ramirez' eyes as he did, watching for the reaction to his comment.

"How could that be," replied Ramirez warily. "I did not expect to see you again after today."

Acevedo smiled at him. "I'm in the business of helping out young girls who get into trouble. Motherly trouble, if you know what I mean. I take care of them, see them through the birth, then take the baby off of their hands. They are better off for it, and no one knows the trouble they're in beyond those that knew it to begin with. And if they're helped early enough, not many people will even know that."

"That all sounds very noble," agreed Ramirez, solemnly nodding his head. He started to smile slightly as he realized what was coming. He spread his hands. "How could I help?"

"Well, if any such girls ever came to your attention, or if you knew of any who'd like to be paid for the privilege of not going through with an abortion, if you would let me know about them, I'd be very grateful to you." Acevedo smiled broadly. "What do you think?"

"I think it will continue to be a pleasure to do business with you," said Ramirez.

The problem now for Acevedo was how to get the baby back across the river and into the care of the nurse who was already taking care of the other one. He'd accepted an offer to go with Ramirez to a nearby restaurant for lunch while he tried to think it through. He was famished by this point, so the invitation was welcome. But by the time the meal of *carnitas* washed down with *Tecate* beer was finished, he was eager to get on the road and back across the border, although his mind was still not made up.

He debated about whether to cross the border this afternoon, or wait until dark, or wait until morning. There were risks involved any way he looked at it. He decided that the sooner he could move, the less chance for things to go bad, or for someone to change their mind and make trouble for him. So he went back to the hospital, discreetly picked up the baby with Ramirez's able assistance, loaded it into his car which still miraculously survived unscathed in the parking lot where he'd left it, and departed as quickly as he had come. He drove only a little ways through Juarez's warren of streets before stopping.

The baby was sleeping soundly. It was bundled up in hospital blankets, and Ramirez had arranged for a mild sedative to help it sleep through the day. So Acevedo had decided to take advantage of that and simply place the baby, wrapped in the blankets, in his trunk and drive across the river as if he had not a care in the world. Having the baby out in the open invited questions about its papers if he was unfortunate enough to be stopped. He counted on the fact that at this time of day traffic would be getting heavy, but not stopped, on the way back north, so that the border agents wouldn't be checking all cars, and particularly not stopping cars with U.S. plates.

He headed back north up the Avenida Abraham Lincoln toward the crossing. Cars were being directed off to the side at random at the U.S. entry point by the Border Control agents. But as Acevedo pulled up to the gate and flashed his passport, he was simply waved through by the bored agent who was already looking past him to the next vehicle. Things were going his way after all. And still not a peep from the baby in back. He quickly accelerated onto the interstate once again and headed away from Juarez.

Traffic was moving along briskly as people left work and began to head home. The sun which he had watched come up this morning was still high in the sky at this point in the day, even though it was beginning its drop into the west. He realized suddenly that he'd been awake for the better part of thirty-six hours now, and he could feel it starting to catch up to him. Fortunately for him, as well as for the baby still hidden in the trunk, he had no intention of going far. Only a few miles to the east side of town and he'd be able to sleep for a bit at the house he kept for the girls and the nurse. He merged into the traffic on I-10 heading east and continued until he reached the exit for Airport Boulevard. He headed toward the airport, then turned east onto Montana Avenue.

He drove slowly along Montana, with the airport off to his left and car dealerships and fast food places on his right. He was headed toward the part of the city that was spreading east out into the desert. The little house he'd bought there was practically at the edge, with not much yet built beyond it. He'd often seen coyotes running down the streets there in the early morning. People had to be careful about letting their cats and little dogs outside unattended.

He drove until he reached Lee Trevino Drive, named after El Paso's favorite son, then turned south into the residential area. A left turn onto Edgemere, followed shortly by two quick rights onto Quintana and then

Raindance, and he was able to see the house. It wasn't much, but it served its purpose. Ranch style, white brick, with a black tile roof. Three bedrooms and a one-car garage that he now pulled into. Hardly any more land than the size of the house itself, just a gravel front yard, and a small enclosed backyard where grass died as quickly as seed was put down and which soaked up water like a dried sponge. He never went out there, but he knew from others living on the street that most of the yards were infested with fire ant nests. Parents always had to be careful that their toddlers didn't disturb a nest and then get covered with stinging bites as the angry ants swarmed. He hated El Paso.

Once in the garage, he quickly closed the door and removed the baby from its hiding place in the trunk. 'Still sleeping soundly, just like a good, little baby should,' he thought. He shut the trunk lid and headed into the house.

As soon as he was in the door, he was confronted by Anita, the nurse he employed to stay with the girls he found while they waited to deliver their babies. He'd been doing this for about six years now; at times he'd had as many as five girls here in this house at once. Anita had been with him that entire time. He looked at her now as she took the baby from him. Thin, early forties, jet black hair just starting to show streaks of gray, with the high cheekbones and flat face that reflected the Indian blood that had commingled with her Mexican ancestors. Not at all attractive, he thought sourly, which was good for him because it left her with no ambition to go elsewhere. She was from a small town in the southern part of Chihuahua, and had moved north looking for work during the sixties. Acevedo had run across her doing scut work at a small medical clinic in Juarez, and had convinced her to work for him. He'd helped her get her work visa, then moved her into this house. She never questioned the details of what he was doing with these girls as they came and departed. She was concerned only with making their time in El Paso easy and in receiving a consistent paycheck, which he made sure she always got.

"I've got to get some sleep," Acevedo said as he handed her the baby and continued past her before she could say a word. "I'll explain everything to you later. Let me sleep for a couple hours and then we'll talk. If I'm not up by six, wake me up." It was a little after four now. He would have liked to sleep the night, but he had more things to do before this day could be done.

CHAPTER 43

El Paso, Texas
Tuesday, 6 May 1975
6:01 p.m. MDT

The knocking on the door to his room woke him up. At first he couldn't remember where he was. Then it all came back as he groggily sat up and looked around. "All right, Anita, all right. I'm awake. Thanks. I'll be out in a couple minutes." He glanced around the room that he used whenever he was out here and that doubled as an office for him. Single bed, nothing on the walls, a chest of drawers and an old desk he'd bought at a flea market up toward Las Cruces which sat against the far wall with a telephone on it. A beat up Apache carpet on the floor that he'd picked up at the same flea market. 'Nothing but the best,' he thought.

Once up and dressed, he headed to the bathroom to splash some water on his face to try to clear his head. He could hear the babies crying and figured it must be dinner time. His stomach was certainly telling him it was dinner time, although he didn't plan to eat here. Although a good nurse, Anita was a horrible cook. That was the consensus of all the girls that had ever come through here, with the result that one of them eventually would at least help out with the cooking. But Anita was cooking tonight, he observed, so that meant he was going to head elsewhere. Anyway, he'd need to meet with Anderson as soon as he could to finish this.

"Where is Elena," asked Anita as she prepared a bottle of baby formula and handed it to Serena. Serena was the third girl that had been staying here, and was now the last. The other girl had delivered several days ago; he'd already paid her off and sent her home during his trip out here last week, but the baby was still here until he could get it into the hands of its new American parents. Serena was about seven months along, so he figured he'd have to be out here again sometime in July. Just the thought of El Paso in July depressed him.

"Unluckily, she's dead in Juarez," Acevedo said matter-of-factly as he sat down at the kitchen table and lit up a Marlboro. Anita and the girl both gasped. "What happened," they cried together at once. "She was here just yesterday afternoon and said she was going to stay with a friend downtown for the night."

"Well, she didn't," said Acevedo. "What she did do was sneak across the river for Cinco de Mayo and got hit by a truck. That's why I told her to stay here," he directed to Serena, "so she'd be in good hands. If she'd done what I told her, she'd still be okay." He pointed a bony, nicotine-stained finger at her. "You better not make the same mistake." Serena was a slight, timid little girl of sixteen who shrank back, cowering, as he glowered at her.

"Anyway," he said, turning back to his cigarette again, "what's done is done. At least the baby survived." He looked at the two infants, one each in the arms of Anita and Serena. "Which one is hers, anyway?" Both babies looked exactly alike as far as he could tell.

"This beautiful one right here," replied Anita as she reached for the bottle to begin feeding. Both she and Serena looked very contented, thought Acevedo. He grunted in reply, and muttered "I'm glad there's no need for me to do any of that" to himself under his breath.

He watched without interest for another moment, then reached for the phone, stubbing out the cigarette in the ashtray on the table. "Take those two into the other room while I make this call, would you? And try to keep them quiet."

The call he was making was to Anderson, an associate of his of long standing from his earliest days in medicine. Acevedo had gone to school initially at Baylor, then transferred to the University of Texas Med School in Houston once that became too hard, and finally finished up at Texas Tech in Amarillo. He did his internship at Presbyterian Hospital in Dallas, which is where he'd met Anderson. Acevedo had not had much good fortune working in hospitals through this early period, moving through several across the state. He'd always seemed to be at odds with the hospital staff, and frequently received adverse counselings about the quality of his work. Fortunately, none of this jeopardized his license as he kept moving out of the way of trouble, and he ultimately began work in his own clinic when the idea came to him that he could make more money by skirting the edge of what passed for right and wrong in the medical world than by holding to the party line. He'd settled into work in San Antonio and had not looked back. Anderson, now the hospital administrator at Eastwood Hospital in downtown El Paso, always was happy to work with Acevedo; they'd done plenty of business in the past.

Anderson answered the phone on the third ring.

"*Que paso, amigo?*" Acevedo began. He knew that Anderson would probably recognize his voice, as always, but they always began their conversations this way then reverted to English. "Acevedo," came the reply. Anderson's gravelly voice sounded as if he'd had a long day. 'Not as long as mine has been, though, my friend,' Acevedo thought to himself. "Are you back in town?"

"Yup, got in a little while ago." A slight exaggeration, but Acevedo didn't want to go into too much detail on the phone. "I need to talk to you. Privately. Preferably tonight."

"Always an emergency, with you, isn't it?" Anderson replied, chuckling. "You eaten dinner yet?"

"Was just about to head out somewhere. You have a suggestion?"

"Why don't you pick me up and we'll head out to Cattleman's?" Cattleman's was a steakhouse about 20 miles east of El Paso out in the desert. It was one of those places that dressed itself up as an old Western ranchhouse, but which had really great food. Acevedo and Anderson had been there before.

"Sounds great," said Acevedo. "I'm ready now, if you are. I'm starving." Anderson lived by himself in a new house in the southeast corner of El Paso, about a mile from Acevedo's.

"I'm definitely ready. I'll see you in a few minutes."

"I'll have the barbecue beef and ribs," said Acevedo to the waiter. Just saying it started him salivating. "And a Shiner Bock." 'You can't go wrong with beer and ribs,' he thought.

"And I'll have the Cowboy, medium rare," continued Anderson, ordering the two pound T-bone that was Cattleman's specialty. "And a Lone Star. I don't know how you can go for that dark beer," he said to Acevedo.

"Just an acquired taste, I guess."

The ride out to the ranch had taken about thirty minutes once Acevedo had picked Anderson up. They had talked about a lot of nothing during the ride, catching up on their lives. Acevedo hadn't seen Anderson in several months, even though he spoke to him fairly frequently on the phone. By the time they had arrived at the ranchhouse, the sun was setting in the west and the torchlights had been lit. 'Just like the good old days in the wild, wild west,' Acevedo chuckled to himself.

They settled into their table and began to talk in earnest as their beers arrived. Acevedo appraised Anderson as he took his first sip. About the same age as he was, late forties, but there the resemblance stopped. Where Acevedo was short and thin, Anderson was tall, about six-two, and wide, about 225 pounds. That had used to be mostly muscle, but was now turning soft and slowly migrating from his shoulders to his middle. They actually made a funny pair when they walked side by side. Anderson had also had some early troubles in the field, but had settled down after his divorce and was now well regarded. The divorce, however, had left him always short of funds, which made him always receptive to Acevedo's offers.

"I'm out here to pick up a couple more kids and take them back to San Antonio," he began. Anderson was aware of the process, having helped Acevedo get girls taken care of at the hospital in the past. He'd also passed Acevedo the names of some girls in need in the past, for which he'd been appropriately rewarded. "No trouble with one, but I need some assistance with the second."

"What do you need, some medical problem looked at?" came the bored response. Their meals arrived and they ate as they continued to talk.

"Nothing that simple, unfortunately." Acevedo proceeded to tell about the events of his day. Anderson said nothing, just chewed and drank and listened as he waited for the punch line. "What I need this time is a birth certificate."

"A birth certificate," sputtered Anderson, nearly choking on a mouthful of beef. "How do you think I can get that done without being noticed? Adjusting schedules and greasing the skids to be seen by a doctor is one thing, but how do you think I can produce a document for a baby that hasn't darkened the doors of my hospital?"

"That's why I'm willing to pay you a thousand bucks for it," replied Acevedo. Despite his objections, he knew that Anderson would help if he made the pot sweet enough. "Those documents all come through you to be verified prior to being sent to the county, don't they? Just type up one more and ship it out with the rest. I'll give you all the information you need."

"But I can't," came the response. The quiet discussion grew more intense as the two progressed through their meal, but by the time they ordered some brandy as 'dessert', they had reached an agreement. The price had gone up a little, but Acevedo was still pleased. Anderson would prepare the document in the morning, and send it out with the other birth certificates when they went to the county to be registered in the afternoon. He even agreed to alter the birth certificate of the other baby that had been born last week to indicate that its birth date was also May 5th. Acevedo knew that a Hispanic couple receiving a baby born on Cinco de Mayo would be overjoyed at their good fortune and would feel that it was worth every penny they were paying, and they were paying Acevedo a lot. Acevedo could get an official copy of both certificates within five working days, which would let the deal for Elena's baby still go down as he'd always planned. Although it had been a very long day, he was going to go home with a bigger profit despite the problems. It almost made coming to El Paso feel like it was worth it. He couldn't help but smile as he sipped the brandy and felt the burn go down to his stomach.

Once back at the house, he was asleep almost before his head hit the pillow. Even the squalling babies weren't able to disturb him.

CHAPTER 44

San Antonio, Texas
Thursday, 8 May 1975
5:12 p.m. MDT

Two days later, Acevedo was back in San Antonio. He'd left El Paso two mornings after his meeting with Anderson. He'd loaded the babies in car seats shortly after dawn, and headed out towards the rising sun with Anita in the car. He always brought her along when he returned home with a new baby so that he could drive and she could attend to it. They didn't normally take two at once, but neither he nor she felt that one more would pose a big problem. As it turned out, they didn't. They made it to San Antonio in a leisurely ten hours, stopping twice along the way, and arriving just before five o'clock. He took both Anita and the babies directly to his clinic on Ashby, where the babies were installed in the nursery and Anita in the room she used whenever she made this quick trip east with him. Tomorrow morning he'd put her on a flight back to El Paso, where she'd take a taxi back to the house on Raindance and resume her care for Serena.

The clinic that he ran was fairly small and non-descript. He didn't want that much attention, and was able to generate sufficient business for himself by word-of-mouth within the Mexican community here. His specialty was helping infertile couples; this ran the gamut from assisting with adoptions, to treating the woman with hormones and artificial insemination, to in vitro fertilization via surrogates. It was this last area that was the most lucrative for him. He had long since figured out that he could work with some couples, particularly those that were either desperate or naïve or preferably both, by 'treating' them unsuccessfully with hormones and then moving on to surrogates. Only instead of actually using a surrogate, he instead rounded up an already pregnant girl from Juarez or Laredo or somewhere else just as bad, and basically 'bought' her baby to present to the happy couple. He just never told them about that little twist, so they all believed they were receiving their biological offspring, simply from a rented womb, one which he never allowed them to get in contact with—that was one of the 'rules' he made for working with him. This is just what he'd finished now with Elena. The whole thing was lucrative because he would charge the infertile couple outrageous sums for the treatments, the surrogacy, and the birth, and pay the birth mother only a fraction of that cost. His profit margin was huge, and he was well on his way to becoming a rich man. He was very circumspect during all of this, carefully identifying couples that would appreciate his service and not ask too many questions about it. His conscience never bothered him a bit about any of this. He always slept well at night.

He was careful as well in using associates in the clinic who would also not ask too many questions. He was the only doctor in the clinic, which was okay since he deliberately chose not to handle too many couples at once. The handful of nurses and technicians that he employed were all paid well, and, happily for him, all had some sort of immigration problem that they chose not to have made public. In some cases, they were the problem, having crossed the border illegally; in some cases, the problem was with a family member. In all cases, after ending up with Acevedo, he ensured their loyalty by making a good life for them possible and by keeping their problems quiet. They all appreciated it, and he'd never had a problem with them.

Done at the clinic for the day after getting everyone settled, he headed home to his house in the Monte Vista area near the university. He'd called his wife from the clinic when he'd arrived with Anita and the babies, and she was waiting for him as he pulled into the garage. The house was a two-story, three-bedroom adobe in the typical southwestern style. It was not overly large, but was comfortable, and Acevedo always looked forward to coming home. His wife, Raquel, was about sixteen years younger than he, and they'd been married now for nearly eight years. She was a pretty girl from Austin, with dark hair and dark eyes and a quick smile, who had worked for him at the clinic until he became besotted with her. They married after they found out she was pregnant, much to the chagrin and ire of her parents, who thankfully were no longer with them, he thought. Ironically, this new wife of the fertility doctor endured a miscarriage, following which she was unable to have more children. They had both adjusted to that reality, and now worked for the day when they could retire to a big house and a good life in the rolling hill country up toward Austin. Raquel ran the clinic for him, although she was not fully aware of all that he did there. He'd already told her of the events of his trip when he'd talked to her by phone the day before, but he had not told her everything. Better that she not know all the sordid details, he thought.

"I've already called the Navarros and the Escondidas and set up appointments for them to come to the clinic tomorrow to sign all the papers and get their baby," she began without preamble as he walked through the door. "They're ecstatic, to say the least; had a million questions for me—what's the baby look like, when was it born, does it have any problems, the usual stuff. Wanted to know if it was a boy or girl, but I told them they'd have to be surprised, just like parents always have to be."

He dumped his bags, gave her a quick kiss, then gratefully accepted the beer she offered him. "Yeah, that probably won't be the case in a few years. With the stuff I've been reading about what's being developed, pretty soon parents will know without a doubt what they're having before it's born. Might even be able to pick what they want if things go the way it looks like they're going. Will take all the suspense out of it." He took a big swig, and sighed contentedly. "Nothing better than a cold beer after a long, hot car ride. Who's coming in first tomorrow?"

"I've got the Navarros in at 10, and the Escondidas in after lunch at 2. Which family does the boy belong to?"

"I'm keeping that as a surprise until tomorrow," he replied wearily. "Even for you." He'd been thinking about that very question ever since he'd looked at the baby boy and girl in El Paso. 'Maybe we'll just have to flip a coin,' he thought, then laughed to himself over that image. No, he'd already made up his mind when he first looked at the babies and figured out which one looked most like which family. No question about it, actually.

CHAPTER 45

San Antonio, Texas
Friday, 9 May 1975
9:57 a.m. MDT

The Navarros pulled up to the clinic in their old Ford a little before 10 in the morning. They'd had to restrain themselves from coming here much earlier, they'd been so happy and anxious about the news. After waiting for years, they were about to take home a baby.

Ramon Navarro was a tall, well-built man of about 45. He was dressed casually, wearing dress jeans, long-sleeve white shirt with a string tie, and Tony Lama boots. Covering the thick dark hair on his head, still with no trace of gray, was a white Stetson. He looked like the prosperous Hispanic businessman that he was.

His wife, Theresa, was about five years younger. She too was dressed casually, although instead of jeans she wore a colorful skirt over her boots. She was tall for a woman of Mexican heritage, about 5 foot 9, and thin. Her long, black hair was pulled back from her face. She easily passed for someone ten years younger.

Both Ramon and Theresa had been born in Mexico in the small town of Sabinas in Coahuila. They'd grown up as neighbors, had married as soon as they could convince their parents to give them their blessing, then had come north with so many other Mexican migrant workers in the years following World War II. They were on the tail end of that wave of illegal immigrants, and had heard all the stories, both good and bad, of those who had come before. They initially had headed up the Rio Grande valley through Mesilla and towards Las Cruces, where they worked in the dry farms of the area, becoming proficient in English in time. It was there that they first realized they were unable to have children, and also where they first decided they wanted to become American citizens. So after working illegally in New Mexico for about four years, they'd applied for work visas and were accepted into the U.S. in a legitimate status. They'd then made their way down toward Houston, where they'd settled and eventually got into the real estate market, at which Ramon had excelled. It was there that they'd become naturalized citizens ten years ago. With their parents in Mexico now dead, they felt no particular ties to the old country, and felt very attached to the new. As they prospered in Houston, they ventured down many avenues in their quest to have a baby, but all had proved unsuccessful. It was only after they had heard of Dr. Acevedo and the success he had in his clinic here in San Antonio that they'd seen a glimmer of hope. And now, after eight months of unsuccessful fertility treatments with him, followed by the nine months of waiting for the surrogate to give birth, they were about to finally get their child.

"Oh, Ramon," Theresa said, as they climbed the steps into the clinic. It was a bright, sunny day, typical of mid-May, and it made her feel like she didn't have a care in the world. "What do you think the baby will be, a boy or a girl?"

"We should find out in a little bit," he replied in a soft voice. He was excited, too, although his nature was such that he typically didn't show much emotion. Despite the three hour drive west on I-10 from Houston this morning, he didn't feel tired. "In you go," he said, holding open the door for her.

The receptionist in the clinic received them warmly and directed them down the hall to their right to Raquel's office. They'd been here several times before as they were going through the fertility hormone treatments, so they knew their way around the small building well. "We're all so happy for you," said the girl.

Once in the office, Raquel presented them with the mountain of paperwork they had to work their way through, received their final check for payment in full, then called the receptionist on the intercom, and asked her to tell Dr. Acevedo that they were ready for him. "I'm so excited I think I'm going to throw up," said Theresa. "I guess that's normal when you're having a baby," Ramon smiled back.

Just then the door opened and in came Acevedo carrying a baby. It was tightly wrapped in a blanket, and was cooing softly. Both Ramon and Theresa got to their feet.

"Congratulations," said Acevedo, smiling. "It's a boy."

Theresa started to cry softly as she reached for the little hand.

PART 4

CHAPTER 46

Washington, DC
Wednesday, 21 December 2022
10:23 a.m. EST

The Press Briefing Room was in an uproar. And for the life of her, White House Press Secretary Barb Singletary couldn't figure out what had happened. One moment things had been moving along normally, and all of a sudden it had become chaos. Reporters were shouting questions at her, shouting at each other, shouting just to be heard. The result of which was that no one could understand anything. Singletary looked to her right from the lectern in the center of the stage at White House Chief of Staff Josh Caldwell, who was leaning against the wall with his arms folded, a deep scowl on his meaty face. He motioned to her to continue. 'Yeah, right,' Singletary thought, 'and just how am I going to make that happen?'

Singletary was a very talented Press Secretary. Everyone agreed with that statement, and in general everyone thought she was doing a great job. Much better than her predecessor, the now departed and not lamented Todd Jenkins of the Thomas administration, who had been roundly detested by the entire press corps. Barb Singletary, on the other hand, was a different breed of animal. Another Texas import who arrived in the White House nearly two years ago with Ray Navarro, she was a young—mid-30s—tall, photogenic, single woman of keen intelligence who had grown up dirt poor near Nacogdoches in east Texas. Through hard work and perseverance, she had been accepted into Baylor University in Waco where she majored in journalism and never looked back. She had begun working for then-Mayor Navarro in Houston in 2015, became enthralled with him and his wife, Julia, as did so many others, and had never even considered leaving his side as his ambitions grew and were fulfilled.

Normally, her press briefings ran smoothly and efficiently, the very definition of control. But not today.

"Ladies and Gentlemen, please," she pleaded, waving her arms at the front of the small room. No larger than a moderate-size living room, the briefing room can seat forty-eight reporters in theater-style leather chairs, but more people were crammed into the room today. "Please quiet down and give me your attention and I'll try my best to answer all of your questions." As she said this, Singletary had the random thought that if things got out of hand, she could make a break for it down the discreet staircase behind her to the unused, but still structurally intact, White House swimming pool that had originally been built for FDR. 'Maybe none of them can swim and they won't be able to follow me,' she thought as she watched the continuing chaos; she had to fight to stifle an urge to laugh maniacally in the face of the uproar.

"Barb," shouted Scott Wallace, a stringer for UPI, "you can't just stand there and tell us the White House and the President think this is nothing. *The Beacon* exposé says he shouldn't even be President. How can you ignore it?"

Jamie Coryell's *Beacon* had published the story a week ago; it had immediately been picked up by the national news services and ballooned from there. *The Beacon* exposé—it was already widely referred to by this name in news accounts—alleged that President Navarro was not only not the natural born child of Ramon and Theresa Navarro, as had already been affirmed in the late Lou Stevenson's reporting, but he was not even a natural born American, coming instead from an unwed Mexican mother in the squalor that was Juarez. Whether the Navarros had been party to the deception, and whether the President himself was aware of it and had hidden his true antecedents throughout his life, was a wildfire debate now raging across America. Newspaper op-ed pages were full of opinions, TV talking heads all seemed compelled to speak of nothing else, and the bloggers and twitterers of the internet were filling the virtual airwaves with chatter. Battle lines were already being drawn and hardening.

"Scott, we're not trying to ignore it. I'm trying to talk with you about it," Singletary shouted over the din. Suddenly the bulk of Josh Caldwell loomed at her side.

"Folks," Caldwell drawled, not shouting but raising his voice to such a level that it dominated the room and caused it to quiet, "either you want to hear what Barb has to say or you don't. And if you don't, then there's no sense in continuing this briefing. This is a serious issue, and it deserves some serious discussion. We believe the President has been ambushed by these scurrilous accusations, and we want to tell our side of the story. So give Barb a chance, would you?" He glared at the room as if daring someone to challenge him.

"Governor, Barb, how can you refute these allegations when everything in *The Beacon* exposé that's been looked at so far has been verified?" asked Wallace, the first to break the silence.

Shortly after Coryell broke the story last week, swarms of investigators had been sent to Texas to look into the allegations that had been made, and no one had found anything thus far to show that Coryell's information was false. Cleverly, Coryell had decided to publish the story as a five part serial, so only the easily corroborated facts had been included thus far. In part one, he had laid out the broad outline of the allegation: that Ray Navarro had actually been born in Juarez, then was smuggled into the United States by a corrupt doctor who'd provided the baby and false papers to the Navarros to raise. And he'd hinted at what was to come, but had provided no details to support most of the accusations in part one. The second part was due out this afternoon, and *The Beacon* promised that details—although not all details—would be included; already hordes of people were waiting outside *The Beacon* office in Lambertville to get the story literally 'hot off the presses.'

"Scott," responded Singletary smoothly, "those few facts that appeared in *The Beacon* last week are not in dispute. We know that the President's parents utilized a fertility clinic in San Antonio, that they received a baby with an El Paso birth certificate, that they raised him as their own. None of that's in dispute. What is in dispute are the extrapolations that have come from those few facts. It is inconceivable to us that the chain of events *The Beacon* exposé lays out could occur."

"But we've already verified some of the names and places that story includes," persisted Wallace. "There was a Doctor Jorge Acevedo who operated a fertility clinic in San Antonio in 1975. There was a Kevin Anderson who was the administrator of Eastwood Hospital in El Paso. Records show that Acevedo owned a house in El Paso at the same time. Why shouldn't we believe what else is alleged?"

"Because they're not true," boomed Caldwell, leaning into the microphone at the lectern. "Seriously, folks, we're talking about a pot shot coming out of the blue at the President of the United States, and you want us to dignify it by turning all of our attention to it. Well, we've got other business to attend to in this government—pressing issues that must be addressed, I might add—and we simply don't have time to waste on this nonsense." He grabbed Singletary's elbow and pulled her toward the door to his right. "Come on, Barb, let's go. The briefing's over."

Caldwell and Singletary hurriedly exited the room, ignoring the cries of protest shouted in their wake as chaos once again reigned.

"Josh, I don't think that was a very wise thing to do," called out Singletary as she hustled to keep up with him as he strode through the corridors of the West Wing, heading to his office. They'd already passed her office, but she wanted to make her point before returning there to do some damage control. "They're now just going to say whatever they want because we gave them nothing. We've got to get out ahead of them on this."

"Oh, can it, Barb," Caldwell said over his shoulder as he moved along the corridor fronting the Oval Office. He stopped suddenly and wheeled to face her. "You want to get out ahead of them, then do it. Get the publisher of that Podunk newspaper on the phone and talk to him. Maybe we can find out what he's going to do next so we're not surprised again." With that, he took off again toward his office.

Singletary stared at his back as it receded down the corridor and then disappeared around a corner to the right. "You know, Josh," she said aloud, "that's not such a bad idea." She glanced at the stone-faced Secret Service agent standing at the entrance to the Oval Office, shrugged, then turned around and headed back to her office to make that call.

CHAPTER 47

Lambertville, NJ
Wednesday, 21 December 2022
4:11 p.m. EST

Jamie Coryell sat as his desk at *The Beacon*, idly staring out the window toward the falling snow. Outside his door he could hear the noise as his people worked to get the final copies of today's issue out the door. Delivery trucks were backed up to the loading docks at the rear of the building, and the final copies were being stuffed into them prior to delivery throughout the area. They'd printed up an additional fifty percent above their normal production run because last week's had sold out so quickly. The hype for this week's run promised that they'd do even better. Jamie was confident these would all sell, too.

The snow was just now beginning to cover the ground, and did not look like it was going to stop anytime soon. 'So much for weather forecasts,' he thought to himself. The forecast had been for light flurries, but this looked like it was going to be a lot more. Once again, he felt grateful that he could walk to work; even when they got a massive dump of snow he didn't have to worry about the roads. 'Hope this doesn't hold up the deliveries,' he mused, still staring out the window.

The past week had been crazy. He'd published the first part of his series in last Wednesday's paper, not imagining the notoriety it would bring. He'd actually started getting calls about it first thing Thursday morning from other local papers; these had graduated quickly to regional and finally national news outlets, all wanting to know the details about 'The Beacon exposé.' He chuckled to himself as he thought about that—'*The Beacon* exposé.' Seemed like everything in the news always had to have a name, something catchy to grab people's attention. This one had been started in Trenton, then got picked up by everybody. He chuckled again, and thought that Lou would be chuckling about it, too.

He'd thought about Lou quite a bit lately, as he put the article together and reported it out. He'd named Lou as the source for his initial information. Told the story of Lou's investigations, and the tragedy of his death. He referred to it as an accident; although he privately had his doubts, he didn't allude to them in his writings. He found himself of mixed mind about the whole thing. On the one hand, this was a great story, and one that needed to be told. As a newspaperman, he had no doubt about that. The initial investigations that Lou had started implied that the information was true, so it should be reported. But on the other hand, Jamie hated that he was being forced into it by *The Shadow's* veiled threats. He'd only spoken to the voice one other time since his initial phone call in October, and in that one Sue'd been threatened again if he didn't publish the story, so he'd agreed in order to protect her. He'd pleaded for time to do background investigation to make his articles tighter, and he'd explained his concept for serializing the story to build interest in it. While *The Shadow* agreed to that concept, liking the way it would draw attention to it, Jamie's real reason for the proposal was to give himself more time to investigate the investigation. Even though everything seemed to be checking out, he couldn't shake the feeling that something was wrong, that he was somehow being set up. And he still seethed with the thought that this story might have resulted in Lou's death. He figured that if he could draw this out over a couple of months, perhaps before the last article was published he'd know what was really true and what was not. More importantly, he might know who *The Shadow* really was. He had listed that in his mind as the most important goal for this entire process, albeit an unspoken one. He would find out who owned the voice, and would find out if he was responsible for Lou's death.

Jamie was also somewhat chagrined to find himself as much a part of the story as what he'd published. He'd fielded a continual stream of phone calls over the last several days, from all manner of people and all manner of organizations, all wanting to interview him as part of their spin on *The Beacon* exposé. Jamie couldn't decide if he liked the attention or not; it was certainly good for business, but he felt it to be a gross imposition on his privacy, as well as a distraction from where the real focus should be. 'Guess this is why celebrities detest we paparazzi,' he'd thought. Thus far he'd managed to keep things low-key, but he wasn't sure if things would stay that way as his next articles became public.

He stood up from his desk and headed for the door to go out into the main office area when his phone rang. He hesitated before picking it up, almost gun-shy about answering calls now for fear of who else would want to interview him on the other end, then decided that, for better or worse, it was just part of the job. He couldn't hide from it, he'd just have to deal with what came his way. 'Won't be in the news business long if I don't talk to people,' he thought as he snatched up the receiver on the fourth ring.

"Jamie Coryell," he answered.

"Mr. Coryell, I'm so glad I caught you. This is Barb Singletary, the White House Press Secretary. Do you have a moment to talk?"

"Sure, Ms. Singletary," he replied, impressed in spite of himself that the caliber of his phone calls had gotten right to the top. "What's on your mind?" And to himself, 'Here it comes.'

"Well, as you may imagine, I've been following your story with interest. And I'm eagerly looking forward to the next installment later today. I wondered if you could perhaps give me a little advance notice about what's in store in that."

Jamie smiled. "Oh, so you want to get some advance warning of what mischief I'll cause this week so you can stay a step ahead of your protégés in the press corps. Is that it?"

"Well," she responded, smiling back through the phone, "I might not have put it exactly that way, but you seem to have gotten right to the heart of the matter. Yes; I want to stay a step ahead. Can you help me out?"

"I'd be happy to, although I don't know what exactly I can tell you. My paper is being delivered around as we speak, so it will become common knowledge pretty soon." He thought a moment. "I could just send you a copy of the article by e-mail. That way you'd have it verbatim right away, and could begin preparing your defense." He laughed softly. "What do you think?"

"Mr. Coryell, that would be great," Singletary responded.

"Please call me Jamie," he interjected. "Mr. Coryell makes me feel very anxious."

"Okay—Jamie. Thanks. I'm Barb."

"Barb. Great. What else might I do for you?"

"Well—Jamie—I would really like to speak with you face to face about this series. As you might imagine, we here have some serious concerns about the veracity of the allegations you're making, and I'd like to better understand how you've determined them to be true. Perhaps you've interpreted things the wrong way—you know, connected the dots but crossed lines to do it. Would you be amenable to meeting me to discuss things?"

Jamie wasn't sure how to respond. He was reluctant to show his hand completely, but at the same time didn't want to appear that he had something to hide. "I guess there'd be no harm in that," he said carefully. "But let's be clear. I'm going to publish what I believe to be true, whether you agree with me or not. And I'll tell you right now—I'm confident that what I've got is true. Fair enough?"

"Fair enough," Singletary answered. "How would it work for you if I came up to your office on Friday. I think that would be much less conspicuous than you coming here. You are becoming sort of a celebrity, you know." Here he heard the smile again. "Plus I'd like to see your paper. I studied journalism in college, but have never actually worked at a paper anywhere."

"Sounds good to me," Coryell replied. "Why don't you plan to get here about eleven, and we can talk and have lunch someplace."

"Okay, eleven it is. Thank you very much, and thanks for the article when you send it. I'll look forward to reading it, and look forward to meeting you Friday. Have a good day."

"You, too, Barb. Goodbye."

He replaced the receiver in its cradle, then walked out into the outer office. Alice Metzger was directing things like a martinet, making sure everything got done and got done right. 'No need for me to be here,' he thought. He walked over to Alice and tapped her shoulder.

"Alice, I'm going to head out. Believe it or not, I just got a call from the White House. The Press Secretary is going to come up here Friday morning to talk to me and see the paper." He smiled and shrugged, as if to say 'Can you believe this?'

Alice was momentarily stunned speechless. Finally she stammered, "The White House called here? Are you kidding me?" She was hopping from one foot to the other like a kid in a candy store trying to make up her mind about what to pick.

"Yep," he said. He could feel a surge of pride welling up in him, despite his efforts to remain low-key and humble; he hoped it wasn't too obvious. "Guess we're in the big time now, huh?"

"I guess so," she grinned. "You better head out and get rested up so you're ready."

"It is two days away, you know," he said, emphasizing the 'is.'

"Take tomorrow off, too, then."

"Well, I'll think about it, but probably not. You sure you don't need me here now?"

"No, Jamie. No problems here. I've got it under control. See you tomorrow." She turned to shout a command to one of the clerks across the room. Then back at him, "And congratulations."

"Thanks. See you tomorrow then." He walked back into his office, grabbed his coat and hat, pulled on his gloves, and went out the back door of the building into the snow. It showed no sign of slacking up. 'Looks like it'll be a white Christmas for a change this year,' he thought as he began trudging toward home through the deepening accumulation.

CHAPTER 48

Washington, DC
Wednesday, 21 December 2022
8:28 p.m. EST

"What do you think, Josh?" President Navarro asked his Chief of Staff, watching yet another analysis of his political life being conducted by a panel on cable news. They were sitting in the President's private study off of the Oval Office. This small room, typically used by presidents as an inner sanctum of sorts where they could escape the public eye and the hustle and bustle of the White House, held only a desk, two overstuffed chairs, and a television. Caldwell occupied one chair, while the President was in his wheelchair at the desk.

"Nothing good, sir," responded Caldwell, scowling at the TV. The general tenor of the broadcasts on every station had been negative all day. They had actually been that way for the last several days, ever since that paper in New Jersey broke the story, and they were getting progressively worse. Some were only mildly critical at this point, merely suggesting that the President explain his side of the story; others were down-right hostile, already openly calling for his resignation. "We're gonna have to address this thing quickly or we'll lose control of it. I already told Barb to talk to the publisher of this paper to find out what's coming next."

"Good thinking." He paused, considering. "Maybe she should go up there to talk to him face to face. Sometimes that works better." Navarro continued to stare at the screen, absent-mindedly massaging his weaker left hand with his right. It was a mannerism that he'd developed once he'd returned to the White House from the hospital, and one which became more pronounced when he was under stress. Caldwell found it somewhat disconcerting to see him doing it now.

"Actually that's what she's planning to do. She's going up there Friday morning to meet him. Try to get on his good side to get us a little advance notice of what's coming."

"Maybe you should go with her," the President said, looking over at Caldwell, seated in the overstuffed chair placed against the wall to his right.

"No, sir, not just yet, I don't think," Caldwell replied. "Let's let Barb take her shot first and see how it goes. Maybe I can visit him sometime in the future if it looks like he needs a little push."

"Okay, I'll be patient." Navarro returned his gaze to the screen, then, seeming to become suddenly agitated, snapped it off with the remote and pivoted his chair to face Caldwell, saying sharply, "But not too long. These are blatant lies that they're spreading about me, and I don't intend to put up with it. Julia doesn't want me to, either." He reached up with his right hand to squeeze his forehead, as Caldwell glanced over at him apprehensively. "Got a little headache coming on," he said, now more calmly. "Time for my next pill, I guess. Come on, Josh, let's head back over to the residence. You can drive this time," he said, motioning with his head toward the handles at the back of the wheelchair.

"Fine, sir," said Caldwell soothingly. "You can get a good night's rest and we'll deal with this tomorrow." He slipped on his coat and cap, gave the President a cap, and helped him get a lap blanket situated around his body and right leg.

They then began the slow roll through the Oval Office, out onto the West Colonnade and around the Rose Garden, and on toward the mansion, with Navarro talking quietly to Julia while Caldwell tried not to listen.

CHAPTER 49

Washington, DC
Thursday, 22 December 2022
7:04 p.m. EST

"Good evening, ladies and gentlemen," intoned Ken Ingalls, the veteran CNN political analyst. "Our top story this evening—new revelations concerning the origins of President Ramon Navarro. In the second part of a continuing exposé, more details were made public late yesterday regarding the alleged birth of the President to an unwed mother in a Mexican hospital. Here to discuss the legal ramifications of this astounding allegation is Professor Matthew Bellis, a legal expert on constitutional law from Georgetown University. Dr. Bellis, good evening and welcome. Tell us, what does this say about President Navarro's claim to his office?"

"It says quite a bit actually, Ken," began Bellis. He was a small man in his mid-sixties, balding with a full grey beard that he kept closely trimmed; the bow tie that was his trademark feature at the university completed his collegial appearance. "The Constitution requires, in Section 1 of Article 2, that the President be a 'natural born citizen'; that is, that he or she be a citizen who has been physically born within the borders of the United States. Now, the citizen part of that requirement is fairly straight-forward. The so-called 'Citizenship Clause' of the 14th Amendment to the Constitution states that 'All persons born or naturalized in the United States, and subject to the jurisdiction thereof, are citizens of the United States and of the State wherein they reside.' So, in the case of President Navarro, if we presume he was born in El Paso to anyone, not necessarily to Ramon and Theresa Navarro as had been heretofore supposed, but still physically born there, then he is therefore a citizen. No problem there. But the 'natural born' part is a little trickier to define. In general, it has been held in legal circles—although never definitively tested in the court system—that if a child is born abroad to American parents, that child is considered to be a 'natural born' citizen, and hence eligible to become president. This was the situation that existed when John McCain, who was born on a U.S. base in Panama to American parents, ran for President in 2008; he was considered to be 'natural born' and therefore eligible to run for the office. But a child born abroad to foreign nationals, and subsequently brought into the United States and adopted by U.S. citizens, is not considered 'natural born.' They can become a citizen through the naturalization process, but they will never be eligible for the presidency. There have actually been several notable, outstanding public servants who fit into this category, former Secretary of State Henry Kissinger and former California Governor Arnold Schwarzeneggar, to name just two. The bottom line here is, if these allegations regarding President Navarro's birth are true, and he was born to a Mexican mother in Mexico, he is simply not eligible to be president and should not be in office."

"You mean to say that Ray Navarro cannot serve, and should not be serving as president if these reports are correct?" asked Ingalls.

"That's precisely the case," replied Bellis. "Furthermore, any actions that he's taken while illegitimately serving as president would be considered invalid. Every law he's signed, every executive order he's issued, every appointment he's made, would be faulty."

"And what a mess that would be," said Ingalls, shaking his head. "It boggles the mind just to think about the impact of what you've just said. Alright, folks. We're going to cut away briefly to a commercial, then be back to talk more with Dr. Matthew Bellis about the ramifications for Ray Navarro's presidency if the recent allegations brought to light regarding his birth prove to be true. Stay with us."

Josh Caldwell snapped off the television he'd been watching in his West Wing office and leaned back in his chair, lacing his fingers behind his head. The unease he had regarding this story was growing with each passing day, and he was ever one to trust his feelings in situations like this. He knew—didn't just think there was a chance, or have an inkling about what was to come—he knew, deep down in his soul, that this was going to explode out of control unless something was done soon to tamp it down. He could already sense the disquiet among some members of the Cabinet and some members of Congress. 'They're all ready to bolt like rabbits,' he thought, disgustedly. 'And they'll turn on Ray in a heartbeat if they think this is going to hurt him.' He snorted in derision at the thought of them.

"Guess I'll just have to deal with this myself," he said aloud, reaching for the phone.

Across town, another television snapped off. Senator Fred Moscone had been watching the news alone. His wife, the Vice President, was on a trip to Chicago at the moment, and would not return to Washington until Sunday. He was sure she'd also been watching the news, something she rarely missed. He could only imagine what her reaction to it would be.

'This keeps getting better and better,' he thought, raising the glass of *Chianti* to his lips. He'd sent the staff home after they'd fixed his dinner, a plate of veal piccata with a Portobello risotto, and was now eating it from a small tray table in the living room. 'Let's see what Franny thinks we should do about all this,' he thought, as he put down his glass and reached for the phone.

CHAPTER 50

Lambertville, NJ
Friday, 23 December 2022
10:53 a.m. EST

The black Chevy Suburban with the tinted windows pulled into Lambertville just before eleven, coming up River Road from the south. The driver headed straight into town and turned left at the first traffic light he came to—one of only three in town, all in a row—and started down Bridge Street toward *The Beacon* office. The car and its occupants had made good time driving north from DC, taking just under three hours to do it. They'd ridden on I-95 the whole way until they crossed the Delaware into New Jersey, when they'd been forced to turn off to pick up River Road. Even the weather, which had been predicted to be ugly like earlier in the week, had cooperated, and a bright sun shone in the clear blue sky as they pulled into the parking lot. Snow was piled high around the edges of the lot, which had been plowed clear.

"Thanks, Jim," Caldwell said to the driver, who also doubled as the Chief of Staff's bodyguard. "We'll be inside for probably an hour, then we're going to eat lunch somewhere around here. You can wait with the car or walk around if you want—just stay with the phone." Not waiting for a response, he opened the rear door where he'd been working as they drove north and clambered out of the big vehicle. "Come on, Barb, let's go give the man our surprise."

Barb Singletary grimaced involuntarily at the look that crossed Caldwell's face as he spoke. He had informed her on the phone last night that he intended to come with her, unannounced, to meet Coryell. She hadn't liked the idea then, and still didn't like it now, but hadn't been able to change his mind. 'I hope this goes well,' she thought doubtfully, exiting out of the car from the opposite side. They both climbed the three steps to the front door of the office and went inside.

The office was practically deserted. Not surprising for the Friday before Christmas they both thought, although neither voiced the sentiment. They saw only a single woman working at a battered desk toward the rear of the room, and they headed her way.

Alice spoke to them before they reached her. "Be with you in just a sec," she said. "Just gotta finish this entry before I lose my train of thought." She scribbled a few more notes at various places in a sheaf of papers that she seemed to be speed-reading, then looked up to them expectantly.

"Good morning," began Singletary. "We're here to see Mr. Coryell. We have an appointment."

Alice recognized both visitors, but stifled any urge to react to the unexpected presence of Caldwell. "Well, I know he's expecting one visitor," she said slowly, looking closely at them and cocking her head to one side, moving her gaze from one to the other, "but I guess he won't care if you brought a friend." She let that comment hang in the air for a moment, then said, "Let's find out." She hopped up from her chair and knocked on a door to her right rear, and called in a sing-song voice, "Jamie, your appointment is here."

"Thanks, Alice," he answered from inside the office, then appeared in the doorway and stopped abruptly when he saw more than one person. He recovered quickly. "Well, you must be Barb," he shook her hand, smiling, "and you, sir, are clearly not. But you're most welcome anyway, Governor." He extended his hand toward Caldwell, smile still in place. Alice, seated back at her desk, and was watching the exchange with a bemused look on her face.

Caldwell laughed at being found out so easily, and because his uninvited presence had had no apparent disconcerting effect on Coryell. Jamie noted that Singletary looked uneasy, though. 'So, you're going to double-team me,' he thought, then said, "Please come inside and we'll talk a little before lunch."

"I see you don't rattle very easily," Caldwell remarked as they entered the office. He looked around the small office with interest, glancing at the framed headlines from old *Beacon* issues on the walls, and the items occupying Jamie's cluttered desk. He believed you could tell quite a bit about a man by the order in which he kept his desk; he was not impressed by Jamie's at first glance.

Jamie was removing a pile of folders from a chair so that they'd all be able to sit; he'd only cleaned up enough space for a single guest. "No, sir," he replied to Caldwell's remark. "I try not to, but I'm not always successful, I'll be the first to admit. There, that should do it,"—he indicated the two vacant chairs for them, while he moved back to sit at his desk—"please sit down." Once they were settled, he opened with "How was the drive up?"

"Not bad at all," Singletary responded. "We made great time and had no problems. This is a great little operation you've got going here, Jamie. I'm impressed. I hope we can get a quick tour before we leave." She glanced around the room as she spoke.

"Thanks, we try to do our best. And I'll be happy to show you around." He smiled again; he felt she was being sincere with her comment. Caldwell, on the other hand, kept his focus squarely on Jamie, and did not appear nearly as appreciative. "But you've come a long way to talk about important things, so why don't we begin. I don't want you to feel I've wasted your time on what must surely be a busy weekend for you."

"That's very kind of you, thanks," said Singletary. "Okay, I'll just dive right in. Jamie, we're concerned with the series of articles you're writing about the President. You've certainly got every right to print them"—here Caldwell fidgeted in his seat as if he was going to make a comment, but he remained silent—"but you must admit that they have the very great potential to cause significant problems. Our concern is two-fold: first, we feel we're being blindsided by them, and second, we're confident that, despite what you may think, they are simply not true. What do you think of that?"

"Barb, believe me that I can appreciate your concerns. If I were in your positions,"—here he extended his hands and arms toward the both—"I would probably feel the same way. So I appreciate the visit today so that we can talk through this one on one, rather than do a lot of name-calling back and forth in public." Caldwell again stirred, but again remained silent and watching. "Let me say that I truly believe that the information I've obtained is accurate. I have attempted to verify it, and although I'll be the first to admit that I have not been able to do so for each and every item, for each item that I have looked into I've come away convinced of its accuracy. So I'm extrapolating somewhat, but I think it's reasonable to do so."

"Mr. Coryell—Jamie, if I may"—here Coryell nodded to indicate that he'd take no offense if Caldwell used his given name—"that is precisely the issue. You're printing things that are perceived by the public at large to be facts, without including any disclaimers to the contrary. Which puts the President in the position of having to defend himself against things which we are equally confident are untrue." Caldwell could feel his anger rising as he spoke to the smug journalist who stared back at him so complacently, and had to will himself to keep it in check as he continued. "Against half-truths and innuendo, so to speak. Surely you can see the dilemma."

They talked back and forth for nearly an hour, Coryell defending himself and his paper, with Caldwell and Singletary playing a form of good cop, bad cop to try to convince him to relent. By the end of the hour, Coryell had not budged from his position that he could and should continue with his series of articles, but had yielded somewhat by agreeing to provide Singletary with a copy of the investigative report that had been prepared by the Trova Agency. They ended their discussion, Jamie gave them a quick tour of the premises, then they were all ready for lunch.

Jamie led them across the street to the Lambertville Station, where he'd reserved a table. His reservation had been for two, but he knew that adding a third chair and place setting would not cause any problem. The Station was the refurbished train station that had once serviced Lambertville, although it had not been used for that purpose for over seventy years. It had been renovated in the eighties and placed into business both as an inn and restaurant. Jamie often went there for lunch when he had business to conduct.

They had an enjoyable meal, filled with good food and small talk. Singletary ate lightly, ordering a Cobb salad, while Caldwell opted for a Black Angus burger and Coryell a Philly cheesesteak. They talked about the weather, about preparations for Christmas, about life in Washington, about everything it seemed but the issue at hand. If they were recognized by any patrons of the restaurant, no one displayed the poor taste to show it. By the end of the meal, Jamie had to admit to himself that they were both good company. Caldwell even picked up the tab.

"I've had a very enjoyable visit," Jamie said sincerely as they returned to the Suburban in *The Beacon's* lot across Bridge Street. Jim, still in place by the driver's door, watched Jamie carefully as they approached. Singletary wondered idly if he'd been there the entire time, or if he'd also gotten a bite to eat somewhere; there was no way to tell. "Thanks for coming such a long way to talk," Coryell continued.

"It was a pleasure," Singletary replied. She found that she'd also enjoyed the visit very much, had been intrigued by *The Beacon's* small operation, and had found Jamie to be very likeable as well. "I'll look forward to getting the report from you," she said, reminding him of his commitment to provide her with a copy of the Trova report.

"Yes, don't forget that," Caldwell added, looking intently into Coryell's eyes. He had not enjoyed the visit as much as Singletary, and still perceived

Coryell as a threat to the President. "That's very important to us. And try to be more circumspect in what you write so that things don't get stirred up for no good reason. Things can sometimes spin out of control before you know it" he said, seemingly in warning. He stuck out a hand, but did not accompany it with a smile. "Pleasure meeting you, Jamie. You take care now."

"I always do, Governor," he replied carefully, a knot suddenly forming in his stomach at Caldwell's words, the thought suddenly coming unbidden to his mind that perhaps Caldwell was indeed *The Shadow* as Lou had feared. "It was a pleasure meeting you, too. And you as well, Barb," he said, extending his hand warily towards hers. "I'll put a copy of the report in the mail today."

As he watched the black car turn left out of the parking lot and head up Bridge Street into town to pick up River Road again, he found himself ill at ease and wondered if he had made a good decision, or if he had just signed a deal with the devil.

CHAPTER 51

Washington, DC
Saturday, 24 December 2022
10:21 p.m. EST

President Navarro sat in his wheelchair staring into the fire, listening to a CD of Christmas carols playing over the sound system. He sat in the Telegraph Room, or the Lincoln Sitting Room as it was sometimes called, which had become his favorite room in the mansion. Originally one of the set of executive offices used by the President in the White House proper before the construction of the West Wing in 1902, the room had been refurbished in a Victorian style during the Clinton years when it served primarily as a sitting room for the famous bedroom next door. Navarro had found himself gravitating to it more and more often in the evenings, particularly now that winter had arrived, so that he could sit before the roaring fire and either work or, more frequently, simply listen to music while he sipped a brandy. Previously a teetotaler, since his return to the White House he had fallen into the habit of having a nightcap in the evenings. Julia had enjoyed reading in this room, and he often felt her presence here; he knew she would understand about his drink.

This evening he was most definitely not working. He had hosted several engagements during the day—a group of Girl Scouts, a group of handicapped children, a group of wounded soldiers—and was worn out. His head hurt, his missing leg ached, and he didn't want to see anyone else. The only one he wanted to see was Julia, and that he couldn't do.

He had thought of going to Camp David tonight once his afternoon engagements had finished, but had decided against it. He and Julia had spent last Christmas Eve there, and he didn't think he could face the memories alone, nor did he want to face them with anyone else. He'd go there some other time, to enjoy the quiet and solitude and brisk mountain air, but not now. Now he would spend the holiday here, alone with his thoughts.

Earlier in the day he had talked with Caldwell about the Trova report that the publisher up in New Jersey had sent to Singletary. He had yet to read it— he would take it with him to Maryland tomorrow and read it while there—but Caldwell had, examining it with a fine-toothed comb, and he was clearly worried about what he'd read.

"Sir, I don't for a moment believe a word of this," Caldwell had said, "but we've got to address it. Just because it's in print, millions will simply assume it's true. Your credibility will be forfeit, and your ability to get things accomplished will become nil." He paused, and had looked at Navarro with concern on his face. Carefully, he'd asked, "From things your parents may have said, is there any of this that rings true at all?"

Navarro had bristled at this, but held his temper. "Josh, other than what is already well known about my birth, I had not heard a word of this until last week when the story came out. I'm confident my parents hid nothing from me. It's simply not true. It can't be." They'd been sitting again in the study off of the Oval Office, and Navarro had glared balefully at Caldwell from his wheelchair at the desk.

"Sir, that's good enough for me. I'll get some folks I know down in Texas to look into this, very discreetly, so that we can head some of this off now that we know what's coming next." He'd been leafing through a sheaf of papers in a briefing folder, and continued, "At least your popularity's still holding up. Despite all the negative press, you're still sitting at over 62%. And your strength in the southwest has even risen a little. The people clearly don't believe this stuff. They are still supporting you wholeheartedly."

Navarro had nodded, and said glumly, "Yeah. That's a good thing, I guess." He'd begun massaging the left hand again unconsciously, although when he'd noticed Caldwell watching him, he'd stopped. "Do you think this Coryell guy is on the level? I mean, do you think this report is really all he's got, or is there more he didn't tell you about?"

Caldwell had said he thought this was it, but that he'd have some folks keep an eye on him. Navarro had not asked what that meant.

'I don't care what Josh does,' he thought now, returning to the present, as the music shifted into a Bach fugue. 'But he'll take care of things for me.' He massaged his hand as he drifted with the music. Suddenly he knew that Julia was there with him, and he smiled. "I've been waiting for you," he said aloud to the empty room, then began to tell her about his troubles.

CHAPTER 52

New Hope, PA
Saturday, 24 December 2022
10:23 p.m. EST

Up north, at about the same time, Jamie and Sue had just finished a late dinner at the Logan Inn in New Hope. Originally established as a tavern in 1722, the Logan is the oldest continuously operated inn in the county, and was one of their favorite places to go for a fancy, romantic dinner. They'd dined tonight at a table for two in the paneled bar, with lights low and soft music, festive in its holiday decorations. They had both enjoyed the snapper turtle soup to begin the meal, then Sue had a veal sorrentino while Jamie enjoyed a New York strip steak *au poivre*. Both were completely stuffed by the end of the meal and decided to forego dessert. They were now relaxing at the table with an after-dinner espresso.

Sue had been up in New York at an art exhibit the day before, so Jamie had recounted his visit with Caldwell and Singletary to her during the meal. While Jamie's take on the visit had been positive, Sue was much more cautious when she heard it. "Be careful of him," she said, speaking of Caldwell. "I'm not necessarily in tune with my parents' sentiments, but I know that they detest the man. Distrust him. They think he'll do anything to protect his boss."

"I didn't get such an extreme impression of him," Jamie replied "but he can make you uneasy. Very intense. Singletary, on the other hand, was a whole different story—very likeable." He took a cautious sip from his drink. "I just hope I made the right decision in giving them the report."

"Very likeable, huh?" Sue said, reaching over to punch his shoulder. "That's what you thought of her? I guess I better not leave town too often."

Jamie laughed. "Yeah, I'm a hot commodity. But seriously, what do you think? Think I should have spilled the beans like that by giving them the report?"

"I don't know, Jamie," Sue said, concern returning to her face. "You said you had an anxious feeling about doing it. Sometimes it's best to follow your first instinct. If you're concerned about it, you'll have to be careful about what comes next."

"Well, I've been thinking about that, actually. Here's what I figure." He sat up straight in his chair and leaned toward her across the candlelit table. "They've got the report, so their attention will be focused on that. They'll check out the facts, point out the weak spots, stuff like that. But I think they won't find much. I think the report will hold up. Want to know why?"

Sue watched him with some amusement. He rarely became overly excited about a subject, but when he did, his eyes twinkled and he acted like a little kid with a secret. With a wry smile on her face, she said quietly, "Tell me why."

"Because I think the report was produced to be perfect. I think the Trova gang fixed it so that all the facts line up if anybody wants to check them. Want to know why?"

Still smiling, she said again, "Tell me why."

"Because I think that it's really not true, and *The Shadow* is somehow using me, just like he used Lou, to discredit Navarro. Even though Lou had used Trova before for some work, I think they're dirty. I think that while Caldwell and Singletary get the facts of the report checked out, I should work on looking into the Trova Agency. And I bet I'll find some dirty laundry when I do."

"And how do you propose to do that?" Sue asked.

"By taking a trip down to Texas and nosing around a little. I've got some friends there who'll help out." He leaned back in his chair. "What do you think?"

"I think it won't work. Wait, wait," she said quickly, seeing his crestfallen face, "not because it's not a good idea, but because you can't do it. Everybody's watching you. You're famous now." They both laughed. "Well you are, sort of. You have to admit, that you're getting plenty of attention now, and if you mysteriously disappear into the wilds of Texas, somebody might notice."

Jamie thought silently. "I suppose you're right," he said finally. "I hate, though, to just turn this over to somebody else. The more people that get involved directly, the more things are likely to leak out." He looked at her, to see her smiling back at him. "What are you smiling about?"

"Well, I think that maybe I should go down there to check things out for you. Want to know why?"

He chuckled. "Tell me why."

"Because nobody will miss me, and I won't leak things to anybody. You can trust me. What do you think?"

Jamie stared silently at her across the table, mulling her amazing proposition over in his mind. Could he take her up on the offer? He could certainly rely on her; if anything, he'd come to realize that Sue was extraordinarily clever about how to do unusual things, and even more tenacious about getting them done. He wasn't sure that she'd be able to uncover whatever there might be to uncover about Trova, but then again she might. And he could continue to probe from this end at the same time. But would it put her at risk? To a certain extent, she already was at risk. In each conversation he had with *The Shadow*, the voice never failed to threaten her if he didn't comply with his demands. He more and more often thought that perhaps he should reconsider and tell her about the threats, urge her to ask for Secret Service protection. But he knew in his heart that wouldn't be acceptable to her, so he never raised the issue. But should he enlist her aid now and up the ante? Certainly two are better than one, and as she said, he knew he could trust her implicitly. He made up his mind.

"Okay, Dr. Watson," he said, referring to her by the name of Sherlock Holmes' long-suffering companion, "you're on. Let's figure out how to do this."

They signaled for their check, paid the bill, and left the Logan to walk down the snowy and icy street to Sue's apartment, where they spent the next several hours figuring out exactly what they would do. By the time they'd finished, Christmas Eve had turned into Christmas morning.

CHAPTER 53

Washington, DC
Wednesday, 28 December 2022
10:23 a.m. EST

Washington had come back to life following the Christmas holiday, and even though Congress was not in session and most government offices were on a reduced holiday schedule, the chatter from the many varied sources that constantly filled the airwaves now grew to dominate the news media in this period of relative inactivity in the capital. Much of that chatter still focused on the continuing story of *The Beacon* exposé, and much hay was being made anticipating what the next installment would reveal. Coryell had indicated in his previous publication last week that the third part would not be published until after the New Year—it was his way to gain a little more time for himself—so the news tended to focus its attentions on last week's publication, slicing and dicing it every which way, and speculating *ad nauseum* about the meaning of it all.

It was notable that media opinions trended in a certain direction depending on what market they were in. Media outlets, whether print, television, or internet, that originated in the Northeast and Midwest—around the New York-Washington and Chicago metro markets—generally were more hostile and condemning of the President. Several speculated openly that he and his parents had known of his illegitimate birth all along, and that he had deliberately hidden that information when he ran for election two years earlier. Media outlets that originated in the Southwest and South—those centered around the L.A., Houston, and Miami markets—tended to be more supportive, many going so far as to say, in essence, 'so what.' It all boiled down to demographics. Where there were significant Hispanic populations, the President still enjoyed considerable support regardless of what any investigation showed. Where Hispanics were not populous, the President was being vilified.

Feelings within Congress were following party affiliations for the moment, although some cracks were beginning to appear. Republicans were calling, loudly and stridently, for an independent investigation by a special prosecutor to look into the allegations put forward in *The Beacon* exposé. Democrats were pledging support for the President and disbelief of the allegations leveled against him, but some murmuring had begun to arise suggesting that an official look into the issue might be warranted.

Interestingly, throughout this entire period of political speculation, popular support for President Navarro continued to remain high. In fact, recent polls showed a trend—weak, admittedly—that his support was actually increasing. This fact maddened the media political analysts, who could not use a report of negative public opinion to support their particular positions. All agreed, though, that things sat on a knife's edge, and it would not take much to start an avalanche rolling downhill.

CHAPTER 54

Washington, DC
Tuesday, 3 January 2023
10:23 a.m. EST
The avalanche began slowly.

On the first workday after the New Year's holiday weekend, when most people were still bleary-eyed and struggling to get back to work, the 118th Congress convened and had its newest members sworn into office. That afternoon, once the Senate was gaveled to order by the President of the Senate—Fran Kerrigan, Vice President of the United States—and a quorum established, Senator Fred Moscone took to the floor of the Senate Chamber and, as a first order of business, called for the appointment of a Special Prosecutor to investigate the allegations regarding Ramon Navarro's eligibility to serve as President of the United States.

Pandemonium ensued. Republicans cheered for the unexpected motion, while Democrats shouted back. Practically everyone in the chamber was on their feet. Of the 33 Senators who were beginning new terms in the 118th Congress, 26 were incumbents returning to office, while 7 new Senators were joining the body on this day. The seven newest Senators who had just been sworn in now stood with mouths agape as they witnessed a memorable first session. The President of the Senate, Fran Kerrigan, presiding over the body on this day, banged her gavel over and over again trying to restore order. Ultimately successful, she proceeded to verbally chastise the entire body for its conduct, threatened all with punishments verging on bodily harm if anything like it ever happened again while she was at the dais, then, to the surprise of none, returned the floor to her husband who had remained patiently at his position at the front of the body while waiting for order to be restored. With the ability to speak once again, he resumed his speech.

"My fellow Senators,' he began, his booming voice echoing through the chamber, "we simply cannot allow these allegations to go unopposed. They must be examined, and the examination must be one which transcends party politics. This cannot be a partisan action. If it is, we fail in our responsibilities to the people." He paused here to look around the room, noticing he had the attention of most, and the interest of all. Placing a solemn look on his face, he resumed. "I, for one, want to believe these allegations are untrue. I, for one, believe in the President and offer him my full support. But we must know, and the country must know, without a doubt, what is the truth."

He continued for several more minutes, exhorting his colleagues to support an investigation, working to convince them that it was necessary and imperative that it be done quickly. Concluding, he stood by as the President of the Senate called for what was a successful voice vote on his motion, and inwardly smiled to himself as she directed that the senator's recommendation be sent to the Permanent Subcommittee for Investigations for consideration, with a report to be sent back to the full body at the subcommittee's earliest convenience.

Looking neither right nor left, with the solemn look still on his face, Senator Moscone returned to his seat on the left side of the chamber, very pleased with his day's work.

CHAPTER 55

Washington, DC
Thursday, 5 January 2023
3:41 p.m. EST

The avalanche gained momentum over the next two days.

On Wednesday, the third installment of *The Beacon* exposé had been printed by Jamie Coryell. This portion identified names and places in Mexico; as with the previous two pieces, it created another frenzy among the talking heads of the national media, who each seemed intent on outdoing their competitors with the depth of their analysis and the seriousness of the inferences they could draw. Wild accusations now started to be bantered about; conspiracy theories were proposed, each more complex than the last. More voices rose in Congress supporting Senator Moscone's call for an independent investigation into the matter, and more voices rose across the country, both supporting and condemning the President.

Inevitably, several lawsuits were filed at various places across the nation seeking an injunction on Ray Navarro's continued ability to serve as President. Most of these were dismissed for one reason or another after filing; however, in a complaint filed in the U.S. District Court for the Virginia Eastern District, the judge ruled on Thursday just after noon in favor of the complainant, and ordered that President Navarro cease to execute the office of President of the United States forthwith until his eligibility for the office could be ascertained. Immediately, the government appealed the ruling to the 4th Circuit Court of Appeals in Richmond, which two hours later issued a stay of the order of the district judge based on the argument that Ramon Navarro's eligibility had been certified by the Texas Secretary of State when his El Paso birth certificate had been authenticated prior to his election. Until such time as that was proven fraudulent, the Circuit Court declared Navarro still to be President and legally fit to exercise his office.

The immediate effect of the district court ruling, and its subsequent abeyance by the circuit court, was to harden the battle lines that were forming across the country.

No one expected that the fight would end there.

CHAPTER 56

Washington, DC
Thursday, 5 January 2023
6:17 p.m. EST

"Mister President," Barb Singletary began tentatively, "I don't believe that's a very prudent course of action."

The President, his Press Secretary, and his Chief of Staff were eating a light 'working dinner' in the Oval Office Dining Room of soup and grilled cheese sandwiches. President Navarro had grown into the custom of beginning his mornings in this room, just down a small corridor from the Oval Office, receiving his daily security briefing from the National Security Advisor, Ollie Holcombe, while he ate his breakfast. He rarely remained in the West Wing to eat his dinner in this room. The events of this day, however, specifically the judicial rulings that had been issued earlier, had caused the President to huddle with these two advisors so that Singletary could issue a detailed statement, a rebuttal actually, later that evening to the press corps.

"And why shouldn't I say that, Barb" Navarro replied in a low, even voice. The President's temper recently had lain just below the surface, and his staff had begun to tread warily around him. He had just indicated to Singletary that he wanted a blunt statement issued, one which said he had been duly and properly elected to office, and no judge was just going to tell him to leave. "Judges don't rule here. Or at least they shouldn't. They should just judge in accordance with the body of law, and not bend it to suit their whim or the whims of the media and the polls." His voice began to rise slightly as he spoke. "Was I, or was I not, certified as eligible for election by Texas two years ago?"

"Yes, sir, you were," she answered contritely.

"And was I, or was I not, duly elected?"

"You were. Yes."

"Then that means that the only way I can be removed from office is by impeachment, if I've committed a high crime or misdemeanor—which I have not—or by virtue of a disability—which the Cabinet has concurred I do not have, despite my injuries. That judge needs to be put in his place." He banged his fist on the table to emphasize his point, rattling the china and silverware.

"Mister President," Caldwell spoke up quickly. "I think all Barb is saying is that we may not want to be quite so confrontational. The issue has been put to rest for the time being. I think we should let it lie where it is and not wave a red flag at the media and goad them into charging at it."

Navarro was silent, mulling over this advice while he idly swirled his soupspoon in the bowl before him. He had been furious earlier in the afternoon when the district court ruling had been announced. It had taken all of Caldwell's power of persuasion to calm him down and get him not to react until the appeal was filed and heard. Navarro had been pacified somewhat by the circuit court's more favorable ruling, but still felt he was being attacked unjustly solely because of an unsubstantiated story that had appeared out of nowhere in the press. That antagonism was rising again in him as he thought over his options.

"Josh, Barb," he said more quietly, having visibly calmed himself with several deep breaths. "I appreciate your advice. Phrase it however you think will be best. But I want the statement to make the following points, and to make them emphatically. One, that I am the legitimate president, having been duly elected as a natural born citizen, any scurrilous allegations notwithstanding. Two, I can only be removed from office by impeachment in the Senate, or by exercise of the 25th Amendment, any scurrilous rulings by an over-zealous judge notwithstanding. And third, if a ruling is made ordering me to cease to exercise my office, I will ignore it as an unconstitutional violation of the separation of powers." He looked them both in the eye, one to the other, trying to gage their resolve. "Make the point that it's the people's will that I remain in office—cite whatever the most advantageous poll for us is—and that I fully intend to live up to their expectations. Any questions?"

"No, sir," Caldwell and Singletary responded in unison.

"Very well," Navarro said. "Barb, go draft up the official statement and get it back here for Josh and me to review within an hour. Then get your thoughts in order for the briefing; I'm sure you'll be flayed in lieu of me." He grinned at her, a gesture that the scars on the left side of his face made somewhat unnerving to her. "The press conference begins at eight-thirty, right?"

"Yes, sir," she replied.

"Plenty of time. Josh and I will watch it from the study there." He jerked his head toward the room next door. "But if they ask why I'm not talking to them myself, tell them I don't intend to dignify any of this with a personal appearance. Clear?"

"Yes, sir," she replied again.

"Good. We'll see you in an hour." Singletary got up from the table without another word, and headed down to her office to work on the statement with her staff. 'Gonna have your hands full trying to put lipstick on this pig, boys and girls,' she thought to herself as she hurried down the halls.

The President and his Chief of Staff remained silent in the room after she'd left, and resumed eating the rest of their meal. Just as they'd about finished, Navarro suddenly said, "Julia, what do you think about all this?"

Caldwell looked over sharply at the President, his friend, and saw him holding his head cocked to one side as if listening. His eyes were focused on the vacant chair to his right; the chair had not had a place setting at it when the three of them had sat down earlier to begin the meal, and Caldwell realized upon reflection that Julia had always sat on the President's right at any meal they had shared as a group. The President began nodding his head.

"I agree, that's what we should do. Thanks, my love, I knew you'd be able to shed some light on this for me." He resumed eating his soup, using his right hand to eat while massaging his forehead with his left.

Caldwell was momentarily speechless. If it weren't for the audible comments he'd just heard, to all appearances the President seemed perfectly normal. Clearly, however, he was experiencing hallucinations to some extent. Caldwell was afraid to even think about how frequently that might actually be happening, and what it meant for the President's mental state. He knew he'd need to speak with Webster about this at once.

"Sir," he said, "do you feel alright?"

"I'm fine, Josh, just a little headache. Time for my next dose, I guess. Would you go into Number 500 and get the pills for me?"

Number 500 was what Navarro called the private bathroom that serviced the Oval Office; 500 was the room number that was emblazoned on its door. It had been reconfigured to accommodate a wheelchair following Navarro's return to work, and so was not used by anyone other than the President. Navarro kept his supply of medications there so he could get to them easily during the day.

"Here you are, sir," Caldwell said once he'd returned to the dining room, holding out the tablet of Vicodin.

"Give me two, Josh. I'm up to two now. One doesn't always work anymore."

"Are you sure that's okay, sir," asked Caldwell warily. "Is that what General Webster said was okay?"

"He's fine with it," Navarro replied nonchalantly, taking the two tablets and downing them with a drink from his water glass. "Well, I'm done here. How about you?" he said, setting down the glass and tossing his napkin onto his plate. Caldwell nodded in agreement. "Okay, then, why don't you wheel me next door and we'll wait there to review Barb's statement, then settle in to watch her performance with the media."

Caldwell obeyed and began to push the President into the study next door. He was not able to miss seeing that the President was absent-mindedly massaging his left hand again, while he murmured inaudibly to himself as they moved. Once he got the President situated at the study's desk and tuned the television to the news, he quickly excused himself to go make the call to Webster.

CHAPTER 57

Washington, DC
Friday, 20 January 2023
12:03 p.m. EST

Nearly two weeks had now passed since the now infamous prime-time press conference. They had been tumultuous weeks, to say the least.

The final installments of *The Beacon* exposé had been published up in Lambertville, so all the details contained in the Trova report were now public. Josh Caldwell had been chagrined to realize that having advance knowledge of what the report contained had done them very little good. The facts contained in it, combined with the presentation packaged by Coryell, had left them little room for maneuver, and he found himself more and more blaming Coryell for their predicament. Caldwell and the White House had found themselves on their heels all the time, futilely fending off attacks from all quarters based on the report's contents. He realized now that until the facts as reported could be definitely rebutted, they were going to continue to lose ground.

Public opinion had begun to divide as the exposé spilled out. The President's approval ratings began to trend downward, to the worry of Caldwell, although throughout the Southwest and Florida they remained strong. Interestingly, many local governments throughout that region of the country began to publicly and officially proclaim their support for the President. It was clear that these people, and the governing bodies that represented them, did not intend to sit idly by and see the President driven from office. They were not interested in the complex legal arguments being debated endlessly on the news and in the press. They only knew that Ray Navarro was one of them and had their best interests at heart, and they proclaimed their continued support for him.

In Congress, the debates had become more rancorous. In the Senate, Senator Moscone's proposal for the initiation of an official investigation into the allegations of *The Beacon* exposé had been approved—barely—although only as a fact-gathering action. No special prosecutor or independent counsel was appointed, though behind the scenes rumblings still continued that stoked those flames. In the House, a bill for impeachment was proposed by a Republican representative from Tennessee; it went nowhere, being buried in committee by the Democratic leadership, but having the impeachment can of worms even cracked open slightly caused eyebrows to raise throughout the capital and alarms to begin sounding in the White House.

The media was basking in it all. Rarely did such a juicy story come their way, one which offered elements of political intrigue, conspiracy, and partisan politics that they could debate and rehash over and over again, and one which promised not to go away anytime soon. Not a night went by that did not have a recap of the day's events, coupled with a detailed round-table analysis. The media fanned into flames the smoldering resentments that existed on both sides of the issue, and then reported gleefully on the fires which erupted.

As the date for the President's State of the Union address neared, those small brushfires soon turned into raging wildfires.

CHAPTER 58

Washington, DC
Tuesday, 24 January 2023
8:22 p.m. EST

"Mister Speaker," announced the Sergeant at Arms of the House in a stentorian voice, "the President of the United States."

All of the assembled Senators, Congressmen, Supreme Court justices, government officials, foreign dignitaries and spectators rose as one and began to applaud as President Navarro was wheeled into the House chamber. He was pushed in the wheelchair by one of his military aides so that his hands could be free to shake hands and wave as he moved slowly from the entryway of the chamber toward the rostrum at the front. Despite the events of the day, the ovation accorded the President by all present was still loud and sustained.

For this evening's speech, special ramps had been installed near the front of the chamber so that the President's wheelchair could easily ascend the steps toward the dais; at the dais itself, another platform was provided to raise the wheelchair higher so the Navarro's head and shoulders would be at a level that would appear as if he was standing. All of these were temporary fixtures that would be removed following the conclusion of the address. The aide guided the President around the left side of the rostrum, past the seats of the Justices and the Joint Chiefs, then was joined by a second aide who assisted in pushing the wheelchair up the ramps and into position for the speech to begin. They locked the wheels in place so there would be no inadvertent motion on the ramp during the speech, then moved aside to take seats from which they could quickly reach the wheelchair if necessary.

President Navarro looked around the chamber as the ovation continued, continuing to smile and wave and point to members of the assemblage, almost as if this was a campaign rally. He also twisted in his chair to his right to offer greetings to the President of the Senate, Vice President Fran Kerrigan, seated behind his right shoulder. He then twisted in the opposite direction to do the same to the Speaker of the House, Congressman Henry Garcia, seated behind his left shoulder. The President turned back toward the front, smoothed the papers before him, then looked up to signal that he was ready to begin. The applause subsided and the chamber was seated.

"Mister Speaker," he began, addressing Garcia first as protocol required, "Vice President Kerrigan, Members of Congress, members of the Supreme Court and Diplomatic Corps, distinguished guests, and fellow citizens. I come before you tonight to report that the state of our Union is strong. Despite the unprecedented events that have occurred during the twelve months since I last addressed you, we remain united in the belief that America continues to grow and to provide a guiding light to the world. Tonight…"

The President's voice was strong as he spoke, although his appearance shocked some who had not seen him in quite a while. He remained gaunt, not having regained the weight and muscle mass that he had possessed before the attack last May. He clearly favored his right side; the right arm waved and pounded the air as he spoke to emphasize points in his speech, while the left largely remained immobile on the podium. The scars on the left side of his face remained visible, although much less livid than they had been immediately after his return from the hospital, but his once jet black hair was now streaked with gray; the left side of his head was almost entirely white. Even though he moved energetically as he delivered the speech, the dark circles under the hollowed eyes vividly showed that he was still not fully recovered.

"…we must remain strong in the face of adversity, and not allow ourselves to be distracted from our solemn obligations to the people of the United States by unsubstantiated rumors and wild speculations that arise. We are a nation of laws, and it is my responsibility to ensure that those laws are faithfully executed. I reiterate to you tonight that I fully intend to do that, and will not be dissuaded from that action by any distractions. The events of today…"

The day's events had been momentous. Huge rallies of thousands had been organized in Los Angeles, Houston, and Miami. Smaller ones occurred in the state capitals of Sacramento, Austin, Tallahassee and Denver. The overarching message of these voices was that they intended to support the Navarro presidency no matter what. The masses shouted that they would not care what a court said, or what a Congress said, they supported Navarro and would broach no attempts to interfere with his presidency. The rallies were largely peaceful; however, some rioting broke out in Sacramento when a counter-protest confronted the Navarro supporters at the Statehouse. Police had restored order quickly, although not before some damage was done to storefronts and parked cars in the area; notably, it was clear to all that the police were not at all sympathetic to the Navarro opponents, and their lack of empathy was born out in arrests and injuries.

"I do not condone violence. And the violence perpetrated against peaceful assemblies, such as occurred in a number of states today, is especially misplaced. I call on all Americans to remember that the right to peaceably assemble is enshrined in our Constitution; it is my responsibility to ensure that that right remains secure, and I pledge to do so."

The audience in the chamber was becoming visibly uneasy as the President spoke. The speech was still interrupted frequently for unnecessary bouts of applause, but the frequency and volume of those ovations noticeably lessened as time went on. It was clear that Navarro's words were touching open nerves, and were not at all what had been expected for the night.

"…the security and safety of our homes and cities in the southwest remains paramount to the security of the nation. For that reason, I have today ordered the Secretary of Defense to send additional military forces into Mexico to set up and administer military governments in the states along the southern border of the United States, specifically Baja California, Sonora, Chihuahua, Coahuila, Nuevo León, and Tamaulipas. These forces will administer those states and establish security there so that our people can be safe in their homes, until such time as a revitalized Mexican central government can become functional. We will no longer tolerate the threat posed by the continuing presence of the narco-gangs that remain in those regions, but will instead root them out and destroy them. We will…"

At this point something unprecedented occurred. While the President continued speaking, six Congressmen and one Senator, all Republicans and all representing states in the Midwest, rose from their seats, moved to the center aisle and left the chamber. All eyes in the chamber watched them go in stunned silence, with only the President's voice continuing on as if nothing had happened. Murmuring began throughout the audience, as neighbor spoke softly to neighbor; all the while the President continued, seemingly unfazed.

"Finally, I want to re-emphasize a point that I have been making for the past couple weeks. There have been recent questions raised about my eligibility to serve as your President. I tell you again tonight that these allegations are all lies. I was born in El Paso, as certified by the state of Texas prior to my election, and I was raised in Houston. I meet all the constitutional requirements for a president, and as such, may only be removed in accordance with that Constitution. I declare to you tonight that I am fully qualified, and fully capable, of serving as President, and will continue to do so, and will not be distracted from that. To the people of the United States, I pledge that I will continue to serve you to the best of my ability; and to those who would distract, I pledge that such actions will not be tolerated."

The chamber was silent. No applause sounded, no one stirred in their seats, no one murmured to their neighbor. None had ever heard such a proclamation uttered by a President before, in public or in private, and none knew how to react.

"So, ladies and gentlemen, I say again to you that our Union is strong. We will continue to move forward. We will continue to act as a beacon of hope to the rest of the world. Thank you all for your attention. May God bless you all and the United States of America. Good night."

The aides jumped from the seats to move to the wheelchair as a slow volume of applause began to rise. Once again, all rose to their feet to applaud, but now, as they watched the President being wheeled out of the chamber and could see the grim expression on his face, they wondered within their applause whether Ray Navarro was fit for the job or not.

CHAPTER 59

Austin, Texas
Friday, 27 January 2023
10:23 p.m. EST

Sue phoned Coryell from Texas late on Friday night to tell him the exciting news.

"Jamie, I found her," she shouted excitedly into the phone. She had been in Texas for nearly two weeks now; Jamie was paying her expenses for the trip, rationalizing that she was functioning as an independent stringer for the paper. 'Why not?' he thought. She'd decided to try to look into Trova via the report they'd produced. If she could find something out of kilter with the report, perhaps that would shed some light on the legitimacy of the Trova Agency. So she'd initially spent several fruitless days in the El Paso area, but had been unable to uncover anything of interest. Eastwood Hospital in El Paso, for example, where the Navarro birth certificate was allegedly forged, had gone bankrupt in 2013 and was razed three years later. Its records had been lost following the bankruptcy proceedings. The drug wars in Juarez had largely destroyed areas in which she was interested south of the border; the Hospital-General de Ciudad Juarez, where Navarro was allegedly born, had been destroyed in a catastrophic fire in the riots of 2018, as had the house of Elena and her grandmother. She'd then moved on to San Antonio, where she was able to find the Acevedo clinic, only to discover that Dr. Acevedo had died in 2012 and that his wife had sold the operation and moved away immediately afterwards. When she'd asked the new managers at the clinic where the wife had gone, Sue'd been invariably told 'Somewhere up north,' whatever that meant. She'd begun to believe that the doctor's wife held the key; if she could track her down—she prayed that she was still alive—then perhaps they'd get some answers about the veracity of the Trova report.

Her break had been purely due to luck. She had tracked down the address of the Acevedo home in the Monte Vista neighborhood of San Antonio by reviewing the records of property transfers in the city archives and had driven out there to see it. As with the clinic, it had been sold shortly after the doctor's death in 2012 by his wife. Sue had found the house easily; it still appeared to be well cared for, as was the rest of the surrounding neighborhood. She had talked with the current owner, who'd told her that they had indeed purchased the house from Mrs. Acevedo, but that they had no idea where she'd moved.

"You know," the owner'd said, pointing off to his left, "you might want to try to speak to old Mrs. McCullough next door. She's been living here forever, and I think she used to be pretty good friends with the Acevedos. She might have kept in touch."

Clair McCullough had proved to be a wealth of information. Small, white-haired but sharp as a tack, she had moved into her home in 1983 and had stayed in it even after her husband died in 1997 and her children had grown up and moved out. She'd remembered Raquel Acevedo fondly, and after a small amount of rummaging through a small desk in the house, had been able to provide Sue with an address near Austin.

Sue had made the hour and a half drive up I-35 from San Antonio to Austin this morning, and by ten o'clock was at the door of the address on Flint Rock Road she'd been given. The house was a two-story adobe with a green tile roof set back from the road on a long dirt driveway, surrounded by cottonwood trees and scrub oaks and with a small pond at the back. The driveway led to a small circle that looped past a detached garage to the front door of the house; Sue had driven up to the door, parked the small Fiat she'd rented near the door, and had rung the bell. Within moments, it was answered by a small, gray-haired woman who appeared to be in her mid-seventies.

Raquel Acevedo in fact had just celebrated her seventy-ninth birthday the week before. Happily, she had not seemed surprised by Sue's visit; in fact, she'd seemed pleased to have a visitor, even an unexpected one. This heartened Sue, who had deliberately not called ahead, hoping rather to speak with Mrs. Acevedo informally. Raquel had invited her inside once Sue had explained who she was and what she wanted.

"You know, you're the second one who's been to see me to ask about Jorge's clinic," Raquel had said. They had moved to the rear of the house and sat on the patio overlooking the pond. "Just a little over a month ago, two nice young men stopped by to talk. They said they were from the health department and were trying to gather information about former doctors in the state. We talked for quite a while about Jorge and his clinic down in San Antonio."

"Did they ask about anything in particular?" Sue'd asked. "Or were they just interested in the work your husband did?"

"Just the work, mostly, I think" Raquel'd replied, then smiled at Sue in embarrassment. "I'm sorry, but sometimes I have a little trouble remembering things exactly any more." She'd insisted on preparing some sweet iced tea for Sue and herself; she had taken a long sip as she struggled to remember the visit. "They only stayed a little while, then said they had to go. Wouldn't even accept any tea from me, they were in such a hurry."

Sue had taken a sip of her tea and could practically feel her teeth begin to rot, there was so much sugar in it; she'd quickly set the glass back down. "Did they ask about any particular work?"

"Not really. They wanted to know if Jorge ever had to travel much, asked if he'd ever gone to Mexico to work. Wanted to know if he ever provided any adoption services. Things like that?" She'd smiled at Sue, clearly enjoying remembering those days which were more vivid in her memory than the present.

"And did he do any of that?" Sue had asked.

"Oh, he never did any adoptions. He was strictly in the fertility business," Raquel had said quietly, looking down at her glass, fidgeting slightly in her seat. "He did travel sometimes, but he never worked anywhere but in Texas."

"I see," said Sue. She thought a moment. She had felt sure that Raquel was hiding something, but did not want to confront her directly about it. Instead, she'd tried a different tack. "Did your husband keep his old files and records once he sold the clinic?"

"Oh, yes," replied Raquel. "Boxes and boxes of them. You know, he worked with hundreds of couples over the years, so many I can't even remember the names anymore. The files are all still stored out in the garage." She had paused then, a puzzled look on her face. "I remember now that those other men asked me about them, too. I asked if they wanted to see them, but they said no."

Sue had felt her excitement rising. "May I see them?" she'd asked.

"And Jamie, it was all there. Boxes and boxes, all intact, all in chronological order. All I had to do was find the records from 1975 and I was in business."

Jamie smiled to himself, hearing her excitement over the line. 'She likes doing this,' he thought. 'Maybe I can make a local reporter out of her when she gets back.' He smiled at the thought.

"What did you find?" he asked.

"There's a complete file on the Navarros and their baby. Names, dates, places, everything. And they all fit perfectly with what's in the Trova report. What do you think of that?"

"Sounds like it's too good to be true," he replied cautiously.

"That's exactly what I thought, too," she said. "So I checked out a few other files and they are definitely different. More disorderly, different handwriting, that kind of stuff. I think this one's been rigged."

Jamie could hear her smile of triumph through the phone. "That's really good work, Sue. Great work. It really confirms this bad feeling I've had." He paused. "Now we'll have to figure out what to do about it."

"Well, I've made copies of all these records. Mrs. Acevedo has been great about that. I'll get them all packaged up and head home tomorrow. Maybe you'll have it figured out by then."

"Yeah, maybe," he said. "You have a good trip home. Can't wait to see you. You've been gone too long, honey. And, again, great job, Sue."

They both hung up, and both sat back, both feeling well satisfied with the day's work.

CHAPTER 60

Washington, DC
Wednesday, 1 February 2023
9:23 a.m. EST

"Josh, I need to talk with you," Vice President Kerrigan said, looking into Caldwell's office from the outer door. "Got a moment?"

"I always have time for you, Madame Vice President," Caldwell said, looking up from the papers scattered across the top of his desk, a sincere look plastered on his round face, although a smile did not accompany it. "Please come in."

"Thanks, Josh," Kerrigan said, entering the office and closing the door behind her. "You don't mind, do you?" She nodded her head toward the closed door.

"Not at all." He remained seated at his desk, while Kerrigan sat down in the straight-backed chair at its front. "What's up?"

"I wanted to talk with you for a couple of minutes about the President before the Cabinet meeting starts." The weekly Cabinet meeting was due to convene in about half an hour. "I'm growing increasingly concerned about his physical and mental condition. Several other Cabinet members are as well. A number of them have come to talk with me about it since the State of the Union last week." She was looking directly into Caldwell's eyes as she spoke. "I plan to bring it up for discussion at the meeting."

Caldwell could feel his temper rise, and knew that his face had reddened involuntarily. He had concerns about the President's health, also, but he didn't want them to be aired in public; even a Cabinet meeting would be too public for him. Some Cabinet members had also come to him on the same topic in recent days, and he had allayed their concerns, at least for the time being. He leaned forward toward the Vice President across the desk. "Let me say that I share your concerns, but I don't think that bringing it up now would be a wise thing to do, Madame Vice President. Not wise at all."

"And why is that, Josh?" Kerrigan could feel her temper rising also, and she began to stand abruptly.

"Please," he said, waving her back down into her seat. "I'm not trying to pick a fight with you. I just don't think we should deal with this publicly. The President is fine for a man who was nearly killed not that long ago. His policies may be making people unhappy, but that does not make him fair game to have his health dissected in front of him." Caldwell let the statement lie in the air.

"Well, how do you think we should address it?" Kerrigan said finally. "We've all seen the President's recent behavior. He's changed from what he was, and I'm concerned about him. We all are. I think he's still sick. The question is how sick." She stared over at Caldwell. "The Cabinet is within its rights to review the President's competency; it has a duty to do so, in fact. If his personality has changed so much that it's noticeably different, so much that his behavior is bordering on the bizarre, then his mental fitness is questionable."

"Not wise," Caldwell said again. He had, in fact, been talking regularly with General Webster about the President. They had become *de facto* conspirators to keep Ray Navarro's issues private, particularly his mental issues, agreeing to do what they could to keep the public from hearing that anything was awry with the President's recovery. Caldwell did not want it to be discussed in a Cabinet meeting.

"Why is that?" she asked. "Tell me, Josh. Does he still talk to Julia? I've seen him do it, you know, when he thinks no one is watching, or when he's unaware he's even doing it. Are the physical tics getting worse? Like the compulsive massaging of his left hand. How about the headaches? Getting worse? How much Vicodin is he up to now?"

Caldwell stared at her with barely disguised anger. "You do what you think you need to do. But it's wrong to do it now. I'm here to tell you, if you push this to a vote by the Cabinet, you'll lose, because most of them can see he's still competent and still on the mend." He hesitated, then added, venomously. "If you want to be President, wait two years and you can run. Don't try to steal it from him now."

Kerrigan stared momentarily at her adversary, then turned and strode silently from the office.

"Good morning, everyone," President Navarro said as he wheeled himself into the Cabinet Room and up to his place at the center of the long table. "Glad to see you could all make it, given the weather outside." It had begun snowing during the night, depositing nearly three inches of heavy, wet snow on Washington by the morning rush hour. Snow could be seen continuing to fall through the windows behind the President that looked out onto the Rose Garden. "On the bright side, though, I don't think Phil will see his shadow tomorrow if the forecast proves correct," the President continued, evoking laughter from around the room. The forecast called for overcast skies and snow flurries for the next two days. Navarro was alluding to the unlikely ability for Punxsutawney Phil to see his shadow up in Pennsylvania tomorrow on Groundhog Day, thereby predicting an early spring. "So some snow for the next several hours will probably be okay in the long run."

Once situated at his position, the President opened the embossed folder waiting there for him and started the meeting. "Okay, folks, let's begin. First up, I'd like to hear from Defense about the preparations for Mexico." He turned to his left where the Secretary of Defense, Aaron Post, sat.

"Mister President, excuse me," interjected Vice President Kerrigan.

Navarro looked across the table at Kerrigan in surprise at the unexpected interruption. He leaned back in the wheelchair, both hands clasped in front of him on the table. "Madame Vice President, what is it?"

"Sir, before we begin with the regular agenda, I and several members of the Cabinet would like to ask about your health." She looked directly at the President's face as she spoke, watching carefully for his reaction. She noted peripherally that most of the other heads around the table were watching him as well. "May I ask how your recovery is progressing?"

"I think it is progressing very well," Navarro replied evenly. "Thank you all for your concern." He looked around the table, no longer smiling. "I'm touched by it, truly touched. Is there anything else?" he said, shifting his gaze back to Kerrigan.

"Sir, allow me to be blunt," she replied. "Many of us are increasingly concerned about your health, and the impact it has on your ability to govern. We see evidence of mood swings, compulsive behavior, and the beginnings of paranoia. From your appearance, you appear to be exhausted. We are concerned for your well-being, sir, and ask you if our observations are cause for concern."

The room remained silent. The President's face had darkened noticeably as Kerrigan spoke, but he responded to her in a calm voice. "Fran. Everyone."

He looked again around the room. "Believe me, I feel fine. Tired, admittedly. I haven't been sleeping all that soundly at night of late, and should probably rest more during the day to compensate. But I don't think the other things you mentioned are justified." He sighed. "Perhaps I am a little moody, at times, but I think that goes hand in hand with not sleeping well. When I am rested, I don't feel irritable. And if I have been short or difficult with any of you," he swung his head from right to left, making eye contact with his Cabinet officers as he did, "please accept my apologies." He paused again, and cocked his head to one side. "Compulsive behavior? I'm not sure I know what you mean. I think you'll have to help me with that one."

"Sir, you frequently—unconsciously—massage your left hand when you appear frustrated or angry. It's become more noticeable, particularly as things have become more stressful lately." She held his gaze. "One member seated here—I won't say who—even likened it to Queeg and his metal balls." She was referring to the eccentric and mentally unbalanced Captain Queeg of *The Caine Mutiny*, who had the compulsive habit of handling a pair of metal balls that produced a clicking sound as he incessantly revolved them in his hand when under stress.

"I massage my hand whenever it hurts, which it frequently does," responded Navarro coolly. "I'm sorry if it appears compulsive; it's not. It's merely quite frequently painful and rubbing it seems to help." He looked around, then back to the Vice President. "I believe you mentioned paranoia also."

"Perhaps that's too strong a word," Kerrigan said hastily. "You do seem to be overly antagonistic recently when challenged or contradicted. It is unlike you; you used to be very receptive of opposing points of view, while now you barely tolerate them. Your remarks last week during the State of the Union, in which you said 'distractions' would not be tolerated, were especially out of character."

"Fran," he interrupted. "Again, I'd say it's due to being overly tired at times. Hearing you say this, I can see where I may be somewhat abrupt at times when things aren't going as I would like, or as quickly as I would like." He swiveled his head again. "Once more, let me apologize." And back to Kerrigan, "Does that allay your concerns?"

The Vice President paused momentarily, inwardly debating whether to press the subject further, or to wait. Finally, she responded "Yes, sir, I believe it does. Thank you for listening to me. And I'm sorry if I've offended you, but I hope you can see where we were concerned." She smiled briefly at him. "May I suggest that you make more time for rest, and allow us to shoulder more of the load for you. Just for a little while."

"Yes, a good idea. I'll try to get more rest." He raised his hands as if surrendering, although he did not smile. "Okay, let's get back to our agenda. Aaron, if you please," he said, turning toward the Defense Secretary.

As the Defense Secretary began to describe the progress in Mexico, Kerrigan looked beyond the President's right shoulder, and saw Caldwell sitting against the wall, staring back at her and slowly shaking his head.

CHAPTER 61

Washington, DC
Saturday, 4 February 2023
11:03 a.m. EST

By the weekend, more unrest had broken out in a number of cities across the country. Word had leaked out to the press about the acrimony in the Cabinet meeting earlier in the week—Kerrigan was sure Caldwell had let it out, while Caldwell was sure it was the fault of Kerrigan and Moscone. Whatever the source, the media people were having a field day with it. Protests and demonstrations had been staged both for and against the President. While most of these were peaceable, in several instances competing protests had clashed, with resulting property damage and injuries. Calmer heads had usually prevailed, and all of these clashes had been ultimately resolved, but police and homeland security organizations were on tenterhooks, anticipating that they had only seen the tip of the iceberg so far, and that the worst was yet to come.

Voices in local and state governments did little to stem the tide. Most seemed to be staking out positions on the issue, expecting problems to continue, and trying to guess what the end result would be so that they could land on the right side of the fence. As the size of the protests grew, many mayors and governors simply forbade the group that they opposed from taking to the streets. In some cases this tactic worked, and there were no clashes between competing groups of protesters, while in others it backfired dramatically. When Hank Schermerhorn, the Governor of Florida, ordered the National Guard to send troops into Dade County to remove pro-Navarro protesters from the downtown areas around the federal courthouse, he was politely told by the Guard's Adjutant General that, regrettably, that would not done because units in south Florida were not ready; Governor Schermerhorn was smart enough not to challenge the general, and the protests continued without further incident.

In Washington, the chatter continued unabated. All were eagerly waiting for the completion of the congressional investigation, although no one could predict with any degree of confidence what the findings of that look would be.

CHAPTER 62

Lambertville, NJ
Saturday, 4 February 2023
11:53 p.m. EST

Jamie and Sue had finished another day of strategizing about how to make public the new information she had uncovered while in Texas. Ever since her flight into Philadelphia last Sunday, they had met every evening, either at his house or her apartment, for dinner and a couple hours of reviewing information and discussing how to best present it. Jamie knew instinctively that he would have to get this right. He wanted to publish it in this week's edition of the *Beacon*, so they had pressed themselves hard to get everything straight in their minds and tie up loose ends.

"I think that should do it," Jamie said, smiling over at Sue and toasting her with his beer. They'd just concluded that the article was as good as they could get it.

Jamie and Sue were seated across from each other on the stools at the island in his kitchen; the dirty dishes and remains of the dinner they'd consumed as they worked were piled in the sink and on the counters behind Sue. They'd had 'party chicken', a meal that had been a specialty of Jamie's mother and which remained one of his favorites, particularly since it was easy to make and tasted delicious. Made of thin sliced chicken breast, rolled together with strips of dried beef, then covered in a mushroom cream sauce—his mother's fancy name for a can of mushroom soup—it was simply broiled in a casserole dish and then served. Most people wouldn't believe it was as simple as that when he'd describe to them how he'd made it. He'd also cooked up a dish of broiled potatoes that he'd covered with butter and rosemary, which he knew Sue especially liked. Jamie'd had beer with his—River Horse, as usual—while Sue'd had a *Tommasi* Pinot Grigio with hers.

"Mr. Coryell," she replied, raising her glass in return, "I do believe you're right." She sipped the white wine thoughtfully. "The other details you found during your research really tie it all together. The stuff I got would be just more hearsay without it. Yours makes it believable."

"I hope it does," Jamie replied to her, pleased that she felt that his efforts had been fruitful.

While Sue had been in Texas, Jamie had researched the Trova Agency extensively on the internet. He was consistently amazed at the information you could find, if you just applied a little logic to the searches you conducted and you displayed a little patience. Of course, the increasingly pervasive digital archives that could be accessed by anyone with a computer, coupled with the increasingly sophisticated search engines that found the desired data in those archives, made it much easier to do than even five years ago. When Jamie thought back to the dark ages when he could only Google a query and hope for the best, he was amazed that anyone had ever successfully found what they were looking for.

What he had been able to glean from the archives were a whole series of strings that he wove into a complete web. The article would show that the Trova Agency had been in existence now for about fifteen years; it was incorporated during the latter stages of the Iraq War, prior to the shift to Afghanistan during the early Obama years, and had received a growing stream of government contracts since then. Much of the agency's work centered around background checks for security clearances; for a while there, a backlog of over half a million investigations had existed, creating a logjam that hamstrung both government and industry from effectively accomplishing classified actions. Trova had helped to conduct those investigations that ultimately resolved the problem. At the same time, though, Trova began receiving other jobs from government agencies that operated in the 'black' world of classified operations. It became clear to Jamie, and to Sue when he described what he'd found, that Trova not only had the special skills that would be needed to fabricate the files that Sue had uncovered, but also that it was guided in its business by people within the U.S. Government. They both knew instinctively that the article would again grab the nation's attention once it was published.

"Where do you think Trova's instructions came from? I mean, who stands to gain by fixing the records like that?" Jamie asked. He had been pondering this question for some time, without being able to come up with an acceptable answer.

"I don't know," she answered after a moment. "Maybe the story will flush them out of hiding."

"Yeah, maybe," he said, staring at his bottle as he swirled the beer around. 'I wonder what *The Shadow* will think?' he thought silently.

CHAPTER 63

Washington, DC
Thursday, 9 February 2023
10:23 p.m. EST

He didn't have to wait long to find out.

The Beacon had hit the streets on Wednesday afternoon, as usual, and by the time the seven o'clock news came on it was being mentioned nationally. As Jamie had anticipated, his story inferring that the Trova Report had been fabricated once more captured people's imaginations; the conspiracy theorists now had even more grist for their mill, and the media lapped up the controversy.

This morning he'd received a call at the office once again from Barb Singletary at the White House.

"Jamie, I can't tell you how surprised we were to see your paper in the news again last night. I thought we'd agreed that you'd give us a heads up prior to printing more stories." Her voice had sounded friendly and matter-of-fact, but Jamie'd thought he could detect an undercurrent of tension behind it.

"No, Barb," he'd replied, "I agreed to share the stories that came from the initial report that we'd received. This was something separate; something additional. Plus, it wasn't something I thought the President would have to worry about. If anything, it tends to vindicate him."

"Well, maybe, but you still put me behind the power curve by not giving us a heads up," she'd said testily. She'd paused, and he'd thought he could almost see her drumming her fingers on her desk. "If you've got anything else coming out, would you please let me know about it so I can prepare myself?"

"You got it, Barb," he'd replied, knowing that it could always be useful to have a friend in high places. Then had added, "Listen, I'd appreciate your honest feeling about the article. Do you think my conclusions about the problem originating somewhere within the government rings true?"

She didn't hesitate. "Jamie, to be honest, I think it's a stretch. Your conclusion is one way to view the information you found, but there can be others, too. For instance, perhaps Dr. Acevedo got a new secretary to help him transcribe files, which is why this one looks different than all the others. Perhaps Dr. Acevedo did it himself, at a different time, to conceal a wrongdoing he'd done in the past. I'll admit that your conclusion does come out as favorable to the President's version of events, but unless you can support it better, it won't end the issue for us."

"Well, I can see your point, certainly," Jamie'd replied, disappointed, "but, if you give me the benefit of the doubt and presume my conclusion is correct, who stands to gain?" This was really the question on which he'd hoped she could provide some insight.

"That's easy," she'd answered. "Whomever opposes the President. And that covers a lot of ground in this town, and around the country, too, for that matter. You'll have to do better, I think." She'd hesitated suddenly, then had asked, "Why, Jamie? Why are you concerned with who stands to gain? Are you worried about something?"

Now it was Jamie's turn to hesitate. 'Should I tell her?' he'd wondered to himself, not sure how far he could trust her. He instinctively felt he could, but if he made a wrong choice things would only go south. He'd decided to test the water with her. "Barb, to be honest with you, I've been getting some threats for a while now. All from an anonymous source on the phone, all very ominous like something you read in some spy novel. It's just got me a little bit anxious, I guess."

"Jamie, if you're being threatened, you should go to the police," she'd said immediately, concern evident in her voice. "Don't try to be brave about it. Let them help you."

"Maybe," he'd said. "I've been considering it. Maybe I will." Then in a brighter voice. "Anyway, I just wondered what you thought. I probably am just being a little paranoid about the government angle. Watching too many movies." He'd laughed.

"Maybe," she'd answered back. "But I'll tell you what I'll do. I'll keep my ear to the ground here to see if anything seems to lend credence to what you're thinking. If I hear about something, I'll give you a call. Okay?" He'd replied affirmatively. "Great. Thanks, Jamie. We'll talk again, I'm sure. And keep me in the loop from now on." The call disconnected.

Jamie had set the phone back into its cradle, and had stared at it speculatively for several minutes, still not sure whether he could trust her or not. 'Time will tell, I suppose,' he thought, then turned back to the work of preparing Saturday's edition.

By the end of the day, he had conducted two phone interviews with national news bureaus, and had fielded numerous other phone calls about the article. Everybody wanted to know if he had more information coming out, and wanted to know how he was able to get this information. He'd been very circumspect in what he revealed, and had kept Sue's name out of the conversation altogether. 'The less visible she is, the better,' he thought. Besides himself, only Alice knew that Sue had been the one in Texas to discover the files, and Jamie was fully confident that she'd never offer up that tidbit of information. All in all, the discussions wore him down, and when he had glanced up from his work to discover it was after six o'clock, he'd decided that he'd done enough for one day and could leave the office, and its phones, behind and head home.

For the first time in what seemed like a long time, he and Sue were not having dinner together. She had left this morning to go down near Baltimore somewhere to a series of art auctions, hoping to collect a few pieces for her gallery; she wouldn't get back in town until Sunday night. As he fixed himself a small meal of leftover spaghetti with sausage and a salad, he realized suddenly that he acutely missed being with her. He'd come to look forward to seeing her at the end of each long day, had come to enjoy the conversations they had and the planning they'd done. To his surprise, Jamie realized that the thought of a life together did not seem that bizarre. He'd always considered himself to be somewhat of a confirmed bachelor, set in his ways and comfortable in them; plus, he was forty now, which meant he'd been enjoying the unfettered, bachelor life for a long time. But now, maybe it wasn't enough. 'Maybe we're meant for each other,' he pondered speculatively as he ate; then thought 'I wonder if she feels the same way?' He vowed to himself that he'd find out.

Just as he'd finished cleaning up the dishes from his meal, and had placed the final dish into the cabinet to the right of the sink, the phone rang. 'Pretty late for a call,' he thought, glancing at the clock on the microwave to see that it was after ten. He snatched the receiver from its cradle on the wall, hoping it was Sue.

"Mr. Coryell," came the metallic voice in response to his 'Hello?'. "We haven't chatted in quite some time, and I see in the news today that you've been busy. I thought we should talk."

"I'm not sure we have anything to talk about," Jamie had replied, sitting down carefully at the island. "What do you want?"

"I want to know what you think you're doing," the voice said ominously. "You did nice work with the exposé. Got people talking. But now this latest thing makes it look like you're trying to discredit that work. I hope that's not the case."

"No, not at all," Jamie replied, suddenly nervous. "I was just trying to flesh out the original story, that's all. People will still be talking," he said hopefully.

"That they will," agreed *The Shadow*. "I was just surprised to hear about it today, and I don't like to be surprised. I think it's time that we meet to talk about what you're going to do next."

Jamie's mouth dried up. His intent in doing the work in Texas was to find out who *The Shadow* was, and what his motivation was. It was the same thing that Lou had wanted when he originally got the story. Now, Jamie was being offered that meeting, and he found himself reluctant. "Why do you think we should meet?"

"Because I think partners should be open with each other," came the response. "I'm sure you want to know if you can trust me. You want to know why I'm giving you this story. Well, I'm prepared to tell you why, but I want to know if I can trust you, too. And I think the best way to do that is to meet face to face. No hiding behind the telephone."

"Why don't you just tell me who you are?" Jamie asked.

"Because these phones can have too many ears," the voice answered. "No, a meeting is what we need."

Jamie considered. In one sense, *The Shadow* was right—he did want to know if he could trust him, and he wanted to know his motivation. On the other hand, he still felt that *The Shadow* had played a role in Lou's death. Would a meeting place him in jeopardy, too? Perhaps, but the advantages outweighed the potential risks, he thought. He'd insist that they meet in a common, public place, so there should be no problem.

"All right, I agree," Jamie finally replied. "A meeting. When and where do you suggest?"

"Not right away," *The Shadow* said. "We need to see what response develops to your latest scribblings. I think in a couple weeks will suffice. And I think somewhere up near you, away from Washington. That would be much more suitable."

"Okay," Jamie said. "Somewhere up here in about two weeks or so. Shall we set a date now, or wait?"

"We wait, but you think of a good place where we can meet discreetly. Once I think the time is right, I'll call again."

"Very well," Jamie said, relieved that the conversation seemed to be ending.

"You have a good night, Mr. Coryell. And no more surprise contributions to the public debate, at least until after we've talked. Remember that I don't like surprises." The call ended.

Jamie hung up the phone, considering the significance of the conversation. He found it somewhat of a coincidence that he'd get this call on the same day that he talked with Singletary. Could it be that she had reported his conversation back to Caldwell, and that Caldwell was this voice? He tried to work out the motive. Caldwell would certainly have the governmental connections in the 'black' world to arrange all of this, but why would he do it? *The Beacon* exposé essentially claimed that the President should not be in office—why would Caldwell give him that? Only if he was trying to hang it around someone else's neck, someone like the Vice President. Sue had told him that the two detested each other. Maybe this was Caldwell's byzantine way to discredit Kerrigan. Or maybe it was truly Kerrigan. Certainly she—and her husband, with his contacts from the Intelligence Committee—would have the necessary government clout to make this happen, and her motive for doing so was obviously much more straightforward. Or maybe it was somebody working on her behalf, like her associate Dougherty that he'd met at her house down in DC; he'd have the right connections, too, and his loyalty to Kerrigan and protectiveness of her was well known. As for calling today, it was probably something he should have expected once this edition was released; that it had happened after he'd talked with Singletary was surely just a coincidence. He thought about it, arguing with himself, comparing all angles against each other, and finally gave up and headed up to bed. 'I'll think some more about it tomorrow,' he thought as he climbed the stairs.

As for a good place to meet, he knew he didn't need to think about that at all. He already had the perfect place in mind.

CHAPTER 64

Washington, DC
Tuesday, 14 February 2023
7:23 p.m. EST

On Valentine's Day, the Senate Permanent Subcommittee for Investigations presented their report on the allegations surrounding President Navarro's birth, although the report did nothing to increase the love between Congress and the White House. The subcommittee's investigators declared that they had been able to corroborate the preponderance of the information presented in *The Beacon* exposé, and averred that they believed the allegations to be true. To their regret, they did not have the opportunity to make any judgments about the *Beacon's* most recent publication; when they attempted to interview Mrs. Acevedo in Austin, and view the files from Dr. Acevedo's clinic, they unfortunately found that the Acevedo garage had been destroyed in a recent fire, along with all of the files stored there, and that Mrs. Acevedo refused to talk with them. "Subpoena an old woman if you wish," she'd told them before slamming the door in their face, "but I'll not say another word that will bring me more trouble." They'd taken her at her word and left.

Nonetheless, even without the Acevedo files, the investigators determined that the overwhelming preponderance of evidence they reviewed supported what *The Beacon* had printed. On that basis, non-binding motions were quickly introduced in both the House and the Senate calling for the President's immediate resignation, both expressing the sentiment that Ray Navarro was illegitimately in the White House. Both were passed by slim majorities in each house. A motion for impeachment was once again introduced in the House, and this time it was not buried but was assigned instead to committee for discussion. No one really believed that an impeachment would proceed, much less lead to a conviction in the Senate, since there was no 'high crime or misdemeanor' in evidence, but the mere discussion of it showed the nation how seriously Congress was now viewing this issue.

By the end of the day, legal actions had also been initiated across the country calling for the President's removal from office. The Supreme Court immediately indicated it would take all these cases under consideration as one action, and promised to issue a ruling posthaste. The mood across the country became dire.

For his part, President Navarro continued to categorically deny that any of the allegations were true. In a primetime news conference, he appealed directly to the nation to stand behind him and not give in to flimsy, and possibly fraudulent, data and not to be swayed by the tocsins sounding on the nightly news and across the internet blogosphere that called for his head. He swore that the adverse information lined up against him was untrue, that he was the legitimate president, and vowed to remain in office and acting as such no matter what. To do otherwise, he claimed, would place the republic in peril, for if duly elected presidents could be removed by Congress or the courts on the basis of lies generated by the media, who could predict which pillar of American society would go next.

In the White House, a bunker mentality prevailed. Caldwell and Singletary worked feverishly to stay ahead of the news cycle, stomping out brushfires where they flared up and trying to come up with a strategy that would keep the President secure. The President stayed obstinately in the Oval Office each day, often eating his meals at his desk, as he telephoned supporters across the country in an effort to shore up their flagging support. The strain of the exercise was taking its toll on him, and General Webster had once again increased his dosage of pain medication and had now additionally prescribed an anti-anxiety medication for him. The doctor was growing increasingly concerned with the mental problems the President was manifesting. The mood swings and the extended conversations with Julia were becoming too frequent and too noticeable to ignore. Webster hoped that the stress of the moment would not send Ray Navarro over the edge.

Across town on this evening, in the Vice President's residence at the Naval Observatory, the Cabinet was once more assembling unbeknownst to the President or his Chief of Staff. These advisors of the President had all had opportunities over the past several weeks to observe the problems that Navarro was having, and all had grown increasingly anxious about his fitness for office. Collectively, they had prevailed upon Kerrigan to host a meeting again to discuss that topic and decide what to do about it.

Seated around the extended table in the dining room as before, the Vice President opened the discussion. "Very well, ladies and gentlemen. We are assembled. Who would like to go first?" It was apparent to all from her demeanor and her tone that she was not happy to be having this discussion again.

"I'll start," said Bob Powell, the Attorney General. Powell was a former U.S. Attorney from Washington state who had made a name for himself when he prosecuted several well-known software corporations for collusion and racketeering about ten years ago. He had ramrodded an intricate government case that spanned several years, had won record damage amounts and had convicted several top executives. He was recognized for having a keen legal mind, with an uncanny ability to sort through the wheat and the chaff when analyzing a case, and was frequently mentioned as a potential Supreme Court nominee whenever the next vacancy might occur. All in the room listened attentively as he spoke.

"I believe what we have before us are two separate issues. One is germane to us, and one, while intriguing, is not. First, the intriguing but irrelevant one. Despite all the notoriety of *The Beacon* exposé, the allegations raised do not matter to us." He waved his hand as murmuring rumbled around the table. "Wait, please, and I'll explain. The 25th Amendment, which is the basis for our meeting here, gives us collectively the responsibility to assess the President's competence on a basis of physical disability. Whether or not Ray Navarro should ever have been permitted to run for president is a moot point as far as we're concerned."

"But, Bob," interrupted Gabe Carkhuff, the VA Secretary, "isn't the 25th less restrictive than that? Doesn't it call on us to determine when he is merely 'unable' to discharge his duties? That's a much looser interpretation of the amendment, obviously, but I don't read it as applying simply to a determination of physical incapacity."

"Gabe, you make a good point, as always," replied Powell, "but to understand how to properly implement the amendment you'd have to read back through the transcripts as it was debated. There I think it's clear that Congress intended the Cabinet to consider both physical and mental incapacities, but not anything broader or more general." He looked up the table toward Kerrigan. "For us to consider something broader, like merely that the President is not fit for office just because we don't like what he's doing, is not the way it was intended. So I recommend we not even talk about *The Beacon* exposé, because it's not applicable to our situation here, and instead focus only on the President's physical and mental condition, because that applies precisely."

"Well spoken, Bob," said Kerrigan. "I tend to agree with your view. Would anyone else like to discuss the issue, or is everyone content that we'll not discuss *The Beacon* exposé and will focus only on the President's condition?" She looked around the table, and although several Cabinet members shifted slightly in their seats in apparent discomfort, none spoke up to press the issue. Even Carkhuff appeared mollified. "Okay," she said, "let's discuss his condition then. Any starters?"

"I'll take this one," the Secretary of State, Mike DiMarco said. "As I argued the last time we met, even though President Navarro clearly has some remaining injuries and a remaining need to have them heal, he is not, in my mind, incapable of executing his office."

"Mike," said Aaron Post, the Defense Secretary. "From a physical standpoint, I'd agree with you. The President's injuries are healing, he's continuing to make progress, and he has no physical impediment that would prevent him from discharging his duties. I've heard some scuttlebutt that, because he's begun taking naps in the afternoon, he should step down. Well just so everyone knows, I take naps, too, and I'm a better man for it." Light laughter sounded around the table; Post was nearing his seventieth birthday, yet could run rings around many a younger man. "However," he continued as the laughter subsided, "I am concerned about his mental state. I am worried that he's making decisions which are not only poor, but which are driving us toward a catastrophe. The orders he's given me to implement in Mexico are a case in point: they exceed his authority by using the military to prop up a foreign government without Congress' approval, and will put thousands at risk, on both sides of the border. I think they're the product of an unstable mind. How many here have seen him talking to himself—out loud, no less—or talking to his dead wife as if she's present and no one else is. We can't accept that he's in his right mind." He looked over to Kerrigan. "Just so you know, I intend to refuse to implement those orders; then we'll see how stable he really is."

"I agree with Aaron," sounded other voices from around the table, while others exclaimed that they agreed with DiMarco. The discussion, while cordial, continued for nearly twenty minutes, until finally it was turned to the Vice President for her opinion.

"Ladies and Gentlemen," Kerrigan began, "let me first say that I share your concerns about the President. He's been traumatized, and is still recovering from it; the recent stress he's been placed under has not been easy on him— nor would it be easy for any of us, if it were directed our way—but I think he's holding up adequately. I'll tell you that I will not vote to remove him. When we did do that originally last spring, there was no doubt that he was incapable of acting. Now it's not so clear. And unless it is absolutely clear, I think we are obligated to support him." She saw some heads nodding in agreement, and some staring straight ahead in obvious displeasure. "I suggest that we leave this in the capable hands of the Supreme Court to rule on President Navarro's eligibility for office, and then move on from there based on their ruling and his reaction to it. I believe that invoking the 25th is the wrong path to head down." She paused, once more looking around the room. "I believe we should still proceed with a vote, but I will vote against it."

When the voting was completed, the Cabinet had once again refused to invoke the 25th and remove Ray Navarro from office in favor of his Vice President. The vote this time, however, was only nine to six; clearly, more were growing convinced that Ray Navarro should go. With any more signs of instability, a majority might just be convinced.

CHAPTER 65

Lambertville, NJ
Thursday, 2 March 2023
9:23 p.m. EST

The metallic voice of *The Shadow* had sounded in Jamie Coryell's ear once again on the Monday of the President's Day weekend, nearly ten days ago now. "Mr. Coryell, I'd like to meet soon. I have some more information to give you, but, as we discussed previously, I think it best that it be done face to face this time. I think that early next week would be a good time."

Jamie had suggested Thursday of that week instead. It would be after he'd finished with the paper's first edition for the week, but before things got hectic with the weekend. "That would work much better for me," he'd said. "I won't be distracted."

"Very well," *The Shadow* had agreed after some thought. "Next Thursday. Have you selected a location, Mr. Coryell?"

Indeed he had. Not far from Lambertville, about five miles south on Route 202, just before it joins with State Road 263, lies Peddler's Village, a tourist mecca of several dozen specialty shops and upscale restaurants that was always crowded with visitors no matter the day or season. It had been in existence for over sixty years, and was a favorite spot of Jamie and Sue when they just wanted to walk around a bit and watch people or simply mindlessly shop. They had ventured out there just last month to enjoy the 'Colonial Dinner,' an annual event that included a savory four-course, 18th-century style dinner. They'd had opportunity to ask questions of food historians as they prepared the dishes over a roaring fire, learning the arcane secrets of baking pies in a Dutch oven, of roasting beef on a 'clock-work jack' or in a 'tin kitchen,' of cooking fish laced onto a plank, of sautéing Maryland crab in a 'spider,' as well as of baking hearty breads and Johnny cakes. Sue, who rarely cooked, had been fascinated by it all, and had taken home some recipes with the vow to learn how to make them.

He'd described the location to *The Shadow*, who had agreed to the meeting there. They'd arranged to rendezvous at eight o'clock in the evening of the 2nd. They would meet in the parking lot just to the rear of the Cock 'n Bull Restaurant, the premier—and always busy—dining location within Peddler's Village, then move inside to the bar for a discreet chat. "I look forward to meeting you finally, Mr. Coryell," the voice had concluded. "And I'm sure you'll be surprised by what I'm bringing you this time."

Jamie and Sue had discussed the meeting several times since that call. She was not at all happy with the arrangement, and had said so to Jamie emphatically.

"I just don't like it," she had argued. "Something's not right about it. Why would this guy want to meet you now? And what can he possibly have to give you that we don't already know? I think I should go to keep an eye on you."

Jamie had immediately put at end to that discussion, categorically refusing to let Sue accompany him to the meeting. Inside, when he was truthful with himself, he knew that she was right. What could be the point? But the journalist in him held out hope for one more missing piece to apply to the puzzle, and he knew he had to try to grab it. But Sue could not be involved. He couldn't allow her to take a risk that was of his doing. He could take it, but that was his job, his chosen job. It wasn't hers. And he had won the argument, much to her displeasure, by refusing to budge.

"All right, be that way," she'd huffed. "But you better make sure you take every precaution imaginable."

"I will," he'd replied, hoping to soothe her apprehension. "It'll be a public place, lots of people around. I promise it'll be okay," he'd concluded, although his thoughts on the subject differed considerably from hers.

His thoughts toward precaution focused on how to protect his information, not how to protect himself. He didn't really believe he was in any danger—he didn't get any sense of that from these latest conversations. Rather, he'd been growing more worried about his data being compromised somehow, just as poor Mrs. Acevedo's had been by what he was sure had been arson. So, unbeknownst to Sue, he and Alice had made copies of all the files that pertained to *The Beacon* exposé however remotely, and he had secured them in a local bank's repository with instructions for their disposition should something happen to him; the originals remained in the *Beacon* office. That way, he figured, the information could not be compromised, no matter what happened.

He also had not shared with Sue the latest results of his research. While continuing to data-mine about Trova, he had stumbled across some intriguing hints as to *The Shadow's* identity. Several documents had surfaced linking the agency to certain officials in government, although Jamie admitted to himself that the links were somewhat tenuous. Nonetheless, they all seemed to point in the same direction and he believed he knew who it was that would be meeting him; he only awaited the face to face confirmation. All of this information was also secured within the copied and secured files that he and Alice had made.

Jamie had remained working at the office this day until about seven o'clock, too keyed up to go home earlier. He was alone in the building; Alice had headed out about an hour earlier at Jamie's urging. He'd eaten a sandwich at his desk, reviewing his thoughts on the meeting and how he thought it would proceed. He wondered about the nature of the new information that *The Shadow* promised him, and had concluded that it could only be data that proved that President Navarro had also known of his illegitimate birth, and was thereby complicit in the deception. Where that information could come from, Jamie couldn't decide, but he knew that if it was indeed the case, his series of stories in this exposé would be the stuff of political legend. He anxiously waited and watched the clock as the hands slowly—agonizingly slowly—moved forward.

Finally, at about a quarter past the hour, he put on his coat and hat, shut off the lights in the office and locked the building as he departed, then headed out into the night. It was dark and overcast, with a light snow beginning to fall; a dusting already covered the ground, although the roads remained bare so far. He got into his car, turned right out of the *Beacon's* lot, and headed the Ford across the bridge spanning the Delaware into Pennsylvania.

He drove slowly through New Hope and out Route 202, the continuing snowfall making drivers cautious. It took him about twenty minutes to reach Lahaska, where Peddler's Village was located. He turned right at the first traffic light in the village, then entered the Cock 'n Bull's parking lot the first block down on his left. He moved the car to the far side of the lot, backing into a space so he could see forward, turned off his lights, and shut off the ignition. Then he waited.

Jamie had debated with himself about how to approach the meeting. Should he be the first one to move to the agreed upon rendezvous spot in the parking lot, and wait to see who approached? Or should he sit back and watch, and only appear once *The Shadow* materialized? He had decided to stake out the ground first so that he could watch as people neared; sitting back in the car and watching could only draw attention to himself, and he still wanted to be discreet about the meeting.

He found himself growing antsy as the wait got longer, so after about fifteen minutes of sitting in the car, he got out and headed toward the restaurant's rear entrance. This was where they had agreed to rendezvous, in the parking lot just outside the rear service door, where deliveries were made. It was still a public place—lighted, common ground—but not an area where they would expect a crowd. From here they'd move to the bar where they could talk, exchange information, and go their separate ways when their business was concluded. He trudged across the parking lot, his footsteps tracing his path in the snowfall, then turned when he reached the far side to await his antagonist's arrival.

As he waited, he shuffled his feet from side to side to keep warm, his hands deep in his pockets. The wind was beginning to pick up slightly, adding a chill to the already damp air. The snow was falling harder now, and he noted that his footprints were already nearly covered. There was no other sign of life in the parking lot. The restaurant behind him was obviously doing a brisk business—the lot was relatively full of cars, and he could clearly hear the noise of voices and music coming from within—but outside it was quiet. He presumed it was that particular time when most people coming to the restaurant had already arrived and been seated, but before the time when they'd finished eating and would be departing. He glanced at his watch, and noted irritably that *The Shadow* was late.

Just as he'd lowered his arm, he heard a noise to his right. Turning, he saw a bulky figure moving toward him through the swirling snow.

"Mr. Coryell," said a familiar voice, not metallic any longer. "We meet again."

"You?" Jamie said, surprised as he recognized his visitor; it was not who he'd expected. "What are you doing…"

As he uttered the words, the night visitor's arm raised and a spit of flame leapt from it, accompanied by a soft coughing sound. A bloody flower erupted in the center of Jamie's forehead, his eyes rolled up into his head, and he dropped soundlessly to the ground. The night visitor stepped forward over the prostrate body, fired another shot directly into the heart, then after unscrewing the silencer and replacing it and the 9mm Glock 26 Subcompact pistol in the pocket of his overcoat, he deftly hoisted the body onto his shoulder, stepped forward, and flipped it backward into the dumpster positioned outside the restaurant's door. He then retrieved three garbage bags that had been sitting on the ground next to the dumpster and tossed them in onto the body, shuffled his feet at the point where the body had fallen to cover the bloodstained snow, and headed back toward the front of the restaurant, his tracks and any sign of the incident disappearing rapidly behind him as the snow fell. No more than ninety seconds had elapsed since he had first appeared out of the gloom.

'With a little luck, my entrée won't even have arrived yet,' he thought, as he reentered the busy restaurant, replaced his coat on the rack in the foyer, and resumed his seat and his meal. No one had even noticed that he'd been gone.

PART 5

CHAPTER 66

Washington, DC
Friday, 3 March 2023
3:23 p.m. EST

On the morning of March 3rd, the day following the as yet unknown murder up in Pennsylvania, the Supreme Court issued its ruling on *Morgan vs Navarro*, the lawsuit brought forward with regard to the President's eligibility to be in office. To the surprise of most, but to the pleasure of none, the Justices basically punted the ball farther down the field and said they would try again in sixty days. The ruling said that although a cursory look at the information which was presented to them—they did not refer to anything from *The Beacon* exposé as evidence—seemed to indicate that Ramon Navarro may indeed be ineligible for the presidency by virtue of a foreign birth to non-citizens, and therefore should not have been allowed to run for President in 2020, they were not yet fully convinced and would wait two months to see if more data surfaced before issuing a final ruling. In the meantime, they decreed that Navarro desist from executing his office until such time as that final ruling was issued, and turn over the reins of government to Fran Kerrigan.

The White House immediately issued a statement from the President saying he refused to comply with the ruling. "This ruling is an embarrassment to all true Americans, and I will not obey it. Either I am the President, or I am not," Navarro said, in a testy, hastily called press conference in the West Wing. "They can't have it both ways. To try to thread the needle and say that I should cease in my responsibilities because maybe I'm ineligible is ludicrous, and a gross breach of the principle of separation of powers within our government. As with all Americans, I am innocent until proven guilty, and in this case, that means that until I'm proven not to be a natural born citizen, I will continue to serve as your President." And with that, he had swiftly and adroitly pivoted his wheelchair and sped it out of the briefing room, leaving a startled Barb Singletary to field questions from the frenzied press corps.

The uproar in Congress was no less frenzied. Interestingly, supporters and detractors appeared on both sides of the aisle. For once, Congress had achieved a degree of non-partisanship—at least in the sense of partisan politics along party lines—even though the stridency of the voices was no less heated. Supporters of the President—most of them Democrats—said he was well within his rights to remain in office, at least until the Court issued a final ruling. Some promised to submit a bill within days calling for a Constitutional Amendment to remove the natural born clause from the presidential eligibility criteria, labeling it a now-obsolete artifact of 18th Century geo-politics. Navarro detractors—most of them Republicans—threatened to press forward with impeachment proceedings, now that they felt the President had shown himself guilty of at least a misdemeanor, if not a high crime, by refusing to abide by the Court's decree. The vitriol that flowed on the floors of both houses of Congress reached new levels.

Across the country, lines remained drawn largely by virtue of politics and demographics. Where Democratic governments were in power, support for the President was professed—although not in all cases. Where Republican governments were in power, calls for the President's removal were heard— although not in all cases. The trump card was clearly the depth of the Hispanic population in a particular area; a state with a Republican governor but a largely Hispanic population came down on the Navarro side of the argument—Florida was a case in point. Support for Navarro hardened considerably across the Southwest, with Governors in Texas and Arizona bluntly stating that they would follow no federal directives which did not issue from President Navarro.

Everyone could see that by no stretch of the imagination had the crisis yet passed. But no one could predict how, or when, it would.

CHAPTER 67

Lambertville, NJ
Thursday, 9 March 2023
10:22 a.m. EST

Sue sat alone by the flower-strewn grave long after everyone else had left the cemetery. It was a comparatively warm day for early March. The temperature had risen up to forty-five, but compared to the wintry days of the past weekend it felt almost balmy. Most of the snow that had been deposited by the weekend storm had melted, although patches of white could still be seen in the shadows where the sun's warmth did not yet reach. But despite the warmth of the almost-spring sun, Sue still shivered as the wind blew in off the river.

Jamie had been buried in Riverview Cemetery, just north of Lambertville, high on a bluff overlooking the Delaware River. It was where he'd purchased a plot several years earlier. "Might as well be prepared for the inevitable," he had told Sue when she had laughed upon finding out what he'd done. He said he was breaking new ground for the Coryells, since he had not found any Coryell headstones in Riverview during the cemetery wanderings he'd done in his youth. Sue idly adjusted a bouquet of flowers at the graveside as she remembered the conversation.

Sue had not initially been concerned when she did not get a call from Jamie on the night of his meeting. He had told her it could run late, and he wouldn't wake her if he thought it was too late. She had remained awake in her apartment until midnight, then had succumbed to sleep. By the next morning, however, when no call still had come, she'd begun to get frantic. She'd called Jamie's house, and had gotten only the answering machine. She'd called his office at the *Beacon*, and got no answer. She'd finally connected with Alice on her cell phone, who'd said she had not seen him since the afternoon before, but hadn't she heard the news? At some point in the night a fire had erupted at *The Beacon* office, apparently caused by an electrical problem in one of the high-speed printing machines within the building. All four of Lambertville's fire companies—the Columbia, Union, Fleetwing and Hibernia—had responded to the alarm and had quickly brought the blaze under control before it spread to any adjoining areas, but the rear of the building, which housed the printing machines, archives and Jamie's office, had been totally gutted. Alice was trying to sort through the debris now with the arson inspector.

Eventually Sue had driven out to Peddler's Village and had found his locked car still in the Cock 'n Bull lot, but found no sign of him. She'd waited until after lunch, then called the police. They'd expressed sympathy for her concerns, but said they could not act until at least forty-eight hours had elapsed; they felt it was likely, or at least possible, that Jamie's meeting had extended much longer, and gone into much more depth, than he had anticipated, and he would reappear once his business was done. It was not until Sunday afternoon, that police forces in Pennsylvania and New Jersey had begun to think there might actually be a problem.

The problem had been resolved when Jamie's corpse was discovered as the dumpster behind the Cock 'n Bull, in which it had lain all weekend, was emptied by the Monday morning garbage crew. Sue had been notified by the police within an hour of the discovery, and had rushed out to Doylestown Hospital where she'd had the morbid task of identifying the body. Immediately afterward, while still in the hospital, she had collapsed and been taken to the emergency room to recover. She'd driven home to her empty apartment from Doylestown after recovering several hours later, late on Monday evening, where she'd gone straight to bed and cried herself to sleep.

The next day she'd found it tough to get out of bed, but finally dragged herself out a little after ten o'clock. She'd phoned Alice, Jamie's assistant at *The Beacon*, to give her the devastating news. Then, not wanting to talk to anyone else, she'd fixed herself a bowl of oatmeal and a mug of coffee, wrapped herself up in a fleece-filled robe, and sat in the cold morning air on her balcony overlooking the river. She couldn't remember the last time she felt so alone. When she had left home to strike out on her own, defying her parents to do so, she had never felt so much at a loss. She'd realized sadly that she hadn't understood the depth of her feelings toward Jamie, and now it was too late.

The ringing of the phone just before noon had brought her back to reality, and she'd roused herself from her chair on the balcony and carried the empty bowl and the ice-cold coffee back into her kitchen to answer it. She'd picked up just before the fourth ring, hoping it might be some word from the police concerning the investigation into Jamie's murder. "Hello?" she'd said quietly.

"Hello, Sue, this is Frank Allen. I'm sorry to disturb you. I heard about Jamie. I'm so very sorry." Allen was a longtime friend of both Jamie and Sue, a lawyer who specialized in probate cases and who hung his shingle on his combined office-home kitty-corner across the intersection from Jamie's house in Lambertville. She and Jamie had occasionally been to his house to visit him and his wife, Clara, and they had occasionally come over to Jamie's for a cookout. He was a couple of years younger than Jamie, and had been practicing law in Lambertville for about ten years; Sue knew that both he and Clara were originally from somewhere in north Jersey, and had moved south to escape the sprawl of the ever-expanding New York suburbs. Clara, too, was a lawyer, although she worked as a public defender down in Trenton. They had no children.

"Hi, Frank," she'd answered into the phone, cradling it against her shoulder while she cleaned her oatmeal bowl. "Thanks for calling. I still can't believe it, it doesn't seem real. Guess I'm in a little bit of shock."

"I can only imagine," he'd replied soothingly. "Listen, I won't bother you long, but I wanted to first let you know that if you need anything—anything— just ask and Clara and I will try to help. Okay?"

"Okay, thanks," she'd answered softly.

"Second, I wanted to let you know that Jamie had provided me with a copy of his will a while back, and had named me his executor. So I was going to start arranging for the funeral. But since you're the closest thing he had to a relative, I wanted to talk with you about it first."

She had broken down in tears at that, and had taken several moments to compose herself while Frank tried to calm her over the phone. Eventually, she'd regained her composure, and they were able to agree on the particulars for the funeral.

All of which had gone exactly as planned, ending in the lonely cemetery today. Dozens of people had attended the service, many of them local, but many from some distance away as well. Some were old acquaintances of Jamie, some merely were aware of him and his role in *The Beacon* exposé and wanted to show their support. Barb Singletary, the White House Press Secretary, had even made the trip up from DC to attend. All had been very cordial to Sue, offering condolences and assistance, but all were now gone and she was once again alone with only her memories.

Sue went to Allen's law office in the house on Coryell Street later that afternoon. She'd gone home after sitting at the cemetery for over an hour, tried to eat some soup but found she had no appetite, then had lain on her couch until three. Frank had earlier told her that he needed to review Jamie's affairs with her, and they had agreed to meet at four o'clock. She had walked over from New Hope to clear her head, taking about twenty minutes to do so. Arriving at her destination, she rang the bell at his door, and he opened it immediately and invited her in.

The Allens' house and office was a unique arrangement. Originally two separate row houses, Frank had purchased both and had then remodeled them so that they were combined, on the inside, into one residence. From all outside appearances, they still appeared to be separate dwellings, but inside they had spacious rooms and open areas. The office occupied the front half of the first floor of the left-hand row house; it could be entered from the outside—as Sue had done from the street—or it could be accessed from the interior, which was how Frank and Clara entered. Sue had never before been in the office, a relatively large room with dark paneling, in-wall bookcases, a big executive desk, and a sitting area with a settee and two upholstered chairs centered on a bow window looking out into a garden.

Allen got her seated, then came right to the point. "Sue," he began, "as I told you before, Jamie had provided me with a copy of his will and had named me as the executor for his estate. I actually drew up the will for him, so I'm very familiar with it. I don't know if he ever discussed any of this with you before?" Sue nodded mutely to indicate he had not. "Okay, then. As you know, he had no living relatives, but did have a fairly sizeable estate. This includes not only *The Beacon*, but also his house across the street, and a fair amount of money in a variety of investments. He had a very substantial life insurance policy, also." He paused momentarily. "He has named you as the beneficiary for all of it. Congratulations."

Sue was stunned. She had thought that Frank was going to offer her support as she dealt with her grief, but had not had an inkling that Jamie would have done anything like this. "Are you sure?" she stammered out. "I would have thought he'd have donated his things to the town, or Columbia, or somewhere."

"No, I'm quite sure," Frank responded, smiling assuredly. "He wanted you to have everything. He's attached no strings. He told me that he didn't care what you did with the estate, but that he wanted you to have it. You're free to retain it all, or to sell it all, as you wish." He paused, then continued. "Whatever you decide, I'll be happy to help you deal with it. It would be my pleasure to do it *pro bono* as a way to honor Jamie's memory."

"Thank you, Frank," she said, reaching out to touch his hand. "You're a good friend, and you're too kind." She let out a whoosh of air. "I really don't know what to say. I'll need to think about things for a while."

"I'd expect nothing less," he answered. He stood up from his chair and walked over to his desk, where he picked up a thick manila envelope. He returned to his seat, then gave it to her. "These are all the documents pertaining to the estate, as well as a copy of all the necessary keys. Jamie even has one in there for his car. Take some time to go through it, and then, when you're ready, we'll talk again and I'll get you to sign a few things for me to send to the Surrogate's Office." The County Surrogate, whose office was at the county seat, Flemington, north of Lambertville, probated all wills. "You're free to enter the buildings, use the car, whatever you wish."

"Frank, again, thanks so much. I really do appreciate it." She opened the envelope, and withdrew a small pouch that contained a number of keys. She smiled as she noticed a small tag on each one describing what it was for in Jamie's neat handwriting. She looked up at Allen. "You know, I think I'd like to go over and walk through the house. Would that be alright?"

"Sure, Sue. As I said, you're welcome to go anywhere. It's all yours now."

"Would you come with me?" she asked. "At least the first time, I think I'd rather not be alone over there."

"Sure," he smiled. "Let's go."

They walked across the street, climbed the steps to the porch, and unlocked the door. It opened easily, the key working perfectly. The house looked as if it was waiting for Jamie to come home. A book sat next to his easy chair in the living room, remote control for the TV close at hand. Back in the kitchen, breakfast plates still sat in the sink. A pile of mail sat on the island; she wondered idly where the rest of his mail was now. As they walked, she reached out to touch an item here and there, lost in memory. They headed back toward the front of the house and began to climb the stairs to the second floor. Peeking into the bedroom, Sue teared up briefly when she saw the neatly made bed—Jamie always was very fastidious—and noticed her framed picture on his dresser. She wiped her cheeks and they moved back toward the office, where Sue stood outside the door looking in. She had grown suddenly still.

"Frank," she said slowly, "something's not right here." She stepped into the room and looked around. Something was out of place, she just couldn't find it.

"What do you mean?" he asked.

"Has anybody else been in here since Jamie died?"

"No one," he replied. "At least not since Monday. I had the police seal the building as soon as I got the news. What's wrong?"

"I don't know," she said, "something just doesn't feel right. Like somebody was here and moved stuff around and then replaced it all. Like they were looking for something." She was walking around the small room as she talked, looking at an item here, and an item there. Finally, her eyes settled on the laptop on the desk; it was open. "There," she said, pointing. "The laptop. Jamie never leaves it open like that. He always closes it when he's done work. Thinks it's going to get dust and dirt in the keyboard if it stays open." She smiled ruefully over at Allen as she said it, as if to say 'You know what he was like.' "Somebody's been using it."

"Sue," Frank said, "how can you be sure? Maybe Jamie forgot to close it, maybe he was in a rush. Could be anything." He looked at her, seeing the set look on her face. "Okay, I'll get the police to come in and check the place out to see if anyone has been here."

"Don't bother," Sue replied. "They won't find anything. There won't be anything to find." And she turned on her heel and left the room, heading down the stairs and out the door, all the while thinking 'But I know you've been here, and I'll find a way to do something about it.' Allen hurried after her, trying to keep up, not understanding what she was talking about.

CHAPTER 68

Washington, DC
Monday, 13 March 2023
11:27 a.m. EDT

As the debate raged across the nation regarding the status of President Navarro, matters soon came to a head regarding orders from the Pentagon.

On the Friday following the impotent Supreme Court ruling, orders were issued from the Office of the Secretary of Defense for all Army, Marine and Air Force units preparing to move into Mexico to stand down and await further instructions. In doing so, Secretary Post indicated that until the issue of the President's authority was completely clarified by the Supreme Court, he would not accede to the President's direction to move forces into northern Mexico for the purpose of establishing military protectorates. On this Friday, as well, the Court had indicated that they planned to issue that ruling on May 2nd.

Close observers of the Washington political scene were not greatly surprised that Post would balk at the President's request, although most did express surprise that the opposition was so blatant. It was an open secret in Washington that the President and his Defense Secretary did not always see eye to eye. It was also a not-so-open secret that Secretary Post had come to believe that Ray Navarro was unfit for office—ineligible for office, if truth be told—and that he was eager to see him on his way back to Houston.

Within hours of the SecDef's statement, the President announced that he had fired Aaron Post as Defense Secretary and issued instructions once again for forces to move south. And within days of that, the problem escalated.

On the following Monday, the Commanding General at Fort Hood, Texas, Lieutenant General John Gribble, announced that he would not comply with the President's orders to move forces to Mexico. He stated that he believed, because of the Supreme Court's order that President Navarro cease to act as president until a final determination was made in May, that the President had no legitimate authority to direct the nation's military. General Gribble was joined in his refusal by several of his senior officers, including three other generals from the sprawling post in the center of Texas. Within hours, a separate set of officers from the post had announced that they would, contrary to their superiors' announcement, obey the Navarro directive. And within hours of that, Military Police units from the Texas National Guard moved onto the post at the direction of the Governor and arrested all those who had refused Navarro's orders. President Navarro, along with his Acting Secretary of Defense, Jared Radcliffe, issued a statement saying that all of those officers had been relieved of their duties, and would be kept in confinement at Fort Hood until a court-martial could be convened; in their place, Texas Army National Guard officers were appointed to assume their responsibilities.

Disturbances flared immediately following this amazing series of events. The President ordered all federal installations to go to a high state of alert and 'lock-down,' thereby preventing anyone from entering or leaving the installations. Most of the officers commanding these bases obeyed immediately. However, the commanders of Hanscom Air Force Base outside of Boston, and Oceana Naval Air Station near Norfolk, Virginia, refused to comply, indicating that they would only accept orders from Vice President Kerrigan, and welcoming 'reinforcements' from the state National Guards which supported their actions.

The most significant confrontation during this extraordinary period arose in New York, the location of the Army's Fort Drum. This strategic base was home to the 10th Mountain Division, which had also received instructions to deploy one of its brigades to Mexico in support of III Corps from Fort Hood. Two days after the mutiny at Fort Hood, the Governor of New York, a vocal detractor of Navarro, ordered his National Guard to enter Fort Drum and prevent any Army units from deploying. The Commanding General of the 10th Mountain issued weapons and ammunition to his troops and prepared for a defense against the state's attempt to seize it, while the Adjutant General of the New York Guard began moving units from across the state into positions from which an assault could be conducted. To the horror of all, shots were fired by the Army defenders when National Guardsmen made an attempt to enter the post; fortunately, no one was injured in the skirmish and both sides settled into a state of watchful waiting as cooler heads prevailed, at least for the time being.

Increasingly, the country began to take sides, and the vehemence of the rhetoric grew louder and angrier. All hoped for a quick resolution to the crisis, although all prayed that their side would prevail. No one wanted to think about what might happen if shots were again fired, but this time hit their mark.

CHAPTER 69

Washington, DC
Thursday, 16 March 2023
10:23 a.m. EDT

"General, what I want to know is whether the military is going to support their President or not?" President Navarro was behind the Resolute Desk in the Oval Office, addressing Sam Fuller, the Chairman of the Joint Chiefs, who was seated in a chair in front of the desk. Flanking him in chairs on either side were Josh Caldwell, on his right, and Jared Radcliffe, the Acting Defense Secretary, on his left. The President fidgeted with the wheels of his chair as he spoke; this was one of those times when he sorely wished he could once again pace about.

"Mister President," Fuller answered evenly in reply, "I can assure you that you have the loyalty and support of the overwhelming majority of officers within the armed forces. They are fully…"

"Then, General, tell me why we're still having to deal with mutinies across the country?" Navarro had been in an angry mood ever since the meeting had begun over an hour ago; his mood had not improved the further it progressed.

"Sir, there will always be a handful of malcontents whenever you have an organization the size of America's military. As those few are identified, they can be dealt with, just as they have been this week. I can assure you…"

"Then tell me, what is being done to eliminate the mutinies that still exist at Hanscom and Oceana. And tell me what is being done to ensure the loyalty of the National Guard."

"Mister President," interjected Radcliffe, "those situations have been contained. Hanscom and Oceana are anomalies, and no other incidents have taken place at any other federal installations." He glanced over at Caldwell, who sat stony-faced, staring out the windows behind the President's head. "The National Guard is more problematic, though. As you know, sir, those militias are controlled by the states until such time as they are federalized, although the federal government does provide them with their funding and other resources. Unless we want to…"

"I know all that, Jared," the President replied acidly. "I want you—and you, General"—here he pointed a finger at Fuller's chest—"to come up with a way to ensure their loyalty. Cut off their funding if need be. Refuse them training if they refuse to obey my orders. Do whatever it takes. But I don't want to hear about anymore state Guards interfering with the business of U.S. military activities. Do I make myself clear?"

"Yes, sir," they both said in unison.

"Good. Then our interview for today is concluded. I'll expect to hear of some substantial progress when we meet again next week, and I'll expect the mutinies at Hanscom and Oceana to be dealt with soon." He looked from one to the other, a scowl on the ravaged face. "You know your way out, I'm sure." They nodded, rose immediately from their chairs and moved quickly out of the office.

Navarro pivoted his chair so that he could also look out the windows behind his desk; he began to massage his left forearm without even realizing it. Caldwell watched him closely, concerned by the tenor of the meeting. He had not expected it to go well, given the unwelcome incidents in Massachusetts, New York and Virginia earlier in the week, but even he had been surprised by the anger and sarcasm in the President's voice. He was glad now that he had excluded Kerrigan from the meeting, even though Radcliffe had wanted her to attend. But he was concerned also with the President's physical appearance. He looked more tired than ever, the strain of his recovery, coupled with the stress generated as a result of the continual attacks in the media on him, clearly wearing him down. He'd have to find a way to convince him to slow down.

"Josh," the President finally said, still looking out the windows toward the South Lawn, "would you get me my pills, please? One of each. After that meeting, I need another dose."

"Mister President, are you sure you should have more so soon?"

"Just get me the pills, Josh," the President shouted, startling Caldwell who jumped up from his chair and went toward Number 500 to retrieve them.

"Here you are, sir," he said on returning, handing Navarro a glass of water along with the pain and anxiety medicine.

"Thanks, Josh," the President replied, calm now. "Sorry about that. The more meetings I have, the more irritable I seem to get lately." He gave his old friend a brief smile, then swallowed the pills. He handed the now empty glass back to Caldwell, then asked, "Josh, are we doing the right thing? I mean, is all that we're going through going to be worth it in the end? Julia doesn't think so, and any more I'm not sure that I do either. Perhaps for the good of the country I should just leave." He turned his head to look at his old friend. "Sometimes I'd just like it all to go away."

Caldwell thought carefully before he responded, then said cautiously, "Sir, you are the legitimate president. No matter what gets printed in the press or tossed about on the Hill, nothing can change that. You're also the right man for the job, which is why you still have such overwhelming support from the people." That remark was somewhat disingenuous on Caldwell's part; Navarro indeed did have overwhelming support throughout the South and Southwest, but his approval ratings had tumbled in the mid-West and Northeast since last week. "You just need to remember that you're still recovering from last year's attack, and you need to get enough rest." He paused, considering his next remark. "I'm sure Julia would agree with me."

"Oh, she does, Josh, she does," Navarro replied, eyes closed but with a smile on his face. "Thanks. I know I can always count on you." He opened his eyes, and turned his head again toward Caldwell. "I'm going to rest here for a little while," he said after a moment, "then I'll make some more of those phone calls you keep pushing on me." He again closed the hazel eyes and leaned his head back in his chair.

Caldwell left the office and headed down the hall to his own. When he arrived, he found General Webster, the White House Physician, waiting for him. Caldwell had asked the doctor to come down from Walter Reed to talk with him this morning, and even though he was thirty minutes early, Caldwell ushered him straight into his office and launched right into the discussion.

"General, do I need to worry about the President or not?"

Webster hesitated a moment before answering. "Governor, if you're asking me if the President is still capable of executing the duties of his office, my answer is yes. None of his physical injuries, and none of his mental stress, preclude that. If you're asking me if his health is being put at risk, my answer is again a yes. The strain that he's under at the moment is adversely affecting his health as his body continues to heal. But that's the dilemma. If he continues in the job, he'll be under stress, and his health, both physical and mental, will suffer. If he gives up the job, even temporarily, the absence of stress will allow his health to improve and his body will heal more rapidly. Pick your poison."

Caldwell considered his next questions, wondering how far he should go. "Are you aware that he talks to Julia?"

Webster nodded. "Of course I am. But I don't think that's anything to be concerned about. Many people, all of them considered perfectly rational and completely well, talk out loud, either to themselves or to an invisible presence. It's simply an outlet. The President does it as a way to relieve some of the stress he's under, which in my mind is much better than trying to hold it all in. Wouldn't you agree?"

"I would," Caldwell replied. "I'm just glad to hear you say it." He paused to jot himself a note in a binder in front of him on the desk, then continued. "And do I need to worry about his medication? It seems to me he's using it very frequently now, more frequently than he has previously. Any problems there?"

"Again, not in my opinion," Webster said. "His use is still within prescribed limits, and he doesn't manifest any ill side-effects from it. I'm keeping my eye on it."

"Good. That's what I was hoping to hear." Caldwell and Webster chatted a few more moments about the President's recuperative program, then Webster departed.

As he exited the West Wing and strode across the parking area to where he'd left his car, he thought to himself, 'I do hope what I told you is true, Governor. But only time will tell.'

That evening in the White House, President Navarro wheeled himself down the long corridor on the second floor and entered the Telegraph Room. He carried a book with him—a political thriller, the genre he most favored— but it was only for show in case someone came upon him there. He had no intention of reading, he only wanted to talk with Julia.

He wheeled himself to the south side of the room, near the darkened windows, where he'd had a space cleared next to a small table with a reading lamp on it. The wireless control for the sound system in the room lay on the table, and he used it to turn on a selection of Mozart violin concertos. He closed his eyes as the music grew around him. He knew she was there with him.

'What am I going to do?' he said to her in his mind. He held the book on his lap, and anyone looking into the room would think that the President was merely taking a nap, tired from his reading. 'Should I stay, or should I go? It's getting to be too much for me. And I want to see you; I've been without you too long.'

'You've got to wait longer, my love,' she replied, her voice clearly heard in his mind. 'When the time is right, I'll ask you to come. Until then, you must continue. Josh will help you.'

'I know,' he replied. 'But I'd rather be with you.'

'Soon,' she answered, 'soon.' And he drifted off to sleep as the sleeping pill he'd taken earlier took effect, a peaceful smile on his face.

CHAPTER 70

Buckingham, PA
Sunday, 19 March 2023
1:12 p.m. EDT

The day after the funeral, Sue had decided she wanted to see her parents. They had met Jamie, however briefly, when he and Sue had visited Washington in the fall, and she felt they'd be able to help assuage her grief. To her surprise, and her secret pleasure, they had insisted on coming north to their Bucks County home to meet her there. She had driven out to it from New Hope this morning, arriving shortly before lunchtime.

The Moscones' Pennsylvania home was a large estate at the end of a long, gated driveway through the woods off of Lower Mountain Road, not too far from the county seat of Doylestown where they'd been married, and about five miles from New Hope. They had purchased the home shortly after Sue had been born, and she had been raised there, although she never really got to know much about the area until she struck out on her own at nineteen. As a child, she had been shuttled between boarding schools and her parent's townhouse in Washington, and only rarely ventured outside of this estate's fenced environs. The Moscones had retained this home and listed it as their principle residence, primarily to meet the residency requirements for his tenure in the Senate and hers in the House of Representatives, but both spent most of their time in Washington and only ventured up here during campaigns. A small caretaker's cottage was also located on the estate, and the elderly couple who lived there kept the house and grounds in good repair, waiting for the infrequent event of their masters' arrival.

Sue always tended to think of the imposing home as a fortress, not just because of her cloistered upbringing but also because of its gothic architectural style, and she'd thought that again as she exited the woods on the long driveway and the mansion came into view. She knew also that the Secret Service had done work to improve the security of the estate when her mother had been elected as Vice President two years earlier, and that knowledge only added to her mindset. Built out of stone, with turrets and gables, the immense two-story house boasted over five thousand square feet of living space scattered about five bedrooms plus the other requisite areas—library, game room, conservatory, gourmet kitchen—as well as a three-car garage, covered swimming pool, and an extensive set of gardens. '*The Clue House*' she'd thought, dredging up the name she always called it, based on the infamous Boddy Mansion from the popular board game and not-so-popular movie. She'd chuckled to herself at the thought as she pulled Jamie's Ford around the circle up to the front door, parked, shut off the ignition, and approached to ring the bell. As had happened in Washington, the door was opened before she could do so by her mother; she wondered if her mother always watched from hiding as guests approached so she could pull that feat.

"Susan," Kerrigan exclaimed, rushing to embrace her only child. "How wonderful to see you. But under such terrible circumstances. Come in, come in and we'll have lunch and talk."

"Thanks, Mother, it's good to see you, too," she'd said sincerely

Her father had been talking quietly on the phone with someone when she entered the main foyer—she could see him in his den which adjoined the main entryway—and he waved to her while he concluded his talk. He soon joined her and Kerrigan on the sunporch at the rear of the house, where a table had been set out for them for lunch.

"Susan," he said, "so good to see you, *bella*." She smiled at the use of the old, familiar pet name for her. "We're so sorry to hear about Jamie. Is there anything we can do for you?"

"No, Daddy, I don't think there's anything. The police are still working on it, but they say it will take time, and they can't promise anything for sure." Her eyes began to tear up at the thought. "But thanks for asking. That means a lot."

They had talked through lunch, and on into the afternoon. Sue could not remember enjoying such a pleasant time with her parents in many years. She described for them the events of the past weekend, her anguish, her grief once the murder was discovered, her surprise at the results of Jamie's will. "I haven't really decided what to do about it all yet," she said. "Maybe I'll get into the newspaper business and pick up where Jamie left off."

"But sweetheart, I don't know if that's such a wise choice," Kerrigan said, concern on her face. "I mean, clearly it's a dangerous profession. I wouldn't want you to put yourself in any danger." She closed her eyes at the thought. "Who could have done such a thing?" she asked. "Who stands to gain?"

"You know who," answered Moscone, grimly. "Your nemesis, Josh Caldwell. All of these stories were hitting Navarro hard, and now that they're stopped, the pressure's off. I'll bet he thinks that things couldn't be better right now."

"But Fred, surely you don't think he could be involved with this murder?" Kerrigan asked. "It must have been someone else."

"*Cara mia*, if there's anything I've learned in Washington, it's not to be too surprised by anything that somebody there does. Could Caldwell have done it? Well, he probably didn't pull the trigger, but he sure has enough contacts who do pull triggers to be able to make it happen." He looked over to Sue. "You be careful of him. He's one ruthless, vindictive man."

"I'll remember, Daddy," she answered dutifully.

The rest of the afternoon had passed quickly, and Sue felt a load of tension had been lifted from her as she drove back to New Hope shortly after five. 'Funny,' she thought as she drove. 'I've been running from them for years, but when I hit bottom, I turn to them. And they make me feel better.' She promised to keep in closer touch from now on. Her parents had suggested she come back to DC with them to stay for a while, at least until she got over this initial stage of grief, but she had politely refused. She knew her home was here, and although she'd be glad to have her parents back in her life, she wouldn't put herself entirely back into theirs.

It was only after she got back to her apartment that she wondered why her father had been so certain that Caldwell stood to gain the most from Jamie's death.

CHAPTER 71

Washington, DC
Thursday, 30 March 2023
4:31 p.m. EDT

Throughout the latter days of March, the mood across the country rapidly declined into a pervasive, pessimistic gloom. The partisans on each side of the stand-off were increasingly angry, and their voices filled the airwaves, the internet, and the written page with their arguments and their demands. Those on the Navarro side of the dispute pledged their continued support for the beleaguered President, threatening to strenuously—even violently, if necessary—oppose any act or group which refused to submit to his authority and comply with his orders. Those aligning themselves against Navarro labeled him a pretender, a usurper, a traitor—and those were the kind terms used— and pledged equally strenuously to see him removed from the White House and to see the rule of law restored. There was very little middle ground in the dispute, and whatever shades of gray had existed which might have enabled some compromise to be suggested were rapidly being defined into stark blacks and whites.

Throughout these tumultuous weeks, the Supreme Court remained mute. Having said they would issue a final ruling on the matter at the beginning of May, the Justices blithely—some said callously—ignored the turmoil sweeping the nation. From both sides of the argument, calls were made urging the Court to accelerate their deliberations and issue a ruling sooner. But they issued no comments, made no off the record remarks. They continued their business as if nothing else was wrong with the world, as if they felt the matter too inconsequential to warrant their attention, while others took matters into their own hands.

More unrest surfaced within the military during this period. More and more, senior officers began to publicly question the legitimacy of any orders originating with the Navarro administration, and instances of outright disobedience to issued orders became more commonplace. During the last week of March, the Republican Governors of six western states—Idaho, Montana, Utah, Wyoming, and North and South Dakota—all declared states of emergency as a result of scattered protests and called out their National Guard units to maintain order. These Governors, all staunch Navarro opponents, were strongly supported in this by the servicemen and women of their militias; almost to a man, they answered the call to duty that the Governors had issued. They were told to enforce curfews and clear the streets in the cities where protests had occurred, and were instructed to either take control of federal military installations within their state or to shut off access to those installations so that they were ineffectual. The Guard went about their tasks enthusiastically and effectively. Malmstrom Air Force Base in Montana, and Mountain Home Air Force Base in Idaho, were handed over to the control of the Guard by the active duty Air Force officers in command there, just as those at Hanscom and Oceana had done earlier. Some pundits noted sarcastically on TV later in the evening following those takeovers that the Governor of Montana now controlled more nuclear missiles than most nations of the world. Other Army and Air Force installations in the Dakotas, Wyoming and Utah, which remained under federal control, were nonetheless surrounded and cut off as units of the state militias moved into positions around them.

The backlash to these actions was swift in coming, and was not confined purely to the military. Across the Southwest, and in Florida, bills were introduced in the state legislatures calling for secession from the Union. At first, these motions were not considered serious, everyone naturally having considered the matter of secession to have been definitively dealt with 170 years earlier. But as the bills advanced in the legislatures and garnered popular support in those states—notably in Texas, Florida, New Mexico and Arizona—concern grew, and grew even further when the Governors and National Guards of those states publically proffered their support for the secessionists, saying they'd rather form a new union than remain in an untrustworthy one. States of emergency were also declared in these areas, but unlike in the north, the federal installations here were fully supportive of the governors' actions.

In Congress, the bill calling for a constitutional amendment to eliminate the natural born eligibility requirement for a president was passed by the required two-thirds majority in both houses in record time—opponents referred to it as 'record haste'—and sent to the State Legislatures for ratification, although no one anticipated that the necessary approval of 38 states—a three-fourths majority—would be forthcoming anytime soon. Calls also began to be heard for the convening of a constitutional convention to make wholesale changes to the document, rather than merely tinkering with it through the amendment process; again, no one expected that this initiative would gain any traction within the states, where two-thirds would have to agree to convene such a meeting. But it was still very discomfiting to hear the calls said aloud.

Battle lines were drawn—literally—and all could see that it would not take much to set the powder kegs off.

CHAPTER 72

Washington, DC
Saturday, 15 April 2023
10:28 a.m. EDT

The mood in the White House fared no better than that in the rest of the country. Tempers were short, and the staff felt they were engaged in a losing delaying action, attempting to forestall the inevitable. Although Barb Singletary conducted daily briefings with the press, at which she put the best spin she could on the accumulating tide of bad news, she admitted to her staff that she felt she was simply keeping fingers in the dike. Although the Cabinet Secretaries continued with the business of government, in private they were considering whether they should bolt to the other side. And although Josh Caldwell was trying to keep everyone in line and everything on an even keel, he was growing ever more concerned about the President's health.

Matters came to a head right around the time that taxes were due. During the buildup to Tax Day, real concerns grew that taxpayers would literally revolt and not only refuse to pay their taxes, but cease to abide by many other laws as well. President Navarro was found working at all hours of the night and day in the Oval Office, refusing to rest as advised by his Chief of Staff and his physician, and taking medication as abundantly as necessary to keep himself going. He grimly referred to his office as the 'bunker,' issued a continual stream of orders to agencies across the nation—most of which Caldwell shortstopped and did not send out—and began to see evil and evildoers everywhere. He refused to meet with the Vice President or the Cabinet anymore; he felt they were all trying to undermine him. He refused to respond to calls from the Congress; he said they were only looking out for their own skins, and had no regard for the nation. He refused to participate in those little trappings of office—such as picture opportunities, meeting visiting groups, hosting social events—which he had previously enjoyed so much, and which meant so much to the people; he claimed he had not the time for such nonsense any longer.

His physical health was now visibly deteriorating as well. People who met him now were shocked by his haggard appearance. For most, his condition brought to mind pictures of Lincoln and FDR that had been taken in the days and weeks prior to their deaths, when these two Presidents looked old before their time. Ray Navarro now had that same look. Dulled hair that was now more white than black; sunken eyes surmounting dark circles; a gaunt face and drained body. And never a smile anymore, which was really what people noticed.

Ultimately, it caught up with him, and in mid-April he collapsed at his desk. He had been working with Caldwell and Ollie Holcombe, the National Security Advisor, when his eyes rolled back in his head and he slumped sideways in his chair. Only a quick move by Holcombe prevented him from tumbling out of it. Medics in the White House were summoned to administer first aid, stabilizing him quickly, but Caldwell called General Webster and demanded that he come immediately from Walter Reed to attend to his most important patient. Webster arrived within twenty minutes, reviewed the situation, and immediately sedated the President and ordered him to bed, with instructions that he should remain there indefinitely.

Caldwell ordered that the President's situation be kept from the public. He was supported in this by Webster, and that evening a decision was made to move the President to Camp David, north of Washington in the Catoctin Mountains of Maryland, where he could recuperate and regain his strength. He also prescribed a regimen of sedatives to keep Navarro at ease, and increased the dosage of his anti-anxiety medication.

A terse press release issued the following day stated merely that the President had gone to Camp David for a change of scenery, and that he would remain there until the end of the month. Vice President Kerrigan, who had been virtually isolated from contact with Navarro for the past several weeks, was watching the television at home with her husband when she heard the news. She had not been given any prior notification of the move by Caldwell, and felt her anger at the man well up anew. She looked over at Moscone, who raised one eyebrow in surprise at the information. "Looks like the time is near, Franny," Moscone said, smiling contentedly while still watching the set from the couch. "You're into the end-game. It won't be long now," he predicted knowingly.

CHAPTER 73

Camp David, Maryland
Sunday, 30 April 2023
3:43 p.m. EDT

Camp David, officially Naval Support Facility Thurmont, is a mountain-based military camp used as a country retreat and for high alert protection of the President of the United States and his guests. First known as Hi-Catoctin, Camp David was originally built during the FDR years as a camp for federal government agents and their families, opening in 1938. In 1942, it was converted to a presidential retreat by President Roosevelt, and received its present name from President Eisenhower the following decade in honor of his grandson.

The camp is very isolated and quiet, which is why presidents and their families have enjoyed it so much over the years. The compound consists of several cabins hidden throughout the woods, connected only by small mulch walking paths; these cabins are all named after various trees, plants, and flowers. Officially a Navy installation, the retreat is maintained by Navy Seabees and guarded at all times by hand-picked Marines.

President Navarro was quartered in the main lodge, currently designated as 'Laurel.' Selected personally by FDR when the presidential retreat was opened, Laurel Lodge had been modified and improved over the years so that now it included a large, combined dining-living room with a huge stone fireplace, a bedroom wing, kitchen wing, and a large screened-in porch that adjoins a flagstone terrace. The exterior is constructed of local stone and hardwood. Surrounding it in close proximity are a swimming pool, bowling alley, putting green, skeet range, and a barbecue area. During the early days of his presidency, Ray and Julia had frequently come up to the retreat on weekends, inviting small groups of close friends who would stay in the guest cabins. Navarro had not been to Camp David since Julia's death.

Webster had forbidden the President to enter Birch Lodge, which was the three-room cottage configured as an office for presidential use. Members of the President's staff had made the trip with him this time, occupying guest cabins and working out of Birch; Caldwell was keeping the government running from there and holding the wolves at bay, continuing to push Navarro's policies forward. But Navarro had yet to venture into the place. Although he was feeling much better, he had given Webster his word that he would completely relax and rest, and he had held to it. At least so far.

Webster, on the other hand, did not share the President's view that he was feeling much better. "You might be more rested," he'd told Navarro bluntly, "but you're far from well. If you don't allow yourself to completely relax, you might never get well." The President had acquiesced, but the doctor still was worried. Navarro's medication dosages remained disturbingly high, and his pain was stubbornly resisting going down. He had attempted periodically to wean the President from the medications, but had always relented when Navarro had said he needed more. Whenever he felt he was making some progress, Navarro would demand more to drown out a pain or a bad feeling. Webster also noted that the President was more frequently invoking Julia, and while Navarro did not admit speaking with her, the doctor knew that he most certainly did. Frequently. Many times he had come quietly up on the President, either in the lodge or on the terrace, and heard him carrying on a lengthy discourse with his wife. 'Time heals all wounds,' he thought, not knowing what other remedy he could employ.

This day, the President had enjoyed a quiet afternoon watching a baseball game on TV, with Caldwell and Barb Singletary in attendance. Navarro had been thrilled to discover that the Astros were on national television that afternoon—he had been an Astros fan for as long as he could remember, even though they had not been real contenders for decades—and had been more thrilled when they ultimately defeated the Phillies in extra innings.

"That makes for a perfect afternoon," he said, smiling at Caldwell and Singletary as the final popup was caught by the Astros' shortstop. He had to admit that he was feeling much more relaxed, not being around Washington and not having to listen to the constant clamor. Caldwell had insisted that the President receive only the minimal amount of briefings necessary while at Camp David, and had personally seen to it that not a word of what was happening in the country reached his ears. Foreign affairs, national security, trade issues—all that was okay. But anything touching on Ray Navarro's legitimacy was off-limits.

Today, however, Vice President Kerrigan was arriving at the compound to meet with the President for a private dinner. The two had been in contact by phone several times during his stay in Maryland, and Kerrigan had insisted that they needed to meet face to face. Navarro felt there could be no harm in that and had agreed, overriding Caldwell's initial inclination to postpone the get-together until an unspecified time in the future. She was due to arrive at five o'clock, approximately another hour.

"Mister President," Caldwell said, "are you sure you'd prefer that I not join you and the Vice President for dinner?" They'd been over this before, but Caldwell thought he'd try one more time.

"No, Josh. Not this time. Fran insisted that we talk privately, and I want to accommodate her." He suddenly reached up to rub his forehead as a pain blossomed behind his eyes. "I don't see any harm in that." He looked over at Singletary, who was watching him carefully. "Barb, would you do me a favor and get me two of my Vicodins from the bedroom? They're in there on the nightstand next to the bed. Thanks," he finished, as she got up from her chair in front of the television and headed back toward the bedroom. "Josh, let's go out on the terrace and enjoy some air, huh?"

"Yes, sir," Caldwell agreed, moving behind the President and reaching to guide the wheelchair through the wide doors onto the flagstones. The sky was perfectly clear and blue, a wonderful spring day. The temperature hovered about sixty-five, but neither of them needed any kind of outer jacket. A slight breeze whispered through the pines surrounding the lodge. "A beautiful day, isn't it, sir?"

"Yes, Josh, it surely is," Navarro replied. He continued to massage his head, looking out into the trees. "Josh," he spoke softly, "remember that last time we had the cookout with you on the balcony at the White House? I just realized that was just about exactly a year ago. Julia was so happy that night," he paused and stopped massaging his head to rub his eyes. He looked over to Caldwell. "Hard to believe it's been a year, doesn't it?"

"Yes, sir, it does."

"You know, I remember telling Julia that night that I didn't know how I'd go on if I ever lost her." He laughed derisively at the sentiment. "But here it is a year later, and I'm still going on without her." He sighed. "I really miss her."

"We all do, sir," Caldwell said, stopping himself from saying anything more as Singletary arrived with the President's medicine. He accepted the two pills from her with a word of thanks, and swallowed them down quickly with a drink of water.

"There, that should hold me for a while, at least," he said, then looked over to Caldwell. "You know, I think I'll take a quick nap before Fran arrives. Want to be on my best behavior with her, you know?"

"Good idea, sir," they both said almost in unison. "I'll take you into the room," Caldwell continued, and began pushing the wheelchair back into the lodge. They entered the bedroom, and Caldwell, assisted by a Secret Service agent summoned from the front door, transferred the President's thin body from the chair and onto the bed, propping him up slightly on pillows so that his head and shoulders were slightly elevated.

"Thanks, guys. Feels good. Josh, I'll just rest about forty-five minutes or so. If I don't ring before then, please have somebody wake me then. Okay?"

"Fine, Mister President. I'll take care of it," he responded. "You get some rest."

And Caldwell and the agent exited the room, quietly closing the door behind them.

Navarro lay in the darkened room for several moments, waiting for all to be silent outside. Then, once he knew that Julia was with him, he began to talk softly with her.

Kerrigan's helicopter settled down on the pad at Camp David shortly after five. She was met there by Caldwell, driving a small golf cart which often served as a shuttle to take visitors from the helipad up to the main compound. They talked as they rode.

"How is the President, Josh?" she asked.

"He's doing well, Madame Vice President, very well. He's resting at the moment, but will be up shortly to meet with you." He glanced sideways at her; she stared straight ahead, watching the dirt path they were on with trepidation as he raced forward. "I asked to sit in on your dinner, and he refused. Says you want to talk in private. Mind sharing with me what's on your mind?"

"Yes, Josh, as a matter of fact, I do mind. But I'll tell you anyway." She now turned to look at him. "I just want to have a simple conversation with him to see how he's doing. Nothing mysterious. No ulterior motives. Just a talk."

"Well, that's good," Caldwell drawled, slowing the cart as they neared the lodge. "Just remember that he's still regaining his strength. I implore you not to upset him about things."

"Not me, Josh," she said, disingenuously. "Just a talk. That's all."

They arrived at the front of the lodge to see that President Navarro had been wheeled out onto the porch by one of the agents. "Greetings, Fran. Welcome to Shangri-La," he said, laughing, invoking FDR's original name for the compound which he had taken from James Hilton's 1933 novel *Lost Horizons* describing a mystical Himalayan valley harboring an earthly paradise. "How was your flight?"

"Very smooth, Mister President," she replied, getting out of the cart and climbing the stairs to the porch. "No problems. You're looking very well, sir, if I may say so. Much better than the last time I saw you. How do you feel?"

"I feel great," he answered, still smiling. "Amazing what some clear, mountain air will do for you. Everybody ought to have a getaway place like this."

They entered the main room of the lodge, where a table for two had been set in front of the window overlooking the terrace. "I thought perhaps we could have a drink first, then eat." Kerrigan nodded her approval. "I asked Josh and Barb to join us for the drinks, then they'll leave so we can talk privately." He ignored Caldwell's scowl at this comment; Kerrigan saw it, too, and smiled inwardly.

They had their drinks on the terrace overlooking the putting green and barbecue area. The President's staff was serving a local white Pinot Grigio from the Linganore Winecellar in nearby Mount Airy, one of a handful of promising wineries scattered throughout central Maryland. They chatted comfortably for about fifteen minutes, with the President needling the Vice President about the Astros' victory over the Phillies, then moved back into the lodge where the meal had been laid out. Caldwell and Singletary bid their farewells, and Navarro and Kerrigan began their meal.

They talked easily as they ate; Navarro was surprised at how comfortable he felt. Over an appetizer of cantaloupe and honeydew melon balls, served with a small wedge of Asiago cheese, they discussed the President's health, with Navarro speaking candidly about his problems and his frustration with his slow progress; Kerrigan shared some of the details of her recent rapprochement with Sue, although not all. They continued their easy talk as the staff brought out a mixed salad topped with pine nuts and feta, and served with a balsamic vinaigrette dressing. And it continued on as their entrees—a sliced pork loin in a peppercorn sauce, with roasted potatoes and succotash—were delivered. But then, after the staff had closed the kitchen door for the final time, the tone of the conversation changed.

"Mister President," began Kerrigan abruptly, setting her fork down on her plate, "I wanted to speak with you about what's been happening across the country during your absence. Will that be alright?"

Navarro looked at her warily; his right hand moved over to the left, seemingly on its own; he moved it away when he realized what he had done, and picked up his fork to spear another piece of pork. "I don't think you'll make Josh very happy, but why not?" He looked at her with haunted eyes. "What's going on?"

Over the next twenty minutes, as they slowly ate, she described to him the unrest that was now engulfing the country. Since his sequester at Camp David, riots had broken out in several major cities, Chicago and Cleveland among them; dozens of injuries had occurred, hundreds of arrests, and millions of dollars in damages as fires blazed and properties were looted. Congress was paralyzed, bogged down in acerbic name-calling that prevented them from trying to find a compromise that would defuse the tensions. The so-called 'natural born' amendment—that bill already passed by Congress and sent to the states for ratification which would eliminate the 'natural born' qualification required of a President—had already been passed by nine state legislatures, mostly in the south and southwest, although surprisingly Washington, Hawaii, and Maryland had also concurred; at the same time, five had already rejected it. Secession movements were gathering strength in Texas, New Mexico and Florida; some analysts were already predicting the demise of the United States and the rise of a new, largely Hispanic nation that would comprise Florida, Texas, New Mexico, Arizona and the southern half of California, plus the northern states of Mexico. Things were unraveling rapidly.

President Navarro had grown more and more somber as Kerrigan's discourse went on. He had stopped eating, and now sat staring at her while rubbing his forehead. "What can we do, Fran?" he finally asked, forlornly.

"Mister President," she began, "you know that I have the utmost respect for you. But sometimes drastic times call for drastic measures." She stared into his eyes, a grim expression set on her face. "You are the problem, sir. You are the cause of this strife that's tearing us apart. Rightly or wrongly, you are to blame. And you are the only one who can fix it."

Navarro blanched and visibly flinched as Kerrigan leveled the accusations. He looked from side to side and around the room, as if seeking assistance or a way out. With his right hand pressed against his forehead, he asked, "How can I fix things, Fran? I haven't caused this to happen."

Kerrigan replied immediately and forcefully. "Sir, you have. You are the problem. It is your questionable legitimacy that has caused all this." He had closed his eyes, wincing with pain, and was slowly shaking his head from side to side. "The only way to resolve this is for you to go away. You must leave all this behind and go away. And you must do it quickly." She let the words hang in the air.

The President was now frantically massaging his left arm, his eyes still squeezed tightly shut. In a strangled voice, he said, "Fran, I need some more medicine to make this pain go away. Would you go into the bedroom and get it for me? Three of each, please."

She hesitated only briefly, then said, "Of course, sir. I'll be right back, then we'll continue to talk." She rose quickly from the table, retrieved the pills from the adjacent room, and returned to her seat. She handed the medication to Navarro, who quickly washed them down with his wine.

"Thank you, Fran," he said, opening the hazel eyes to look at her. Then, with a pained expressions, said, "I can't resign. I'm not wrong. Why can't everyone see that?" He turned his head toward his right and asked, "What do you think I should do?"

"Right or wrong at this point doesn't matter. It's all about perception now, and you've lost the confidence of most of the country. They all perceive that you're the problem. The only solution is for you to go away." She paused, then asked, "What is Julia telling you to do?"

He looked back at her. "She's telling me you're right. It's time for me to end this." His face had taken on a defeated look.

"I think you should listen to her. You must. She's never steered you wrong before, has she?"

"No, never," he replied. "Never." They had finished most of the meal, but neither was eating anymore. The President's eyes had now taken on a glazed look; tiredness was etched on the gaunt face. "I'm sorry, Fran, but I've got to rest again. I'm sorry; I hope you understand. Would you ask the agent to get me settled?"

"Surely, Mister President." She stood up from the table and began to move toward the door to call the agent waiting outside, then paused. "Ray," she said softly, "you know what you must do. For the good of the country. Ask Julia. Listen to what she says. She'll tell you that I'm right."

Navarro didn't answer. Nor did he speak to her again as the agent wheeled him into the bedroom and settled him into the bed.

"Good-bye, Mister President," Kerrigan said quietly as he disappeared into the room. Then she turned and quickly left the lodge, eager to be on her way back to Washington.

In the dark of his room, Ray Navarro lay again with his pain, waiting for Julia to come. The talk with Kerrigan had caused his head to throb and his missing leg to ache. He felt short of breath, and vaguely nauseous. "Julia," he cried aloud to the empty room, "talk to me. I need you."

As he said the words, he knew suddenly that she was there. He could feel her presence by the bed. He opened his eyes and saw her standing in front of him, shimmering, blonde hair gleaming, with arms open wide.

"Ray," she said, "you've done enough. Come to me and rest. The pain will end. The problems will end. And we'll be together again."

"Yes," he said, "yes, my love, I've waited so long. I've missed you so much."

"Come to me, Ray, and you're troubles will be over."

He nodded his head slowly in the dark, then reach to the nightstand to pick up the bottle of Vicodin once more.

EPILOGUE

Washington, DC
Wednesday, 3 May 2023
11:17 a.m. EDT

Fran Kerrigan quietly entered the Oval Office and immediately sat down behind the Resolute Desk. She had not been in the office for some time, and then only briefly for photo ops. She had not sat in this chair at all since that day last spring after the assassination attempt on Navarro. She remembered what she had thought then, that someday she'd be seated in this chair in her own right. 'That day is now,' she thought.

She swiveled in the big chair behind the desk to face the tall doors that opened out to the Rose Garden, and thought back on all that had happened in the past twelve months. 'Things couldn't have turned out better,' she thought to herself.

The door to the left of the desk that led into the president's private office suddenly opened. She spun in the chair to see her husband entering the office, a smile of pride on his broad face.

"Madame President, please allow me to be the first to congratulate you. You've finally got what should have been yours in the first place." He stopped in front of the desk and faced her. "You look good there, Franny, really good. It all turned out just as we'd hoped, didn't it?"

Kerrigan rose from the chair and came around the desk to embrace her husband. "Indeed it did, Fred, indeed it did. And none of it would have happened if it hadn't been for you. I knew I could count on you."

President Navarro's death on Sunday had shocked the weary nation and made people see each other in a new light. Differences which had seemed so crucial, but which were now seen as so petty, were put aside, and voices which had been shouting in opposition now joined together to remember the President as a man of principle who always did what he thought was best for America. With his passing, the root cause of the dispute of the last several months passed

JOHN SCOFIELD PRALL JR.

as well, and the legitimacy and authority of the federal government was recognized once more.

President Kerrigan went to great lengths to assuage the nation's wounds. Speaking at Navarro's funeral as he was laid to rest in Arlington next to Julia, to a crowd of mourners that included not only senior officials from his administration, members of Congress, and foreign dignitaries, but West Point classmates, comrades in arms, and other past associates, she hailed him as a good man, a true American hero, one who literally gave his all for the United States. "We must now resolve our differences, bind up our wounds, and move forward in the spirit of this good man. To do otherwise will negate everything that Ray Navarro stood for, what he worked so tirelessly for, and what he gave his life for. We must do him proud."

The official report of the cause of his death stated that it was due to complications from the injuries he had received a year before during the attack in California. Scar tissue in his head, when coupled with the strain he'd been under for the past several weeks, had combined to kill him with an unexpected aneurysm. There was no mention of any overdose of pain medication, and no intimation that this was anything other than a tragic, unfortunate death. By order of the President, all medical records relating to Ramon Navarro Jr. were permanently sealed.

President Kerrigan and Senator Moscone had just returned from the funeral in Arlington, venturing into the White House for the first time. She had taken the oath of office at the Vice President's residence at the Naval Observatory early on Monday morning, following the discovery of the President's body when his staff had entered his room to rouse him for the day. Kerrigan had been notified of the death by seven that morning. She had been briefed within an hour by General Webster about its cause—he told her it appeared he had died in his sleep, and mentioned nothing about suicide—and had summoned the Cabinet, as well as Chief of Staff Josh Caldwell, to her home to watch her be sworn in at ten o'clock. She had gone on television that afternoon to formally announce the death and to describe the funeral arrangements the government would make. She deliberately did not enter the White House until Ray Navarro's body had been buried in Arlington's earth.

Yesterday, she had announced that she intended to make no immediate changes to government policy or to government agencies, other than to say that Josh Caldwell would be replaced as White House Chief of Staff—at his request, she said, so that he could return to Texas. He would be replaced by Jess Dougherty, her long-time Chief. No one was surprised by the announcement, and Caldwell had made no comment. He left Washington immediately after Navarro's funeral.

She reached out to all sides of the recent dispute, offering to restore confidence and soliciting thoughts on how best to do that. She stated her support for the proposed 'natural born' constitutional amendment. She restored to good standing all officers of the armed forces who had recently been at odds with President Navarro. She affirmed her support for Navarro's Mexican initiative. And she was rewarded with an outpouring of support from Congress, state and local government, and people from all walks of life. The media hailed her almost as a messiah who had come to lift the nation from its own self-destruction. The relief that the crisis was past was almost palpable.

On Tuesday, May 2nd, in an anticlimax, the Supreme Court issued their final ruling in the case of *Morgan vs Navarro*. They concluded, having examined all available evidence, that it was not proved that the certification provided by the Secretary of State of Texas regarding the legitimacy of Ramon Navarro Jr.'s birth in El Paso was improper, and that therefore Ramon Navarro Jr. was eligible for the presidency. In an astounding aside, the Chief Justice, Ephraim Runyon, regretted any dismay the Court's tardy ruling had caused, explaining that justice simply could not be rushed.

But Fran Kerrigan could not have cared less about that, for she was now legitimately in the Oval Office where she had always wanted to be. "You handled this whole ordeal so well throughout," she said to her husband, eyes glowing. "And with no one the wiser. You were masterful."

"Ah, *cara mia*, but you had to play your part, too, and you played it well. We couldn't have done it if you'd seemed too eager or pushed too hard. It had to come off just right. Pushing Caldwell's buttons so that he'd overreact. Playing coy with the Cabinet. And then the other part. All those phone calls you made, using that voice synthesizer with the background noise. And finally giving Navarro the push over the edge. You were the masterful one."

Kerrigan continued to hold him in an embrace. "But the work your agency did down in Texas really got things rolling. If they hadn't created such a believable report, something that could really catch the attention of those meddling reporters, none of this would have ever worked."

Moscone chuckled. "They did do nice work, didn't they? Having those connections from the Intelligence Committee is quite often a great benefit. It helped, too, that at least part of the story was true. That Acevedo did actually bring a baby over from Juarez. Just happens that it was a girl he brought, and that Navarro had actually been born in that hospital in El Paso a few days earlier. Just shows that if there is just a little bit of truth to a story that can be supported with some facts, most people will believe it even if little bits of it are changed." He smiled contentedly, remembering the work he'd done.

"And then you took care of two birds with one stone when you got Susan to return to us. And got rid of that wretched reporter, too." She released him and looked up into his eyes. "I've never been more proud of you for having the guts to do something that important. It was very brave."

"Oh, *carissima*, it was nothing. It was even easier than the first one. Went just like clockwork, just like we thought. I was able to finish my meal and get back to the estate there before the snow even got deep."

"And now Susan is back with us again. It's wonderful." She smiled.

A knock on the door to the Oval Office stopped their reminiscing. Both turned toward the door to see the bulky form of Jess Dougherty enter.

"Madame President, please excuse me, but it's time for the Cabinet meeting to begin." The first official Cabinet session of her presidency was about to start.

"Well, Fred, I've got to go to work. Wish me luck."

"Madame President, you'll be great. No need of luck anymore." He leaned over to kiss her forehead.

She smiled, then turned and strode confidently out the door, master of her world.

New Hope, PA
Friday, 5 May 2023
2:28 p.m. EDT

Sue had been tempted to head to Washington to see her mother installed in office, but she'd decided, given the circumstances, that it would be better not to. 'Too much turmoil down there right now,' she thought. 'I'll wait until later in the spring, then make a quiet visit.' She'd called instead, and they talked for a long time, and both were happy.

So, instead, she'd watched her mother on television, her father at her side, and in spite of herself, felt proud of the moment. 'I know this is what you always wanted—what you both always wanted—and I'm glad for you,' she'd thought at the time. But in her heart she wished it could have happened differently.

In New Hope and Lambertville, people still did not connect her with Fran Kerrigan, and she was more than content to keep them in the dark. She went about her business with no one the wiser, and hoped it would remain that way.

Since Jamie's funeral, Sue had come to grips with her grief and was getting on with her life. She had made the decision to get *The Beacon* up and running again, and to become involved with its operation as a publisher; she thought Jamie would have been pleased about that. She knew she had lots to learn about how to do that, but counted on Alice Metzger to help. The fire had ultimately been ruled an accident—an electrical short—although a whiff of arson still hung about it. Nonetheless, the insurance company had paid up and Sue was now using that money to refurbish the office building and to purchase new replacement printing machines. Nothing could replace the old archives, of course, but one had to play the cards that life dealt you.

She'd also decided to move into Jamie's house in Lambertville. Her apartment had been almost too small for her to begin with, and she had always liked Jamie's old house on Coryell Street and the quiet neighborhood it was in. She was actually planning to move across the river next week, having used some of the insurance money Jamie had provided for her to spruce the place up a little.

She still intended to keep her gallery in New Hope, though. Whether or not she'd be able to both run that and publish a newspaper would remain to be seen, but she wanted to give it a try. She was working in the gallery, preparing a new exhibit for a weekend exhibition that began tomorrow, when her cell phone rang.

"Hello?" she answered.

"Hello, Sue? Frank Allen here. I hope I'm not disturbing you."

"Not at all, Frank. I could use a little break anyway. What is it?"

"Well, there's one final item of Jamie's estate that I need to give you today. It's a lot of files and documents that he had placed in a safe deposit box with me for safekeeping shortly before he died. He had left instructions with me to release them to you sixty days after his death, should that ever occur. And today is the sixtieth day." He paused. "You should pick them up here, rather than having me deliver by mail or Fedex. I'd be more comfortable seeing them directly into your hands."

"Of course, Frank," she answered, "it's no problem. How about if I swing by after work and pick them up at your office? Would four o'clock be okay?"

"That would be perfect. I'll see you then." They both hung up, and Sue spent the afternoon wondering what Jamie could possibly have thought she would want.

Sue arrived at Frank Allen's office shortly after four, and found the lawyer waiting for her.

"Come in, Sue," he said, holding open the door to his office as she entered. It was a fine spring day, with a temperature in the mid-seventies and no humidity; Sue had enjoyed the slow walk across the bridge from New Hope, enjoyed it so much in fact that she had to speed up at the end just to get to the office close to the appointed time. "Great day, isn't it?"

"A beautiful day," she agreed. "Is this it?" she asked, pointing at the four boxes on his floor. They were all still sealed, and neatly labeled 'Coryell files', with a 1 through 4 for each appropriate box. "They must be his family records," she said to Allen. "I know he had collected a lot of stuff about the Coryells."

"Maybe," Frank said. "I guess you'll find out. What do you want to do with them?"

She smiled and batted her eyes at him. "Do you think you could assist a poor, helpless girl to carry them across the street?"

He laughed. "Sure, Sue, if that's where you want them. That'll be easy. I was afraid you were going to say 'carry them to New Hope.'" They each grabbed a box, finding them heavy, but not too heavy, and began the first of two trips across to Jamie's house. To her house, she had to keep reminding herself.

They carried them up the stairs to the room Jamie had used as an office, then Frank headed home. "Good luck with all that," he called out as he climbed down the porch and crossed the street. "Let me know if you need anything else."

"Thanks, Frank. I will." She went back inside the house, closed the door, and headed up to examine her treasures, first making a stop in the kitchen to pour herself a glass of Chablis.

"Alright, Jamie," she said to the room once she'd settled down in front of the boxes, "what's so important?" She grabbed Box #1 and slit open the sealed top with a pair of scissors, then gasped at what she found. "Well, aren't you clever?" she said aloud again, for she found herself looking at a complete copy of *The Beacon* exposé files, the originals of which had been destroyed in the fire. She flipped through them quickly, working through the boxes in numerical order, seeing Lou's initial notes, the Trova report, her findings from Texas, as well as much more supporting documentation that Jamie had uncovered. When she got to Box #4, however, she found herself reading new information that she hadn't seen before, and that she hadn't known existed.

The final box's contents were the data that Jamie had unearthed regarding the Trova Agency. It documented its progression from the time of its incorporation, and the growth of its secretive government business. To her horror, she also found documents signed by her father, some in his own handwriting, directing the agency to do illicit work, to include instructions for fabricating the Acevedo files. She was stunned.

"Oh, no," Sue moaned, sinking back into her chair, realizing the implications immediately. "You couldn't have. Just when I changed my mind about you, you show me I was right in the first place." The more she read, the more she realized she'd been deceived. 'They're both in it together,' she thought, sure that her mother was involved as well, for although nothing in the file named her specifically, she knew that when one of her parents did something, the other was involved with it, too. And at last, shocked as the ultimate realization finally came to her, she could only quietly say "Jamie" as the tears fell down her cheeks again.

She remained there in the small room as day turned to night, staring at the pages but not seeing them. She saw Jamie again, exuberant about his paper. Saw him wanting to do what was right. And she saw her parents, always lusting for power, never satisfied with what they had, and again wondered 'How could you?' She saw all that had gone on across the country over the last several months as a result of that lust, and slowly realized what she must do. What Jamie would have wanted her to do.

Searching back through the files, she found the number she wanted. Dialing it on her cell phone, she waited silently as the phone searched for a connection. Finally, a gruff voice sounded on the other end.

"Hello?" the voice drawled.

"Hello, Governor Caldwell. My name is Susan Malone. I'm the daughter of Fran Kerrigan and Fred Moscone, and was a friend of Jamie Coryell. I believe you were acquainted with him and his work. I have some information that I think you'll be interested in."

THE END